THE PROMISED LAND

Erich Maria Remarque was born in Osnabrück in 1898. Exiled from Nazi Germany and deprived of his citizenship, he lived in America and Switzerland. The author of a dozen novels, Remarque died in 1970.

Michael Hofmann is a poet, reviewer and translator from German (Benn, Fallada, Junger, Kafka, Roth and others). In 2012 he won the Thornton Wilder Prize from the American Academy of Arts and Letters. He teaches at the University of Florida. He is also the author of a book of essays, *Where Have You Been.*

ERICH MARIA REMARQUE

The Promised Land

TRANSLATED FROM THE GERMAN BY
Michael Hofmann

VINTAGE BOOKS
London

Published by Vintage 2014

2 4 6 8 10 9 7 5 3 1

First published in Germany as *Das gelobte Land* © 1998 the Estate of the
late Paulette Remarque © 1998, 2010, Verlag Kiepenhauer & Witsch GmbH
& Co. KG, Cologne/Germany

The translation of this work was supported by a grant from the
Goethe-Institut which is funded by the German Ministry of Foreign Affairs

Vintage
Random House, 20 Vauxhall Bridge Road,
London SW1V 2SA

www.vintage-classics.info

Addresses for companies within The Random House Group Limited can be
found at: www.randomhouse.co.uk/offices.htm

The Random House Group Limited Reg. No. 954009

A CIP catalogue record for this book
is available from the British Library

ISBN 9780099577089

The Random House Group Limited supports the Forest
Stewardship Council® (FSC®), the leading international
forest-certification organisation. Our books carrying the FSC
label are printed on FSC®-certified paper. FSC is the only
forest-certification scheme supported by the leading environmental
organisations, including Greenpeace. Our paper procurement
policy can be found at www.randomhouse.co.uk/environment

Typeset by Palimpsest Book Production Limited,
Falkirk, Stirlingshire
Printed and bound in Great Britain by
Clays Ltd, St Ives PLC

Contents

1

The city was dangled in front of me for three weeks, but it might as well have been on a different planet. It was no more than a couple of miles away, the other side of a narrow sea channel I could almost have swum across; but it was so far out of my reach, it might have been surrounded by an armoured column of tanks. It was defended by the strongest walls the twentieth century could devise: walls of paper, passport and visa regulations, the inhuman laws of an indifferent bureaucracy. I was on Ellis Island, it was the summer of 1944 and the city in front of me was New York.

Ellis Island was the mildest internment camp I had ever known. There was no beating or torture, and we were neither gassed nor worked to death. There was even good food, which didn't cost anything, and beds to sleep in. There were guards everywhere, but they were almost friendly. Ellis Island was where those immigrants were kept whose documentation was doubtful or incomplete. In America it wasn't enough to have a valid visa from an American consulate in Europe – no, it had to be approved and endorsed by the immigration authorities in New York. Only then would you be admitted to the country, or, if you were undesirable, sent back on the next boat. Being sent back wasn't as straightforward as it used to be. Europe was at war, America was at war, German U-boats lurked in the Atlantic and very few passenger liners sailed to European ports. For those emigrants who were sent back, it might even have felt like a stroke of luck, being able to remain a little longer on Ellis Island – they who, for years, had seen their lives only in terms of days and weeks – but there were too many other rumours for them to feel much relief: rumours of phantom ships full of desperate Jews criss-crossing the oceans for month after month, being turned away wherever they tried to make land. Some of the emigrants had personally seen the rows of screaming and desperate faces off Cuba and various South American ports, begging for mercy, pressing up against the railings of the ramshackle hulks outside the locked ports – dismal contemporary versions of the Flying Dutchman, on the run from submarines and human hard-heartedness, consignments of living dead and damned souls, whose only crime was to be human and to want to live.

There was the usual quota of nervous breakdowns. Oddly, they were even a little more frequent on Ellis Island than in the internment camps in France, practically under the noses of the Germans and the Gestapo. That was probably to do with having made the adjustment to the acute danger in France, which was such that it kept off breakdowns; whereas here the shattering effect from the prospect of imminent rescue being cast in doubt once more tended to bring them on. There were no suicides here, as there were in France; for that, the sense of hope (even hope mingled with despair) was too strong. But a collapse could be brought on by something as little as an interview with a harmless immigration inspector – the carapace of suspicion and alertness learned over the years suddenly cracked, and the immediate setting on of a counter-suspicion swelled into panic lest you had made a mistake. As always, there were more breakdowns among men than women.

The city, so near and so unattainable, became a torment – it beckoned and mocked, promised everything and kept nothing. Sometimes it was no more than a foggy monster, a thing garnished with scraps of clouds and the noisy ships screaming around it like so many steel ichthyosaurs. In the evening, in the storm of artificial light, it became a glittering carpet dangling between the horizons, alien and disconcerting after the dark wartime nights of Europe. When, late at night, it turned into an austere white moonscape, a ghostly, silent Babel bristling with hundreds of towers, then in the dormitories the refugees would often get up, woken by the sobs and gasps and screams of the sleepers, who were hounded in their dreams by Gestapo, gendarmes and SS killers, and they would gather at the windows in drab little groups, mumbling or silent, staring with burning eyes across at the quivering panorama of lights of the Promised Land of America, in a community and fellow feeling that is known only to misery, never to joy.

I had a German passport, valid for another four months. It was made out in the name of Ludwig Sommer and it was almost genuine. I had come into it from a friend who had died almost two years before in Bordeaux; since our height, hair and eye colour were a match, Bauer, the onetime mathematics professor and passport forger in Marseilles, had urged me not to change the name on it. There were excellent lithographers among the emigrants who had helped the odd undocumented refugee to a workable passport; but nevertheless, I took Bauer's advice and renounced my own name, of which little enough was left to use. On the contrary, it was on the Gestapo lists and it was high time to lose it. So my passport was almost genuine, only the picture and I were false. The expert Bauer explained the advantages to me a tampered-with passport, however expertly done, would only stand up to fleeting scrutiny at best – and the moment it was taken to a proper police lab it would give up its secret and the outcome would be prison, expatriation or worse. A real passport, though, with a false holder, was much more difficult and time-consuming to check; you would have to go back to the authority that had issued it – and that was no longer possible in the war. All ties with Germany were broken. Since then, the experts advised you to change your identity; stamps were easier to copy than names. The only difference in my passport was the religion. Sommer had been a Jew; I wasn't. To Bauer the difference was negligible.

'If the Germans catch you, throw the passport away,' he said. 'Since you're not circumcised, you might be able to talk your way out and avoid the gas chamber. Perhaps it will even be useful to you on the run to be thought of as a Jew. You can always explain your ignorance of the religion by saying that you and your father were freethinkers anyway.'

Bauer was caught three months later. A friend, Robert Hirsch, himself furnished with the papers of a Spanish consular official, tried to get him out of prison. He was too late. Bauer had been put on a train to Germany the night before.

On Ellis Island I met two emigrants I'd known slightly from before. We had run into each other here and there on the 'Via Dolorosa'. The Via Dolorosa was the name given to the escape route from the Hitler regime. It went from Holland and Belgium and northern France down to Paris; there it forked. One fork dropped down from Lyons to the Mediterranean coast; the other went via Bordeaux, Marseilles and the Pyrenees into Spain, Portugal and the port of Lisbon. Emigrants and refugees from Germany gave it the name. They weren't just on the run from Hitler's Gestapo – they

4

also had to hide from the police in the countries they fled to. Most of them had no visas and no valid papers. If the police caught them, they would be locked up, imprisoned and thrown out of the country. At least many of the countries were sufficiently humane not to repatriate them to Germany, where they would have died in concentration camps. Since only a small minority of the refugees had valid passports, most were on the run all the time. Nor could they work, without papers. Most were hungry, isolated and wretched; hence they called the road of their wanderings the Via Dolorosa. The stations of the cross were the post offices in the various towns and the white walls along the streets were their newspapers. At the post offices they hoped for poste restante news of friends and family members. And then in charcoal and chalk on nearby walls they would find messages from the lost and missing, warnings, advice, screams into the void. This was during the brief period of indulgence that preceded the epoch of inhumanity when the Gestapo and the various national police forces made common cause against them.

One of the two emigrants I met on Ellis Island was Rabinovitz, a man I had run into on the Swiss border, where a customs official threw us out into France four times in a single night. We were chased back each time by the French border police. It was terribly cold, and finally Rabinovitz and I managed to persuade the Swiss to put us in a cell. Swiss prisons were heated; they enjoyed a paradisal reputation and we would happily have spent the whole winter there, only the Swiss were practically minded. They quickly bundled us out over the Italian frontier of the Ticino, where we parted ways. Both the emigrants had relatives in America who would guarantee their support. Therefore they were able to leave Ellis Island after not many days. When

5

he left, Rabinovitz promised me to try to look up other Via Dolorosa associates in New York. I didn't expect much. It was the usual promise that was forgotten as soon as the man making it found himself at liberty.

Still, I wasn't unhappy. A few years before, in a museum in Brussels, I had learned to sit still for hours on end without getting in a panic. I was able to put myself into a state of self-induced blankness that was close to autohypnosis. It produced a kind of dull, out-of-the-body feeling, which made long suspenseful waiting bearable, because – in that benign version of schizophrenia – it no longer concerned me, as I didn't exist. That way I wasn't crushed by the solitariness of a very small lightless room where I was hidden for a few months. The museum director had given me refuge there while the Gestapo went through Brussels with a fine-tooth comb. I only saw him briefly in the morning when he would bring me something to eat; and sometimes in the evening, when the museum was closed and I had the run of the place. In the daytime the space was kept locked; the director was the only other person with a key. Of course, I had to suppress coughing, sneezing and all sorts of noisy movement when there were people in the corridor. That was simple enough, but the nervous tickle of fear could have emerged as full-blown panic if I had been in actual danger. Therefore I went further than I had to into my state of blankness so as to have a kind of shock reserve and for a time ignored my watch so that I no longer knew if it was day or night, particularly on Sundays, when the director didn't come in; but I had to give that up as well. It tended to unbalance me and brought me close to self-abandonment. Not that I was too far from that at the best of times. The thing that pulled me through was not any belief in life anyway, so much as the desire for revenge.

★

A week after Rabinovitz's departure, a lean, cadaverous man spoke to me. He carried a green crocodile attaché case and looked like one of the lawyers who fluttered through the big day room like so many crows.

'Are you Ludwig Sommer?'

I gave the man a suspicious look. He had asked in German. 'Why?' I asked.

'Don't you know whether you're Ludwig Sommer or not?' The man burst into a creaking sort of laugh. He had unusually large white teeth in a lined grey face.

By now I had concluded that I had no need to keep my name secret. 'Of course I know,' I replied, 'but what's it to you?'

The man blinked owlishly once or twice. 'I'm here on behalf of Robert Hirsch,' he finally vouchsafed.

I looked up in surprise. 'Hirsch? Did you say Robert Hirsch?'

The man nodded. 'Who else?'

'Robert Hirsch is dead,' I said.

The man looked at me in puzzlement. 'Robert Hirsch is in New York,' he said. 'I spoke to him two hours ago.'

I shook my head. 'That's not possible. It must have been someone else. Robert Hirsch was shot dead in Marseilles.'

'Nonsense! Hirsch sent me here to help get you out.'

I didn't believe him. I sensed a trap from the immigration inspectors. 'How did he know I was here?' I asked.

'He had a call from a man by the name of Rabinovitz; that's how he heard you were here.' The man took a card out of his waistcoat pocket. 'Levin and Watson, law firm. I'm Levin. Now are you satisfied? You're not exactly trusting, are you? Why? Have you got so much to hide?'

I took a deep breath. Now I believed him. 'All over Marseilles, the word was that Robert Hirsch was shot by the Gestapo,' I said.

7

'Marseilles!' sneered Levin. 'This is America!'

'Are you sure?' I looked around the room with the barred windows and the huddled masses. Again, Levin launched into his cackling laugh.

'Well, maybe not quite. As I see, you haven't quite lost your sense of humour. Mr Hirsch gave me some information about you. You were together with him in an internment camp in France? Is that right?'

I nodded. I still felt stunned. Robert Hirsch alive and in New York!

'Is that right?' repeated Levin a little impatiently.

I nodded again. It was half true; Hirsch had only been in the camp for an hour. He had turned up in the uniform of an SS officer and had demanded that the French commandant hand over two German politicals who were wanted by the Gestapo. That was when he spotted me; he hadn't known I was in the camp. Without a hitch, he had then demanded my release as well. The camp commandant, who was a timid major in the reserve and hated all this, had only insisted on a formal written request. Hirsch gave it to him; he always kept a supply of blank forms on his person. Then he gave the Hitler salute, packed us into his car and sped away. The two politicals were picked up a year later; they were caught in a police trap in Bordeaux.

'Yes, that's right,' I said. 'Would you mind showing me the material Hirsch gave you?'

Levin hesitated momentarily. 'Of course. Why, if I might ask?'

I didn't answer. I wanted to establish whether Robert's statement corresponded with what I had said to the immigration inspectors. I read the document through carefully and gave it back.

'Is that what happened, then?' asked Levin again.

'Yes,' I said and looked around. In an instant, everything seemed to have changed. I was no longer alone. Robert Hirsch was alive. A voice had called to me, a voice I thought had died. Everything was changed. Nothing was lost.

'How much money do you have?' asked the lawyer.

'A hundred and fifty dollars,' I replied cautiously.

Levin inclined his bald head. 'It's not very much – even for a short-term visitor's visa, to go on to Canada or Mexico. But we can fix that. Do you see what I'm saying?'

'No. Why would I want to go to Canada or Mexico?'

Levin flashed his horsy teeth at me again. 'No reason, Mr Sommer. The main thing is just to get you into New York. A short-term transit visa is easiest to arrange. Once you're in the country you can fall ill. Be incapable of travel. And we can make further applications on your behalf. The situation can change. What matters is getting your foot in the door. Now do you understand me?'

'Yes.'

A loudly crying woman walked by. Levin pulled a pair of black horn rims out of his pocket and watched her. 'It can't be much fun sitting here,' he observed.

I shrugged. 'It could be worse.'

'Worse? How so?'

'Much worse,' I said. 'You could be here and have stomach cancer. Or Ellis Island could be in Germany and they could be nailing your father to the floor to get confessions out of you.'

Levin stared at me. 'You have a morbid imagination,' he said.

I shook my head. 'Not at all,' I said, 'just morbid experiences.'

The lawyer pulled out a large patterned handkerchief and trumpetingly blew his nose. Then he folded it up carefully and pocketed it. 'How old are you?'

'Thirty-two.'

'And how long have you been a refugee?'

'For almost five years.'

It wasn't true. I'd been on the run for longer than that; but Ludwig Sommer, the proprietor of my passport, had only been going since 1939.

'Jewish?'

I nodded.

'You don't really look it, you know,' said Levin.

'That's as may be. But would you say that Hitler, Goebbels, Himmler and Hess looked particularly Aryan?'

Levin emitted his cackling laugh again. 'Ha, you've got a point there! Well, it doesn't matter anyway. Why would you want to claim to be a Jew if you weren't one? Now of all times! Right?'

'Could be.'

'Were you in a German concentration camp?'

'Yes,' I said unwillingly. 'Four months.'

'Are you able to prove that?' Levin asked with a strange avidity.

'There weren't any documents. I was released and then I ran away.'

'Too bad! They would have come in handy.'

I looked at Levin. I could understand him; but the idea of utilising something like that in a transaction was a little repugnant to me. It had been too grim. So grim that I made an effort to efface the memory. Not to forget it, only to erase it in me until such time as I needed it. Not here in Ellis Island – later, in Germany.

Levin opened his attaché case and pulled out some pieces of paper. 'I still have what Mr Hirsch gave me by way of testimony and statements from people who knew you. Everything duly notarised. By my partner Watson, for the sake of convenience. Would you like to take a look at what we have?'

I shook my head. I'd seen these statements in Paris. Robert Hirsch was a past master at getting up such things. I didn't want to see them now. I had an odd feeling that, with everything that was going for me today, I ought to leave something up to chance. Whoever fights at odds of a hundred to one will want to leave a little chink for chance. It would have been absurd to try to explain something like that to Levin.

The lawyer returned the papers to the case. 'Now we need to find a sponsor, someone who will guarantee that you won't fall burden on the state, as we like to say, while you're in America. Do you know anyone?'

'No.'

'But maybe Robert Hirsch would know someone?'

'I wouldn't know.'

'He'll find someone all right,' said Levin with strange confidence. 'He's very good at such things. Where will you be staying in New York? Mr Hirsch suggests the Hotel Rausch. He stayed there himself.'

For a moment I said nothing. Then I said, 'Mr Levin, are you telling me that I'm going to get out of here?'

'Why not? That's what I'm here for.'

'You really believe that?'

'Of course. Don't you?'

I closed my eyes for a moment. 'Yes,' I finally said. 'I do too.'

'Well, then. Never lose hope! Or does that not apply to emigrants?'

I shook my head.

'There, see! Never give up hope – a good old American principle! You understand?'

I nodded. I didn't feel like explaining to this naive son of the law how destructive hope could be. It could gnaw away at a weakened heart, the way swinging and missing saps the reserves of a boxer in a losing fight. I'd seen more people go down with misplaced hope than in a tense resignation that concentrated everything on naked survival and left no place for anything else.

Levin shut his attaché case. 'I'm going to take these documents to the inspectors, then. I'll be back in a few days. Chin up, now! We'll get you there.' He took a sniff. 'The smell in here! Like a poorly disinfected hospital.'

'It smells of poverty, bureaucracy and despair,' I said.

Levin took off his glasses and rubbed his eyes. 'Despair, eh,' he said ironically, 'can you smell that?'

'You're a happy man if you don't know that,' I replied.

'That seems to be starting your classification of happiness quite a long way down.'

I didn't answer; there was no point in trying to explain to him that you couldn't start low enough and that, in fact, that was the secret of survival. Levin gave me his big, bony hand. I wanted to ask him what price he was charging, but I didn't. You could wreck everything by asking too many questions. Hirsch had sent Levin, that was enough.

I stood up and watched the lawyer leave. I still couldn't quite believe his assurances that everything would be fine. I had been through too much and had often come a cropper. But all the same, I felt a surge of feeling that got stronger and that I was unable to keep down. It wasn't just the thought that Robert Hirsch was alive in New York – it was something else, the thing that a moment before I had tried to resist and that, with the arrogance of unhappiness, I had dismissed from my presence: a desperate hope. It was abruptly, silently there, just now come into being, a perverse, unjustified, wild hope, an anonymous hope almost without focus, save perhaps a nebulous freedom, but a freedom for what, or from what? I didn't know. It was a nameless hope that without my doing anything took the thing in me that said 'I' and saddled us with such a primitive lust for life that it was almost nothing to do with me. What had become of my resignation? My mistrust? My pathetically constructed spurious superiority? I didn't know.

I turned round and saw the woman who had cried just a moment ago. She was holding a red-haired boy by the hand. He was eating a banana.

'What did they do to you, then?' I asked.

'They don't want to admit my little boy.'

'Why not?'

'They claim he's—' She hesitated. 'He's slow,' she hurriedly finished. 'But he'll get better! After everything we've been through. He's not retarded! He's just a bit slow. He'll get better. He just needs time. He's not disturbed. But they won't believe me.'

'Was there a doctor present?'

'I don't know.'

'You must ask for a doctor. A specialist. He'll help you.'

'How can I ask for a specialist?' muttered the woman. 'I'm poor.'

'You must make an application. You can do that here.'

The little boy folded up his banana peel and popped it in his trouser pocket.

'He's so tidy,' whispered his mother. 'See how tidy he is! How can he possibly be mad?'

I looked at the boy. He seemed not to hear his mother. His lower lip drooped and he was scratching his flame-red hair. The sun glinted in his eyes as though they were made of glass. 'Why don't they want to let him in?' the mother muttered. 'He's even worse off than the rest.'

13

There was no answer to that. 'They let in a lot of people,' I said finally. 'Almost everyone. Every morning some people are admitted. You just have to be patient.'

As I said it I despised myself. I could feel myself trying to hide from those eyes that were looking to me in their need, as though I had a real explanation. I had none. Awkwardly I reached into my pocket, took out some money and gave it to the apathetic boy. 'Here you are, go and buy yourself something nice!'

It was the oldest emigrant superstition; the attempt to bribe fate by a foolish gesture. I felt promptly ashamed of myself. A few pennies' worth of humanity in return for my freedom, I thought. What else? With the arrival of Hope, did her corrupt twin sister Fear arrive at the same time? And Fear's vile daughter, Cowardice?

That night I slept badly. For a long time I stood at the window, looking at the northern lights of New York quivering and flashing, and thinking of my broken life. Towards morning an old man had felt faint. Excited shapes moved around his bed. Someone went looking for nitroglycerine. The old man had lost his trunk. 'He mustn't get sick,' whispered his relatives. 'Otherwise everything is lost! He has to be able to get up in the morning!' They couldn't find the trunk; but a melancholy Turk with a long moustache helped them out with medicine. In the morning the old man was able to hobble into the day room again.

2

The lawyer came again three days later. 'You look awful,' he cackled. 'What's the matter with you?'

'Hope,' I quipped back. 'It kills a man faster than misfortune. You should know that, Mr Levin.'

'You and your émigré humour! You really have no reason to be downcast. I've got news for you.'

'What news would that be?' I asked cautiously. I was afraid that something might have come up to do with my passport.

Levin flashed his giant teeth. He does laugh a lot, I thought. 'We've found someone to guarantee your stay,' he said. 'Someone who will undertake to see that you do not fall burden on the state. A sponsor! What do you say now?'

'Hirsch?' I asked disbelievingly.

Levin shook his bald head. 'Hirsch doesn't have that sort of money. Do you know Tannenbaum the banker?'

I didn't say anything. I wasn't sure what I should admit to.

'Maybe,' I said.

'Maybe? What do you mean maybe?! You and your evasions! You must know him! He's going to sponsor you!'

A flock of seagulls suddenly squalled across the flashing sea, very close to the windows. I didn't know any banker called Tannenbaum. I didn't know anyone in New York, except Robert Hirsch. He must have fixed it for me. The way he did in France as a Spanish consul.

'I probably do,' I said. 'You meet so many people when you're on the run; you forget the names.'

Levin looked at me doubtfully. 'A name like Tannenbaum?'

I laughed. 'Yes, a name like Tannenbaum! Why not? Tannenbaum most of all. Who wants to share the name of a German Christmas tree!'

Levin blew his hooked nose. 'It doesn't really matter if you know him or not. The important thing is that he's prepared to sign for you.'

He opened his attaché case. A few newspapers tumbled out. 'The morning papers. Have you read them yet?'

'No.'

'Why on earth not? Can't you get the papers here?'

'Sure. I just haven't read them.'

'Extraordinary. I'd have thought you couldn't wait to see them every day. Isn't that what all you people do here?'

'Probably.'

'But not you?'

'No, not me. My English isn't good enough.'

Levin shook his head. 'You're a strange fellow all right.'

'Maybe so,' I replied. I declined to explain to this apostle of straightforwardness that I was in no hurry to read about the war while I was locked up here. I preferred to keep my scant reserves intact by not subjecting them to pointless emotions. If I'd told him that my current reading matter was an anthology of German poetry that I had lugged the length of the Via Dolorosa, he might have stopped wanting to represent me on the grounds that I was insane. 'Thanks a lot,' I said and took the newspapers.

Levin went on rooting about in his attaché case. 'Here are two hundred dollars that Mr Hirsch gave me for you,' he said.

'A down payment on my fee.' He produced four bills, spread them out like a hand of cards and put them away again.

I watched them go. 'Did Mr Hirsch give you the money specifically as a down payment?' I asked.

'Not specifically, but you want me to have it, don't you?' Levin grinned again, this time not just with his teeth and wrinkles but even with his ears. They flapped like an elephant's. 'You wouldn't want me to work for you for nothing?' he asked coyly.

'Certainly not. But didn't you tell me that my hundred and fifty dollars aren't enough to get me admitted to America?'

'Not if you have a sponsor. Tannenbaum's changed the game for you.'

Levin was positively dazzling. He was so dazzling that I feared an attack on my hundred and fifty dollars. I resolved to defend them tooth and claw till I got my passport back with visa. Levin seemed to sense my position. 'I'm going to take these papers to the inspectors,' he said baldly. 'If everything goes well, my partner Mr Watson will come to see you in a day or two. And he'll settle the rest.'

'Watson?' I asked.

'Watson,' he replied.

'Why Watson?' I asked suspiciously.

To my surprise, Levin was a little thrown by the question. 'Watson's family has been in America for many generations. They are among the oldest Americans,' he explained. 'They came on the *Mayflower*. In America, that's like aristocracy. It's a helpful circumstance that one should make the most of. Especially in your case. Understand?'

'I understand,' I said, surprised. Presumably Watson wasn't Jewish. So they had that over here as well.

'He'll give the whole thing the right sort of setting,' said Levin with dignity. 'It's useful for subsequent applications

17

too.' He got up and held out his bony hand. 'All the best! You'll be in New York before you know it!'

I didn't say anything. I didn't like this latest turn. I was as superstitious as anyone who lives on chance and I thought the confidence with which he anticipated the future was unlucky. He had been like that the first day too, when he asked me where I was going to live in New York. You didn't do that sort of thing among emigrants, it was unlucky. I had seen things go wrong too often. And Tannenbaum – what was that about? I couldn't quite believe in something as odd and spectacular as that. And the fellow had just helped himself to Robert Hirsch's money! It couldn't have been meant like that. Two hundred dollars! A fortune! It had taken me two years to put aside a hundred and fifty. Maybe Levin would take them off me next time. The only thing that inspired any confidence in me was the fact that this hyena with too many teeth had been sent to me by Robert Hirsch.

Hirsch was the only real Maccabee I knew. One day, shortly after the truce at Vichy, he had turned up in Provence in the guise of a Spanish vice consul. From somewhere he had got his hands on a diplomatic passport under the name Raul Tegner and he would show up in that capacity with fearless impertinence. No one knew to what degree the passport was genuine or not. People assumed he had got it via the French Resistance. Hirsch himself gave nothing away, but everyone knew that in his meteoric career he had also worked for the Resistance. He had a car with CD plates, wore a sharp suit and, at a time when petrol was about as scarce as hens' teeth, he always seemed to have plenty of it. He could only have laid his mitts on all these things with help from the Underground. He smuggled weapons, handbills and little single-sheet fold-over pamphlets for them. It was the time the Germans were in breach of the agreements about partial Occupation and broke into Free France to arrest emigrants. Hirsch tried to save as many as he could. His car, his passport and his boldness were all helpful to him. As an ostensible representative of a friendly dictator he played the Franco card whenever he was stopped. He gave tongue-lashings to patrols, appealing to his diplomatic immunity, invoking the General and his close ties to Hitler. The German patrols generally preferred to let him go rather than risk the possible consequences from higher-ups. With their innate feeling of subordination they were in awe of his title and ID; and their obedience training only reinforced their reluctance to take any responsibility, especially in the lower ranks. But even the SS wobbled when Hirsch started yelling at them. He was counting on the fear that every dictatorship inculcates in its own supporters, its way of turning the law into something unpredictable and personal, and thereby dangerous for its supporters if they failed to keep up with the endlessly mutating paragraphs. In this way he profited from the scourge of cowardice, which along with brutality is the inevitable concomitant of any violent regime.

For a few months he was a virtual legend among the emigrants. He saved a few lives with the help of some blank forms he had got hold of from somewhere and filled in according to need. People were able to escape over the Pyrenees, even though the Gestapo were already there. Others were hidden in Provençal monasteries until such time as they could be moved along. He was able to fish a couple out of a detention cell and let them escape. He carried whole bundles of Underground literature practically openly in his car. And then – this time disguised as an SS officer – he had got me and the two politicals out of the internment camp. Everyone was waiting for this one-man campaign against violence to end with the inevitable violent death. Then things went a bit quiet. It was said he had been shot by the Gestapo. As ever, there were people who claimed to have witnessed the scene personally.

After my liberation from the internment camp I had run into him the odd time and we spent a few evenings together, till daybreak. Hirsch was beside himself at the way the Jews had let themselves be rounded up by the Germans like so many rabbits; that so many thousands of them were stuffed – without any resistance – into overcrowded cattle cars and hauled away to the death camps. He couldn't understand why there were almost no attempts made to disobey or to resist; that they died meekly, without even a minority revolting, knowing they were about to be killed anyway, if only to take a few of the killers with them. We both understood that this wasn't explainable in terms of the superficial notions of fear, last-ditch, desperate hope, much less cowardice – more the opposite – because it seemed to take more bravery to go silently to one's death than to die fighting in a last desperate parody of Teutonic vengeance. Even so, Hirsch was beside himself about the two-thousand-year-old tradition of meekness, ever since the time of the Maccabees. He hated his own people for it and understood it with a painful love. His private war against brutality had more than personal motivations; he was also in rebellion against himself.

I picked up the newspapers Levin had left me. I was a halting reader. A Syrian had lent me a French-language English grammar on the boat and given me some lessons; when he was released, he had left me the book and I continued to study it. I picked up pronunciation as best

I could with the aid of a portable gramophone that a family of Polish emigrants had brought with them to Ellis Island. There were about a dozen records with it, making up an introduction to English. In the morning it was carried downstairs from the dormitory into the day room, and the entire family would huddle round it and practise their English. Reverently and effortfully they followed the drawling, plummy voice of the speaker, who slowly related the life of an imaginary English family called Brown, who had a house and garden, sons and daughters who went to school and did homework, while Mr Brown owned a bicycle on which he cycled to work and Mrs Brown watered the flowers, prepared the meals, wore a kitchen apron and had black hair. The desperate emigrants eagerly took part in this placid life, their mouths opening and closing in time with the speaker on the records as in a slow-motion film, while others sat with them in their circle, trying to learn from it as well. Sometimes in the gathering dusk, it looked as though people were sitting round a pond with old carp that slowly broke the surface, and opened and closed their mouths and waited to be fed.

Of course, there were also some who were fluent in English. Their fathers had had the foresight to enrol them in trade schools where they learned English, instead of the Latin and Greek that were taught in the gymnasiums. They now became highly sought-after teachers and would some-times practise with the others, sitting over newspapers, spelling out articles about mass murder to learn to count – ten thousand dead, twenty thousand wounded, fifty thou-sand missing, hundred thousand taken prisoner – in that way the tragedy of the world was reduced to a school lesson in which the students did their best to pronounce the 'th' in 'thousand'. The champion linguists kept patiently demonstrating it, that difficult sound that doesn't exist in German and by whose mangling you can always tell a foreigner – 'th' as in thousand, fifty thousand dead in Berlin, in Hamburg, until suddenly someone went pale, gulped, forgot phonetics and muttered in dread, 'Hamburg? That's where my mother is!'

I had no idea what kind of accents I was picking up on Ellis Island, but after a while I started to hate the notion of using the war as material for a language primer. I would rather expose myself to the stupidity of my grammar, and to learn that Karl wore a green cap, that his sister was twelve years old and was fond of cake, and that his grandmother still went ice-skating. These profundities from bygone schoolmasters' imaginations at least constituted a banal idyll, in among the bloody lessons in the newspapers. It was heart-wrenching seeing how the refugees turned against their own languages and were ashamed of them, how as soon as possible – even among themselves – they stammered in their broken English, not just to learn, but also to rid themselves of the last thing they had brought with them: the language of the murderers. Two days before my release I couldn't find my German poetry book. I had left it in the day room and found it later in the toilet, shredded and covered in filth. I thought it served me right; this enchanting poetry here was a terrible mockery of what had been done to these people by the selfsame Germany.

Levin's partner, Watson, did indeed turn up a couple of days later. He was a stately-looking man with a large, fleshy face and a carefully trimmed white moustache. As I had assumed, he was no Jew and had nothing of Levin's curiosity, and nothing of his intelligence either. He could speak neither German nor French, but he had an expansive line in gesture and a bland, foolish smile. We communicated as best we could. He didn't ask me for anything, but motioned to me imperiously to wait while he went to the inspectors' office.

There was a commotion in the women's section. Warders came running. Women had formed a circle round one woman who was lying on the floor, screaming.

'What's going on?' I asked an old man who had hurried over and was now back. 'Another nervous breakdown?'

The man shook his head. 'It seems one of the women is giving birth.'

'What? Giving birth? Here?'

'It looks that way. I wonder what the inspectors will have to say.' The man pulled a mirthless grin.

'A premature birth!' said one woman in a red velvet blouse. 'She's a month before due. No wonder, with all these excitements.'

'Is it born yet?' I asked.

The woman looked at me condescendingly. 'Of course not. Those are just the first contractions. She could be hours.'

'Will the child be an American if it's born here?' asked the old man.

'What else?' asked the woman in red.

'I mean, here on Ellis Island. We're only quarantined here, we're not in America proper. America's over there!'

'This is America all right,' said the woman indignantly. 'The guards are Americans! And the inspectors!'

'It would be a boon for the mother,' said the old man. 'That way she'd have an American relative: her baby! It would make it easier for her to be admitted. Emigrants who have American relatives are admitted.' The man looked around cautiously and grinned awkwardly.

'If he's not an American, then he'll be the first real world citizen,' I said.

'The second,' the man countered. 'The first I saw on a bridge between Austria and Czechoslovakia in 1937. The German emigrants had been chased on to the bridge by the police forces of both countries. They were penned in and couldn't go forward or back; the police sealed off both ends of the bridge. They were stuck on the frontier for three days. One woman had her baby there.'

'What happened to it?' asked the woman in the red blouse with interest.

'It died before the two countries could come to war over it,' replied the old man. 'This was during the more humane period before the German annexation,' he added apologetically. 'Later, they would have clubbed mother and child like wet cats.'

I saw Watson come out of the office. In his light, chequered suit he towered over the refugees bunched around the door. I walked quickly towards him. All of a sudden my heart was beating fast. Watson waved my passport at me. 'You're in luck,' he said. 'A woman is apparently giving birth out here; the officials were completely distracted. Here's your visa.'

I took my passport. My hands trembled. 'For how long is it good?' I asked.

Watson laughed. 'They wanted to give you a transit visa of four weeks; I've got you two months as a tourist. You should thank the woman in labour. I think they couldn't wait to see the back of you and me. A motorboat has been ordered for the woman. We could ride in with her. What about it?' Watson thumped me vigorously on the back.

'Am I free, then?'

'Sure! For the next two months. Then it's the next round.'

'Two months!' I said. 'An eternity!'

Watson shook his leonine head. 'No eternity. Two months. Best thing we start to reflect on our next steps right away.'

'Once I'm over there,' I said. 'Not now.'

'All right, but don't leave it too long. There are still some expenses, travel, the cost of the visa and one or two more things. Fifty dollars altogether. Best to take care of that right away. You can pay the rest of the bill once you've settled in to your new life.'

'How much is there still owing?'

'A hundred dollars. Very modest. We're not monsters.'

I made no reply. At that moment I just wanted to get out of here as fast as possible. Away from Ellis Island! I was afraid the door to the inspectors' room might open at the very last moment and I might be called back. Quickly I pulled out my wallet and took out a fifty-dollar bill. Now I had ninety-nine left – and a hundred-dollar debt. Presumably I would spend the rest of my life servicing the interest to those lawyers, I thought fleetingly. But I didn't care; everything was pushed aside by a wave of trembling, violent impatience.

'Can we go now?' I asked.

The woman in the red velvet blouse laughed. 'It might be hours till the baby's born. Hours! But those men don't know that. Those inspectors! They know all about every-thing, but not that. And I'm not about to clue them in now either. Every little creature that comes into the world here represents a ray of hope to the others. Isn't that right?'

'Right,' I said. I saw two people supporting the pregnant woman. 'Can we go along with them?' I asked Watson.

He nodded. The woman in the velvet blouse shook my hand. The old man came out too and congratulated me. We went out. I had to show my passport at the exit. The policeman handed it back to me right away. 'Good luck, sir!' he said and gave me his hand. It was the first time in my life that a policeman had wished me luck and shaken my hand. It had a strange effect on me – only now did I begin to think I was truly free.

We piled into a motor launch. The pregnant woman lay in the back between a couple of warders; Watson, I and a few more of the new releases stood at the front. The moans of the woman were drowned out by the noise of the motor and the ships' sirens all around us. The sun and wind bounced light and shade at the boat from all sides, so that it seemed to be floating between sky and water. I didn't look around. I clutched at the passport in my pocket. The skyscrapers of Manhattan took off into the dazzling sky. The crossing didn't last more than a few minutes.

When we docked, one of the released detainees burst into tears. He was a man with thin legs and an old-fashioned green felt hat. His moustache trembled, he dropped to one knee and spread his arms in a helpless gesture. In the strong morning sunlight he looked both moving and a little ridiculous. His wife, a brown and wizened-looking woman, pulled him to his feet in irritation. 'You'll get your suit dirty! It's the only one you've got!'

'America,' he murmured.

'Yes, we're in America,' she replied in a shrill voice. 'And where's Josef? And Samuel? What's keeping them? And where's Miriam, where is everyone? We're in America,' she repeated. 'And where are they? Get up and look after your suit!' She looked along the row of us with dead, impassive beetle eyes. 'We're in America! And where are the others? Where are the children?'

'What is she saying?' asked Watson.

'She's pleased to be in America.'

'So I should think. This is the Promised Land. I guess you're pretty happy too.'

'Very much! Thank you for all your help.'

I looked around. There seemed to be a battle of cars on

the roads. I had never seen so many vehicles at one time. In Europe since the outbreak of war, there had only been a few around; there was hardly any petrol. 'Where are the soldiers?' I asked.

'Soldiers? How come?'

'America's at war!'

Watson smiled broadly. 'The war is in Europe and in the Pacific,' he explained unctuously. 'Not here. There is no war in America. We're at peace here.'

I had forgotten that for a moment. The enemy was on the other side of the globe. There were no frontiers to be defended here. There was no shooting here. There were no ruins here either. No bombs. No destruction. 'Peace,' I said.

'Not like in Europe, eh,' remarked Watson proudly.

I nodded. 'Not at all,' I agreed.

Watson pointed across the street. 'There's a taxi rank. And a bus stop. I don't expect you want to walk.'

'Absolutely! I want to walk. I've been locked up for too long.'

'All right. Suit yourself. You won't get lost in New York. Almost all the streets have numbers. It's very practical.'

I walked through the city like a boy of five – that about corresponded to my knowledge of the English language. I walked through a shining rain of noise, words, traffic, laughter, shouts and the arousing din of a life that had nothing to do with me, but that battered my senses like a storm. All I registered was the noise, not the meaning, just as I registered the light but not how it came to be, or what it was there for. I walked through a city in which everyone seemed to be an unknown Prometheus, performing familiar gestures in an unfamiliar way, and with words I had no idea what to do with. There was a multiplicity of possibilities but I wasn't sure, because I didn't know the language. It was different from Europe, where there was just one language, and I understood that. It felt like crossing a huge stage in the round, with passers-by, waiters, drivers and vendors putting on a baffling play among themselves, that was going on all around me but to my exclusion because I didn't know how to interpret anything. I saw that it was a unique moment that would never come round again. By tomorrow morning, perhaps even by the time I reached the hotel, I would be part of it, and the struggle would recommence with evasions and lies and haggling, and that cluster of half-truths that made up my day-to-day life – but now, at this very moment, the city was showing me its face, wild, noisy, strange and unconcerned, without having taken me in at all, and therefore clear, objective, imposing and at the same time sheer as filigree, a vast and dazzling crucible. Time briefly held its breath, everything was possible, any turn was open, there were no rules, it was entirely in my own hands whether I would crash or not.

I walked terribly slowly through the fizzing city; I both saw it and didn't see it. I had been taken up with basic survival for so long; my way of getting by was based on ignoring all life outside my own. There was a ruthless urge to survive, it was like the panic on a sinking ship, with always the one aim: not to go under. But now, at this signal hour, I felt that life might begin to unfold before me, that there was some sort of future, however briefly measured, and that, along with the future, the past too might return to haunt me with its smell of blood and graves. I felt vaguely that it was a past that might easily destroy me, but I didn't want to know, not now, I was too taken with the sparkling shop windows and the wild smell of freedom, the crush of strangers and the noontime rush, the anonymous din, the appetites and the fabulous light – for this one hour, in which I blundered around like an illegitimate wanderer between two worlds, not belonging to either one. I was in a film with the wrong soundtrack, subject to an astounding alchemy of light, colour, incomprehension and – within the incomprehension – a childish feeling of security. It was as though life itself, so long pressed in on itself like the kernel of a nut, was about to open itself to me again, to respond to clamour and question, to look and insight, across the soft mulch of memory to a shy and still impalpable hope. Did such things really exist? I wondered, as I stared into a huge open hall full of shiny chrome slot machines, jingling and flashing coloured lights – could it be? Wasn't everything desiccated and dead, could survival morph into living on and then become just – life? Was it possible: to begin again, from the beginning, to be interpreted like the language before me, unknown and full of possibilities? Was it possible, without being treason and a kind of twofold murder of the dead, who wanted not to be forgotten?

I walked on. I followed the streets with the numbers and not the names, they became dingier and narrower, till I found myself standing in front of a building set back from the street with the sign Hotel Rausch over the door. The doorway had fake marble cladding, one side of which was cracked. I walked in and stopped. Emerging from the harsh glare of the street, I could make out little more than a sort of counter, some red plush chairs and a rocker, from which a hulking bear-like form got up. 'Are you Ludwig Sommer?' the bear asked me, in French.

'Yes, I am,' I said in surprise. 'How do you know?'

'Robert Hirsch told us you'd be along one of these days. My name is Vladimir Moikov. I'm the manager here, and the head waiter and just about everything else.'

'It's as well you speak French. Otherwise I think I'd just have gaped back at you like a fish.'

Moikov and I shook hands. 'Apparently, fishes are great underwater conversationalists,' he said. 'Anything but mute. Recent scientific discovery. But you can talk German with me too, if you like.'

'Are you German?'

Moikov's broad face crumpled. 'No. I'm a survivor of many revolutions. Now I'm an American. Before, I was Czech, Russian, Polish, Austrian, according to whoever was occupying the tiny hamlet my mother came from. I was even a German for a while. But you look thirsty. Would you like a vodka?'

I hesitated, thinking of my dwindling finances. 'What do you charge for a room?' I asked.

'Our cheapest is two dollars a night. It's no more than a tiny bedroom.' Moikov went over to the board with the keys. 'Basic, no luxuries. But there's a bathroom on the landing.'

'I'll take it. Is it cheaper by the month?'

'Fifty dollars, forty-five paid in advance.'

'Fine.'

Moikov smiled like an ancient baboon. 'The vodka is part of the deal. It's on the house. I make it myself, by the way. It's good stuff.'

'We made some in Switzerland one time, fifty per cent proof, with a cuvée of blackcurrant flowers on a piece of sugar,' I replied. 'A pharmacist supplied the alcohol. It cost way less than the cheapest schnapps. Those were good times, winter of 1942.'

'In prison?'

'In prison in Bellinzona. Unfortunately I was only in there for a week. For illegal border crossing.'

'Blackcurrants, eh?' mused Moikov. 'Interesting! But where would I find blackcurrants in New York?'

'You barely taste them,' I replied. 'The guy who had the idea was a White Russian. This vodka is very good.'

'I'm glad. Do you play chess?'

'Prison chess. Not grand master level. Refugee chess, to distract myself.'

Moikov nodded. 'And then there's language chess,' he said. 'We play a lot of it here. Chess is so abstract that it's good to go over English grammar at the same time. I'll show you to your room.'

The room was very small, it didn't get much light and it faced the back. I paid the forty-five dollars and unpacked my case. The room had a cast-iron overhead light fixture and a little green table lamp; you could leave it on overnight. That calmed me. Ever since my time in the museum in Brussels, I've hated sleeping in utter darkness. Then I counted my money again. I didn't know how long a man could live off forty-nine dollars in New York, but it didn't worry me. Many times I had had just a fraction of that. As long as you were alive, you were never completely lost, the late Mr Sommer had said shortly before he died – curious how true that was and how completely untrue at the same time.

'There's a letter for you from Robert Hirsch,' said Moikov when I came back down. 'He wasn't sure when you'd be arriving. I suggest you go over and see him tonight. He works in the daytime – most people do, here.'

Work, I thought. Legal! The bliss of that! What a thing it would be. All I knew was off-the-books black market labour, always on the lookout for the police.

3

I went to see Hirsch at lunchtime. I couldn't wait till evening. I found a little business with two windows full of wirelesses, electric irons, hairdryers, mixers and electric cookers; gleams of shiny metal and chrome – but the door was locked. I waited for a while; then I thought about it and guessed that Robert Hirsch had probably stepped out for lunch. A little disappointed, I turned round. Suddenly I felt a keen hunger. I looked around helplessly. I wanted something to eat, but not to spend too much money. On the corner I saw a shop that looked like a pharmacy. Enemas, bottles of eau de toilette and aspirin advertisements stood in the window; but through the open door I saw a kind of bar at which people were sitting and eating. I went in. 'What can I do for you?' asked a youth in white impatiently behind the bar.

Just then I wasn't able to give him an answer. I had never ordered anything in America before. I pointed to my neighbour's plate. 'Hamburger?' yapped the youth.

'Hamburger,' I replied in bewilderment. I had never expected my first word of English to be German.

The hamburger was juicy and good. It came with a toasted bun. The youth barked something else. I didn't understand his staccato; but I saw that my neighbour was given a dish of ice cream. I hadn't had ice cream in years.

But 'yes' wasn't enough for the boy. He pointed to a long board behind him and barked again.

My neighbour looked at me. He was bald and had a walrus moustache. 'What flavour?' he enunciated, as to a child.

'The usual,' I replied, to get off the hook.

The walrus smiled. 'There are forty-two sorts of ice cream here,' he explained.

'What?'

The man pointed to the board. 'Choose.'

I made out the word 'pistachio'. In Paris, the wandering carpet sellers hawked pistachio nuts round the cafés. I wasn't familiar with the ice cream. 'Pistachio,' I said. 'And coconut.'

I paid and slowly went out. It was the first time I had eaten lunch in a pharmacy. I walked past other counters for prescriptions and medicines. You could buy rubber gloves, paperbacks and goldfish here. What a country, I thought as I emerged on to the street. Forty-two flavours of ice cream, war, and not a soldier in sight.

I went back to the Rausch. I recognised the crumbling marble façade from a distance, amidst so much that was unfamiliar it seemed almost like home. Vladimir Moikov was not around. No one was around. The hotel was deserted. I walked through the lobby with plush armchairs and a few dusty potted palms. No one. I picked up my key, went up to my room and lay down fully dressed on my bed for a little nap. I awoke with no idea where I was. I had had a dream, a bad dream. The room was now filled with a pinkish, floating dusk. I got up and looked out of the window. Two Negroes were carrying out rubbish bins downstairs. A lid fell off and clattered on the cement. Now I remembered something in my dream. I was being pursued across the ocean. I went downstairs. Moikov was back; he was sitting at a table with a frail-looking old lady and waved. I looked at my watch. It was time to see Hirsch. I had been asleep for longer than I thought.

A small crowd of people was milling around Robert Hirsch's shop. I thought there might have been an accident, or something involving the police; the usual catastrophe. I pushed through the crowd and then I heard an unnaturally loud voice talking. There were three loudspeakers now beside the window and the door was wide open. The voice was coming from the loudspeakers. The shop was deserted and dark.

Then I saw Hirsch. He was standing outside, among the listeners. I identified his narrow head and reddish hair right away. He hadn't changed. 'Robert,' I said softly, just behind him in the powerful sound of the triple loudspeakers.

He didn't hear. 'Robert!' I called. 'Robert!'

He spun round. His expression changed. 'Ludwig! It's you! When did you get here?'

'Just this morning. I came once earlier, but there was no one around.'

We shook hands. 'Good you're here,' he said. 'Damned good, Ludwig! I thought you were dead.'

'I thought you were, Robert. They were all saying you were killed in Marseilles. There were even people who claimed to have been there when you were shot.'

Hirsch laughed. 'Emigrant gossip. Anyway, it lengthens one's life to be supposed dead. I'm glad you're here, Ludwig.' He pointed to the triple row of loudspeakers in the window. 'Roosevelt!' he said. 'Your saviour. Let's hear what he has to say.'

I nodded. The mighty, amplified voice drowned out all expressions of feeling anyway. We weren't used to it either;

on the Via Dolorosa people lost each other from sight so often, and met and re-met or didn't, that it tended to make you discreet and cool, as if seeing each other were an everyday occurrence. You died or you were arrested or you met up again down the road. You were alive – wasn't that the point? It was, in Europe, I thought. Here it was different. I was excited – and anyway, I found it very hard to follow what the President was saying.

I noticed that Hirsch didn't appear to be listening very closely. He watched the people in front of his windows. Most of them stood there placidly, listening; a few made remarks to one another. A fat woman with a high heap of blonde hair laughed dismissively, tapped her temple and sashayed away with her thick hips. 'They should lynch that bastard!' growled a man in a chequered sports jacket next to me.

'What is "lynch"?' I asked Hirsch.

'Lynch,' he mused, 'put to death, hang. You should know that.'

Just at that moment the loudspeakers fell silent. 'Is that why you wanted to run all your equipment?' I asked. 'As a kind of compulsory tolerance training?'

He nodded. 'My old weakness. I don't seem to be able to stop. But it's hopeless. Wherever you go.'

People dispersed quickly. Only the man in the sports jacket stayed put. 'What's that language you're talking to each other in?' he growled. 'German?'

'French,' Hirsch replied coolly. We had been talking German. 'The language of your allies.'

'Allies, my ass! And we're fighting for those people. It's all Roosevelt's fault!'

The man swayed off. 'It's always the same,' observed Hirsch. 'Xenophobia is the surest sign of primitiveness in people.'

Then he looked at me. 'You've lost weight, Ludwig. And you look older. I really thought you were dead! Strange, always to jump to that conclusion when you're left without news of someone for a while. We're not even that old!'

I laughed. 'It's the way we've been made to live, Robert.'

Hirsch was roughly my age, thirty-two, but he looked much older. And he was smaller and slighter than me too. 'I was sure you were dead too,' I said.

'That was a rumour I started myself, to make it easier to get by,' he replied. 'It got to be time for that.'

We entered the shop, where the radio was broadcasting a sanctimonious advertisement for a cemetery. 'Well-drained, sandy soil,' I caught. 'And magnificent views!' Hirsch switched off the voice, and produced glasses, a bottle and ice from a small refrigerator. 'The last of my absinthe,' he commented. 'This is a good day to crack it open.'

'Absinthe?' I asked. 'The real thing?'

'No, not really. Ersatz, like everything: Pernod. But it's all the way from Paris. Cheers, Ludwig! To life!'

'Cheers, Robert.' I hated Pernod. It tasted like liquorice or aniseed. 'Where were you last in France?' I asked.

'I was hidden for three months in a cloister in Provence. The abbé was charming. They were keen to make a Catholic out of me, but didn't insist. In addition to me, there were a couple of shot-down English fighter pilots hidden there. We went around in monk's robes, just in case. I used the time to improve my English. Hence the Oxford accent, don't you know; the pilots had studied there. Did Levin take all your money off you?'

'No. But he did keep the money you gave me.'

'Good! I thought he would. That's why I used him,' Hirsch laughed. 'Here's the rest, which I kept back. Otherwise he'd have had that as well.'

He produced two fifty-dollar bills and shoved them in my pocket. 'I don't need anything,' I said. 'I've got enough. More than I ever did in Europe! You should let me try to get by on my own.'

'Rubbish, Ludwig! I know exactly how much you've got. Anyway, a dollar will get you half as much here as it would in Europe; and to be poor in America is twice as hard as it is anywhere else. Did you have any news of Josef Richter? He was in Marseilles when I went to Spain.'

I nodded. 'That's where they caught him too. Outside the American consulate. He didn't have a chance to flee into the building. You know what it was like.'

'Yes,' he said, 'I know.'

The streets around the foreign consulates in France were the preferred hunting grounds for the Gestapo and the police. Most emigrants were trying to obtain exit visas. As long as they were on diplomatic premises they were safe – but they were often picked up the moment they walked out of the door.

'And Werner?' asked Hirsch. 'What happened to him?'

'Beaten to a pulp by the Gestapo and put on a transport.'

I didn't ask Robert how he had managed to get out of France. That was a habit from before, if you didn't know something, you wouldn't be able to betray it; no one could tell whether they could stand up to modern torture methods or not.

'That nation!' Hirsch exclaimed. 'That bloody nation, persecuting its citizens like that. And we belong to it.'

He stared into space. For a while, neither of us said anything. 'Robert,' I finally asked. 'Who is Tannenbaum?'

He emerged from his introspection. 'Tannenbaum is a Jewish banker,' he replied. 'Been settled in the States for years. Rich. And well-disposed, if you give him a nudge.'

'Good. And who gave him a nudge in my direction? Was it you, Robert? More compulsory compassion training?'

'No, Ludwig, it wasn't me. The mildest emigrant soul in the world: Jessie Stein.'

'Is Jessie here too? How did she make it over?'

Hirsch laughed. 'She made it all by herself. In some comfort. Heck, in luxury. She got to America the way Vollberg got to Spain. You'll come across lots more old friends here. Even in the Hotel Rausch. Not everyone was arrested or killed.'

Two years ago, Vollberg had laid siege to the Franco-Spanish border for several weeks. He could obtain neither an exit visa from France nor an entry visa to Spain. While the other emigrants clambered across the Pyrenees on goat tracks, the desperate Vollberg, who couldn't climb, ended up renting an ancient Rolls-Royce with about twenty miles' worth of petrol and took the high road into Spain. The owner of the car became his chauffeur, lent Vollberg his best suit and his war decorations, which Vollberg proudly displayed, sprawled in the back of the car. It worked. Not one of the customs people asked the ostensible owner of a Rolls-Royce for his visa. Instead, they all clustered avidly round the engine, while the chauffeur patiently told them about its performance.

'Are you telling me Jessie Stein drove to America in a Rolls-Royce?' I asked.

'No, Ludwig. But she was on the last sailing of the *Queen Mary* before war broke out. Her visa was valid for just two days when she got here. Then it was extended to six months. And then renewed every six months.'

Suddenly breathless with excitement, I stared at Hirsch. 'Does that happen, then, Robert?' I asked. 'Can you get a visa extended here? Even a tourist visa?'

'Only a tourist visa. You don't need to extend the others. They're proper entry visas with so-called quotas; a kind of preliminary stage to full citizenship in five years. Oversubscribed for decades! With a quota visa you're even allowed to work; not with a tourist visa. How long is yours good for?'

'Eight weeks. Do you really think I could get it extended?'

'Why not? Levin and Watson know their stuff.'

I leaned back in my chair. All of a sudden, for the first time in many years, I felt deeply relaxed. Hirsch looked at me and laughed. 'Tonight we celebrate your entry into the respectable phase of emigration,' he said. 'I'll buy you dinner. The Via Dolorosa days are over, Ludwig.'

'Until tomorrow at least,' I said. 'Then I'll have to start hunting for work and will be in breach of the laws again. What are the prisons like in New York?'

'Oh, thoroughly democratic. In some you even get given a wireless. If not, I can supply you with one.'

'Do they have internment camps in America?'

'Yes, they do. But just for a change they're reserved for suspected Nazis.'

'There's a turn-up!' I got to my feet. 'Where shall we eat? In an American pharmacy? I had lunch in one. It was very good. There were condoms and forty-two flavours of ice cream, or was it the other way round.'

Hirsch laughed. 'Those places are called drugstores. No, I've got something else in mind.'

He locked the door. 'Does this shop belong to you?' I asked.

He shook his head. 'No, I'm just a poor little salesman,' he said in a fit of bitterness. 'A humdrum shopkeeper from morning till night. Who'd have thought it would come to that!'

I made no reply. I'd have been happy to be a shopkeeper here. We went out on the street. There was a thin wisp of red between the buildings, it was as though it felt cold and didn't belong here. Two aeroplanes buzzed up in the clear sky. No one paid them any regard, no one took refuge in doorways or dropped to the ground. A double row of street lamps came on. Neon advertisements clambered up and down the sides of some of the buildings like great apes. In Europe at this time everything would have been pitch dark. 'You know, there really isn't a war on here,' I said.

'No,' replied Hirsch. 'There isn't. No ruins, no danger, no bombs, that's what you mean, isn't it?' He laughed. 'No danger – but all the despair that comes from hanging around doing nothing.'

I looked at him. His face gave nothing away. 'I think I could get used to it,' I said.

We turned into a long avenue where red, amber and green traffic lights sparkled at various depths. 'We're going to a fish restaurant,' said Hirsch. 'Do you remember the last time we ate fish together, in France?'

I laughed. 'I remember exactly. It was in the old port of Marseilles, at Basso's. I had the bouillabaisse with saffron and you had the crevettes. You were treating me. It was the last meal we had together. Unfortunately we weren't able to finish it, because we noticed some policemen among the clientele and we had to slip away.'

Hirsch nodded. 'This time, I promise you you'll be able to finish your meal. It's no longer a question of life and death.'

'Thank God!'

We stopped in front of a brightly lit restaurant. Two big plate-glass windows had displays of fish and seafood. They lay on beds of shaved ice. The fish were in long silver rows with sightless eyes; the prawns shimmered pink, because they had already been cooked; but the lobsters, which looked like primordial knights in black armour, they were still alive. To begin with, we didn't realise they were alive; then we saw the feelers and then the eyes that stood out like little buttons, moving. They were looking at you; moving around and looking at you. Their great claws moved languidly. Little wooden pegs had been driven into them, so that the animals didn't cut each other to pieces.

'What a life!' I said. 'To be laid out on ice, made fast and disabled! Like so many emigrants without passports.'

'I'll order you one. The biggest they have.'

I declined. 'Not today, Robert. I don't want to kill something on my first day here. I think we should let those poor creatures live! Even that wretched existence is life of a kind and they would defend it if they could. I'll order prawns. They're cooked already. And what'll you have?'

'Lobster. I want to relieve it from its sufferings!'

'Two views,' I said. 'Yours is more practical. Mine is more hypocritical.'

'They'll change.'

We walked in. A wave of warm air came out to greet us. There was a strong smell of fish. Almost all the tables were occupied. Waiters rushed past carrying enormous platters, from which enormous crabs' legs stuck out like so many bones at a cannibal feast. At one table sat a couple of policemen, elbows on the table, crabs' legs in their fists like harmonicas. I stopped involuntarily and looked for the exit. Robert gave me a nudge. 'No need to run any more, Ludwig,' he said and laughed. 'But a lawful existence demands courage as well. Sometimes more courage than running away.'

★

I sat in the red plush alcove that passed for a drawing room in the Hotel Rausch, studying English grammar. It was late already, but I didn't feel like going to bed. Moikov was fussing around in his little lobby. After a time, I heard someone come in, seemingly with a limp. It was an odd sort of limp, a syncopated stagger, and it reminded me of someone I'd known in Europe. In the darkness, I didn't have a good view of the man.

'Lachmann?' I ventured.

The man stopped. 'Lachmann,' I said again and switched on the overhead light. It dribbled down yellow and dull and glum from a three-armed art nouveau chandelier.

The man blinked over in my direction. 'Good God, Ludwig!' he said. 'Since when have you been here?'

'For three days. I recognised your footfall straight away.'

'My rotten trochee rhythm?'

'Your three-four waltz time, Kurt.'

'How did you make it over? Did Roosevelt give you a visa? Are you on the list of important European intellectuals who have to be rescued?'

I shook my head. 'None of us are. Poor buggers like us aren't famous enough.'

'I'm sure I'm not,' said Lachmann.

Moikov came in. 'You know each other, gentlemen?'

'Yes,' I said, 'we've known each other for a long time. From many prisons.'

Moikov turned off the overhead light and got a bottle. 'This calls for a vodka,' he said. 'When there is an occasion, we celebrate. This is on the hotel. We are very hospitable here.'

'I don't drink,' said Lachmann.

'That's right!' Moikov poured me a glass. 'One of the points of emigration is that it affords so many opportunities for greetings and leave-takings,' he said. 'That creates the illusion of a long life.'

Neither Lachmann nor I said anything. Moikov was from another generation – the one that had fled Russia in 1917. What was still flaming in us had long since cooled and stabilised in him.

'Cheers, Moikov,' I said. 'Why weren't we born as Yogis? Or in Switzerland?'

Lachmann laughed drily. 'I'd be happy enough not to have been born as a Jew in Germany.'

'You are in the first wave of world citizens,' countered Moikov unmoved. 'You should at least comport yourselves like pioneers. One day people will erect monuments to you.'

He went to the registry desk to give out a key. 'A joker,' Lachmann said when his back was turned. 'Are you doing anything for him?'

'What?'

'Vodka, heroin, gambling, that sort of thing?'

'Is he into all that?'

'They say.'

'Is that what you're here for?'

'No. But I used to live here too. Like almost every new arrival in New York.'

Lachmann gave me a conspiratorial look and sat down next to me. 'I'm keen on a woman who's living here,' he whispered. 'Imagine: a Puerto-Rican, forty-five years old, with a bad foot, traffic accident. She's going out with a Mexican pimp. For five dollars he's willing to throw us into bed together. Money's not the problem, it's the woman. She's religious. It's such terrible luck! She's faithful to him. He beats her for it, but she won't change her mind. She thinks God's watching her from the clouds. Even at night. I told her God was short-sighted; always has been. Nothing doing. But still she takes my money. And she makes promises. And gives it to the pimp. And breaks her word and laughs. And makes new promises. I'm being driven crazy! It's hopeless.'

Lachmann had a complex because of his limp. He apparently used to be a prodigious skirt-chaser once, in Berlin. An SS brigade, who had heard about his exploits, had hauled him back to their headquarters to castrate him and was just in the process of doing so when – this was in 1933 – they were disturbed by the police. Lachmann had lost four teeth, had a scarred scrotum and a multiply-broken leg, which healed badly because the hospital was already refusing to take Jewish patients. Since then he's walked with a limp and had a preference for women with mild physical defects like himself. He didn't really mind, so long as they had a big, taut derrière. He claimed to have had a woman with three breasts once, in Rouen. That was the love of his life. The police had caught him twice with her and expatriated him to Switzerland. He had gone back to her in Rouen a third time – just as an emperor moth flies many miles to his female in a wire cage. He was caught, put in prison for four weeks and extradited again. The only thing that kept him from going back a fourth time was the fact that the Germans by then had overrun much of France. Without knowing it, Hitler had saved the life of the Jewish Lachmann.

'You haven't changed, Kurt,' I said.

'People don't change,' Lachmann replied glumly. 'You make a thousand resolutions when you're on the floor; but the moment things are so you can breathe again, you forget them.' Lachmann himself took a breath. 'I'm not sure if it's heroic or plain stupid.'

'Heroic,' I said. 'In a situation as bad as ours we should reach for the finest attributes.'

Lachmann mopped his brow. He had a head like a seal. 'You haven't changed either!' He sighed and pulled out a parcel wrapped in tissue paper. 'A rosary,' he explained. 'I deal in them. Relics and amulets; also icons, statues and holy candles. I have a good base in the Catholic market.' He lifted up the rosary. 'Real silver and ivory,' he said. 'Blessed by His Holiness in person. Do you think that might break her resistance?'

'Blessed by whom?'

He looked at me tetchily. 'By Pius! Pius the Twelfth – who did you think?'

'Benedict the Fifteenth would have been better. First, he's dead, which, as with stamps, increases the value. And second, he wasn't a fascist.'

'You and your damnfool jokes! I'd forgotten about that side of you. The last time in Paris—'

'Hold it right there,' I said, 'no reminiscing!'

'Whatever you say.' Lachmann hesitated for a moment, then his indiscretion won out. He unwrapped another tissue-paper-sheathed object. 'A piece of an olive tree from the garden of Gethsemane in Jerusalem! An original, with official stamp and written authentication. Tell me that won't melt her heart!' He looked at me beseechingly.

I looked at the things with fascination. 'Do you make a living out of that stuff? Is there money in it?'

He was instantly suspicious. 'Just enough to keep from starving. Why? Are you going to set up in competition?'

'I'm just curious, Kurt. Nothing more.'

He looked at his watch. 'I'm supposed to pick her up at eleven. Cross your fingers for me.' He got up, straightened his tie and limped up the stairs. Then he came down again. 'What can I do?' he said plaintively. 'I'm such a passionate man! It's awful. I'm sure it'll be the death of me. But what else is there?'

I shut my grammar and leaned back. From where I was sitting, I had a view of the street. The door was open, it was hot and the light of an arc lamp reached in from outside, as far as the front desk; thereafter it was extinguished in the dark stairwell. The mirror opposite was a pale grey, aspiring to silver. I stared at it absent-mindedly. In the counter light the plush armchairs seemed almost violet and the stains on them had a momentary look of dried blood. Where had I seen that before? Dried blood in a small room, with the window lit by a majestic sunset that leached all the colours away, in a reflection of vague grey, black, and this dark red and violet. Broken, bloodied bodies on the floor and a face in the window that suddenly turned away, and caught the setting sun on one side, while the other remained in shade. A high, bored-sounding, nasal voice that said, 'Keep moving! Next one!'

I got up quickly and turned on the overhead light. Then I looked around again. The thin light of the chandelier once again dripped like a yellow grey rain over the chairs and the plush sofa, maroon and ugly as before. There wasn't any blood. I looked into the mirror; it cast a dim and wobbly reflection of the front desk – nothing more.

'No,' I said aloud. 'No! Not here!'

I went over to the door. From the front desk Moikov looked up at me. 'What about our game of chess?'

I shook my head. 'Later. I'm going out for a bit now. Take in the shops and the lights of New York. At this time of night, Europe was dark.'

Moikov looked at me doubtfully. Then he tilted his great skull. 'Don't try and chat up a woman,' he said. 'She might cry for help and you'll get in trouble with the police. New York isn't Paris. Europeans tend not to appreciate the difference.'

46

I stopped. 'Aren't there any prostitutes in New York, then?'

The creases deepened in Moikov's face. 'Not on the streets. The police chase them away.'

'And in brothels?'

'Same deal. The police chase them away.'

'How do Americans manage to reproduce?'

'In respectable bourgeois marriages under the sanction of all-powerful women's clubs.'

I was astonished. Apparently prostitutes were persecuted here the way they persecuted emigrants in Europe. 'I don't have enough English to talk to a woman anyway.'

I stepped out on to the street, which lay in front of me, bright and sterile. At this time in France, the whores would be out in force, teetering through the streets on their high heels, or standing under the blacked-out light of the air raid lanterns. They were a tough breed all right, not even afraid of the Gestapo. They were the fleeting companions of lonely refugees who couldn't stand their own company any more and had a little money for a swift hour of perfunctory intimacy. I looked at the delis, which were stuffed full of hams, salamis, pineapples and cheeses. Finished, I thought, you night birds of Paris! A future of celibacy and masturbation lay ahead of me.

I stopped in front of one shop with a sign: Hot Pastrami. It was a deli. The door was open, even though it was late at night. There seemed to be no curfew hour in New York.

'One portion of hot pastrami,' I said.

'On rye?' The seller pointed to a rye loaf.

I nodded. 'With a pickled cucumber.' I pointed to a gherkin.

The man pushed the plate across to me. I sat down on a bar stool and started to eat. I hadn't known what pastrami was. It was hot corned beef and it was very good. Everything

47

in those days tasted very good to me. I was always hungry and I could always eat. The food on Ellis Island had an odd taste sometimes; it was rumoured that it contained bromide, to inhibit the sexual drive.

Apart from me, there was a striking-looking girl at the counter. She sat there so still as though her face were marble. Her hair was lacquered like that of an Egyptian sphinx; she was heavily made up. In Paris, one might have taken her for a prostitute; only prostitutes used that much make-up.

I thought of Hirsch. I had seen him that afternoon. 'You need a woman,' he said. 'Soon! You've been on your own too long. Best thing is you find an emigrant. She'll understand you. You'll have someone to talk to. German and French. English too, eventually. Loneliness is a proud and appalling illness. We've had enough of it to last a lifetime.'

'Not an American?'

'Not for the moment. Maybe down the road. Don't get someone else's superfluous complexes on top of your own.'

I had a chocolate ice cream. Two queers came in with apricot-coloured poodles, and bought cigarettes and a Sara Lee cake. Funny, I thought. Everyone expecting me to throw myself at the nearest woman; I don't feel like it at all. The unfamiliar light on the streets was much more stimulating.

Slowly I made my way back to the hotel.

'Didn't you find anything?' asked Moikov.

'Wasn't looking.'

'Just as well. Then what about a quiet game of chess now. Or are you too tired?'

I shook my head. 'Freedom keeps you from getting tired.'

'Or not,' responded Moikov. 'Usually, the emigrants collapse when they get here and sleep for days. Exhaustion through safety, I'd say. But not you?'

'No. Or at least I don't feel at all tired.'

'Then it'll catch up with you later. But it will.'

'Fine.'

Moikov got his board and pieces. 'Has Lachmann gone already?' I asked.

'Not yet. He's still upstairs with his lady love.'

'Do you think he'll get lucky tonight?'

'Why would he? She'll take him to dinner with her Mexican and he'll pay the bill. Was he always like that?'

'He claims not. He says it gave him a complex when he got his limp.'

Moikov nodded. 'Perhaps so,' he said. 'It doesn't matter anyway. You wouldn't believe how many things cease to matter when you get old.'

'How long have you been here?'

'Twenty years.'

I saw a shadowy figure pass through the door. It was a young woman, leaning forward a little, with a fine-boned face. She was pale, with pale-grey eyes and chestnut hair that looked dyed. 'Maria!' said Moikov, surprised, and got up. 'When did you get back?'

'Yesterday.'

I got up as well. Moikov kissed the girl on both cheeks. She was almost my height, wore a tailored suit and had a slightly flustered way of speaking. Her voice was rough and a little loud, almost metallic. She paid no attention to me. 'What about a vodka?' asked Moikov. 'Or a whiskey?'

'A vodka. But just one finger. I have to go. Modelling.'

'At this time of night?'

'The photographer wasn't free any sooner. Dresses and hats. Tiny little hats.'

I saw that she was herself wearing a hat; it was like a little cap, a scrap of black, sitting askew on top of her head.

Moikov went back for the bottle. 'You're not American, are you?' she asked. She and Moikov had been speaking French.

'No. I'm German.'

'I hate the Germans,' she said.

'So do I,' I replied.

She looked at me in surprise. 'I didn't mean it like that!' she said quickly. 'Not personally.'

'Nor did I.'

'You know what I mean: on account of the war.'

'Of course,' I replied indifferently. 'There's a war on, I know.'

It wasn't the first time I had come under attack for my nationality. It had happened to me often enough in France. Wars were boom time for simple generalisations.

Moikov returned with the bottle and three small glasses.

'None for me,' I said.

'Are you offended?' asked the girl.

'Not at all. I just don't feel like drinking. I hope that doesn't bother you.'

Moikov chortled. 'Cheers, Maria,' he said, raising his glass.

'Divine,' said the girl, and knocked back her glass with a quick jolt and a shudder.

Moikov picked up the bottle. 'Another? They're very small glasses.'

'Merci, Vladimir. It's enough. I must go. Au revoir.'

She held her hand out to me as well. 'Au revoir, Monsieur.'

The pressure of her hand was unexpectedly strong. 'Au revoir, Mademoiselle.'

Moikov, who had escorted her outside, came back. 'Did she annoy you?'

'No. It was my fault. I could have said I had an Austrian passport.'

'Don't take it amiss. She doesn't mean anything by it. She speaks faster than she thinks. First time out, she annoys almost everyone.'

'Really?' I said crossly. 'She's not pretty enough to afford to do that.'

Moikov blinked at me. 'It's not a good day for her. She improves on acquaintance, believe me.'

'Is she Italian?'

'I think so. Her name is Maria Fiola. A mix of nationalities, like many here; I believe her mother was a Spanish or Russian Jewess. She works as a fashion model. She used to live here.'

'Like Lachmann,' I noted.

'Like Lachmann, like Hirsch, like Löwenstein and lots more,' replied Moikov. 'This is a cheap, cosmopolitan sort of place. A cut above the national ghettoes of the immigrants when they first get here.'

'Ghettoes? Do they have those here too?'

'They use the word. Lots of emigrants prefer to live with their compatriots. Later on, their children move out.'

'Is there a German ghetto?'

'Of course. Yorktown. That's the area around 86th Street and the Hindenburg Café.'

'You're joking. The Hindenburg Café? With a war on?'

Moikov nodded. 'American Germans are often worse than Nazis.'

'But the emigrants?'

'A few live up there, yes.'

There was the sound of footsteps down the stairs. I heard Lachmann's limp. Then I heard a very low, sonorous woman's voice. That would be the Puerto-Rican. She walked ahead of Lachmann, not seeming to care if he followed or not. I didn't think she had a bad foot. She talked only to the Mexican at her side.

'Poor Lachmann,' I said, when the group had gone on its way.

'Poor?' replied Moikov. 'Why? He has what he doesn't have, but would like to have.'

'You always hang on to that, don't you?' I asked.

'You're only poor when you stop wanting. Do you want the vodka now that you declined a moment ago?'

I nodded. Moikov poured. He was very liberal with his vodka, I thought. He had a striking way of drinking it as well. The little glass disappeared completely into his enormous hand. He didn't knock it back. Instead, he passed it very slowly across his mouth, so that you didn't see the glass, then he set it down carefully on the table, empty. You simply didn't see him drink. Then he opened his eyes, which looked briefly lidless, like those of a very ancient parrot.

'Now what about that game of chess?' he asked.

'Sure,' I said.

Moikov set out the pieces. 'The pleasant thing about chess is that it's so utterly neutral,' he explained. 'There's no hidden moral anywhere in it.'

4

Over the course of the following week my sense of a double age brought on by New York changed quickly. If the first time I walked through the city I'd felt like a five- or six-year-old because of my English, a week later already I felt like an eight-year-old. Every morning I sat down for a few hours in the lobby's red plush with my grammar and every afternoon I took whatever opportunity offered of a halting conversation. I knew I had to learn to communicate before my money ran out, to earn something. It was a race against time. In order, I had a French, German, Polish, Jewish and finally, once I was sure that the waitresses and chambermaids I met were real Americans, a Brooklyn accent.

'You should start a relationship with a teacher,' said Moikov, with whom I was now on first-name terms.

'One from Brooklyn?'

'Boston would be better. They're supposed to speak the clearest English in America. Here in the hotel, the accents fly around like typhoid germs. You seem to have a good ear for variations, unfortunately, and not for norms. I'm thinking a little emotion would help you learn.'

'Vladimir,' I said, 'I'm changing quickly enough as it is. Every day my American identity gets a year older. Unfortunately, it causes the world to lose some of its magic. The more I understand, the more the mystery disappears.

Exotic figures in a drugstore turn out to be hot-dog sellers. Another couple of weeks and my two selves will be caught up. Then I'll feel disillusioned. New York won't be Peking, Baghdad, Atlantis and Athens rolled into one any more – and I'll have to go to Harlem or Chinatown to experience the Pacific. So, give me some time with accents. I don't want to grow out of my second childhood too quickly!'

I soon knew the antique stores on Second and Third Avenue. Ludwig Sommer, to whose passport I was giving a new lease of life, had been an antique dealer. He had known a lot and I had learned from him.

There were hundreds of shops in that part of New York. My favourite time to visit them was the late afternoon. The sun would be low on the other side of the street and seemed to amuse itself by making prisms of bright dust in the shop windows, like a magician who fords glass walls like water. As at a secret command, the old mirrors on the walls seemed to wake up, and in the space of a second acquired silver and depth. What a moment before had been stained surface was now a window into infinity, juggling gaudy impressions of the other side of the street. As if by magic, the dusty collections of old junk came to life. Normally, time in melancholy fashion seemed to stand still in them, they were quiet backwaters in the noisy avenue, which rushed past them and barely seemed to touch them. They were extinguished, like small stoves that no longer gave warmth, just an illusion of former warmth. They were dead, but not in a sad way, just like bits of the past are no longer tragic, just memory that no longer hurts and perhaps never hurt. Their owners moved slowly behind the glass panes, staring out often in thick glasses, like carp, among Chinese mandarin robes and tapestries, or hunkered between Tibetan lacquered devils, or read thrillers or newspapers.

But all that changed when the slant sun of late afternoon gave the right side of the avenue a honeyed charm, while on the shady side the windows filled with the spiders' webs of evening. It was the moment when the soft light gave the shops an illusory life, a mirror existence on borrowed light, at which they awoke, just as the painted clock in an optician's shop comes to life for a second a day, when the painted time and the real time coincide.

I was standing in front of one antique shop when its door suddenly opened, and a thin little man with a hooked nose and pepper-and-salt trousers stepped out. He must have been watching me for a while already. 'Nice evening, eh?' he said.

I nodded. He gave me a sidelong look. 'Is there anything here that catches your eye?'

I pointed to a Chinese bronze vase on a fake Venetian pier table. 'What's that?'

'A Chinese bronze vase. Cheap. Come on in and have a proper look at it.'

I followed him in. The man got the bronze out of the window. 'How old is it?'

'Not that old.' He looked at me for a while. 'It's a copy of a much older original. Ming Dynasty, I should say.'

'How much does something like that cost?' I looked blankly out of the window on to the street. Alexander Silver & Co. I spelled out, reading the back of the letters.

'You can have it for fifty dollars,' said Alexander Silver. 'With a teak base thrown in. Hand-carved.'

I took the bronze in my hands. It felt good. The edges were sharp, but they didn't look new; the patina wasn't buffed, hence didn't have that jade shimmer of the big museum pieces. I closed my eyes and felt the vase all over.

It didn't have any malachite encrustations either. I had often done this in Brussels at night; the museum had a good collection of Chou bronzes. One of them was a piece like this one and that too you might have taken for a Tang or Ming Dynasty copy to begin with. It was pardonable. The Chinese had started making copies of Chou and Shan bronzes as early as the Han era, round about the time of the birth of Christ, and buried them in the ground to get them a genuine old patina in double quick time. Sommer had told me about it. The rest I had picked up in Brussels.

Silver was watching me. 'Are you quite sure this is a copy?' I asked.

'I could say no,' he replied. 'But this is an honest business. You obviously know a thing or two about these things.' He set one foot on a Dutch footstool. I saw that he was wearing patent leather loafers and purple socks with his pepper-and-salt trousers. His feet were very small. 'I bought the piece as an eighteenth-century copy,' he said. 'I don't think that's what it is, but I don't think it's older than sixteenth century either. All AD, of course.'

I put the bronze back on the fake Venetian pier table. It was very cheap and I would like to have bought it; but I didn't know where I could sell it and I could only afford to invest my little bit of money for a brief time. And I needed to be very sure of myself before I did so.

'Could I take it away with me for a day?' I asked.

'You can keep it for the rest of your life, for fifty dollars.'

'On approval. One day.'

'Listen, sir,' said Alexander Silver. 'I hardly know you. The last time I let something go on approval it was to a very trustworthy lady. She took two beautiful Meissen figurines. Eighteenth century.'

'And what happened? That was the last you saw of all three of them?'

'No, she came back. The figurines were in pieces, though. She was on a crowded bus and a man with a toolbox knocked them out of her hand. An accident. She was crying as though she had lost a child. What could I do? She didn't have any money. She just wanted to annoy her friends in the bridge club. We had to write it off.'

'Bronzes don't break so easily. Especially if they're copies.'

Silver looked at me hard. 'I'll even tell you where I bought it. A museum upstate let it go. As a copy. Could anyone be as frank as that?'

I didn't answer. Silver shook his head. 'All right,' he said. 'Ornery fellow, aren't you? I like that. I'll make you another suggestion. Pay me fifty dollars and you can take the bronze with you and give it back to me at the end of the week. Then I'll either pay you your money back, or you can keep it. Can't say fairer than that.'

I thought quickly. I wasn't altogether sure I could trust my judgement: Chinese bronzes were no simple matter. Nor could I be sure if Silver's offer was sincere. But I had to risk something and all at once this was a possibility. I couldn't make my way in America by doing dishes; for that I would have needed a work permit; and I didn't have one. Even if the police didn't catch me, I'd find myself on the outs with the unions.

'Agreed,' I said and pulled out my skinny wallet.

After the Brussels museum closed for the evening, the director would let me out of my little room. I wasn't to switch on any lights and had to steer clear of the windows, but I was allowed to go to the bathroom and wander around in the dark. In the morning, before the cleaning women arrived, I had to lock myself up again. It was a uniquely solitary and fearful shadow education in art history. To begin with I would just squat down behind the curtains and watch the Brussels street through the window, the way I had stared at New York from Ellis Island. I gave that up once I noticed SS uniforms among the soldiers and civilians. So as to think as little as possible about my situation, I occupied myself instead with the paintings and artefacts all around me. The time before the war when I had worked as a tout for Ludwig Sommer gave me a solid foundation. I had in fact studied art history for two semesters in Germany before deciding to become a journalist. When I had to flee Germany that meant the end of that as a profession. I didn't know any other language well enough to be able to write in it. Now, during the silent and ghostly nights in the echoey museum corridors I forced myself to muster as much interest in art as I could. I knew I was lost if I carried on staring at the street. I had to keep on the move. The Chinese bronzes were the first things to attract me. I tried to study them on bright, moonlit nights. They glimmered like jade and like green and blue silk. The patina changed with the light. In those months I learned that you had to look at things for a long time before they would begin to speak to you. I learned this in despair, to overcome my fear, and for a long time it was nothing but a self-induced attempt to flee myself, till one stormy moonlit night I realised that I had for the first time forgotten my fear, and for a few moments had felt oddly close to a bronze I was looking at. Nothing parted me from it and for the short duration of this spell I was aware of nothing except the turbulent night, the peaceful bronze, the moonlight that animated it and some emanation from the thing itself; a being that lived and breathed and listened and forgot all about itself. From that time on I regularly managed to escape myself and switch myself off. A few weeks later the director brought me a battery torch I could use at night in my little cubbyhole. He had realised he could trust me and that I wouldn't use the torch in the galleries, but only in my broom cupboard. It was as though he had restored the gift of sight to me. And the gift of reading, for that matter. He allowed me to borrow books from the museum library and study them overnight. In the morning he would take them back. When he noticed my interest in the bronzes, he would occasionally let me keep one overnight in my room and I would give it back to him in the morning, when he brought me my sandwiches for the day. Apart from him, the only person who knew I was hiding in the museum was his daughter Sibylle. He had had to tell her one day when he was sick and couldn't go in. She picked up his mail and brought me sandwiches wrapped in greaseproof paper, which she'd kept between her breasts. Sometimes they were still warm from her skin and the paper had a faint scent of carnations. I was madly in love with Sibylle, but it was an almost impersonal feeling she was barely aware of. I loved in her the things I no longer had: freedom, insouciance, hope and the sweet turmoil of a youth I had outgrown. I couldn't imagine an actual life with her; she was too exclusively a symbol; a warm, near, unattainable symbol of everything I had lost. My own youth had come to a sharp end amidst the death cries of my father. He had cried for one entire day and I knew who had ordered his death.

'Do you know something about these things, then?' asked Moikov. 'Fifty dollars is a lot of money!'

'Not a lot, but a bit. Anyway, I have no choice. I need to do something.'

'Where did you learn about them?'

'In Paris, and in a museum in Brussels.'

'Were you employed there?' asked Moikov, surprised.

'No, hidden.'

'From the Germans?'

'From the Germans, after they had taken Brussels.'

'What else did you do there?'

'I learned French,' I said. 'I had a grammar. Just like now. In the summer, after the museum closed, it wasn't completely dark. Later on I had a torch.'

Moikov nodded. 'Weren't there guards in the museum?'

'What for? Against the Germans!? They would have helped themselves to what they wanted anyway.'

Moikov laughed. 'Strange how you acquire an education. When I was a refugee in Finland, I happened to have a little pocket chess set with me. I played all the time I was in hiding, to distract myself. I got to be a half-decent chess player. Later on, in Germany, I even made a living from it. I gave chess lessons. I'd never have expected it. Were you always an art dealer?'

'Yes – in about the same way as you were a chess player.'

'That's what I thought.'

I couldn't tell him anything about Sommer, or my false passport. The passport admittedly gave Sommer's profession as antique dealer and on Ellis Island I'd been tested in my knowledge by an immigration inspector. I must have picked up enough from Sommer and in Brussels, because I passed the test. The decisive factor was my knowledge of Chinese bronzes. Oddly enough, the inspector knew something about them. Devout Christians would have called this the kind agency of providence.

I heard Lachmann's unmistakable footfall outside. Moikov was called away to the telephone. Lachmann limped into the plush lounge. Right away he spotted the bronze. 'Bought?' he asked.

'Sort of.'

'A mistake,' he declared. 'You're a beginner. You should begin by dealing in little things, cheap things that everyone needs. Stockings, soap, neckties . . .'

'. . . rosaries, icons,' I continued his list. 'Like you, Jew.'

He gestured dismissively. 'That's something else. That takes expertise. You don't have that; you're just hard up! But what am I saying?' He looked at me with watery eyes. 'Nothing helped, Ludwig. She took the presents and claims she wants to use the relics in her prayers for me at night! What good is that to me! And the woman has a bottom like an empress! All in vain! Now she says she wants Jordan water. Water from the River Jordan! How am I going to get that for her? She's crazy! Do you have any idea where I can find Jordan water?'

'From the tap.'

'What?'

'Take an old bottle, a bit of dust and a sealed cork. In Bordeaux there used to be a firm of petty crooks who sold Lourdes water like that. Five francs a bottle. Exactly as I described. You take it from the tap. I read about it in the paper. They weren't even punished. The whole court was laughing.'

Lachmann was lost in thought. 'Isn't it sacrilegious to do that?'

'I don't think so. Just dishonest.'

Lachmann scratched his bumpy skull. 'It's strange, ever since I've started selling medallions and rosaries, my sense of God has completely changed. I've become a sort of Catholic Jewish schizophrenic. So you reckon it's not sacrilege? Not blasphemy? What faith are you?'

I shook my head. 'I think God has a better sense of humour than we usually imagine. And much less compassion.'

Lachmann stood up. He was persuaded already. 'It's not as though I'm selling the water. So it's not for gain. It's just a present. I'm sure that's lawful.' In a quick, pained grin he showed his spotted teeth. 'It's for love. And God is Love! Fine. My last attempt. What sort of bottle would you advise?'

'Not one of Moikov's vodka bottles, she's certainly familiar with those.'

'Of course not! A plain, anonymous-looking bottle. The kind that sailors drop in the sea. A bottle for a message. And sealed! That's it. I'll get Moikov to give me some sealing wax. He uses it for his vodka. Maybe he has some old Cyrillic coin that I can stamp it with. Something that would suggest it came from some Armenian cloister in Palestine. Do you think that'll work on her?'

'No. I think you should just ignore her for a week or two. I think that would help more.'

Lachmann turned round. All at once his expression was despairing. The pale-blue eyes bulged like those of a dead haddock. 'Wait!? How can I do that?' he exclaimed. 'I'm in a race against time as it is. I'm way past fifty already! In a few years I'll be impotent! Then what? Just the wild urge and regret, and no appeasement. Hell! Don't you understand? What has my life given me to date? Fear, misery and flight. And I have only the one life!' He pulled out his handkerchief. 'And it's three-quarters over,' he whispered.

'Don't wail,' I answered him. 'That's no good. You should have learned that long ago.'

'I'm not wailing,' he countered angrily. 'I just want to blow my nose. Emotion opens my sinuses instead of my tear ducts. If I was a weeper, I'd have had more success. But who wants a Romeo who parps through his nose like a tuba when he's emotional? I can't breathe otherwise.' He trumpeted loudly several times in succession. Then he hobbled off to Moikov at the front desk.

I picked up the bronze and carried it up to my room. I set it down on the windowsill and looked at it in the vanishing light. It was roughly the time the museum closed in Brussels in the summertime and I was able to leave my little room.

I slowly turned the bronze to all sides. I had read almost the whole, not very extensive, literature on the topic and knew many of the illustrations. I knew that you could sometimes identify copies by little anachronisms in the design; by tiny decorations on a Chou-style bronze that were only developed in the Han epoch, or much later, in the Ming or Tang eras, and thereby gave the pieces a much later date. I didn't find any of those. The piece seemed to me to date from the middle of the Chou period, maybe 500 or 600 BCE.

I lay down on my bed and put the bronze on the bedside table. From the yard I could hear the clatter of the metal bins, and the shouts of the kitchen assistants, and the soft, guttural bass of the black man who carried out the trash.

Involuntarily I fell asleep. When I awoke it was night time. It took me a moment to get my bearings. Then I saw the bronze and thought for a second I was back in my cubbyhole in the museum. I sat up, breathing shallowly, and remembered a bad dream; enough to know I didn't want to remember any more. I got up and went over to the window, which was wide open. There was the yard and down there were the bins. I'm free, I said into the darkness and I repeated it a couple of times, quietly and intensely, as I had often done when I was on the run. Once I had calmed down a little, I looked at the bronze again, which just caught the reddish light of the night city. Suddenly I had the feeling it was alive. Its patina wasn't dead, it didn't feel stuck on or artificially produced by acids on a roughed-up surface; it had grown, naturally and organically, over hundreds of years;

it came from the water it had lain in, from the minerals of the earth that had merged with it and probably the strip of pure blue at its base was a phosphorus reaction from a corpse over a thousand years ago. The patina had the weak sheen that the unpolished Chou pieces in the museum had by virtue of their porosity, which was a porosity that didn't swallow light, like the artificially treated vases, but that made it look more silky, not in a smooth way, but like raw silk. And it didn't feel cold to the touch either.

I sat down on the bed again and set the bronze aside. I stared into space, realising that with all these thoughts I was just trying to numb my memory. I didn't want to recall that last morning in Brussels, when Sibylle tore open the door to my room, and charged in and whispered that her father had been picked up and I had to flee, right away, no one knew whether they would torture him or not, and if they did whether he would break down and give me up. She pushed me out through the door, and called me back and stuffed a handful of money into my pocket. 'Go out, leave, as though you were a visitor here, walk, don't run!' she whispered. 'God protect you,' she said, instead of cursing me for bringing her father and probably herself into ruin. 'Go! God protect you!' And to my hurried question, who had given him away, she merely replied, 'It doesn't matter! Go now, before they search the museum!' and she kissed me hurriedly and pushed me out and whispered after me, 'I'll straighten out the room! Leave! Don't write. Ever! They check everything. God protect you.'

I walked down the stairs, slowly so as not to attract attention. I didn't see many people; no one had an eye for me. I crossed the street. I looked back. At a window, I thought I caught the white fleck of a face.

★

I got up and went over to the window. The opposite wall of the hotel was now in darkness. There was light on in one window alone. The curtains were open. I saw a man in briefs standing in front of a golden mirror, powdering his face. Then he took off his briefs and stood there naked. His chest was tattooed but not hairy. He pulled on a pair of black silk knickers and a black brassiere, and began stuffing the brassiere lovingly with tissue paper. I stared across the well aimlessly, not really aware of what was going on there. Then I retreated into my room and switched on the overhead light. When I drew my own curtains, I saw that the curtains opposite were also being drawn, only they were of red silk. All the other curtains in the hotel were brown cotton.

I went downstairs to look for Moikov. I couldn't find him. Perhaps he had gone out. I sat down in the lounge to wait for him. After some time I thought I could hear someone crying. It wasn't loud and to begin with I didn't pay it much attention, but it tugged at my nerves all the same. Finally I went to the back of the lounge where I saw, curled up on the sofa in the darkness, next to the plant stand, Maria Fiola.

I thought I should turn round and go; that aggressive so-and-so was really all I needed. But she had seen me. She was crying with eyes wide open, not missing a trick. 'Can I help?' I asked.

She shook her head and looked at me, like a cat about to hiss.

'The blues?' I asked.

'Yes,' she said, 'the blues.'

Weltschmerz, I thought. A property of a different, more romantic century. Not this one, characterised by genocide and torture and total war. Probably man trouble. 'I expect you're looking for Moikov,' I said.

She nodded. 'Where is he?'

'No idea. I was looking for him too. Perhaps he's out delivering some of his vodka.'

'Yes. When you need him he's not there.'

'A grave shortcoming,' I said. 'Unfortunately all too prevalent. Did you want to have a drink with him?'

'I wanted to talk to him. He understands everything! And what about vodka? Where is the vodka here?'

'Maybe there's a bottle in reception.'

Maria Fiola shook her head. 'The cupboard's locked. I tried.'

'He should have left it open. As a Russian, he should have sensed the hour of despair. But then his Irish stand-in, Felix O'Brien, would have got drunk and muddled up all the keys.'

The girl pulled herself up. I stared at her in surprise. She had a shapeless silk turban on, studded with bits of metal like so many revolver barrels.

'What is it?' she asked in perplexity. 'Do I look like a monster?'

'Not at all – but very military.'

She reached for her turban and undid it with a single movement. Her hair was studded with wire and metal curlers like miniature German hand grenades. 'Do you mean this?' she asked. 'My hair? I'm having my picture taken later; so I'm curling it.'

'It looks as though you could shoot from all those barrels.'

She laughed harshly. 'I wish I could.'

'I've got a bottle of vodka in my room,' I said. 'I can go and get it. There's plenty of glasses around.'

'What a sensible thought! Why didn't you say so right away?'

★

The bottle was still half full. Moikov had sold it to me at cost price. I wasn't a solitary drinker; I knew that would only make my mood still more desolate. Nor was I expecting much from the girl with the pistols in her hair; but I expected least of all from my room. As I walked by, I took the bronze off the bedside table and stowed it in my cupboard.

Maria Fiola was a different person when I returned. Her tears were gone, her complexion was powdered and clear, and her hair was freed of its metal rollers. It wasn't tumbling down in innumerable little curls as I'd imagined, but it was straight and had a wave at the neck. Nor was it dyed, as I'd thought originally, it didn't have that brittle straw-y texture. It was brown with mahogany lights.

'How come you drink vodka?' she asked. 'They're not vodka drinkers where you're from.'

'I know. The Germans drink beer and schnapps. But I've forgotten my country and I don't drink beer or schnapps. What about you? The Italians aren't vodka drinkers either.'

'My mother's Russian. And vodka's the only drink that doesn't smell on your breath.'

'There's a good reason,' I said.

'It's important for a woman. What do you drink?'

This is a stupid conversation, I thought. 'Whatever's around,' I said. 'In France I used to drink wine when there was wine.'

'France!' said the girl. 'I wonder what the Germans will have done to France.'

'I wasn't there to see it. I was sitting in a French intern-ment camp at the time.'

'Of course! As an enemy!'

'As a refugee from the Germans.' I laughed. 'You seem to have forgotten that the Germans and Italians are on the same side. They attacked France together.'

'That was Mussolini's fault! I hate him!'

'So do I,' I said.

'And I hate Hitler!'

'So do I,' I said. 'That makes us kind of negative allies.'

The girl looked at me wonderingly. 'That's one way of looking at it, I suppose.'

'Sometimes it's the only way. Until recently, Moikov was one of us as well. The Germans had occupied the village he was born in and made the inhabitants Teutons. That's over now. The Russians conquered it back and he became a Russian once more. An enemy, as you say.'

Maria Fiola laughed. 'You have a funny way of seeing things. What are we really?'

'Human beings,' I said. 'But most of us have forgotten that long ago. Human beings who will one day die – most have forgotten that as well. There's nothing we are less convinced of than that we will die. Another vodka?'

'No, thanks.' She stood up and shook hands. 'I have to go now. Work,' she said.

I watched her go. I heard nothing: she didn't walk or step, she seemed to glide through the ugly furniture untouched. Probably that too was an aspect of her job as mannequin. She had pulled her cloth tightly round her head and looked slender and supple, though not frail – of a tough, almost dangerous elegance.

I took the bottle upstairs, then went out on to the street. The stand-in porter Felix O'Brien stood there, reeking of beer like an entire dive. 'How's life, Felix?' I asked him.

He shrugged. 'Get up, eat, work, go to bed. What else is there to report? It's always the same. Sometimes I really don't see why I bother.'

'Yeah,' I said. 'But you do.'

5

'Jessie!' I said. 'Sweetheart! Benefactress! I'm so happy to see you!'

The round face with its red cheeks, black eyes and grey fringe was the same as ever. Jessie Stein stood in the doorway of her little flat in New York, just as she had once stood in the doorway of her big flat in Berlin and later, on the run, in the doorway of various rooms in France, Belgium and Spain – always smiling, always helpful, as though she had no worries at all. And it was true, she had none of her own. Her whole life was helping others.

'My God, Ludwig!' she said. 'When did we last see each other?'

It was the typical emigrant question. I didn't know the answer. 'Before the war, of course, Jessie,' I said. 'In the happy time when it was only the French police that were after us. But where? Somewhere on the Via Dolorosa. Was it Lille?'

Jessie shook her head. 'Wasn't it 1939, in Paris? Just before the war?'

'Of course, Jessie! It was in the Hotel International, now I remember. You made pancakes in your room for Ravic and me. You even had raspberries to go with them. They were the last raspberries in my life. I've never had any since.'

'Tragic,' said Robert Hirsch. 'And there aren't any in America, just a substitute: loganberries. But they aren't the same. I only hope you don't go back to Europe for something like that, the way Egon Fürst the actor did.'

'What was Fürst's story?'

'He couldn't find lamb's lettuce in New York. He had emigrated here, but it was driving him to distraction. He went back to Germany. To Vienna.'

'That's not true, Robert,' replied Jessie. 'He was homesick. And he couldn't work here. His English wasn't good enough. No one had heard of him. In Germany everyone knew him.'

'He wasn't a Jew,' said Hirsch. 'Only Jews are homesick for Germany. It may sound hideously paradoxical, but it's true.'

'He's referring to me,' said Jessie, laughing. 'Isn't he wicked! But it's my birthday, so I don't mind. Come in! We've got apple strudel and fresh coffee. Just like at home. Not the stewed dishwater that Americans call coffee.'

Jessie, the protectress of the emigrants. Before 1933, in Berlin, she was already a mother to all needy actors, artists, writers and intellectuals. A naive enthusiasm, impervious to criticism, kept her positive at all times. Her enthusiasm was shown not only in her salon where she laid siege to directors and producers, but in the way she patched up broken marriages, listened to those in despair, gave small loans, helped lovers, arranged for publication and did much by her stubbornness. Publishers, producers and theatre directors of course found her irritating, but they couldn't resist her selflessness and goodwill. So she lived in myriad commitments on all sides, as a mother figure to artists, all the while she had no proper life of her own. For a while in Berlin there was a husband at her side, an unobtrusive man called Stein, who made sure the guests always had enough to eat and to drink, and who otherwise stayed in the background. He died, as discreetly as he had lived, of a lung infection caught somewhere on the Via Dolorosa.

Jessie went into life as a fugitive as though it concerned someone else. She didn't seem to care that she had lost her house and her fortune. She continued to look after expatriated and fugitive artists she ran into on the road. Her ability to radiate a sort of petit bourgeois comfort was quite astonishing; as much as her unflappable good humour. The more she was needed, the more she beamed. With the aid of a couple of cushions and a spirit cooker, she managed to turn a wretched hotel room into something homey; she cooked and baked and washed for impractical and improvident artists on the run; and when it turned out, following the death of Mr Tobias Stein, that the deceased had planned ahead and quietly left a sum in dollars with the New York Guaranty Trust Co. in Paris, Jessie used the sum for her protégés, all except a small bit for herself and the cost of a ticket to New York on the *Queen Mary*. Never having exercised herself much about politics, she didn't know that ships' berths tended to be sold out months in advance and wasn't astonished when she managed to obtain one. She happened to be standing at the counter when the extraordinary thing happened: a ticket was returned. Its intended user had suffered a heart attack. Since Jessie happened to be next in line, the ticket was sold on to her; others would have shelled out a fortune for it. At the time Jessie had no thought of staying in America; she was just there to collect her money and go home. She had been at sea for two days when the war broke out, so Jessie wound up staying in New York. I knew all this from Hirsch.

★

Jessie's drawing room was not large, but it was absolutely in her style. Cushions everywhere, lots of chairs, a chaise longue, and plenty of photographs on the walls, almost all of them with lavish dedications scribbled across them. A few of them were in black frames.

'Jessie's casualties,' said a delicate woman, seated beneath them. 'That's Hasenclever!' she pointed up at a photo in a black frame.

I remembered Hasenclever. The French had shut him in an internment camp, like all the emigrants they could lay their hands on in 1939. One night, when the German forces were within a few miles of the camp, Hasenclever took his own life. He didn't want to be captured and tortured to death in a German concentration camp. But then the Germans didn't advance, as everyone thought they were going to. At the last moment they changed direction and the camp didn't fall into the Gestapo's clutches. But Hasenclever was already dead.

I saw that next to me Hirsch too was staring at the photo of Hasenclever. 'I didn't know where he was,' he said. 'I wanted to rescue him. But there was so much confusion at the time that it was hard to find anyone, harder still to get them out. That mix of French slovenliness and bloody bureaucracy! It wasn't necessarily ill-intentioned, at least some of the time, but it was certainly fatal to the people who were caught up in it.'

To one side of the casualty section I saw a photo of Egon Fürst, which had a black ribbon, but no frame. 'What does that mean?' I asked the frail-looking woman. 'Has he been murdered in Germany or something?'

She shook her head. 'No, then he would have had a black frame too. It just means Jessie's grieving for him. Hence the black ribbon. And the place away from the others. The dead people are all over there, with Hasenclever. There are a lot of them.'

Evidently Jessie kept her memories in good order. Even death could become clutter, I thought, looking at the colourful cushions on the chaise longue under the photographs. Some of the actors were dressed for some part or other they had played to acclaim in Germany or Vienna. Jessie must have brought them all with her. In fading velvet or chain mail, with swords and crowns, they smiled happily and heroically out of their black frames.

On the opposite side were photos of Jessie's friends who were still alive. Here too the majority were performers. Jessie had a weakness for celebrities. There were just a couple of doctors and writers among them. I didn't know which was the more ghostly, the collection of the dead, or facing them the collection of living, who had yet to graduate to death, as Wagner heroes with ox horns on their heads, or Don Juan or William Tell, in their old accolade of past performances, surely much more modest now, and far too old to play the parts in which they were photographed.

'The Prince of Homburg!' said a bowed little man behind me. 'That was me once upon a time! And now?'

I looked round; then at the photo again. 'Is that really you?'

'That was me,' replied the elderly-looking man with some bitterness. 'Fifteen years ago. In Munich. The Kammerspiele. The papers said I was the definitive Prince of Homburg for the decade. They promised me a glittering career! As if! Career!' He bowed jerkily. 'Gregor Haas: quondam actor!'

I muttered my name. Haas stared at the photograph he no longer resembled. 'Prince of Homburg! Can you recognise me? Of course not! I had all my hair then, and no wrinkles. I just had to be careful not to put on weight. I had a weakness for cake. Apple strudel with whipped cream. Today—' The little manikin opened his jacket. It was too big for him and inside it was a scrawny, concave belly. 'If only Jessie would burn those old pictures! But she clings to them as though they were her children. This is "Jessie's Club"! Did you know that?'

I nodded. That was what Jessie's protégés were known as, even back in France. 'Were you one?' asked Haas.

'Sure, sometimes. Who wasn't?'

'She found me a job here. I take care of German correspondence for a company that does a lot of business with Switzerland.' Haas looked worriedly around. 'But I can't say how much longer. These Swiss firms are taking on more and more English-speaking staff; soon my job here won't exist any more.' He looked up at me. 'If you survive one lot of fears, the next lot is ready and waiting. Is it like that for you as well?'

'More or less. But you get used to it.'

'You get used to it or you don't,' Haas retorted brusquely. 'In which case you hang yourself one fine day.'

He made an abrupt movement and bowed again. 'Goodbye,' he said. Only then did it occur to me that we'd been speaking German. Most of the people in the room were speaking German. I remembered that that had been important to Jessie, even in France. To her it wasn't just absurd, it was almost treasonable if the emigrants didn't talk to each other in German. She belonged to that group of refugees who saw the Nazis as Martians who had taken over the defenceless Fatherland – as opposed to the other group that claimed there was a bit of a Nazi in every German. There was a third school as well, which went further and claimed that every human being had a bit of Nazi in them, though it might be called something else. This school had two branches

74

– the one philosophical, the other militant. Robert Hirsch belonged to the militant wing.

'Did Gregor Haas tell you his story?' Robert asked.

'Yes. He was unhappy when Jessie pinned up her pictures of him. He'd sooner not remember all that.'

Hirsch laughed. 'Gregor's papered the walls of his little flat with pictures of himself in his brief prime. He'd rather die than forget how unhappy he is. He's a real actor. Only now he's not playing the Prince of Homburg any more, but a poor temp with no greasepaint.'

'And what about Egon Fürst?' I asked. 'Was that really why he went back?'

'He wasn't able to learn English. And he couldn't get his head around the fact that no one here had heard of him. Some actors are like that. Fürst was very famous in Germany. He didn't understand that he had to spell his name for everyone, starting with the immigration authorities, because no one had ever heard of him. It did him in. Something that's perfectly banal for one person is a full-blown tragedy for someone else. When a film company insisted that he do a screen test like some beginner, that did it for him. He had to go back. Presumably he's still living there now. Jessie would know. But I don't know if he's getting work in Germany or not.'

Jessie came bustling up. 'Coffee's ready!' she announced. 'And apple cake! Come and sit, boys and girls.'

I grasped her by the shoulders and gave her a big kiss. 'You saved my life again, Jessie. You got Tannenbaum to intervene in my case.'

'Poppycock!' she said, freeing herself. 'You don't die as quickly as that. You least of all.'

'You saved me from having to take ship on our contemporary "Flying Dutchman". Sailing from port to port, unable to dock anywhere.'

'Are there really such vessels?' she asked.

'Yes,' I said. 'Full of emigrants, mainly Jews. Full of children, too.'

Jessie's round face darkened. 'Why don't they leave us be?' she murmured. 'We're not a threat, there aren't very many of us.'

'That's exactly the point,' said Hirsch. 'You can massacre us with impunity. And you can be deaf to our cries with impunity too. We are the most patient victims there are.'

Jessie spun round. 'Robert,' she said, 'it's my birthday. I'm an old woman. Can we please have just one afternoon of self-deception. I baked the strudel myself. I made the coffee myself. And here are the Dahls, Erika and Beatrice. They helped me and they're going to serve. Do me a favour, and just eat and stop spreading gloom. If only you political donkeys would fall in love for once!'

I saw the petite woman who had been sitting under the dead photographs approaching now with a coffee pot. She was followed by another woman, who looked identical. They were wearing the same clothes as well. 'Twins!' said Jessie proudly, as if it somehow reflected credit on her. 'Real twins. And both so pretty. They have a wonderful career in the cinema ahead of them.'

The twins danced attendance on us. They had long legs, dark eyes and bleached hair. 'You really can't tell them apart,' said someone next to me. 'Even though one is supposed to be a tart, and the other a terrifyingly austere puritan.'

'Surely they have different first names,' I said.

'That's just it,' said the man. 'They play with their names. One claims to be the other. They get a kick out of it, but if you happen to be in love with them, it's hellish.'

I looked at him with interest. This was a new variant: to

be in love with twins. 'Are you in love with one of them, or both?' I asked.

'Leo Bach,' said the man. 'Pleased to meet you. To be perfectly honest, it's the tart I'm after. Only I don't know which one is her.'

'It must be simple enough to find out.'

'That's what I thought too. Especially today, when they've both got their hands full with coffee and cake. I pinched one in the bottom, and she went and spilled coffee all over my blue suit. Then I tried pinching the other and she poured coffee all over me as well. Now I'm not sure; did I make a mistake and pinch one of them twice, or not? They are so quick. The way they dart in and out of rooms. What do you think? What makes me wonder is the identical reaction – the coffee on the suit. That would suggest it was the same twin, wouldn't you think?'

'Couldn't you try the experiment again? And this time without losing them from sight?'

Leo Bach shook his head. 'My suit's too far gone. And I've only got the one.'

'I always thought coffee didn't leave stains on blue suits.'

'I couldn't care less about the stains. I keep my money in my inside pocket. Any more coffee and it'll be sodden. Perhaps it'll run. I can't allow that to happen.'

One of the twins came along with cake. Leo Bach flinched; then he helped himself greedily. The other twin was carrying the coffee pot; she refilled my cup. Bach stopped eating and watched her till she was gone. 'Actresses!' he cursed. 'Holy innocents! You can't even tell their voices apart.'

'It's really too bad,' I said. 'But perhaps neither of them likes having her bottom pinched. There are certain circles where that's thought of as a rather crude expression of interest.'

77

Leo Bach dismissed the thought. 'Oh, get along with you! We're not "certain circles" here. We're emigrants. Desperate people.'

I accompanied Hirsch back to his store. Outside, the early evening in the city roared by with noise and light and people. We didn't turn on a light; there was sufficient coming in from outside. The windowpane kept out enough of the noise. We sat there as in a cave, with the scene outside reflected in the quiet bulbous eyes of the televisions. They were just sitting there, none of them was switched on. We seemed to be bunkered in a silent future world of robots, in which the world outside – sweat and pain, panic and aggression – had already given way to a cool, technical solution.

'Strange, how different everything feels here in America,' said Hirsch. 'Don't you think?'

I shook my head. He got up and fetched the Pernod bottle and a couple of glasses. Then he went to his refrigerator and produced a tray of ice cubes. The fridge light briefly illuminated his thin face with the reddish-blond tuft of hair above it. He still looked like a fading poet, rather than a furious Maccabee.

'It was all so different when we were on the run,' he resumed. 'In France, Holland, Belgium, Portugal, Spain. The least scrap of settled existence seemed like the greatest adventure. A room with a bed; a stove; an evening with friends. Or Jesse, like the angel of the annunciation with a packet of potato pancakes and a pot of proper coffee. Those things felt like revelations, beacons of comfort against the flickering background of threat. And now? What's it all turned into? A perfectly harmless coffee round. Smugness. Cosiness. Don't you think?'

'No,' I replied. 'The danger has lost its edge, that's really all. Other things show in stronger relief. I'm all in favour of the coffee and the security. We at least know there'll be a next time. In Europe we never knew that.' I laughed. 'Or are you missing the danger, because it gave the bourgeois side of things its heroic aspect? The way doctors are more heroic in a cholera epidemic than during a flu?'

'Of course I don't. What gets my goat is the atmosphere. That mixture of humility, impotent rage, futile protest, resignation and black humour. Hopeless jokes and emigrant reminiscences – they should all be hopping mad!'

I looked at Robert Hirsch attentively. 'What else should they do?' I finally asked. 'Perhaps they're not what you expected them to be here. But they're all to some extent adventurers in spite of themselves. They have their security here, but they're still second-class citizens. Here on sufferance – enemy aliens, they call them. They'll remain that all their lives, even if they should one day return to Germany. They'd be just the same in Germany.'

'Do you think they will go back?'

'Not all of them, but some will. Unless they happen to die here first. It takes a strong heart to lead a deracinated life. And unhappiness is rarely heroic. They lead borrowed lives, without a home, without much more future than a merciful illusion.' I pushed my glass away. 'Damn, Robert, I'm starting to preach. I think it's the absinthe. Or the darkness. Haven't you got anything else to drink?'

'Cognac,' he replied. 'Courvoisier.'

'A gift from Heaven!'

He got up to fetch the bottle. I saw his shape against the lit-up window. My God, I thought, what if he should feel such a secret yearning for that old life of hopelessness and excitements? I hadn't seen him in a long time before I reached New York, and I knew how quickly such nostalgia came about. Memory was the biggest falsifier there was; everything a man survived was logged as 'adventure' – otherwise we wouldn't keep having new wars all the time. And Robert Hirsch had led a different sort of life from the other emigrants anyway; that of a Maccabee, a life of revenge and rescue, not that of a victim. Could death have gone down like the sun, against an inglorious backdrop of dailiness and security? I wondered, with a little touch of envy – because in my own damned sky, it was still there almost every night, so that I had to leave the lights on for the moment when I awoke out of my terrifying dreams.

Hirsch opened the cognac. The aroma spread immediately. It was good, pre-war cognac. 'Do you remember the first time we drank cognac?' asked Hirsch.

I nodded. 'In Laon. In a poultry coop, on the run. That was the time we decided to compile the Laon Breviary. It was a night of ghosts: full of clucking hens, cognac and fear. You had confiscated the bottle from a wine merchant who was a collaborator.'

'Basically, I stole it,' said Hirsch. 'The other term was a euphemism. Just like the Nazis.'

The Laon Breviary was a collection of practical rules for refugee life, based on our experiences as emigrants on the Via Dolorosa. Each time refugees met up, they exchanged new tricks and new defences. Hirsch and I finally started collecting them in the form of a compendium for beginners on how best to keep out of the clutches of the police. There were addresses where you might find help and others that were best avoided; easy and hazardous border crossings; kindly customs officials and sadists; safe letter-drop locations for messages; museums and churches the police didn't check;

80

ways of deceiving the police. In addition, later, there were names of reliable link men to escape the Gestapo, the simple practical philosophy of the hunted and the bitter humour of naked survival.

Someone knocked on the window. A bald man was staring in. He knocked again, louder. Hirsch got up and opened the door. 'We're not robbers,' he explained. 'We live here.'

'Really? And what are you doing in the dark so long after closing time?'

'We're not homosexuals either. We're making plans for the future. The future's dark, which is why we didn't put a light on.'

'I don't understand,' said the man.

'Call the police if you don't believe me,' said Robert and slammed the door in his face.

He came back to the table. 'America's a land of conformists,' he said. 'Everyone does exactly the same thing as his neighbour and at exactly the same time. If you don't that's accounted suspicious.' He put the absinthe away and got himself a brandy glass. 'Forget what I said earlier, Ludwig. I have moments like that from time to time.' He laughed. 'Laon Breviary, Paragraph 12: Emotion clouds judgement; anxiety too. It may never happen.'

I nodded. 'Did you ever think of volunteering for the army here?'

Hirsch took a mouthful of cognac. 'Yes,' he said. 'They didn't want me. "Once a German, always a German," they said. Maybe they're right. They were prepared to have me fight the Japanese in the Pacific, but that didn't interest me. I'm not a mercenary who shoots at people for a living. Perhaps they're right. Would you shoot Germans if the army took you?'

'Some Germans, for sure.'

'Ones you know,' he countered. 'What about the others? What about the lot of them?'

I thought about it. 'That's a hard question to answer,' I said.

Hirsch laughed bitterly. 'There is no answer, is there? There rarely is, for cosmopolitans like us. We don't belong anywhere. Neither the country we've left behind, nor the new one we find ourselves in now. Uncle Sam's damned well right not to trust us.'

I said nothing. There was nothing to say. We found ourselves in a situation that was defined by others. For most of us it was already decided. Only for the rebellious heart of a Robert Hirsch was it not yet decided. 'The French Foreign Legion took Germans,' I finally said. 'They even offered them French nationality. Once the war was over.'

'The French Foreign Legion,' scoffed Robert. 'And then they sent them to Africa to build roads.'

We sat at the table, neither of us speaking. Hirsch lit a cigarette. 'Strange,' he said. 'Cigarettes never taste good in the dark. You don't feel them. Wouldn't it be great if you couldn't feel pain in the dark either?'

'You feel it twice as bad. Wonder why? Because you're afraid in the dark?'

'You feel more alone. At the mercy of your imagination.'

I stopped listening. I had seen a face that broke my heart. It happened so suddenly that I was caught cold. I had an impulse to jump up and run after it, but I stayed where I was, and then I knew I was mistaken. I had seen something. The face I thought I saw, tipped at an angle, smiling back over her shoulder, in the light of street lamps, was in reality dead. The face I thought I saw wasn't smiling any more either. The last time I had seen it, it was stiff and cold, and there were flies on its eyes.

'What did you say?' I pulled myself together.

It's not real, I thought. It was an illusion, I was bound to wake up in a minute. The dark, secluded space with its many glass eyes on their shiny cabinets was so unreal for a moment that everything outside seemed unreal too, and so did I.

'Do you mind if I switch the light on?' I asked.

'Go ahead.'

We blinked at each other as the chill neon drenched us, as though we had been exchanging improper confidences. 'What were you saying?' I asked.

Hirsch looked at me with surprise. 'I said you shouldn't think too hard about Tannenbaum. He's a sensible fellow and he knows you need time to adjust. You don't need to go out of your way to thank him. His wife sometimes lays on meals for hungry emigrants. I happen to know there's one coming up. They'll invite you. We'll go together. That's better for you, isn't it?'

'Much better.'

I got up. 'And how about a job?' asked Hirsch. 'Have you found something yet?'

'Not yet. But I've found an opening. I'm not going to throw myself on Tannenbaum's mercy.'

'There's no need to worry about that. You can always stay with me. I can feed you.'

I shook my head. 'I want to make it on my own, Robert. All of it! All of it!' I repeated. 'Paragraph 7 of the Laon Breviary: Help only comes to those who don't need it.'

★

I didn't walk back to the hotel. I wandered aimlessly through the streets, as I did most evenings. I looked at the light and I thought about Ruth who was dead. We had met up by chance and stayed together. Things were pretty bleak. We didn't know anybody else, there were just the two of us. Then one day I was arrested, locked up for a fortnight and deported across the Swiss border. It had taken me a lot of trouble to get back into France. When I got back to Paris, Ruth was dead. I found her in her room, the fat, metallic flies buzzing round her, evidently she had been lying there for days. I had never been able to shake the feeling that I had somehow left her in the lurch. She had no one else, and I had gone and got myself arrested. Ruth had taken her own life. Like many emigrants she had kept poison on her in the event that the Gestapo took her in. She hadn't even needed it. A couple of tubes of sleeping pills had been enough for her tired, discouraged heart.

I stopped and stared at a newspaper stand. Huge banner headlines on all the papers. Bomb plot to kill Hitler! Hitler assassinated!

A cluster of people ringed the kiosk. I pushed my way through and bought a paper. It was still wet with printer's ink. My hands were shaking. I looked for an entryway and began to read. I didn't understand all of it. I felt madly impatient because I was making such slow headway. I crumpled the newspaper up, smoothed it out again and hailed a taxi. I went over to Hirsch's place.

He wasn't in. I knocked on the door for a long time. It was locked. Nor was he in the store either. Probably he'd gone out just before I got there. I went to the King of the Sea. The dead fishes were glittering, the chained lobsters shifted on their freezing beds of ice, the waiters balanced tureens of fish soup on their shoulders, the place was full, but Hirsch wasn't there. Slowly I walked on. I didn't want to go back to the hotel; I was afraid I'd run into Lachmann again. Nor did I want to sit in the plush lounge; maybe Maria Fiola was there. Moikov would be out, I knew that.

I walked up Fifth Avenue. Its breadth and dazzling brightness calmed me. It was as though all the lit-up buildings gave out little electrical pulses that caused the air to vibrate. I could feel them on my face and hands. Outside the Savoy Plaza I bought another special edition from a dwarf with a pencil moustache. The reports were more or less the same as before. There had been an attempt on Hitler's life in his headquarters. By an officer. It wasn't quite certain that Hitler was dead; but he was gravely wounded. It was an officers' revolt. Part of the army was rebelling in Berlin, other generals had joined the plot. It could well be the end.

I stood in front of a brightly lit shop window to read the finer print. It was as though there was a magnetic storm all round me. I could hear the lions in the zoo. I stared into the window without seeing anything. After a while I noticed that I was in front of a jewellery store called Van Cleef & Arpels. Two diadems that had belonged to dead queens lay there among emeralds, diamonds and rubies in a cave lined with black velvet: cool and apathetic, a closed, crystalline world, immaculate, come into being long before the restlessness of life began, and remaining immaculate since, without murder, silently growing by its own baffling laws. I felt the newspaper crumple in my hand, I saw the banner headlines, then I glanced down Fifth Avenue again, this gleaming street of excess and glittering golden displays, floor upon floor, sparkling with a flip, hybrid and Babylonian conceit. Nothing had changed, while I had supposed an emotional cloudburst had occurred. The newspaper in my hand was all I knew of the war, this shadow conflict without destruction, this ghostly revisiting of a Battle of Chalons against a modern-day Attila over the water, this invisible war, whose bare echo resounded in the imperturbable newspaper kiosks at night.

'What time do the morning editions come out?' I asked.

'In two hours. The *Times* and the *Tribune*.'

I resumed my restless wandering up Fifth Avenue, past Central Park, to the Sherry Netherland, and from there to the Metropolitan Museum and on to the Hotel Pierre. It was an indescribable night: high and quiet, warm, full of late July, the florists' shops overflowing with roses, carnations and orchids, with bunches of lilacs on the pavements of the side streets, with a sky full of stars arcing over Central Park, supported on the tops of trees, lindens and magnolias, echoing with peace, horse-drawn carriages for late-night lovers, the melancholy roars of the lions and the buzz of cars, inscribing their scribbled lights in the avenues flanking the park.

I walked down to the little lake in the park. It twinkled in the light of the invisible moon. I sat down on a bench. I couldn't think clearly. I tried; but without warning the past was all around me, everything was whirling, reeling, approaching, staring at me out of its dead eyes, then dipping away into the shadow of the trees, rustling, creeping on inaudible feet into the future, talking with quenched voices of ashes and grief, urging and whispering and drifting through the wanderings of the years, till I almost believed in hallucinations and thought I saw them, in a ghostly mix of guilt, responsibility, omission, impotence, bitterness and a flickering desire for vengeance. Everything was torn open again on this warm July night, full of the smell of greening and flowering plants and the mouldering damp of the flat, black lake, on which somnolent ducks drily quacked back and forth, a shadow parade of pain, guilt and unfulfilled promises. I stood up; I couldn't bear to sit there quietly and feel the bats' wings so close to my face that they stifled my breathing with the cold whiff of graves. I walked further into the park, scraps of memories fluttering round me like an ancient torn coat, not knowing where I was going. I stopped in an open sandy spot. Nestled into the clearing was a little merry-go-round with coloured lights and shadows. It was sheeted over with canvas, but only partially; I could see the horses with their golden harnesses and their flowing manes and the gondolas, the bears and the elephants. They were frozen in violent motion, their gallops were petrified, and they stood there silent and still, charmed as in a fairy tale. I stood there for a long time staring at this frozen life, which had a strangely demoralising effect, because it was meant so blithely and joyfully. There were many things it reminded me of.

I heard footsteps. Two policemen emerged from the darkness behind me. Before I could think whether to try to run away or not, they were flanking me. I stood there. 'What are you doing here?' the larger of them asked calmly.

'I'm going for a walk,' I replied.

'Here at night? In the park? Why?'

I couldn't think of an answer. 'Papers?' asked the other one.

I had Sommer's passport on me. They shone a torch at it. 'So, you're not American then?' asked the second one.

'No.'

'Where are you living?'

'At the Hotel Rausch.'

'You've not been in New York for long?' asked the bigger one.

'No.'

The smaller one continued to study my passport. I felt the butterflies in my stomach that I always had whenever I ran into the police. Ten years now. I looked at the merry-go-round and a lacquered grey horse rearing up in permanent protest, then I stared up at the night sky and thought how perverse it would be if I were picked up now as a German spy. The smaller policeman was still looking at my passport. 'Done yet?' asked the taller one. 'I don't think he's a mugger, Jim.'

Jim said nothing. His colleague started to get impatient. 'We'd better go on, Jim.' He turned to me. 'Don't you know it's dangerous to walk here alone at nights?'

I shook my head. My notions of danger were different. I looked at the carousel again. 'Bad people like to hang around here at night,' explained the taller policeman. 'Bag snatchers, thieves, stuff like that. Things happen here all the time. Or were you hoping to get beaten up?'

He laughed. I said nothing. I just looked at my passport, which was still in the hands of the shorter policeman. That passport was the only thing I had if I ever wanted to return to Europe. 'Come with us,' said Jim finally. He didn't give me my passport back. I followed the two policemen. We came to a police car parked by the side of the road. 'Get in,' said Jim. I got in the back seat. I wasn't thinking of anything at all.

In no time we emerged from the park at 59th Street. 'We're philanthropists,' said the taller policeman. 'Real philanthropists, buster. As much as we are able.'

Suddenly I felt my neck was sweaty and I nodded mechanically. 'Are the morning papers out yet?' I asked.

'Yes. The son of a bitch got away. Some bastards have all the luck.'

I walked down the street, past the Hotel St Moritz with its little courtyard with tables and chairs – the only one I had seen in New York. New York didn't have cafés with newspapers, not like Paris or Vienna or even the smallest European town. Probably no one had the time.

I came to a kiosk. All at once I felt very tired. I scanned the front page. Hitler was not dead. All the other reports were contradictory. It was an army coup; it wasn't. Berlin was in the hands of the rebels; the ringleaders had been rounded up by generals loyal to Hitler. But Hitler was alive. He wasn't captured. He had already given orders to hang the rebels.

'When do the next lot of newspapers come out?' I asked.

'In the morning. The noon edition. These are the morning papers already.'

I looked at the newspaper vendor in perplexity. 'Wireless,' he said. 'Turn on your wireless. The stations broadcast the latest news all night.'

'That's right.'

I didn't have a wireless. But Moikov had one. Maybe he was back by now. I caught a cab back to the hotel. All at once I felt too tired to walk. I was in a hurry to be back as well. I was full of a trembling excitement and oddly uninvolved at the same time; it was as though I were hearing and feeling everything through cotton wool.

Moikov was back. He hadn't gone out at all. 'Robert Hirsch was here,' he said.

'When?'

'Two hours ago.'

Just when I was looking for Robert in his flat. 'Did he leave anything for me?' I asked.

Moikov motioned to a wireless set glittering with chrome buttons. 'He brought you this. It's a Zenith. Very good make. He thought you'd be able to use it tonight.'

I nodded. 'Did he say anything else?'

'He was here until about half an hour ago. He was excited and still pessimistic. He said the Germans had never managed to pull off a revolution in their history. Not even a rebellion. Their god was order and obedience, not conscience. He described the coup as an inside job – it wasn't that the Nazis were mass murderers and had turned the rule of law into a bloody farce, no, these people were just upset about losing the war. Up until half an hour ago, we were listening to the news together; when it was confirmed that Hitler had survived and was screaming for revenge, Hirsch went home. He left you the radio.'

'Has anything happened since?'

'Hitler is going to give a speech. To prove to the people that he was spared by Providence.'

'Of course. Anything relating to the troops at the Front?'

Moikov shook his head. 'Nothing, Ludwig. The war goes on.'

I nodded. Moikov looked at me. 'You look green around the gills. I split a bottle of vodka with Robert. I'll split another one with you, if you like. This is a night for nervous breakdowns. Or vodka.'

I declined. 'No, Vladimir. I'm falling-over tired. But I'll take the radio upstairs. Is there a socket in my room?'

'You don't need one. It's a travel radio.' Moikov was still looking at me. 'Don't make yourself crazy,' he said. 'At least have a mouthful. And maybe some of these—' He opened his hand, in which lay three tablets. 'To help you sleep. Tomorrow morning's plenty early to find out what's true and what's not. Tip from an old emigrant who's been through false hopes like that ten times over and had to bury them eleven times.'

'You think this is a case like that?'

'We'll find out tomorrow, won't we? Hope produces strange bedfellows. I found that out – and a murderer often changes his colours – it depends if it puts someone on your side or against you. I've given up that game long ago – I'd sooner just believe in the Ten Commandments. And God knows, they're patchy enough.'

A shadow of a woman came in. She was very old, with skin like grey, wrinkled tissue paper. Moikov got to his feet. 'Can I help you, Contessa?'

The shadow nodded hastily. 'My cordial, Vladimir Ivanovitch. I've run out. These July nights! I can't sleep. They remind me of the summer in St Petersburg in 1915. The poor Tsar!'

Moikov handed her a small bottle of vodka. 'Here's your cordial, Contessa. Good night. Sleep well.'

'I'll try.'

The shadow hurried out. It was wearing a deeply old-fashioned grey lace dress with ruffles. 'She lives in the past,' said Moikov. 'Time stopped for her with the Russian Revolution of 1917. Since then she's been dead; only she doesn't know it.' He looked at me alertly. 'Too much has happened in these past thirty years, Ludwig. There is no justice for so much bloodshed. Never was. One would have to eliminate half the world. Take the word of an old man who once felt as you do.'

I picked up the wireless and went up to my room. The windows were open. On the nightstand stood the Chinese bronze. It felt like a lifetime ago. I put the radio down next to it and listened to the news, which came at irregular, breathless intervals in between jazz, advertisements for whiskey, toilet paper, cold cream, summer sales, petrol and high-class cemeteries with light, well-drained soil and splendid views. I tried to find some foreign stations, England or Africa, and sometimes I was almost there, I picked up a word or two, but then it was drowned out by static, or a storm over the Atlantic, lightning beyond the horizon, or maybe even the echo of a terrific battle. I got up and stared out of the window, into the silent starry July night. Then I turned on the radio with its mishmash of propaganda and tragedy which it so utterly failed to separate, only that the advertisements got louder and ever more urgent, and the news just got worse. The assassination attempt had failed, the army was rounding up the guilty parties, it was generals against generals and the party of the murderers was coming up with new methods of torture, of hanging the conspirators or beheading them very slowly. The name of God was often invoked in the course of the night; but He seemed to be on Hitler's side. I fell asleep in the early morning, dog tired.

At noon, I heard from Moikov that someone had died that night in the hotel, an emigrant who never left his room. His name was Siegfried Sahl and he had suffered a heart attack. His body had already been taken away. I had never seen him. 'You can have his room if you want,' said Moikov. 'It's a bit bigger than yours. And better. Closer to the bathroom. Same price.'

I declined. Moikov didn't understand me. I wasn't sure I understood myself. 'You look awful,' he said. 'I guess sleeping tablets don't agree with you.'

'I haven't had trouble in the past.'

He looked at me critically. 'When I was your age, I used to think about personal vengeance and personal justice,' he said. 'Today, that feels to me like a kid after a terrible earth-quake asking what happened to his lost ball. Do you understand me, Ludwig?'

'No,' I said. 'But, lest you think I'm completely crazy, I'd like to swap rooms after all.'

I wondered whether or not to call Hirsch. But then I didn't want to talk about the conspiracy any more. It had failed and nothing had changed. There was nothing to talk about.

6

I took the bronze back to Silver. 'It's genuine,' I said.

'Fine. But you still shouldn't pay me any more than we agreed,' he replied. 'All sales are final. We're honest people here.'

'I still want to bring it back,' I said.

'Why?'

'Because I want to make a deal with you.'

Silver reached into his pocket, pulled out a ten-dollar bill, kissed it and put it back in a different pocket. 'What can I treat you to?' he asked merrily.

'How do you mean?'

'I made a bet with my brother whether you would return the bronze or not. I won. So let's have a coffee together? Not American coffee, but Czech coffee. The Americans boil their coffee to death. The Czech bakery over the road doesn't. They make it fresh, with hot water, without bringing it to the boil.'

We crossed the busy avenue. A street-sweeping machine was squirting water in all directions. A purple delivery van for children's diapers almost killed us. Silver avoided it with a dextrous leap. Today he had yellow socks under his patent-leather pumps. 'Now, what sort of deal do you have in mind?' he asked, once we were sitting in the bakery, in the beautiful bakery smell of cake, chocolate and coffee.

'I want to give you back the bronze and share the profits with you – sixty-forty. Sixty for me.'

'You call that sharing?'

'I call that generous.'

'Why do you want to cut me in at all, if you're so convinced the bronze is really old?'

'Two reasons. First, I can't sell it. I don't know anyone here. And second, I'm looking for a job. A particular kind of job: a job for someone who's not allowed to work. A job that an emigrant could do.'

Silver looked at me. 'Are you Jewish?'

I nodded.

'A refugee?'

'Yes. But I've got a visa.'

Silver thought for a moment. 'What do you like to do?'

'Whatever needs doing. Clearing up, organising, cataloguing – any sort of cash-in-hand job. Just to tide me over for a few weeks, till I find something else.'

'I see. Interesting suggestion. We have an enormous basement under the store. Full of all sorts of junk, we don't even know what. Do you think you have any sort of expertise that would help?'

'Absolutely. Enough to organise and catalogue, I would think.'

'Where were you trained?'

I got out my passport. Silver looked at the space: occupation. 'Antique dealer,' he said. 'I thought so all along. A colleague!' He finished his coffee. 'Let's go back to the shop.'

We went back across the street. It was almost dry again, after its recent sprinkling. The sun was warm, and there was a smell of steam and exhaust.

'Are bronzes your speciality?' Silver asked.

I nodded. 'Bronzes, rugs and a few other things.'

'And where did you study?'

'In Brussels and Paris.'

Silver offered me a thin, black Brazil cigar. I hated cigars; but I took it anyway.

I unwrapped the bronze from its tissue paper and looked at it in the sun. I felt a flashback to my panicked nights in the echoing corridors of the museum – then I set the bronze down on a table next to the window.

Silver watched me. 'Here's something we might do,' he said. 'I'll show the vase to the owner of Loo & Co. I know he's due back from San Francisco any day. I don't know much about it. Is that all right with you?'

'Absolutely. And what about work? The clearing away and classifying?'

'What do you make of this piece here?' asked Silver, pointing to the table I had put the bronze on. 'Good or bad?'

'So-so Louis XV, provincial, old, but with a new inlay,' I replied, quietly blessing the late Sommer who had had an artist's love for all old things.

'Not bad,' said Silver and gave me a light for the cigar. 'You know more than I do. To be frank, I've inherited this business,' he went on to explain. 'My brother and I. We were both lawyers. It didn't suit us. We're honest men, not legal weasels. We've had the shop for a couple of years and there's still a lot of the business we don't understand. But we get a kick out of it. It's like living in a gypsy caravan that we've parked here. With the bakery opposite, from where we can always see a customer walk in. Do you understand me?'

'Absolutely.'

'The business stays where it is, but the street is in constant motion,' said Silver. 'Like a film. There's always something going on. It suits us much better than defending villains and obtaining divorces. It's more decent as well. Don't you think so?'

'I do,' I replied, surprised at a lawyer thinking art was a more honourable field than the law.

Silver nodded. 'I'm the optimist of the family. I'm a Gemini. My brother is the pessimist. He's Cancer. We run the business together. I have to ask his permission regarding you. Is that all right?'

'It has to be, Mr Silver.'

'Good. Well, I suggest you come by in two or three days. Then we may know more. Concerning the bronze as well. How much are you looking to be paid for working here?'

'Enough to live off.'

'In the Ritz?' asked Silver.

'No, the Rausch. It doesn't have so many stars.'

'What about ten dollars a day?'

'Twelve,' I said. 'I'm a heavy smoker.'

'It will only be for a few weeks,' said Silver. 'No more than that. We don't need help with the selling side of the business. My brother and I are already too many. There's usually only one of us in the shop at any given time. But that's another reason why we like it; we want to make money, but not flog ourselves to death. Am I right?'

'Of course you are!'

'We seem to understand each other very well. Even though we've only just met.'

I didn't explain to Silver that two people always understand each other very well when one agrees with everything the other says. A woman in a feather hat walked in. Everything about her seemed to rustle. She must have been wearing layers and layers of silk petticoats. Everything rustled. She was heavily made up and curvaceous. An old Playmate with a puddingy face. 'Do you have any Venetian furniture?' she asked.

97

'The best,' Silver assured her and gave me a discreet signal to leave. 'Goodbye, Count Orsini,' he said to me fairly loudly. 'We'll send you the pieces tomorrow.'

'Not before eleven,' I replied. 'Between eleven and twelve, at the Ritz. Au revoir, mon cher.'

'Au revoir,' replied Silver, with a pretty rough accent. 'Say, half-past eleven.'

'Enough!' said Robert Hirsch. 'Enough. Don't you think?'

He switched off the television. A fleshy-faced announcer with dazzling teeth was just confidently intoning something about the latest news from Germany. We had already heard it twice from other stations. The oleaginous voice faded and the face melted away in astonishment into the fog that spread from the edge of the screen.

'Thank God!' said Hirsch. 'The best thing about these machines is the off button.'

'Radio is better,' I said. 'You don't see the faces.'

'Shall I turn on the radio?'

I shook my head. 'It's over, Robert. It failed. Nothing caught. No revolution.'

'It was just a coup. Started in the army, beaten back by the army.' Hirsch looked at me with his bright, despairing eyes. 'It was a mutiny among technocrats, Ludwig. They knew the war is lost. They wanted to save Germany from destruction. It was a patriotic uprising, not a humanitarian one.'

'You can't keep them apart. Nor was it a purely military matter; there were civilians involved as well.'

Hirsch shook his head. 'It's no good. If Hitler had gone on winning, nothing would have happened. This wasn't a rebellion against a murderous regime – it was a revolt against a bunch of incompetents. They weren't opposed to

98

concentration camps and gas chambers; they rose because Germany was being wrecked.'

I felt sorry for him. He felt it more keenly than I did. His life in France had been compounded of rage, retribution, adventure and compassion rather than morality and politics. If he'd been a moralist, he would have been trapped much earlier. Instead, odd as it appeared, he met the Nazis on something close to their level, only he had been better than they were. The Nazis, while utterly without scruple, were still moralists weighed down with political baggage – dark morals and sweaty, dark politics, that drew its responsibility from blind obedience and the automatic authority of any sort of order. Hirsch had been in the advantage against them; instead of heavy moral baggage, he carried only a light infantry pack and he followed his intelligence instead of falling prey to emotions. It wasn't for nothing that he came from a people who already venerated science and philosophy at a time when their persecutors were still crouching on tree limbs like monkeys. He had the advantage of quick reflexes, so long as he forgot the tradition of his people, which consisted of two and a half thousand years of perse-cution and suffering and resignation. If he had attended to that, he would have lost his certainty and been destroyed.

I looked at him. He appeared calm and collected. But so had Josef Bär, when I had been too tired in Paris to sit up and drink with him one more night. The next morning he was found hanging from the window in his room, dangling in the breeze, while the open half of the window clattered back and forth like a slow death-watch beetle. A rootless individual was sensitive and exposed to coincidences and moods that most people didn't feel. Intelligence, too, could become dangerous when turned on itself, the way millstones could grind each other to pieces when there was no corn. I knew that; that was why I had almost violently forced myself to a dumb resignation after the excitements of the night. Whoever had learned to be patient was better armed against the ravages of disappointment. But Hirsch had never been able to wait.

In addition, there was a further side to his character: that of the *condottiere*. It didn't only rile him that the assassination and popular uprising had failed, he couldn't cope with the thought that they had both been amateurish in their preparation. It was almost the professional indignation of an expert who had identified serious mistakes.

An apple-cheeked housewife walked in. She was looking for an electric toaster. I watched as Hirsch demonstrated the gleaming equipment. He was patient with her and even managed to talk her into buying an electric iron as well; even so, I couldn't imagine he would have a long career as a salesman.

I looked out on to the street. It was the hour of the accountants. At this time they flocked out to lunch in the drugstores. They escaped the air-conditioned cages of their offices and briefly imagined themselves as a couple of pay grades better off than they were. They went around in confident little clusters, gabby and bold, their jackets flying in the warm breeze, they were full of midday life and the illusions of men who would have made boss long ago, if there were anything like justice in this world.

Hirsch looked over my shoulder. 'The accountants' parade. In about two hours we'll get the housewives'. They fly out – from one shop window to the next, from one store to the next – they besiege the sales staffs without the least intention of buying anything, they relay the latest gossip from the newspapers. Their promenades follow the simple hierarchy of money; the wealthiest in the middle, flanked by a couple just a tad less well off. In winter you can see it at a glance, from the fur coats – mink in the middle, two black astrakhans on either side, eager and stupid. Meanwhile, their husbands are heading for early coronaries from their unremitting pursuit of the dollar. America is the land of rich widows, all soon to remarry; and young, ambitious, penniless men. That's the great wheel of becoming.' Hirsch laughed. 'What a difference from the hazardous existence of the flea, which leaps from one planet to the next, from man to man, and from dog to dog; and the locust, which passes over whole continents; not to mention the Jules-Verne-like adventures of the mosquito, which covers the distance from Central Park to Fifth Avenue.'

Someone knocked on the window. 'The dead are alive,' I said. 'It's Ravic. Or his brother.'

'It's the man himself,' said Hirsch. 'He's been here for a long time. Didn't you know?'

I shook my head. Ravic had been a noted doctor in Germany. He had fled to France and had had to work illegally for a French doctor of lesser gifts. I knew him from that time, when he was also moonlighting as medical examiner in the biggest brothel in Paris. He was a very good surgeon. The French doctor would hang around the operating room until the patient went under, then Ravic would come in and perform the operation. It didn't bother him; he was happy to have work and to conduct operations. He was a patient surgeon.

'Where are you working now, Ravic?' I asked. 'And how? New York doesn't have any brothels, at least not officially.'

'I'm working in a hospital.'

'Illegal?'

'Semi-legal. I'm a sort of superior nurse. I need to retake my exams. In English.'

'Just like in France?'

'Bit better. In France it was harder. Here at least I don't have to retake my school-leaving certificate.'

'Why ever not?'

Ravic laughed. 'Dear Ludwig,' he said. 'Do I need to remind you that the philanthropic professions are the most jealous there are? Theologians and doctors. Their organisations protect mediocrity with fire and sword. I wouldn't be surprised if I had to redo my exams in Germany, if I ever went back there.'

'Do you want to?' asked Hirsch.

Ravic shrugged. 'I'll cross that bridge when I come to it. Paragraph 6 of the Laon Breviary. Before that there's the year of despair. Let's get past that first!'

'Why the year of despair?' I asked. 'Don't you think they've lost the war?'

Ravic nodded. 'I do! But just because. The assassination failed, the war's lost, but the Germans are fighting on. They are being pushed back on all fronts; but they fight for every foot of ground as if it were the Holy Grail. This will be the year of lost illusions. No one will be able to argue any more that the poor Germans were taken over by Nazis from Mars. The poor Germans are themselves the Nazis and they are fighting for them with their lives. A lot of crockery will come to grief because of the illusions of the emigrants. Whoever fights like that for his ostensible oppressor loves his oppressor.'

'And the assassination?'

'Well, it failed, didn't it,' said Ravic. 'Fizzled out. The last chance hopelessly botched. There was never a chance really. The Hitler loyalists among the generals destroyed it. The bankruptcy of the officer corps following the bankruptcy of

German justice. And do you know what the worst thing of all will be? It will all be forgotten when it's over.'

We were silent for a while. 'Ravic,' said Hirsch. 'Did you come to depress us? We were feeling bad enough before you came.'

Ravic's face changed. 'I came here to get a drink, Robert. The last time, you still had a bit of Calvados.'

'Well, I finished that myself. But I have cognac and absinthe. And a bottle of Moikov's American bison grass vodka.'

'Give me the vodka. I'd prefer the cognac if it were up to me, but they won't be able to smell vodka on my breath. I have to conduct an operation this afternoon for the first time here.'

'On behalf of another doctor?'

'No. But in the presence of a chief surgeon. To make sure I do it properly. It's an operation that was named after me twelve years ago, when the world was still in one piece.' Ravic laughed. 'If you live dangerously, you should beware of irony. Wasn't that in your Laon Breviary as well? Have you forgotten it by now, or are you still living by it?'

'We're just dusting it off,' I said. 'We thought we were safe here and didn't need it any more.'

'You're never safe anywhere,' said Ravic. 'And least of all when you think you might be. "This is good vodka! Give me another one!" "Here's to you!" Those are sayings that are safe. Don't stand there like chickens in the rain. You're alive! So many people had to die who wanted to live. You must think about them and not much else, at least until the year of despair is over.'

He looked at his watch. 'I have to go. Some time when you're really feeling low, come and see me in the hospital. I'll give you a tour of the cancer ward that'll cheer you up.'

'Good!' said Hirsch. 'And take the vodka with you.'

'What for?'

'As payment,' replied Hirsch. 'We love instant analyses, even if they're not always correct. And curing depression by worse depression is at least original.'

Ravic laughed. 'It's not a cure for neurotics or romantics.' He picked up the bottle and packed it in his almost empty doctor's bag. 'And one last piece of advice, free of charge,' he said. 'Don't be so damned superior with your fate – what you need, both of you, is a woman, but preferably not an emigrant. A sorrow shared is a sorrow doubled – and that's really more than you need.'

It was early evening. I had just eaten the cheapest meal in the corner drugstore – two franks and two rolls. Then I had spent a long time staring at an advertisement for ice cream. America was the country of ice cream; you saw soldiers on the streets, nibbling choc ices. It was most unlike Germany where the soldiers slept at attention and when they farted it sounded like a machine-gun volley.

I walked back to the hotel down 42nd Street. That was the street of strip joints. The walls were covered with posters of nude or nearly nude dancers who at night would take their clothes off onstage for the heavy-breathing crowd. Later in the evening porters and barkers would stand in front of the doors in wadded coats like Turkish generals, and extol what was to be seen inside. The street would be crawling with fantasy uniforms, but you never saw the giveaway umbrellas and overnight bags of the whores of Europe. They didn't go out on the street and the spectators in the strip joints seemed to be exclusively dim wankers. The whores here were called call girls because they were procured over confidential closely guarded phone numbers;

but even that was against the law and the police were as hot on their trail as if they were an anarchist conspiracy. The morals of America were set by the women's league.

I left wankers' row and found myself among brownstones. These were narrow, cheap buildings, usually up some stairs, and people would sit on the stairs by the iron railings. The aluminium bins stood on the pavement in front of the steps, overflowing with garbage. Kids dodged in and out among the cars, trying to play baseball. Their mothers sat in the windows and on the steps like roosting hens. Smaller children clung on to them, tired and trustful, like dirty white butterflies in the dusk.

The reserve porter Felix O'Brien was standing outside the Rausch. 'Is Moikov not around?' I asked him.

'It's Saturday,' he replied. 'My day. Moikov's on the road.'

'Of course!' Saturday, I'd forgotten. A long, empty Sunday stretched ahead of me.

'Miss Fiola's been asking for Mr Moikov as well,' said Felix casually.

'Is she there still? Or has she gone away again?'

'I don't think she's gone. At least I didn't see her go if she did.'

Maria Fiola came towards me from the dim light of the plush lounge. She was in another one of her opulent turbans; this time, a black one.

'Are you modelling again?' I asked.

She nodded. 'I forgot today's Saturday, that's when Vladimir makes delivery of his nectar. But I've planned ahead. Since last time, I've had my own bottle. It's hidden in Vladimir's fridge. Not even Felix has unearthed it yet. Though that's only a matter of time.'

She walked ahead of me and got the bottle out of the corner fridge. I put two glasses on the table next to the mirror.

'You've picked up the wrong bottle,' I said. 'That's hydrogen peroxide. Highly poisonous.' I pointed to the label.

Maria Fiola laughed. 'No, it's the right bottle. I put the label on myself, to throw Felix off the scent. Hydrogen peroxide doesn't smell, any more than vodka does. Felix has a keen nose but even he won't be able to identify something he hasn't tasted. Hence the label. Highly poisonous! Simple, isn't it?'

'All the best ideas are simple,' I said admiringly. 'That's why they're so hard.'

'I had some more vodka of my own a couple of days ago. As an anti-Felix device, Vladimir Ivanovitch poured it into a dusty old vinegar bottle and stuck a sign on it in Cyrillic. The next morning it was gone.'

'Lachmann?' I guessed.

She nodded, surprised. 'How did you know?'

'Natural powers of deduction,' I said. 'Did he confess?'

'Yes. He felt so bad, he brought me this bottle instead and it's quite a bit bigger. The other one was half a litre, this is over three-quarters. Cheers!'

'Cheers!' Lachmann's Lourdes water, I thought. He wouldn't have been able to smell it; and he was teetotal. Who knew what happened to him with the Puerto-Rican woman. But maybe he had billed it as grappa from the Mount of Olives.

'I like sitting here,' said Maria Fiola. 'It's a habit from before, when I was living here. I've always liked sitting in hotels. Something is always happening. People coming and going – hellos and goodbyes, those are probably the most exciting things in life.'

'Do you reckon?'

'Don't you?'

I thought about it. I'd had enough goodbyes and farewells to last me a lifetime. Too many. Especially farewells. I thought a quiet life was much more exciting. 'Perhaps you're right,' I replied. 'But isn't a big hotel better for that?'

She shook her turban, setting the metal curlers clinking. 'I think big hotels lack character. Not like here. Here no one hides their feelings. You could see that with me the other day. Have you met Raoul yet?'

'No.'

'What about the Contessa?'

'Not really.'

'You've got a lot to look forward to, then. What about another vodka? These glasses are really very small.'

'Same size as last time.'

I couldn't help it; thinking of Lachmann gave the vodka a faint taste of incense. I remembered the Laon Breviary: Distrust the imagination; it makes things bigger, smaller, distorted.

Maria Fiola reached for a parcel beside her. 'My wigs! Red, blonde, black, grey and even white. You know, a model can't look forward to a long career. And I don't enjoy it; so I always stop off here on my way before dressing up. Vladimir is kind of like a still pole in a turning world. We're taking colour pictures today. Why don't you come along? If you haven't got anything else planned?'

'No. I don't. But surely your photographer would throw me out.'

'Nicky? What an idea! There'll be at least another dozen people there. If you get bored, you can leave any time. It's not like a party, you know.'

'All right.'

I would have grabbed at anything to avoid the solitude of my room. It was the room the emigrant Sahl had died in. I had found a couple of letters from him in the closet: he hadn't got around to mailing them. One was to Ruth

Sahl in the labour camp at Terezin near Vienna: 'Dear Ruth, it's been so long since I heard from you – I hope you're doing well and are in good health.' I knew that Terezin was one of the collection points for Jews who were then shipped on to the ovens at Auschwitz. Ruth Sahl had probably been incinerated long ago. I was going to send the letter anyway. It was full of love without hope: despair, guilt and questions.

'Shall we take a taxi?' I asked when we were outside. My wallet was pretty thin these days.

Maria Fiola shook her head. 'Only Raoul takes taxis at the Rausch. I remember that from my time there. Everyone else walks everywhere. I do. I enjoy it. Don't you?'

'I walk everywhere too. Especially in New York. Two or three hours are nothing to me.' I didn't mention that I only walked in New York because I didn't have to worry about the police. It gave me a sense of freedom that hadn't worn off yet.

'It's not that far,' said the girl.

I offered to carry her parcel of wigs, but she didn't let me. 'I'll carry them myself. These things are sensitive. You need to hold them firmly but gently, otherwise they'll slip out and fall on the pavement.' She laughed. 'Women! I love the banality sometimes. It's so refreshing when you're surrounded by geniuses and comedians all day.'

'And are you?'

She nodded. 'It comes with the territory. Paradoxes, aphorisms, irony – all to dispel the slight whiff of homosexuality in the fashion industry.'

We walked against the prevailing flow. Maria Fiola walked quickly, with long strides. She didn't mince and she held her head up like a figurehead on a ship; it made her look taller than she was. 'It's a big day today,' she said. 'Colour pictures. Evening dresses and furs.'

'Furs? In this heat?'

'That doesn't matter. We're always a season or two ahead anyway. In summer, we work on the autumn and winter fashions. The designs are photographed. Then the clothes have to be manufactured and distributed. That takes months. It means we're always mixed up with time. We live through two seasons at once – the one we're in and the one whose clothes we're photographing. Sometimes we get muddled up. It's all a bit gypsyish and never completely true.'

We got to a dark side street, lit only by the white light of a hamburger stand and a drugstore on the corner. It occurred to me that this was the first time I'd been out walking with a woman in America.

About a dozen people were gathered in a huge, almost bare room, with a number of chairs, a stage and a few white screens, the whole thing lit by Klieg lights. Nicky the photographer gave Maria a hug, a little cloud of speech fragments flew up, I was briefly introduced, whiskey was passed around and I found myself on a chair, quite a way from the action and quite forgotten.

But it meant I got to see a scene I had never witnessed before. Big boxes were unpacked, carted behind a curtain and opened one by one. They were followed by coats and fur wraps, and an intense debate began as to what should be photographed first. There were two other models in addition to Maria Fiola, a blonde who was wearing very little except a pair of silver shoes and a dark-skinned girl with black hair.

'The coats first,' said an energetic elderly woman.

Nicky protested. He was a thin, sandy-haired man with a gold chain round his wrist. 'The dresses first! Otherwise they'll be crushed under the furs!'

'The girls don't need to have them on under their coats. They can wear their own clothes. Or nothing at all. The furs have to go back first. Later tonight.'

'Very well,' said Nicky. 'The furriers seem not to trust us. Start with the furs. The mink cape. The tourmaline.'

A further debate started, in English and French, as to how the cape was to be photographed. I listened with half an ear. The artificial excitement reminded me of the theatre – as though a scene from *A Midsummer Night's Dream* or *Der Rosenkavalier* were being rehearsed. At any moment, I thought, Oberon might appear to a fanfare.

In that instant all the lights focused on one wall. A vase of artificial delphiniums was brought on. The blonde model with the silver shoes came out in a honey-coloured fur cape. The director smoothed out the fur, two high beams came on and the model froze, as though a policeman had threatened her with a pistol. 'Camera!' called Nicky.

The model moved again. The director too. Nicky said, 'And again! A little to the right. Look past the camera. Good!'

I leaned back. The contrast between my own position and the scene in front of me projected me into a feeling of unreality that had nothing of confusion, alertness and reverie. It was more like a deep calm, a mild rapture that I had rarely if ever experienced. It occurred to me that since leaving home I had hardly ever been inside a theatre, much less an opera house. The odd trip to the cinema was the most I could claim, and even that had been so that I could disappear from sight for a couple of hours.

I followed the various shots of the cape and the blonde model, who seemed to grow more and more ethereal. I couldn't imagine her having human needs. It must be the very strong white light that played over everything and robbed her of her physicality. Someone brought me another glass of whiskey. I was glad I had come along. For the first time I felt relaxed, without the tension that I was more or less aware of the rest of the time.

'Maria!' called Nicky. 'The beaver!'

And then all at once there was Maria Fiola on the stage, slim and petite, bundled up in a matt black coat, with a sort of beret of the same thin, gleaming fur set rakishly on her head.

'Good!' called Nicky. 'Hold the pose! Hold very still.'

He shooed the director away as she came on to tweak at the coat. 'No! No! Hetty! There's time for that later. This isn't the last shot. I wanted her as she was, unposed.'

'But you can't see—'

'Later, Hetty! Take!'

Maria didn't freeze the way the blonde model had. She just stayed still, as though she had already stopped moving. The sidelights scanned her face and were caught in her eyes, which were suddenly terribly blue.

'Good!' said Nicky. 'And now with the coat falling open.'

Hetty fluttered up. Maria spread the coat, as though it was just two butterfly wings. It had looked narrow; in fact it was very wide, lined with white silk with big grey squares printed on it. 'Hold that!' said Nicky. 'Like an emperor moth. Wide!'

'Emperor moths aren't black. They're purple!' objected Hetty.

'Here they're black,' retorted Nicky superbly.

It seemed that Hetty was knowledgeable about butterflies. She insisted that what Nicky had in mind was a Camberwell Beauty. But Nicky won out. In fashion, there was no such thing as Camberwell.

'How are you liking it?' asked a voice next to me.

A pale, heavyset man with strangely gleaming round black

eyes flopped on to a camp stool, which quaked and settled. 'Fabulous,' I replied honestly.

'Of course we can't lay our hands on the work of the great French couturiers right now,' said the man. 'Consequence of the war. But Mainbocher and Balenciaga show up pretty well, wouldn't you agree?'

'Very much so.' I had no idea what he was talking about.

'Well, I hope the war will be over soon, so that we can get more first-rate fabrics. These silks from Lyons—'

The man got up, people were calling him. It didn't seem to me particularly ridiculous to offer that as a reason for ending the war; on the contrary, to me, sitting there, it made perfect sense.

The evening dresses were photographed. Then without warning Maria Fiola was standing next to me. She was wearing a tight white sheath that exposed her shoulders. 'Are you horribly bored?' she asked.

'Not in the least.' I looked up at her. 'I think I must be having a benign hallucination,' I said. 'Otherwise I surely wouldn't have the sense that I'd seen the diadem you're wearing before, in the windows of Van Cleef & Arpels this afternoon. It was on display as having belonged to Empress Eugenie. Or do I mean Marie Antoinette?'

'You have a good eye. It is from Van Cleef & Arpels.' Maria laughed.

'Did you buy it, then?' I asked. Just at that moment nothing seemed impossible to me. Perhaps Maria was the runaway daughter of a Chicago corned-beef millionaire. I had read about such characters in gossip columns.

'No. And I haven't stolen it either. The magazine we're doing the pictures for has borrowed it. The man over there will pick it up from me at the end of the night. He works for Van Cleef and he's guarding it for them. What was your favourite?'

'The black and white velvet cape you wore. The Balenciaga.'

She turned round and looked at me in surprise. 'It is a Balenciaga,' she said slowly. 'How did you know that? Are you in the business? How else would you know that was a Balenciaga cape?'

'Only five minutes ago I didn't know. I would have thought a Balenciaga was a make of car.'

'How do you know, then?'

'The pale-looking man over there told me the name. The rest was conjecture.'

'It really is a Balenciaga,' she said. 'It was flown over here in a bomber. A Flying Fortress. Smuggled in.'

'That's a good use for a bomber. If it happened more often it would be the beginning of a golden age.'

She laughed. 'So you aren't carrying a mini camera in your pocket, and you're not a spy to steal the secrets of next winter's fashions for the competition? A pity, really! But it seems you want watching closely. Have you got enough to drink?'

'Thank you, yes.'

'Maria!' called the photographer. 'Maria! Next shot!'

'We're all going to El Morocco for an hour afterwards,' she said. 'Will you come? You have to walk me home, after all.'

She was standing on the stage before I could reply. Of course I couldn't come. I didn't have any money. But there was time for that. For now, I was drifting along in this atmosphere in which a spy was not someone who was shot at dawn, but someone who was out to steal the cut of a velvet cape. Even time here seemed to shift. While the heat was beating down outside, in here we had midwinter; mink coats and fur jackets shimmered under the lights. Nicky repeated one or two shots. The dark model came on in a red wig; Maria Fiola in a blonde one and then a white one. In a few minutes she seemed to have aged by decades. It gave me the strange feeling of having known her for many years. The models no longer bothered to go behind the curtain to change. They were tired and they had no defences anyway against the harsh, pure light. The men weren't interested; at least some of them were homosexual and the rest were probably used to seeing naked women.

As the boxes were being packed up, I told Maria Fiola I wouldn't be able to come. I had heard it said that El Morocco was the best nightclub in New York.

'Why not?' she asked.

'I haven't got enough money on me.'

'You idiot! We're all invited. The magazine's paying. And you're my friend. Do you really think I'd let you pay?'

I wasn't sure whether to take that as a compliment or not. I stared at the strange, made-up woman in the blonde wig and the emerald and diamond diadem as if I'd never seen her before. I felt a rush of warmth for her as though we were accomplices of a kind. 'Don't the jewels have to be returned first?' I asked.

'The man from Van Cleef is coming with us. Apparently it's good PR if they're worn in public.'

I stopped protesting. Nor was I surprised later to be sitting in El Morocco, with its lights and music and dancers; the benches were zebra patterned, and an artificial night sky in which the stars came on and went out glistened over this unreal world. In a side room a man from Vienna sang Viennese songs in German, even though America was at war with both. It could never have happened in Europe.

The singer would have been thrown in prison or concentration camp, or he might have been lynched on the spot. Here such soldiers and officers as were present and happened to know the words sang along in raptures. For someone who had seen the word tolerance move from a noble cause in the nineteenth century to a crass insult in the twentieth, it was like coming upon a strange kind of oasis in the unlikeliest place. I wasn't sure whether to put it down to super-confidence or lack of imagination – and I didn't want to know. I was sitting among dancers and singers, my new best friends, in candlelight, next to a woman I barely knew in an outrageous blonde wig and a borrowed diadem with real emeralds. I was a little parasite, basking in quasi-benevolence and quaffing free champagne. Really, the whole evening had been borrowed from Van Cleef & Arpels and had to be returned tomorrow morning. In my pocket I could feel the letter from the emigrant Sahl that I wanted to post: 'My darling Ruth, I am in agonies of remorse, because I tried too late to rescue you; but who would guess that they would go after women and children as well? I didn't have any money and what could I do anyway. I so badly hope that you are alive, even if you are unable to write back. I pray—' At that point the letter was illegible with tears. I hadn't sent it off, because I wanted to consider first whether it might harm the woman, if she should still be alive. I knew now that I wouldn't send it.

7

Alexander Silver was already waving to me from the shop. His head was between a nineteeth-century mandarin robe and a Ghiordes carpet hanging next to it. He pushed them both aside and waved harder. Below him, the stone head of a Khmer Buddha contemplated the street. I walked in.

'Any news?' I asked, looking around for the bronze.

He nodded. 'I showed the piece to Frank Caro at Loo's. It's a fake.'

'Oh?' I said in surprise. I didn't see why he was waving to me so energetically.

'Of course I'll take it back anyway. I don't want you to lose out.'

Silver reached for his wallet. I thought he was a bit quick about it. Something in his face didn't chime with that news either. 'No,' I said, taking a chance that I was risking half my capital. 'I'd rather keep it.'

'Very well,' said Silver. Abruptly he was laughing. 'Then you know the first law of the art dealer: not to fall for bluff.'

'As it happens, I knew that already, not as an art dealer, admittedly, but as a human being. So the vase is genuine?'

'What makes you draw that conclusion?'

'Three unimportant factors. But let's cut to the chase anyway. The bronze is genuine?'

'Caro thinks it's genuine. He doesn't understand how anyone could have thought otherwise. He says sometimes young museum people eager to show off their understanding can be too critical. Especially when they're newly hired; they think they have to prove they know more than their predecessors.'

'How much is it worth?'

'It's not an important piece. But good mid-period Chou. At an auction at Parke Bernet it might go for four or five hundred dollars. Not more. Chinese bronzes have fallen.'

'Why?'

'Because everything's cheap. There's a war on. And there aren't many collectors of Chinese bronzes.'

'Same reason: because there's a war on?'

Silver laughed. I saw a lot of gold in his mouth. 'How much were you going to ask for your share?'

'What I paid. And half the profit. Not sixty-forty though, fifty-fifty.'

'Well, we'll have to sell the bronze first. Caro's quote was an auction price; it might only fetch half that. Or even less.'

He was right. There was a big difference between what the bronze was worth and how much someone was actually prepared to pay for it. I wondered about offering it to Caro.

'Let's go over the road,' said Silver. 'It's time for coffee.'

'How so?' I asked. It was ten o'clock.

'It's always time for coffee.'

We crossed the road. Silver was wearing purple socks with his patent-leather pumps. He looked like a Jewish bishop. 'I'll tell you what I'm going to do,' he said. 'I'll telephone the museum I acquired it from and explain that I've sold the bronze. My buyer then took it to Loo, who told him it was genuine. I'll offer to try and buy it back for the museum.'

'For the old price?'

'For a price we can discuss over a second cup of coffee. How is the coffee today?'

'Good so far. But why do you want to offer the bronze to the museum that sold it to you? You'll only embarrass or infuriate the man who told you it was fake.'

'You're right. He can turn it down. But I'll have done my duty. The worldwide art business is like a village; and art dealers are terrible gossips. The museum man might hear the story from the next buyer; then the museum would be finished for me as a client. Do you see?'

I nodded cautiously.

'Whereas if I offer him the bronze first, he has cause to be grateful to me. He owes me, really. If he then turns it down, it frees us to sell to anyone we can. There are certain unwritten laws, of which this is one.'

'How much are you going to ask him for?' I asked.

'The price you supposedly paid. Not fifty dollars, but two hundred and fifty.'

'And how much of that is for you?'

'Seventy-five,' said Silver, with a magnificent gesture. 'Not a hundred – just seventy-five. We're human beings here. What do you say?'

'It has style, but I'm still losing out. Loo says Parke Bernet would sell it at auction—'

Silver interrupted me. 'My dear Mr Sommer, in the stock exchange and the art market it's a mistake to take things to extremes, because you might end up losing everything. Don't be a gambler! If a good profit beckons, take it. That was the Rothschilds' motto. Bear it in mind.'

'Very well,' I said. 'But I need an incentive for my first deal. Don't forget, I risked half my fortune.'

'We're arguing about a sum that has yet to be realised.

The museum may refuse. Then we'll have to go to a lot of trouble to locate a buyer. In these times!'

'What would you be prepared to offer if you knew the piece was genuine?' I asked.

'A hundred dollars,' replied Silver instantly. 'And not a penny more.'

'Mr Silver! And at ten-thirty in the morning!'

Silver beckoned to the Czech waitress. 'You should try the almond sponge,' he said to me. 'It's excellent.'

'At ten-thirty in the morning?'

'Why not? You need to take your own decisions in this life. Otherwise you're a machine.'

'All right. What about my job for you?'

Silver forked a piece of sponge on to my plate. It was dense, with a thick crust of sugar and almonds. 'I had a word with my brother. You can start tomorrow. Whatever happens with the bronze.'

I took a deep breath. 'For fifteen dollars a day?'

Silver looked at me reproachfully. 'We agreed twelve and a half. You know, I'd almost take you for a goy. No Jew would try damnfool tricks like that.'

'A believing Jew might not. But I'm a miserable free-thinker and I'm fighting for my life, Mr Silver.'

'So much the worse. Are you really so hard up?'

'You have no idea. I have debts. Starting with the lawyer who got me into the country.'

'Lawyers can wait. They're used to it. And I used to be one, remember.'

'I still need him, though. Soon, too, to extend my leave to stay. I'm sure he's expecting to be paid off first.'

'Let's go back to the store,' said Silver. 'You're breaking my heart!'

We plunged into the traffic like the Jews into the Red

Sea and made it safely to the other side. Silver seemed to have a rebel heart. He scorned traffic lights. I told him he was dicing with the hospital. 'If you like sitting in the café and watching your business from there, then you have to be quick when a customer comes,' he explained. 'Hence my death-defying way of crossing the street.'

He pulled out a scuffed wallet. 'So. It seems you need an advance,' he said. 'How would a hundred dollars suit you?'

'For the bronze or for the job?'

'For both.'

'All right,' I said. 'But just for the bronze. I want the job treated separately. Probably best you pay me by the week in arrears.'

Silver shook his head in disapproval. 'Any other wishes? Silver dollars or pieces of eight?'

'No. I'm not a greedy shark. But this is the first money I'll have earned in America! It makes me hope I won't finish up as a beggar or starving. You understand? It's a little childish.'

'A good way of being childish.'

Silver pulled out ten ten-dollar bills. 'A down payment for our joint enterprise.' He paid down another five. 'And the price you paid for the bronze. Better?'

'Very generous. What time do you want me to start tomorrow?'

'Not at eight. Nine. That's another advantage in our line of business. No one buys antiques at eight in the morning.'

I stuffed the money into my pocket and took my leave. The street outside was a dazzle of noise and light. I hadn't known freedom for long enough to have lost the connection between money and existence. To me they felt like one and the same. The notes felt like life itself. I had three weeks of life in my pocket.

★

It was lunchtime. We were sitting in Hirsch's store: Ravic, Hirsch and me. Outside, the hour of the accountants was just getting under way.

'A human being,' Ravic was saying, 'is difficult to put a price on. Let's leave emotions out of it, they're impossible to measure and vary so much by individual that someone who to you is worth more than the whole world is barely worth the price of a bullet to the next person. From the point of view of chemistry, there's not much there either – seven dollars' worth of calcium, protein, cellulose, fat, a lot of water and tiny amounts of this and that trace element. It's only interesting when you want to destroy him. In Caesar's day, in the Gallic Wars, it cost about seventy cents in today's money to kill a soldier. In the time of Napoleon, with rifles and artillery and so on, it was already about two thousand dollars all told, with a very small sum included for training. In World War One it is estimated that the sum per dead soldier had gone up to ten thousand dollars apiece, with vast sums for artillery, fortification, warships and munitions. And for the war currently in progress the experts think the sum will be around fifty thousand dollars to kill a simple accountant bundled into a uniform.'

'In that case war will gradually be priced out of existence,' said Hirsch. 'Very moral.'

Ravic shook his head. 'Unfortunately not. The generals are pinning their hopes on the atom bombs that are now being worked on. They reckon they will break the inflationary spiral of mass death. They have hopes of returning to Napoleon-era prices.'

'Two thousand a pop?'

'Yes, or even less.'

The midday news flickered across the TV. The announcer reported the number of casualties with grim satisfaction.

They did that every noon and night; it was a kind of hors d'oeuvre.

'They are even expecting a collapse in the price,' said Ravic. 'They've invented total war. That means they no longer need to go to the trouble of shipping expensively trained men to the front. The hinterland comes into play. Bombers have helped a lot. Now women, children, the old and the sick join the ranks of the casualties. We're already getting used to it.' He pointed to the announcer on the screen. 'Look at him! Unctuous as a priest.'

'Higher justice,' declared Hirsch. 'The army always had a line in it. Why should soldiers be the only ones to risk their lives? Why not spread the risk a little? It's only logical. Children grow up and women give birth to future soldiers – why not kill them right away, before they become dangerous. The humanity of generals and politicians is truly immeasurable! A sensible doctor doesn't wait till an epidemic gets out of control either. Isn't that right, Ravic?'

'That's right,' said Ravic, suddenly looking very tired.

Robert Hirsch looked at him. 'Do you want me to turn off the announcer?'

Ravic nodded. 'Yes, turn him off, Robert. This happy machine-gun fire of words isn't tolerable for very long. Do you know why there will always be war?'

'Because memory is a romantic falsifier,' I said. 'It's a sieve that lets horror through, and forgets it and turns it into an adventure. Everyone is a hero in his own memory. The only ones who are really qualified to talk about war are the dead: they're the only ones who got to experience all of it. And they don't talk.'

Ravic shook his head. 'One man doesn't feel another's pain,' he said. 'That's all it is. Not even another's death. After a little while, all he'll know is that he's managed to get away himself. It's our damned skin that separates us and makes us into so many egoistic islands. You experienced it in the camps; pain for the dead doesn't keep you from choking down a piece of bread you've managed to get hold of.' He raised his glass. 'Could we drink this cognac otherwise, while the fat announcer goes on blathering about the human cost as though it were so many kebabs?'

'No,' said Hirsch. 'We couldn't. But could we even live?'

Outside the window a woman in a teal blouse was smacking a boy of about four. The kid broke away and kicked her on the shin. Then he ran off and managed to stay out of range, all the while making faces at her. They disappeared among the stiffly striding accountants.

'In their humanity the generals have come up with a new term,' said Hirsch. 'They don't like to talk about millions of dead; instead, the word megadeath will soon be gracing their reports. Don't you think ten megadeaths sounds so much better than ten million dead? How far gone are the days when the soldiers in ancient China were accounted the lowest class, lower than hangmen, because while hangmen killed only criminals, generals killed innocents! Today they're at the top of the tree and the more people they kill, the greater their fame.'

I looked around. Ravic sat slumped in his armchair, eyes closed. It was a doctor's habit. He could fall asleep and wake up by the second.

'He's asleep,' said Hirsch. 'The hecatombs, the megadeaths and the grimacings of fate that we call history fall into his slumber like a silent rain. That's the blessing of the skin that separates us and that he was so furious with. The luck of the non-participant.'

Ravic opened his eyes. 'I'm not asleep. I'm going one by

one through the issues raised by a hysterectomy in English, you incorrigible theoreticians. Have you forgotten the paragraphs of the Laon Breviary? Grief for the inevitable weakens a man at times of danger.'

He got up and looked out at the street. The accountants were gone; the popinjay parade of wives had begun. They fluttered out to the shops in their flowered dresses. 'Is that the time already? I've got to be at the hospital.'

'It's easy for you,' said Hirsch. 'At least you've got a respectable job.'

Ravic laughed. 'But a hopeless one, Robert.'

'You didn't talk much today,' said Robert Hirsch to me. 'Are you bored by our lunchtime symposiums?'

I shook my head. 'I joined the ranks of the employed today. The bronze has been sold and I'm going to start in Silver's basement tomorrow morning. I can't help feeling a little stunned.'

Hirsch laughed. 'The work we do!'

'I've got nothing against mine,' I said. 'It has a symbolic valency. Tidying up and dealing with old things.' I pulled Silver's money out. 'Why don't you take half of it, Robert. I'm still massively in your debt.'

He refused. 'You should use that to pay Levin and Watson. You'll be needing them before long. Don't fritter it away. Authorities are authorities, war or not. How's your English coming on?'

I laughed. 'Since this morning, everything has picked up in the most extraordinary way. I think it's the step into bourgeoisification. For rapture read earning power; breathlessness is now the daily trot. The future is at hand. Working, earning, security.'

Hirsch looked at me critically. 'Do you really think we're cut out for all that?'

'Why not?'

'Don't you think the years on the run spoiled us for it, Ludwig?'

'I don't know. This is my first day as a bourgeois – and it's work off the books. I'm not clear of the police yet.'

'There are soldiers who can't adjust to peacetime,' said Hirsch.

'We'll have to wait and see,' I said. 'Paragraph 19 of the Laon Breviary: Concern for tomorrow weakens the power of judgement today.'

'What's going on here?' I asked Moikov, as I walked into the hotel lobby.

'A disaster! Raoul! Our best customer! The man with the luxury suite with living room, dining room, marble tub and TV in his bedroom. He wants to take his own life!'

'Since when?'

'Since this afternoon. He's lost Kiki. His dear friend of four years.'

Someone sobbed loudly and heart-rendingly between the potted palm and the Swiss cheese plant. 'There's a lot of crying in this hotel,' I said. 'And always under the palm tree.'

'People always cry in hotels,' claimed Moikov.

'In the Ritz as well?'

'In the Ritz they cry when the Dow falls. Here it's when someone realises he's all alone in the world when he thought he wasn't.'

'Surely that might just as well be a reason to be happy. You can celebrate your liberty.'

'Or your heartlessness.'

'Is Kiki dead?' I asked.

'Worse! He's got engaged. To a woman! For Raoul it's a tragedy. If he'd eloped with another homo, the whole thing would have been in the family, so to speak. But a woman! The enemy camp! Betrayal! The sin against the Holy Ghost!'

'The poor devils. Having to defend themselves on both sides. Against competition from men and women alike.'

Moikov sniggered. 'Raoul just delivered himself of some interesting opinions regarding women. The most repeatable one was: seals with skin. He had unkind things to say about the part they so admire in America, the full bosom. "Hypertrophic udders" was about the mildest of them. Every time he imagines his Kiki attached to one, it makes him roar. I'm glad you're back. You're used to disasters. We have to get him back in his room. We can't keep him down here. Help me, will you? He must weigh two hundred pounds.'

We went to the palm corner. 'He'll come back to you, Raoul,' Moikov said beseechingly. 'You need to get a grip on yourself. Tomorrow everything'll be sorted out. Kiki will be back.'

'Polluted!' groaned Raoul, who was lying like a shot hippo on the sofa.

We tried to prise him up. He slumped against the marble-top table, wailing. Moikov kept trying to talk to him. 'It's just an error. Forgivable, Raoul. But he'll be back. I've known it to happen so many times. Kiki will be back, full of regret.'

'The filthy bitch! What about the letter he wrote me? He's not coming back! He took my gold watch as well, the minx.'

Raoul started crying all over again. As we picked him up, he trod on my foot. All two hundred pounds of him. 'Watch what you're doing, you old woman!' I swore reflexively.

'What?!'

'Yes,' I said, calmer now. 'You really are behaving like an emotional old biddy.'

'Me an old woman?' said Raoul, in an instant sounding rather more like himself.

'Mr Sommer doesn't mean it like that,' put in Moikov. 'It's his English. In French it means something very different. It's a great compliment.'

Raoul wiped his eyes. We were waiting for the next hysterical outcry. 'A woman,' he said, quietly and mortally offended. 'Me a woman.'

'He meant it the French way,' lied Moikov. 'It's an honour. Think of a *femme fatale*.'

'Abandoned!' declared Raoul and he got up without help. 'Abandoned by everyone.'

We got him to the stairs easily enough now. 'A few hours of sleep,' said Moikov encouragingly. 'Two or three seconal. Then a nice cup of coffee. Everything will look completely different in the morning.'

Raoul didn't reply. We too had deserted him. The whole world. Moikov walked him up the stairs. 'Everything will be simpler tomorrow. Kiki's not dead. Just a youthful aberration.'

'For me he's dead. And he took my cufflinks!'

'But they were a present from you. For his birthday. Anyway, he'll give them back, I'm sure.'

'Why do you go to so much trouble over that mooncalf?' I asked Moikov when he came back down.

'He's our best lodger. Have you ever seen inside his apartment? If we didn't have him, we'd have to raise everyone's rents. Including yours.'

'My God!'

'Anyway, mooncalf or not,' said Moikov. 'Everyone suffers

in their own way and there are no distinctions in pain. And above all there's no absurdity. I'm surprised you don't know that.'

'I do know it,' I said, feeling a little ashamed of myself. 'But there are distinctions.'

'Only relatively speaking. We had a chambermaid here once who drowned herself in the Hudson, because her son had stolen a few dollars. She couldn't endure the shame. Was that ridiculous?'

'Yes and no. Let's not argue.'

Moikov listened up the stairs. 'I hope he doesn't do anything stupid,' he murmured. 'These extremists often blow a fuse.'

'Was she an extremist, your chambermaid?'

'She was a poor wretch. She could see no way out – where everything was open. How about a game of chess?'

'Yes. And let's drink a vodka. Or two. Or as many as we want. Sell me a bottle. I'll pay you right now.'

'What's this about?!'

'I've found work. For a month or two.'

'Good.' Moikov pricked up his ears.

'Lachmann!' I said. 'I'd know his footfall anywhere.'

Moikov sighed. 'I don't know if it's the moon or what, but this seems to be an evening for extremists.'

After Raoul, Lachmann seemed quite piano. 'Sit down,' I said. 'Don't talk, have a drink and consider this text: God is in the detail.'

'Eh?'

I repeated my sentence. 'What nonsense,' said Lachmann.

'Good. Because we don't have to die, we should be brave, another motto. All our emotions here have already been lavished on Raoul.'

'I don't drink vodka. I don't drink at all, as you ought to know. In Poitiers you once tried to get me drunk on a bottle of cherry brandy you'd stolen from somewhere. Just as well my stomach rebelled, otherwise I'm sure the police would have caught me.' Lachmann turned to Moikov. 'Is she back?'

'No. Not yet. Just Sommer and Raoul. Both as nervous as kittens. Full moon, I think.'

'What?'

'Full moon. Raises the blood pressure. Enhances illusions. Inspires murderers.'

'Vladimir!' replied the tormented Lachmann. 'After darkness, you should go easy on jokes at other people's expense. We all have enough on our own plates. Was no one here otherwise?'

'Only Maria Fiola. She stayed for an hour and twelve minutes. Drank one and a half vodkas. Said goodbye and headed for the airport. Will be back in a few days. Will be modelling clothes and getting herself photographed. Is that enough for you, Mr Lachmann, spy in the house of love?'

Lachmann, crushed, nodded. 'I'm a pest,' he muttered, 'I know I am. But I'm a bigger pest for myself.'

Moikov listened in the direction of the stairs. 'I'll just go and see what Raoul is doing.'

He got up and went upstairs. For his age and weight, he was surprisingly light-footed.

'What am I going to do,' said Lachmann. 'Last night I had a dream. The old dream. I was being castrated. By the SS in their headquarters. With a pair of scissors, not a knife. I woke up screaming. I suppose that's the full moon too. The scissors, I mean.'

'Forget it,' I said. 'The SS didn't succeed, as everybody knows.'

'Everyone knows? Of course they do! I got a shock to last me a lifetime. Anyway, they were partially successful. I bear the scars. And a multiply-broken leg. Women laugh at me. There's nothing worse than to be laughed at by a woman when you're naked. You never forget! That's why I make a beeline for women who have flaws. Can't you understand?'

I nodded. I knew the story; he'd told it to me a dozen times. Nor did I ask him how the Lourdes water had gone down. He was too jumpy. Instead I asked him, 'What are you doing here?'

'They were going to come by here. Stop in for a drink. They probably went to the cinema to get rid of me. I bought them dinner.'

'Don't wait for them. Let them wait for you if they want.'

'You think? Yes, you're probably right. Just it's hard. If only I wasn't so all alone!'

'Doesn't your job help you at all? Dealing in rosaries and icons, and meeting so many sanctified persons? Doesn't God help?'

'Are you crazy? What good is that supposed to be?'

'It could make it easier to resign. God was a conservative invention to avert revolutions against the injustice of human institutions.'

'Do you think so?'

'No. But in our exposed situation, we can't afford much in the way of fixed principles. You have to reach for whatever offers.'

'You're so damned superior,' said Lachmann. 'Big deal! How's your job?'

'I'm starting tomorrow, clearing and cataloguing for an antique dealer.'

'For a regular wage?'

I nodded.

'A mistake,' said Lachmann, cheering up immediately at the prospect of dispensing advice. 'You should be in trade. An inch of trade is worth a yard of work.'

'I'll try and remember.'

'Only people who are afraid of life are after a fixed wage,' Lachmann explained offensively. It was remarkable how quickly he could move from lamentation to spite. Another extremist, I thought.

'You're so right. I have as many fears as a dog has fleas,' I declared amiably. 'But that's the way I am. What's a little bit of sexual anxiety compared to that. Be glad!'

Moikov came down the stairs. 'He's asleep,' he announced. 'Three Seconal did the trick.'

'Seconal?' asked Lachmann. 'Do you have any left?'

Moikov nodded and produced the packet. 'Two enough for you, I suppose?'

'Why? Raoul gets three; why shouldn't I get the same?'

'Raoul lost Kiki; twice over. Whereas you, you've still got hope.'

Lachmann made to protest; his sufferings didn't like to be minimised.

'Hurry home,' I said. 'The pills have twice the effect on full moon nights.'

Lachmann limped out.

'I should have been an apothecary,' said Moikov.

We recommenced our game of chess.

'Was Maria Fiola really here earlier?' I asked.

Moikov nodded. 'She wanted to celebrate her liberation from the Germans. The place she was born in Italy has just been taken by the Americans. Up until now it had been in German hands. So she's no longer a reluctant ally of yours any more – she's a newly minted enemy. She says to say hello. I think she would have liked to tell you herself.'

'Bless her!' I replied. 'I would only have accepted her declaration of war if she'd worn Marie Antoinette's diadem.'

Moikov laughed. 'I've got some more bad news for you,

Ludwig. The village I was born in has just lately been freed as well – by the Russians. So I too have gone from being a forced ally of yours to being a forced enemy. Will you be able to stand it?'

'With difficulty. How many times have you changed your nationality, would you say?'

'About ten. Unwillingly. Czech, Polish, Austrian, Russian, and some back and forth. Mostly it just passed me by. This won't be the last time, either. You're mate, by the way. Your game's off today.'

'I was never any good, Vladimir. You're fifteen years of emigration and eleven fatherlands ahead of me. I'm counting America.'

'Here comes the Contessa.' Moikov stood up. 'The full moon's bringing them all out.'

The Contessa was wearing a feather boa with her old-fashioned, high-necked lace dress. It made her look like a very old bleached bird of paradise made of crumpled tissue paper. Her face was small and pale, and full of delicate little lines.

'A cordial, Contessa?' asked Moikov with grave politeness.

'Thank you, Vladimir Ivanovitch. Does it work with Seconal?'

'Do you want Seconal?'

'I can't sleep, as you well know,' lamented the little lady. 'Migraine and grief. And now this moon! As over Tsarskoe Selo. The poor Tsar.'

'This is Mr Sommer,' said Moikov.

The Contessa looked me up and down with her rapid bird's eye. She didn't recognise me. 'Another refugee?' she asked indifferently.

'Another one,' replied Moikov.

She sighed. 'First we are refugees from life, then from death.' Suddenly her eyes were full of tears. 'Give me a cordial, Vladimir Ivanovitch. A very small one. And two Seconal.' She shook her bird's head. 'Who can understand? When I was a young girl in St Petersburg the doctors gave me up. Tuberculosis. I was past help. I had days to live. And now? They're all dead, the doctors, the Tsar and his officers. Only I go on living and living and living.'

She stood up. Moikov went out with her and returned. 'Did you give her the Seconal?' I asked.

'Yes. And a bottle of vodka. She's already drunk. You didn't notice? She's old school,' said Moikov admiringly. 'The little lady drinks a bottle of vodka a day. She's over ninety. She has nothing left but shadow memories of a shadow life that makes her feel sad. Things that are only present in her old head. First she lived in the Ritz. Then in the Ambassador. Then in a Russian pension. Now she's here with us. She sells an item of jewellery a year. First they were diamonds. Then rubies. Then sapphires. Smaller and smaller as she got on. She doesn't have many left now.'

'Apropos, do you have any Seconal left?' I asked.

Moikov looked at me. 'You too?'

'Just in case,' I replied. 'It being a full moon and all. Really just as a precaution. You never know. You can't instruct dreams. And I need to get up early tomorrow. Work, you know.'

Moikov shook his head. 'It's remarkable where a human being gets his sense of superiority from, don't you think? Did you ever see an animal crying?'

8

I'd been working for Silver for a couple of weeks. The store had a vast basement that reached way under the street. It had galleries and halls, and was full of all kinds of junk. There were prams down there, hanging from the ceiling. The Silvers had inherited all of it, and had made a couple of vain attempts to put it in some kind of order and catalogue it, but they'd soon given up. They hadn't given up the law in order to become filing clerks in a catacomb. If there was anything of value there it would only appreciate with age, they thought, and they went across the road for coffee. They were serious about becoming bohemians.

I burrowed down into the catacombs in the morning, usually not to emerge till noon. The basement was scantily lit by a few bare light bulbs. It took me back a little to my time in Brussels and to begin with I was afraid it might take me back too strongly; but I decided to get accustomed to it slowly and deliberately, so as to reduce my anxiety. I had several times performed such experiments on myself, bearing down on the intolerable by force of habit and making it just barely tolerable.

The Silvers paid me frequent visits, coming down a flight of stairs that was little better than a glorified ladder. First I saw the pepper-and-salt trousers, the patent-leather pumps, the episcopal socks of Alexander Silver; then the pumps, silk socks and black trousers of his brother Arnold. Both were sociable and curious; they weren't keeping an eye on me. They just wanted to chat.

I got used to the dimmed sounds of the cars and trucks passing overhead. Eventually I was able to clear a little space. Some of the things were so poor that there was no sense in keeping them, like broken kitchen chairs and a few factory-made sofas in poor shape. The Silvers just put them out on the sidewalk for the garbage men to pick up in the morning.

After a few days in the basement, in a heap of worthless carpets, I came upon a pair of Ghiordes prayer rugs, one with a blue the other a green prayer niche. These were no modern copies; they were originals, perhaps a hundred and fifty years old and in good condition. Like a terrier I proudly lugged them upstairs.

In the store was a customer, a stately old dame dripping with gold. 'May I introduce you to our expert, Madam,' said a perfectly straight-faced Alexander Silver on my appearance. 'Monsieur Sommer, from the Louvre in Paris. He speaks mostly French. What do you make of this table, Mr Sommer?'

'Prime Louis XV. Very pure lines. Good condition. A rare piece,' I replied in a strong French accent. Then, for effect, I said my piece again in French.

'Too much,' said the woman with the gold chains.

Silver was briefly taken aback. 'But I didn't quote you a price, Madam.'

'Doesn't matter. Too much!'

'Very well,' said Silver, quickly adjusting. 'Then why don't you tell me what you'd be prepared to pay for it?'

Now it was the woman's turn to be caught out. She hesitated for a while. 'How much for the rug?' she asked, pointing to the green Ghiordes.

'No price,' replied Silver. 'It's an heirloom from my mother. Not for sale.'

The woman laughed.

'Only the green one is an heirloom,' I explained. 'The blue one belongs to me. I brought it along to show to Mr Silver. If he buys it, he'll have a companion piece for his green one. That raises the value by twenty per cent.'

'Is there nothing for sale here?' asked the woman bitterly.

'The table and everything else you see here,' said Silver.

'Including the green rug?'

The trouble with the rugs was that Silver didn't know what they were and that I didn't know what they were worth in dollars. There was no possibility of our communicating. The woman with the gold sat between us and kept her eyes on both of us.

'All right,' said Silver at a venture. 'For you, I'll sell the rug.'

The woman laughed. 'As I thought. How much?'

'Eight hundred dollars.'

'Too much,' said the woman.

'You seem to be very attached to the phrase. How much would you like to pay?'

'Nothing,' declared the woman, standing up. 'I just wanted to hear it from you. You're all crooks.'

Her chains jingled as she beetled out of the shop. On her way, she upset a Dutch lantern and made no effort to pick it up. Silver did so. 'Are you married, Madam?' he asked sweetly.

'What's that to do with you?'

'Nothing. My colleague and I just wanted to be sure to include your poor husband in our prayers tonight. In English and French, of course.'

'You won't be seeing her again,' I said. 'Or if you do, accompanied by a policeman.'

Silver motioned dismissively. 'I wasn't a lawyer for nothing. And that sledge horse never bought anything anyway. There are tens of thousands like her. They're bored, and they make storekeepers and salesmen wish they'd never been born. Usually they sit in shoe shops and clothes shops, and try things on and never ever buy anything.' He looked at the rug. 'So tell me about my mother's heirloom.'

'Ghiordes, early nineteenth century, perhaps even late eighteenth, Asia Minor. Pretty things. In the trade they're accounted semi-antique. Antique would be sixteenth and seventeenth century. There are very few that old still in existence. And those are usually Persian.'

'What would you say these are worth, then?'

'In Paris, from a carpet dealer before the war, maybe five hundred dollars.'

'The pair?'

'No, each.'

'Wow! Don't you think that calls for a coffee?'

We made our way across; Silver suicidally brought a Ford to a squealing halt and got himself a tirade from the driver. 'You stupid ass' was about the mildest term. Silver blew the man a kiss. 'There,' he said. 'Now my confidence is restored. It suffered from the encounter with the sledge horse.'

I looked at him blankly. 'I happen to be a temperamental man,' he said. 'A choleric of the worst sort. The driver was well within his rights to call me what he did; the sledge horse wasn't. They balance out. My inner peace is restored. What about a croissant with your coffee today?'

'Sure.'

I couldn't quite follow Silver's logic, but I was happy to take the croissant. The war years in France and the hunger years of the emigration had left me with a bottomless hole in my stomach; I was always able to eat, at any time of day, and I didn't much care what. On my wanderings through the city I would stop and stare at the food stores to see the things they had in their displays: great hams, delicatessen, fancy cakes.

Silver pulled out his wallet. 'The affair of the bronze has been settled,' he announced triumphantly. 'The museum wired me back. They will take it. At a higher price than we thought. The curator has been replaced – though not on account of our little matter. It seems he made a few more mistakes besides. Here is your share.'

Silver put two hundred-dollar bills next to the plate with my croissant. 'Satisfied?'

I nodded. 'What about the advance?' I asked. 'Do I have to pay you back out of this, or will you apply it to my weekly wage?'

Silver laughed. 'It's earned. You've made three hundred dollars.'

'Two hundred and fifty,' I corrected him. 'Fifty was my own money.'

'Right. And if we sell the carpets, you'll earn a premium for them as well. We're human beings here, not moneymaking machines. We used to be when we were lawyers. Everything all right?'

'Very much so, Mr Silver. You're a mensch!'

'Another croissant?'

'Why not? They're delicious, and there's not much of them.'

'Lovely here, isn't it?' said Silver. 'It's something I've always wished for – a good café close to work.' He kept peering across the avenue at the store, lest any customers stepped inside. He was like an eager sparrow pecking for food among great horses' hooves. Unexpectedly he heaved a deep sigh. 'Everything would be wonderful, if my brother hadn't had that ridiculous idea,' he said.

'What idea?'

'He has a lady friend. A shiksa. And now, just imagine, he wants to marry her. A tragedy! It would spell ruin for all of us.'

'What's a shiksa?'

Silver looked at me in astonishment. 'You don't know what a shiksa is? What kind of Jew are you? Well, an agnostic, I suppose. A shiksa is a Christian. A Christian with bobbed peroxide curls and eyes like a boiled herring, and a mouth with forty-eight teeth because she's so avid for our precious saved-up dollars. A bottle-blonde hyena with two crooked feet.'

It took me a while to see the portrait as a whole. 'My poor mama,' Silver continued. 'She would turn in her grave if we hadn't had her cremated eight years ago. In a crematorium.'

This was too much for me. The word gonged in my head like a bell. I pushed my plate away. I suddenly sniffed the sweetish dull smell that made my gorge rise irresistibly. 'Crematorium?' I asked.

'Yes. It's the simplest thing here. And the most hygienic. She was an observing Jew, born in Poland. She died here. You know—'

'I know,' I put in hastily. 'But tell me about your brother? Why shouldn't he get married?'

'But not to a shiksa!' said Silver indignantly. 'There are more nice Jewish girls in New York than in Palestine. New York is one-third Jewish. Don't tell me he can't find one. Where else, if not here? But no, he has to have his way. It's like marrying a Brünnhilde in Jerusalem.'

I listened to his outburst in silence and was careful not to draw Silver's attention to the phenomenon of reverse anti-Semitism. Some things you can't joke about, you can't even suggest ironic comparisons.

Silver got a grip on himself. 'I didn't mean to tell you all that,' he said. 'You probably don't see the full scale of the tragedy.'

'Not directly. With me tragedies are always something to do with death. Not with weddings. Call me old-fashioned.'

He nodded. He didn't laugh. 'We are devout Jews,' he said. 'We don't marry outside the community. That's our religion.' He looked at me. 'I don't suppose you were given a religious upbringing?'

I shook my head. I kept forgetting that he thought I was a Jew.

'Atheist,' he said. 'Freethinker! Are you really?'

I thought about it. 'I'm an atheist who believes in God,' I said. 'At night.'

Ludwig Sommer, whose name I went by, had worked as a picture restorer – cash in hand – for a French antique dealer. He had traded in antiques himself on the side. I was his tout for a long time, seeing as he had a dickey heart and couldn't get around much. His great speciality had been old rugs. He knew more about rugs than most museum directors. He took me along to shady Turkish and Armenian rug merchants, and told me about the tricks that were used in faking carpets and how to spot them. It was the same as with the Chinese bronzes: you had to have a detailed knowledge of the weaving styles and the colours and patterns, and compare them; the fakes were the ones that tended to make the least mistakes, since they were usually untrained weavers who were working from an original and, as they went along, often corrected the irregularities of genuine old carpets. But it was precisely these irregularities that proved a thing was genuine; there was no such thing as a perfectly symmetrical old carpet. It averted misfortune, thus the belief of the weavers, and it made the carpets look more alive. The fakes always tended to look somehow laboured and never sang. Sommer had a small collection of tiny scraps by means of which he would point out the differences to me. On Sundays we would go to the museums to study the masterpieces. It was in some ways an idyllic time; the best I'd known on the run. But it didn't last. Just one summer. Here I learned what I knew about the Ghiordes rugs I'd turned up at the Silvers'.

It was the last year of Sommer's life. He knew it, he had no illusions. He knew too that he was working for a crook, restoring paintings that would later be passed off as genuine, and he didn't even bother to ironise his situation. There wasn't the time. He had been through so much, and lost so much, but he had remained so rational that he had even banned bitterness from his last few months. He was the first to try to teach me to ration my struggle with destiny, so that I wasn't prematurely destroyed by it. I never learned this fully – any more than I learned the other thing: that revenge is a dish best served cold.

It was a weird, floaty sort of summer. Mostly we sat around on the Ile St Louis, where Sommer had his workshop. He loved sitting on the banks of the Seine, silently, under the great cloudy skies, with the bridges and the barges and the river flickering in the sun. In his last weeks he was already beyond words. Words didn't matter, compared to what he was leaving behind, and anyway he no longer wanted to explain or lament or sentimentalise anything. There was the sky and breath, there were his eyes and life, which was slipping away from him and which he could only oppose with one thing, which was his placid, almost unthinking cheerfulness, a gratitude that was almost beyond gratitude and the steadiness of a human being who faced his approaching death with eyes open, without dread, without struggle, mastering pain with serenity, abdication before the claw of extinction choked off his breath.

Sommer was the master of the relativising existential comparison. This was a melancholy emigrants' idiom: everything could have been just the way it was – only worse. One wouldn't just have lost one's fortune, one might have been locked up in Germany; one wouldn't just have been tortured, one would have been worked to death; one wouldn't just have been worked to death, one might have been handed over to SS doctors for experiments and slow vivisection; and so on and on, until death, which existed in two forms; you were incinerated, or you rotted away in a mass grave.

'I could have been struck down with bowel cancer,' said Sommer. 'With throat cancer too. Or I could have been struck blind.' He smiled. 'So many possibilities! The heart – that's a clean disease! That blue! Do you see that blue! The sky! The blue of an old carpet.'

I didn't understand him at the time. I was too vehement and too trapped in my thoughts of injustice and revenge. But he moved me. As long as he was able to, we sat out in churches and museums. They were old sanctuaries for him, the police never bothered going to such places. The Louvre, the Musée des Arts Decoratifs, the Jeu de Paume and Notre-Dame became our second home. They were shelter, company and education all at the same time. The churches too; though not so much the divine mercy aspect of them – we entertained reservations about that – but their art.

Those summer afternoons in the bright museum, among the paintings of the Impressionists! The peace of an oasis in the storm of inhumanity. We sat in front of the peaceful pictures, next to me the dying Sommer, neither of us speaking, and the pictures were windows cut into endless-ness. They were the best that mankind had made, seen at a time of the worst of which they were capable. 'Or I could have been burned alive in an extermination camp, in the land of Goethe and Hölderlin,' said Sommer after a long while, slowly and happily.

'Take my passport,' he said. 'May it keep you alive.'

'You should sell it,' I replied. I knew that one of the emigrants who had no papers at all had offered twelve hundred Swiss francs for it, a staggering sum, for which Sommer could have got himself to hospital. But Sommer didn't want that. He wanted to die in his workshop on the Ile St Louis, among his precious scraps of carpet and the smell of turps. Guggenheim, a former professor of medicine who was currently dealing in stockings, was his doctor; he could hardly have found a better. 'Take my passport,' said Sommer. 'There's still a bit of life left in it. And take this as well: it's a piece of death.' He pressed into my hand a little metal container on a thin chain. Inside the container was a cyanide capsule, bedded on cotton wool. Like a number of the emigrants, Sommer carried one around with him everywhere, in case he should fall into the hands of the Gestapo; he suspected he was unable to stand up to torture and he wanted to die swiftly.

He died in his sleep. He left me his clothes, a few lithographs and the collection of carpet scraps. I sold the clothes, the lithographs and the scraps for money to give him a burial. I kept the cyanide capsule and the passport. Sommer was buried under my name. And I kept one little fragment of a Ghiordes rug – a piece of the edging with some pale-blue prayer niche, blue as the August sky over Paris and blue as the carpet I found at the Silvers'. I carried the capsule around with me for a long time; I finally threw it into the sea as we were approaching Ellis Island. I wanted to be spared unnecessary questions. I felt a bit odd going around with Sommer's passport – a bit like a dead man on holiday. Then I got used to it.

Robert Hirsch refused a second time to be paid back the money he had lent me. 'But I'm swimming in money,' I protested. 'And I've got a full-time underground job for at least another six weeks.'

'Pay your lawyers first,' he replied. 'Messrs Levin and Watson. That's important. You still need them. Pay your friends last. They can wait. Paragraph 4B of the Laon Breviary!'

I laughed. 'You're mistaken! The Laon Breviary said exactly the opposite. First your friends, then the others.'

'This is the revised New York edition of the Laon Breviary. Your residence permit is the most important thing. Or do you really want to wind up interned as an enemy alien? They have internment camps all over California and Florida. California for the Japanese, Florida for the Germans. How do you fancy being bunged up together with a load of German Nazis?'

I shook my head. 'Would they really do that?'

'You bet. If you're suspicious. And it doesn't take much. A dodgy passport is enough, Ludwig. Have you forgotten the old saying: that it's easy to wind up in the claws of the law, but almost impossible to get out?'

'No,' I replied uneasily.

'And do you want to be beaten up in these camps? By the Nazis, who will be in the majority?'

'Aren't the camps guarded?'

Hirsch smiled pityingly. 'Come on, Ludwig! You know there's no protection at night, even in a little bijou camp with two hundred inmates. The "Holy Ghost" comes round with a rubber truncheon that leaves no trace. Or worse. Who gives a shit about an apparent suicide when every day there are thousands of Americans dying in Europe?'

'And the camp commandant?'

Hirsch gestured impatiently. 'The commandants of these camps are usually old warhorses who've done their time. Quiet lifers. The Nazis with their smart salutes, and standing to attention and all that military discipline, impress them much more than the odds and sods who come to them whingeing about being molested. You know that.'

'Yes,' I replied.

'The state's the state,' said Hirsch. 'We're not persecuted here. We're tolerated. That's progress. But don't get light-headed. And don't forget we're second-class citizens here.' He pulled out his pink passport: 'Enemy alien. Second-class human being.'

'And what about when the war's over?'

Hirsch laughed. 'Even if you became an American citizen, you'd still be second rate to them. You could never become President. And you'd keep having to run back to America when your papers ran out, to get them renewed. Born Americans don't. Who can afford that?'

He produced the bottle of cognac from a corner. 'OK. Time to knock off,' he said. 'No more drudgery. Today I've sold four radios, two vacuum cleaners and a toaster. It's no good. I'm not cut out for this work.'

'What else?'

'Believe it or not: I wanted to be a lawyer. In Germany! In a country whose founding principle was: law is whatever suits the state. The land of the happy executioners. That's over. Then what? What else can a man put his trust in, Ludwig?'

I shrugged my shoulders. 'I can't think very far ahead, Robert.'

He looked at me: 'You're a lucky man.'

'What's that?'

He smiled ironically. 'For not knowing.'

'All right, Robert,' I said impatiently. 'Man is the only creature that knows it must die. And what did he do with the knowledge?'

'Invented religion.'

'Right. And hence intolerance. Every religion claims to be the only true religion.'

'And then wars. The bloodiest ones were always the ones that were conducted in God's name. Even Hitler had to seek an accommodation with Him.'

We were going tit for tat like a litany or ping-pong. Suddenly Hirsch laughed. 'Do you remember how we practised ourselves in this litany in the chicken shed in Laon, so as not to fall victim to despair? And ate raw eggs and drank cognac? I don't think we're good for anything any more. We're going to be gypsies till the end of our days. Sad, cynical, desperate gypsies. Don't you think?'

'No,' I replied. 'I told you, I can't think that far ahead.'

Outside, the hot summer night drifted past; an air conditioner was going in the shop. It hummed softly and gave me the sense of being on board ship. We sat there in silence for a while. The cognac didn't taste as it should in the cold, artificial air. Its aroma suffered too. 'Do you dream sometimes?' Hirsch asked finally. 'Of before?'

I nodded. 'More than in the old country?' he asked.

I nodded again. 'Beware of your memories,' he said. 'They can be dangerous to you here. There weren't so many of them before.'

'I know,' I said. 'But who can control sleep?'

Hirsch got up. 'Because we're safer here, they're more dangerous to us. Over there, we were set on survival; they couldn't get so deep into us. Here, we feel less worried.'

'What about Bär in Paris? And Ruth? And Gutmann in Nice? There are no rules,' I said. 'But you have to watch out.'

'That's what I mean.' Hirsch turned on a light. 'Your patron Tannenbaum is having a little party on Saturday. He asked me to bring you. At eight o'clock.'

'OK,' I said. 'Has he got air conditioning in his place, like you?'

Hirsch laughed. 'He's got the lot. New York is hotter than Paris, isn't it?'

'Tropical! And it's as humid as a launderette with all its washers and dryers going full tilt.'

'And in winter it's as cold as Alaska. That's how we miserable salesmen of electrical equipment make our living.'

'I imagined the tropics differently.'

Hirsch looked at me. 'Isn't it possible,' he said, 'that this here will one day come to seem among the best times in our wretched lives?'

When I turned into the hotel an unusual scene met my eyes. The lounge was festively lit. There was a big table in the room with the palm and the cheese plant, round which was gathered an interestingly mixed company. Raoul was doing the honours. He was sitting at the head of the table, looking like a sweating giant tortoise in a beige suit. There was a fancy white tablecloth and a waiter I had never seen before; Moikov was sitting beside Raoul; on his other side was Lachmann, next to his Puerto-Rican woman. The Mexican was there as well, in a pink tie, shifty eyes and a stone face. Then there were two dark-haired, Hispanic-looking women in their thirties; a young man with curled hair and a deep bass voice, though he looked more like a treble; the Contessa in her grey lace; and on Moikov's other side Maria Fiola.

'Mr Sommer!' exclaimed Raoul. 'Give us the pleasure of your company!'

'What's going on?' I asked. 'Is it someone's birthday? Someone getting citizenship? Or has someone won the lottery?'

'None of the above! Just a party. Sit with us, Mr Sommer,' replied Raoul, slightly the worse for wear. 'One of my saviours,' he explained to the blond youth with the bass voice. 'Shake! This is John Bolton.'

I felt something like a wet fish in my hand; on the basis of the low voice, I'd expected something more sinewy. 'What would you like to drink?' asked Raoul. 'We've got everything: Scotch, bourbon, rye, Coca-Cola, even champagne. What did you say the other day, when my heart was sweating with sadness? "Everything flows!" And nothing is for ever, the best-looking Jew turns into an old yid. And the same in love. Too true! So, what'll it be?' Raoul waved imperiously to the waiter. 'Alfons!'

I sat down next to Maria Fiola. 'What are you drinking?'

'Vodka,' she replied happily.

'All right, then, give me a vodka,' I said to Alfons, who looked like a somewhat shattered rat.

'A double!' announced Raoul with shining eyes. 'Doubles all round today.'

I looked at Moikov. 'Did the mystery of the human heart stir in him again?' I asked. 'The power of celestial love?'

Moikov giggled and nodded. 'It has! But you could equally call it the illusion where everybody thinks the other is his prisoner.'

'That was quick work!'

'A *coup de foudre*,' said Maria Fiola. 'One-sided as it always is. Only the other person never knows.'

'How long have you been back?' I asked, looking at her. Surrounded by Spanish-looking people, she seemed Spanish herself.

'Since the day before yesterday.'

'Are you having your picture taken?'

'Not tonight. Why? Did you want to come along?'

'Yes.'

'At last an unambiguous word in all the symbolical emotionalism here. Cheers!'

'Cheers!'

'Cheers! Salut! Bottoms up!' cried Raoul and bumped glasses with everyone. 'Cheers, John!'

He tried to get up, but sank back with a crash into his chair of state. In addition to its other horrors, the plush lounge had been refurbished in neo-Gothic.

'It's tonight!' Lachmann whispered to me. 'I'm going to get the Mexican drunk. He thinks I'm drinking tequila with him, but I've bribed Alfons. He's giving me water.'

'And the woman?'

'She doesn't know. First things first.'

'I'd drink with the woman if I were you,' I said. 'She's the one who's opposed. The Mexican doesn't mind, so you say.'

He was unsettled, briefly. 'Never mind,' he then hurriedly proclaimed. 'It'll work. One shouldn't try and calculate everything in advance, that's a sure road to failure. Leave room for chance.'

I looked at him with a kind of envy. He leaned across to me. His breath in my ear felt hot and wet. 'If you just want someone badly enough, it'll happen,' he whispered. 'It's tapping pipes in prison. The slow lightning of emotion.

Cosmic rebalancing. Of course Nature remains impersonal and moody. You have to help her along.'

For a moment I was speechless. This new surge of conviction was unexpected. Then I bowed. His black and white magic commanded respect, his hope derived from hopelessness. 'Well, all hail to you in love's starry cavern,' I said. 'The well-aimed *coup de foudre*. Not the blind dart.'

'No jokes!' retorted the pained Lachmann. 'I'm deadly serious. A life is at stake. At least for the moment.'

Lachmann waved to the waiter for another glass of water. 'Another *coup de foudre*,' Maria Fiola said to me. 'We seem to be surrounded by them, like summer lightning. You haven't had one yourself, have you?'

'No,' I said. 'Sadly not. What about you?'

'Some time ago.' She laughed and gripped her glass. 'The sad thing is they don't last.'

'That depends. Life is the more colourful for them being there.'

'What's even sadder is that they recur,' said the girl. 'They're not unique. Each time they become a little more ridiculous and more painful. It's no paradox. Miracles shouldn't be repeatable.'

'Why not?'

'It weakens them.'

'A weak wonder is still better than no bread, especially Wonder bread. Why must weakness automatically seem undignified?'

Maria Fiola gave me a sidelong look. 'Playboy, huh?' she asked ironically.

I shook my head. 'Horrid word,' I said. 'Plain gratitude would be better.'

She looked quickly into her glass. 'Someone's been giving me water instead of vodka.'

'That can only have been Alfons the waiter.' I looked over at Lachmann. 'Can you taste something funny in your drink?'

'Yes. It doesn't taste like water. I can't put my finger on what the taste is, but it's not water. You know I never drink. This burns. What is it?'

'You're lost, you smartass,' I said. 'It's vodka. Alfons has made a mistake and mixed up the glasses. You'll notice very soon.'

'What effect does it have?' asked Lachmann, pale with terror. 'I knocked back my glass. I drank to the Mexican. My God! I was hoping to make him finish his tequila.'

'You ended up fooling yourself. But it could be lucky for you!'

'It always hits the innocent ones,' whispered a doomed-looking Lachmann. 'How could it be lucky?'

'Perhaps the Puerto-Rican lady will like you better if you're a bit drunk. Less aimed. More confused and charming.'

Raoul had struggled into the vertical. 'Ladies and gentlemen,' he declared. 'When I think that a little while ago I was on the brink of suicide over that little punk Kiki, I could kick myself. What idiots we are, especially when we think we're at our noblest and best!'

He gestured expansively and upset a large glass of green crème de menthe in front of one of the Hispanic ladies. The syrupy stuff flowed across the tablecloth on to her dress. At that instant we had the feeling of being in a jungle in which a couple of hundred roosting parrots had been disturbed. Both Hispanic girls squawked violently at Raoul. Arms laden with costume jewellery flew through the air.

'I'll buy you another one!' cried Raoul. 'A prettier one! Help! Contessa!'

Renewed cries. Flashing eyes and teeth right in front of the Buddha Raoul.

'I never get involved in this sort of thing,' the Contessa said quietly. 'Too many bad experiences. In Petersburg, in 1917—'

The squawking stopped in an instant as Raoul flourished his wallet. He opened it slowly and with dignity. 'Miss Fiola,' he said. 'You're in the rag trade. I want to be generous, but not exploited. How much is the dress worth?'

'She can get it dry-cleaned,' said Maria Fiola.

The noise started all over again. 'Careful!' I said and intercepted a bowl of whipped cream that had been launched at Maria. The Hispanic ladies had quit Raoul and were trying to get at her with their teeth and claws. I pulled her under the table. 'They're throwing red wine glasses,' I said and pointed to a large stain in the tablecloth. 'So far as I know, you can't get rid of those. Or can you?'

She struggled to free herself. 'Don't try to fight those hyenas,' I said. 'You're much better off down here!'

'I'll strangle them with the Swiss cheese plant! Let me go!'

I held her fast. 'You're not especially fond of your sisters, are you?' I asked.

Again, she tried to get free of me. She was much stronger than I'd thought. Nor was she as thin as she looked either. 'I'm not fond of anyone,' she snapped. 'That's my sorrow. Now let me go!'

A plate of boloney smacked down on to the floor next to us. Then things got a little quieter. I held Maria fast. 'One more minute,' I said. 'We're not in the clear yet. Behave for one minute like Empress Eugenie, whose diamonds you wore so magnificently.'

Maria Fiola started to laugh. 'Eugenie would have shot

the pair of them,' she said. I pulled her up from under the tablecloth, which had a savage stain. 'Nasty!' I said. 'Californian burgundy.'

Like the gifted general he was, Raoul had put an end to hostilities. He had scattered a few dollar bills in the far corner of the plush lounge, where the Hispanic ladies were picking them up like cross hens.

'Now, ladies,' he said. 'It's time for us to go. I apologise for my clumsiness, but it's bedtime now.'

He beckoned to Alfons the waiter. Moikov rose. Whoever expected fresh strife was disappointed. With a short volley of lisping oaths and great swishing of skirts, the two ladies vacated the field.

'Where did they come from?' asked Raoul.

No one knew. Everyone thought they had been invited by somebody else. 'Never mind,' said the magnanimous Raoul. 'Where does anything come from in life? Now do you understand what I have against women? Somehow things always lapse into farce when they're around.' He turned to Maria. 'Were you hit, Miss Fiola?'

'Only spiritually. Mr Sommer caught the worst of the cold meat platter.'

'And you, Contessa?'

The old lady pooh-poohed. 'There wasn't even any shooting.'

'Very good. In that case, Alfons, what about nightcaps all round.'

The Puerto-Rican lady suddenly started to sing. She had a low powerful voice and while she sang she kept her eyes fixed on the Mexican. It was a ballad of a vehement, natural lust, almost mournful, and it was so far from any sort of ratiocination and civilisation that it acquired something of the grimness of death, long before mankind had learned its most human quality, humour and laughter: just direct and shameless and innocent. The Mexican didn't budge. The woman too remained motionless, but for her eyes and mouth. The two of them looked at each other, neither blinking an eye, and the melody grew stronger and stronger and flowed. It was a consummation, without touch, and everyone took it as that. No one spoke, I saw tears in Maria Fiola's eyes while the song poured out, and I saw everyone staring at their feet, Raoul, John, Moikov, even Lachmann and the Contessa, for an instant everyone was taken out of themselves by this woman, who could see nothing but her Mexican, and the life in him, in his dirty gigolo face, and it was neither peculiar not ridiculous.

9

I collected Robert Hirsch early for the party at my sponsor Tannenbaum's. 'This isn't the usual monthly feeding of poor emigrants,' said Hirsch. 'It's more. It's a celebration. Farewell death, welcome birth and new life! The Tannenbaums are becoming naturalised Americans tomorrow. The celebration is today.'

'Have they been here so long?'

'Five years. Really. They came here under the quota system.'

'How did they manage that? The quotas have been over-filled for years in advance.'

'I don't know. Perhaps they had been here once before; or they had influential relatives in America; or they were just lucky.'

'Lucky?'

'Sure. Lucky. Why the question? Haven't we depended on luck for years?'

I nodded. 'I wish I didn't keep forgetting. Life would be simpler.'

Hirsch laughed. 'You of all people can't complain. Your beginner's English gives you the illusion of a second childhood. Enjoy it and stop moaning.'

'All right.'

'We'll be burying the name Tannenbaum tonight,' said Robert. 'It won't exist any more, come tomorrow. When you acquire American citizenship you can change your name. Of course Tannenbaum will take the opportunity.'

'I can't blame him. What's he changing it to?'

Hirsch laughed. 'He thought about it for a long time. He suffered so long under the name Tannenbaum that nothing but the best new name would do. He wanted to come as close as he could to the great names of history. Usually, he's a reserved sort of character; but at this point a lifelong anxiety expressed itself. His family came forward with Baum and Tann and Nebau, all cut down versions of the original name. Tannenbaum wasn't having it. He reacted as though someone had suggested sodomy. You won't understand.'

'No, I do. But try to leave out the anti-Semitic remarks!'

'Sommer's easier to live with,' replied Hirsch. 'You were lucky with your Jewish double. There are loads of Christian Sommers. Hirsch is a bit harder. And Tannenbaum requires a heroic effort even to exist. And that all your life.'

'Well, so what did he decide to change it to?'

'First he thought of changing just his first name. He's an Adolf, wouldn't you know it. Adolf Tannenbaum as in Adolf Hitler. But then he remembered all the sneers he had suffered in Germany and he wanted to have a typically English surname. Then that phase passed. All at once Tannenbaum wanted something as anonymous as possible. He looked in the phone book for the commonest name in America. He chose Smith. There are tens of thousands; Fred Smith. It's a bit like being called Noman. He couldn't be happier. He's looking forward to disappearing into a sea of Smiths. Tomorrow's the big day.'

Tannenbaum was born in Germany and grew up there, but he never quite trusted the Germans or the Europeans. He had lived through the German inflation of 1918 to 1923 and come out of it penniless.

Like a lot of Wilhelmine Jews, he was a fervent patriot, it was a time when anti-Semitism was seen as vulgar and Jews could rise into the aristocracy. He had invested his fortune in 1914 in war loans. When at the end of the Inflation the currency was stabilised at a rate of four marks per billion, he was forced into bankruptcy. He had never forgotten it and had subsequently invested whatever he could spare in America. He had observed the French and Austrian Inflations and had survived them both handily. When export restrictions were suddenly slapped on the German mark – this was in 1931, two years before the Nazi takeover – Tannenbaum had already managed to expatriate most of his fortune. Still, he kept his business in Germany. The restrictions on the mark were never lifted. That spelled the ruin of many thousands of Jews who were unable to transfer their money abroad and were hence condemned to stay in Germany. The appalling irony of the situation was that the tottering bank that had precipitated the crisis was a Jewish bank – and the government that slapped a ban on currency exports was democratically elected. The Jews in Germany were prevented from fleeing and duly met their ends in concentration camps. In high-up Nazi circles this was viewed as proof that history had a sense of humour.

It didn't take long in 1933 before Tannenbaum saw which way the wind was blowing. He was falsely accused of all sorts of financial shenanigans. An underage trainee he had never seen had him accused through her mother of raping her. Trusting to what was left of German justice, he rejected the mother's attempt to extort 50,000 marks from him and went to court. Then he learned quickly. He was blackmailed again. A police inspector, acting on behalf of a high-up Party figure, visited him one evening and told him what he would be letting himself in for if he didn't see sense. The sum involved was rather higher. In return, Tannenbaum and his family would be given a chance to flee across the Dutch border. Tannenbaum didn't believe it, but he had no other option. He ended up signing everything that was put in front of him. Then the unexpected happened. His family was shipped across the border. First his wife and daughter. Two days later, after he received a postcard from them in Amsterdam, Tannenbaum made over the rest of his German shares to the blackmailers. Three days later he was in Holland. He was lucky: his crooks were honest. In Holland the next act of the tragicomedy began. Tannenbaum's passport expired before he could get an American visa. He tried to get an extension at the German consulate. He had little money in Holland. His fortune in America was set up in such a way that only he personally had access to it. So in Amsterdam Tannenbaum found himself a millionaire without funds. He had to borrow money. It was surprisingly easy. He was able to get an extension on his passport and finally an American visa. When he got to New York, lifted the stack of shares he owned out of the safe and kissed the top one, he decided to become a naturalised American citizen, to change his name and to forget Germany. He didn't altogether forget it, though; he continued to help stranded emigrants.

He was a delicate man, quiet and unassuming, not at all what I had expected. He waved away my thanks for his sponsorship. 'You didn't cost me a penny,' he said, smiling.

He led us to the drawing room, which opened into a huge dining room. I remained in the doorway. 'Good God!' I said.

Three huge tables had been arranged into a horseshoe-shaped buffet. They were so thickly covered with bowls, dishes and platters that the tablecloth underneath them was invisible.

The left-hand table was covered with all kinds of cakes, among them two great gateaux, one a dark chocolate one, with 'Tannenbaum' written on it in icing, the other in pink marzipan, with marzipan flowers in the middle and the name 'Smith'. 'It was our cook Rosa's idea,' explained Tannenbaum. 'We couldn't talk her out of it. Tannenbaum will be cut and eaten today. Smith is for tomorrow, when we return from the ceremony. Our cook conceived of it as a sort of symbolic act.'

'How did you happen to choose the name Smith?' asked Hirsch. 'Meyer would have been as common. And a bit more Jewish.'

Tannenbaum was sheepish. 'This is nothing to do with our Jewishness,' he explained. 'We're not denying it. We just didn't want to be called Christmas tree any more.'

'In Java, people go through several names in the course of their lives,' I said. 'Depending on how they feel. I think that's eminently sensible.' I couldn't take my eyes off a chicken in port wine sauce that happened to be in front of me.

Tannenbaum was still a little concerned that he had upset Robert's religious feeling. He had heard about his heroics in France and had great respect for him. 'What would you like to drink?' he asked.

Hirsch laughed. 'Well, on such an occasion as this, the best champagne. Dom Perignon.'

Tannenbaum shook his head. 'I'm afraid we don't have any of that. Not today. We have no French wines. We didn't want anything that reminded us of the past. We might have been able to offer Dutch gin and Moselle wine. We turned them down. We've been through too much. America has adopted us. So all we have are American wines and spirits. You understand, don't you?'

Hirsch appeared not to. 'What happened to you in France?' he asked.

'I was turned back at the border.'

'So now you're taking revenge with your one-man boycott of France? A wine war! What an idea!'

'Not revenge,' corrected Tannenbaum. 'Just gratitude for the country that took us in. We have Californian champagne, New York and Chilean white wine and bourbon. We want to forget, Mr Hirsch! At least today! How else can we go on living? We want to leave everything behind us. Including our damned name. We want to start over.'

I looked at the rather impressive little man with his garland of white hair. To leave everything behind, consign it to oblivion, I thought. How grand and how impractical! But no doubt everyone had a different version of that.

'That's a wonderful display of eatables, Mr Tannenbaum,' I said. 'There's enough there to feed a company. Will we manage to get through it all tonight?'

Tannenbaum smiled with relief. 'Our guests always come with healthy appetites. Why don't you make a start? It's a buffet. Just help yourself to what you want.'

I reached for a chicken leg in port and aspic right away. 'What have you got against Tannenbaum?' I asked Hirsch, while we slowly made our way round the great buffet.

'Nothing,' he said. 'I've got a grouse with myself.'

'Who doesn't.'

He looked at me. 'Forgetting!' he said vehemently. 'As if it were easy! Just forget, so that your cosy lifestyle isn't disturbed. The only people who can forget are those who have nothing to forget.'

'Maybe that's the case with Tannenbaum,' I suggested in a spirit of conciliation, and helped myself to the chicken breast as well. 'Perhaps he just has financial losses. No deaths.'

Hirsch looked at me again. 'Every Jew has his or her dead. Every one!'

I looked around. 'Robert,' I said. 'Who is supposed to eat all this? It's such a waste.'

'Oh, it'll be eaten all right,' replied Hirsch, calmer now. 'There are two waves. Tonight there's the first wave. Emigrants who have already achieved something here, academics, doctors, lawyers who have yet to make their mark, actors, writers and scientists whose English isn't up to snuff, or who can't seem to learn – in a word, the intellectual proletariat of the evicted, most of whom don't get enough to eat.'

'And tomorrow?' I asked.

'Tomorrow, whatever's left goes to a charitable organisation for even poorer refugees. A primitive but effective form of help.'

'What's wrong with that, Robert?'

'Nothing,' he said.

'That's what I think. Is everything prepared here on the premises?'

'Everything,' replied Hirsch, 'and it's all so good. In Germany, Tannenbaum had a Hungarian cook. She was allowed to go on working, though it was for a Jewish family. When he left Germany she remained loyal to him. She followed him discreetly a couple of months later, to Holland, with Mrs Tannenbaum's jewels in the form of single, perfect, unadorned stones that Mrs Tannenbaum had left her, in her stomach. Before crossing the border, Rosa swallowed them with two cups of coffee and cream and a couple of slices of light sponge cake. It turned out not to have been necessary. She was a plump blonde with blue eyes and a Hungarian passport, no one checked her. Now she cooks here. Without help. No one knows how she does it. A jewel, as they say. The last of the great Viennese and Budapest tradition.'

I took a spoonful of sautéed chicken liver and onion. Hirsch came sniffing along. 'It's not possible to resist that,' he said and heaped a spoonful on to his own plate. 'Do you know, the last time I had chicken livers they saved me from suicide?'

'With mushrooms or not?' I asked.

'Without. But with a lot of onions. You'll remember from the Laon Breviary that life consists of several layers, any of which may break at any time. Usually these breaks don't coincide, so that the other layers act like splints to the one that just happens to have cracked. Only when there are multiple breaks is there danger. That's the time for motive-less suicides. I had one time like that. That was when the aroma of fried chicken livers with onions saved me. I decided I would eat before making an end. I had to wait a little till they were done. Washed them down with a glass of beer. The beer wasn't cold enough and I waited for it to cool down. Got involved in a conversation. Still felt hungry and I ordered another portion. One thing led to another and by the end I was functioning again. It's not a story.'

'I believe you.' I reached for the spoon to help myself to more. 'Purely a precaution!' I said. 'To make sure I don't kill myself.'

'I'll tell you another story that the sorry mangled English of the emigrants always puts me in mind of. There was an old emigrant lady, who was poor and sick and alone. She wanted to take her life and probably would have done, but when she turned on the gas, she thought how incredibly difficult she had found it to learn English and how for the past few days she had had the feeling she was getting a little better at it. All at once it seemed a pity to give up. Her little bit of English was all she had, she stuck to it, she didn't want it to be lost, and that pulled her through. Since then I've always thought of her when I hear the painstaking English of the emigrants with their heavy German accents.

It both disgusts me and moves me to the core. I think comedy protects against tragedy, not the other way round. Look at the line of them standing there, grateful and emotional, already vulnerable but still full of wretched courage, helping themselves to herring and Italian salad and roast beef. They think the worst is over! They're trying to muddle along over here. They don't know the worst is still ahead.'

'What's that?' I asked.

'They still have a little hope. Going home! That's the dream. A kind of happy ending. Even if they don't admit it to themselves. It keeps them going. But it's an illusion. They don't really believe in it. It's just a fond hope. No one at home will want to know them if they do decide to go back. Not even the so-called good Germans. People will either hate them directly, or indirectly because they have a bad conscience. In their former homeland they will be even more wretchedly alien than they are here, where they get by because they believe they will one day be able to go home as celebrated victims.'

Hirsch looked at the lines of guests at the buffet. 'I feel so sorry for them.' he said, more quietly. 'They are so well-behaved. I feel sorry for them and they make me livid, because they're so well-behaved. Come on, let's go. I always get like this here.'

We couldn't do it. I found some Wiener schnitzel, which I hadn't tasted for years as good as this. 'Robert,' I said. 'You know the first Commandment of the primer of Laon: Never allow emotions to wreck your appetite. With a little training we can manage to keep them both. That may seem cynical, but in reality it's only wisdom. Permit me to sample this schnitzel.'

'Sample away,' said Hirsch. 'But hurry! I can see Mrs Tannenbaum coming.'

A frigate under full sail – red – whooshed up to us. She was round, big, bounteous, cheerful and beamed at us. 'Mr Hirsch!' she said breathlessly, 'Mr Sommer! Come over here! They're cutting the cake. The chocolate cake. Help me to wreck it!'

I looked at the splendid Wiener schnitzel in my hand. Hirsch saw it. 'Paragraph 10 of the Breviary,' he said. 'You can always eat anything at any time. That includes Wiener schnitzel and chocolate cake.'

The chocolate cake was swiftly demolished. I had the impression Tannenbaum looked happier after it was gone. 'How are you keeping body and soul together, Mr Sommer?' he asked me shyly.

I told him about my work for the Silver brothers. 'Is that a permanent job?' he asked.

'No. Maybe another two weeks, then I'll have finished there.'

'Do you know about paintings?'

'Not enough to be able to sell them. But some. Why?'

'I know someone who's looking for help. More or less the kind of thing you're doing now. Not declared to the authorities. The way you want it. There's no particular rush. But call me once you know when you'll be free.'

I looked at him in surprise. I had been racking my brain for days about what I would do when I was finished working for the Silvers. It had to be cash in hand; and while that was easily found, it was very badly paid. 'I am free,' I said hurriedly. 'I can quit the Silvers any day.'

Tannenbaum demurred. 'As I say, there's no particular rush. If you call in a week, that's plenty of time. I need to talk to my acquaintance first.'

'I'm anxious not to pass up the opportunity, Mr Tannenbaum.'

'So am I,' he replied, smiling. 'It's my name on your sponsorship papers, after all.' He stood up. 'Are you a dancer, Mr Sommer?'

'Only with my principles. Not otherwise. To be honest, I didn't think the opportunity would present itself again.'

'We invited a few young people along. It's not easy to plan a congenial evening at this time. You feel guilty. But I'd like my family to have some fun. Especially my daughter Ruth. You can't always wait for the right moment to come along, can you?'

'Certainly not. And after all, this is a kind of charitable occasion. They happen in wartime. Every week or two in New York.'

Tannenbaum's face lost its air of concern. 'Do you think so? Yes, perhaps you're right. Well, tuck in. My wife will be happy. Not to mention Rosa, our cook. There's a little late supper at eleven. The goulash will be ready. It's been on the go since this afternoon. Two sorts. I would recommend the Szeged!'

'Did he invite you to stay for goulash?' asked Hirsch.

I nodded. 'It's cooked in great vats,' he said, 'and eaten in small groups. Friends of the household get little bowls of it to take home. It's the best goulash in America.' He stopped. 'Do you see the person over there tucking into apple strudel and whipped cream as if her life depended on it?'

I looked where he was pointing. 'That's no person,' I said. 'That's an extraordinarily lovely young woman. What a wonderful face!' I looked at her again. 'What's she doing here, I wonder? At this wake? Does she have hidden flaws? Thick ankles or hips like a timpani?'

'Not a bit of it! Wait till she stands up! She's perfection. Ankles like a gazelle. Knees like Diana. Breasts of marble.

All the clichés fit her. Even her toes without the ghost of a corn!'

I looked at him in astonishment. I wasn't used to these hymnal tones from him. 'Stare away!' he said. 'I know what you're thinking. And, to set the seal on everything, her name is Carmen.'

'Well?' I asked in suspense. 'What else does she have going for her?'

'She's stupid. The gorgeous creature is thick! Not just thick, but of a fabulous thickness. Her performance just now with the apple strudel, that was actually a considerable intellectual feat, after which she should really take a little rest.'

'That's too bad,' I said.

'On the contrary,' replied Hirsch. 'It's fascinating.'

'Why?'

'Because it's so utterly unexpected.'

'A statue is stupid.'

'Statues don't talk. This one does.'

'But what, Robert? And how do you know her?'

'From France. I got her out of a tricky situation there. It was high time she disappeared. I wanted to take her with me. I had a car outside with diplomatic plates. But she wanted to have a bath and change her clothes first. All this, while the Gestapo were practically on their way. It wouldn't have surprised me if she had wanted to get her hair done as well. Luckily there were no hairdressers. But she wanted to have breakfast. She thought skipping breakfast was unlucky. I felt like smacking her in the face with her damned croissants. She had her breakfast. Then she wanted to pack up the leftover croissants and jam for the flight. I was shaking with nerves. Finally she climbed in, all in her own good time, fifteen minutes before the Gestapo patrol showed up.'

'That's not stupidity,' I said appreciatively. 'That's the

protective magic cloak of inspired indolence. A gift from the gods!'

Hirsch nodded. 'I heard news of her later from time to time. Like a beautiful indolent ship she sailed through all the obstacles, through Scylla and Charybdis. She was in incredible situations. Nothing happened to her. Her incredible candour disarmed murderers. She wasn't even raped. She arrived — wouldn't you know it — on the last plane from Lisbon.'

'What is she doing now?'

'With the good fortune of a sacred cow, she got a job straight away. As a model. She didn't find this job — that would have been too much trouble. No, she was handed it on a plate.'

'Why isn't she in the movies?'

Hirsch shrugged. 'Doesn't feel like it. Too demanding. No ambition. No complexes. An astonishing woman!'

I reached for a piece of cheesecake. I could understand Hirsch's fascination with Carmen. What in his case had been achieved by brazenness and death-defying courage she had done by nature. It was bound to exert an irresistible attraction on him. I watched him for a while. 'I understand you,' I said at last. 'But how long could you endure such stupidity?!'

'Oh, Ludwig, as long as you like! It's the biggest adventure there is, the new frontier. Intelligence is predictable. Before long you know its ways and can predict its reactions. But radiant stupidity is unfathomable. It's always new, it defies rationality and it's a mystery. What more could a man wish for?'

I didn't say anything. I wasn't sure if he was pulling my leg, or if he was half-serious about what he was saying. All at once we found ourselves joined by the twins, along with other acquaintances of Jessie's. They were all so bubbly and overexcited that the overall effect was rather melancholy. The unemployed actors were there who sold stockings in the daytime and every morning studied their reflections in the hope that their wrinkles weren't so deep as to prevent them from being cast as the romantic leads that they had played ten years ago, before they had left Germany. They talked about that time and about their audience as though they had trodden the boards only yesterday, and under the Tannenbaums' chandeliers imagined for an hour or two what it might be like to be welcomed back at home. A particularly vengeful, unemployed bon vivant by the name of Koller was there too. He stood there with Ravic, grimly eyeing what remained of the buffet.

'Have you been adding to your bloodlist?' Hirsch asked him ironically.

Koller nodded darkly. 'Half a dozen more will face the firing squad as soon as we're back!'

'Who'll do the shooting?' asked Hirsch. 'You?'

'All in good time. The courts will see to it.'

'The courts!' retorted Hirsch contemptuously. 'You mean the German courts who for the last ten years have passed iniquitous judgements? You should reserve the stage rights to your list, Mr Koller. It's a comedy!'

Koller went pale with fury. 'And if it was up to you, the murderers should get off scot-free, I suppose?'

'No, but you won't find them. When this war is over there won't be any Nazis anywhere. Only good Germans who went around helping Jews. And if you should happen to find one, Mr Koller, then you won't hang him either. Not you with your naive list. You will suddenly understand him. And maybe even forgive him.'

'Like you, you mean?'

'No, not like me. But like some of us. That's the wretched thing about us Jews. All we can do is understand and forgive.

But not avenge ourselves. That's why we're the everlasting victims.'

Hirsch looked around, as though he were waking up. 'What am I saying,' he said. 'What the hell am I saying. Excuse me,' he said to Koller. 'I didn't really mean it, it was just emigrant Koller![1] Everyone gets an attack of it from time to time.'

Koller looked at him haughtily. I tugged at Hirsch's sleeve. 'Come on, Robert,' I said. 'Tannenbaum's waiting in the kitchen with the Szeged goulash.'

He nodded. 'I couldn't stand to hear that lousy comedian go on and forgive you,' I said.

'I don't know what's wrong with me,' he muttered. 'It must be all that talk about forgetting and beginning again and not forgetting that's making me crazy. Everything is being talked to pieces.'

The Dahl twins appeared. One of them was carrying an almond cake, the other a tray with coffee cups and a coffee pot. Involuntarily I looked around for Leo Bach. He wasn't far to seek and was eyeing the sashaying twins hungrily.

'Did you ever find out which of the twins is the tart and which is the saint?' I asked.

He shook his head. 'Not yet. But I've made another discovery. The moment they arrived in America, they were whisked away from the dockside to a plastic surgery clinic and had their noses operated on using their last money, to start a new life. What do you say to that?'

'Great!' I replied. 'Let's hear it for the new lives! The Tannenbaum-Smiths, the Dahl twins! I'm all in favour. Long live the adventure of the second reality!'

---

[1] *Koller* is a German word for a fit or tantrum, which makes possible the pun on the character's name here.

Leo Bach looked at me uncomprehendingly. 'It doesn't even show,' he lamented.

'You should try to find out the address of the clinic,' I said.

'Me?' said Bach. 'Why me? I'm fine the way I am.'

'That's some claim, Mr Bach. I wish I could say the same for myself.'

The twins were now standing laughing in front of us, with their coffee and cakes and their pretty bottoms. 'Courage!' I said to Bach.

He shot me a furious glare, took a piece of cake and pinched neither of the twins. 'Never you worry, it'll catch up with you too, you frigid lump,' he growled.

I looked around for Hirsch. He was just being beset by Mrs Tannenbaum. Mr Tannenbaum joined them. 'The gentlemen aren't dancing, Jutta,' he said to the imposing frigate. 'They claim they never learned. There was no time. It's like wartime children, growing up without chocolate.' He smiled shyly. 'We asked the American soldiers to come and dance. They all know how.'

Mrs Tannenbaum bustled away. 'It's for the sake of my daughter,' explained Tannenbaum. 'She has so little opportunity to dance.' I followed his look. His daughter was dancing with Koller, the keeper of the bloodlist. Koller seemed to bring the same commitment to his dancing that he brought to everything else. He was dragging the little girl right across the room by main force. I had the impression that one of her legs was shorter than the other. Tannenbaum sighed. 'Thank God, by this time tomorrow, we'll be Americans,' he said to Hirsch. 'Then I'll be rid of the weight of three names.'

'How three?' asked Hirsch.

Tannenbaum nodded. 'I have two given names. Adolf and

Wilhelm. Wilhelm was an idea of my patriotic grandfather's – it was still in the Empire. But Adolf. Who would ever have guessed!'

'I knew a doctor in Germany by the name of Adolf Deutschland,' I said. 'And he was a Jew.'

'My goodness!' exclaimed Tannenbaum with sympathy. 'He's even worse off than I am. What became of him?'

'He was forced to change his name. Both his names.'

'And nothing else?'

'Nothing else. They took away his practice and he was able to escape to Switzerland. Admittedly, this was as far back as 1933.'

'What's his name now?'

'Niemand,' I said. 'Doctor Niemand.'[2]

Tannenbaum gasped. I saw he was wondering if he'd made a mistake: 'Niemand' sounded tempting to him. A touch more anonymous even than Smith. But then he became aware of some signals from the kitchen door. The cook Rosa was standing there, waving a large wooden spoon. He pulled himself together. 'The goulash is ready, ladies and gentlemen,' announced the former Adolf Wilhelm. 'I suggest we eat in the kitchen. It tastes best there.'

He went on ahead. I was setting off after him. Hirsch held my sleeve. 'Look, Carmen's dancing.'

'And there goes the man on whom my future depends,' I replied.

'The future can wait a minute or two.' Hirsch held me fast. 'Beauty never. Paragraph 87 of the longer, revised Laon Breviary, New York edition.'

I looked over at Carmen. Like a dream image of cosmic melancholy she lay in the orang-utan arms of a lanky,

[2] "No one", still playing on the theme of Odysseus.

red-haired sergeant with double-jointed knees. 'Probably she's thinking of how to make potato pancakes,' said Hirsch. 'Or not even that. And I adore the cow!'

'Don't moan,' I replied. 'Act! Why didn't you do something long ago?'

'I didn't know where she was. On top of everything else, this magical creature has the quality of disappearing without trace for years on end.'

I laughed. 'That's a quality not even kings possess. Much less women. Forget your wretched past and do something right away.'

He looked at me doubtfully. 'I'm going to have my goulash now,' I said. 'Szeged! And shore up my barren future with Adolf Wilhelm Smith.'

It was midnight when I got back to the Hotel Rausch. To my surprise, Maria Fiola was sitting in the lounge, playing chess with Moikov.

'Do you have a late-night date with your photographer?' I asked.

She shook her head. 'Note the question!' replied Moikov in her stead. 'A manifest neurotic. No sooner does he show up somewhere than he starts asking questions. A destroyer of happiness! Happiness is silence and no questions.'

'A bovine form of happiness, if you ask me,' I replied. 'I've seen that in action tonight. The greatest beauty is pure imperturbability – no doubt about it.'

Maria Fiola looked up. 'Really?'

I nodded. 'The princess with the unicorn.'

'Then he needs a vodka,' explained Moikov. 'We simple people were just enjoying the sweetness of our melancholy. Unicorn worshippers usually shy away. From the dark side of the moon.' He set a glass down on the table and filled it.

'Real Russian, endless *Weltschmerz*,' said Maria Fiola. 'Not the German kind.'

'That died out with Hitler,' I remarked.

The bell rang in the office. Moikov got up wheezingly. 'The Contessa,' he said, with a look at the board above the room numbers. 'Another nightmare about Tsarskoe Selo. I'll take a little bottle with me.'

'Why have you got *Weltschmerz*?' I asked Maria.

'Just today I haven't. Vladimir has it now because he's become a Russian again. The Communists murdered his parents. A couple of days ago they retook his village from the Germans.'

'I know. But hasn't he long since become American?'

'Can you become that?'

'Why not? And maybe sooner than you can become some other things?'

'Maybe. What else do you want to ask, you questioner, you? What I'm still doing up at this time? In this wretched caff? Didn't you want to ask me that?'

I shook my head. 'Why shouldn't you be here? You itemised it for me once anyway. The Hotel Rausch is halfway between your flat and your place of work, Nicky's atelier. It's the last possible place for a stirrup cup before or after the battle. And Vladimir Moikov's vodka is first-rate. Plus, you used to live here off and on. Why shouldn't you be here?'

She nodded and looked at me alertly. 'There's one thing you forgot,' she said. 'If you don't much care about anything, then your own whereabouts are going to be a matter of indifference too. Isn't that right?'

'Not at all! There are big differences there. I'd rather be rich, healthy, young and desperate than poor, old, sick and without hope.'

Maria Fiola suddenly burst out laughing. I had sometimes seen that in her – the abrupt transition from one mood to its opposite. It fascinated me every time; I wasn't at all like that myself. In an instant she could look like a beautiful girl without a care in the world. 'I'll tell you,' she said. 'When I'm unhappy I come here, because when I stayed here I was much unhappier. There's a kind of comfort involved. And apart from that, this is a tiny piece of pseudo-home for me. The only one I know.'

Moikov had left us the bottle. I poured for Maria Fiola and me. Vodka tasted like life itself after the Szeged goulash of Rosa the cook. The girl drank it with the pony-like jerk that I had noticed in her right at the beginning. 'Happiness and unhappiness,' she said. 'Those are such big, pathos-laden, nineteenth-century terms. I don't even know what else to say in their place. Maybe solitude and the illusion of not being alone? I don't know. What else?'

I didn't say anything. We had different views on happiness and unhappiness. Hers were apparently aesthetic, mine were real. Also, it was a question of what you had been through and not so much of the imagination. Imagination lied, altered, falsified. Anyway, I didn't set too much store by what Maria Fiola said; she changed too quickly.

Moikov came back. 'The Contessa is reliving the storming of the Winter Palace,' he reported. 'I left her half a bottle of vodka.'

'I need to go,' said Maria Fiola. She looked at the chessboard. 'I was in a hopeless position anyway.'

'So are we all,' said Moikov. 'It's never a reason to give up. On the contrary: it gives you extraordinary freedom sometimes.'

Maria Fiola laughed tenderly. She was always that way with Moikov; it was as though he were a distant relative.

'Not at my age, Vladimir Ivanovitch,' she said. 'Maybe I'm desperate, but I still believe in gods and devils. Do you want to take me home?' she asked me. 'Not by taxi. Walk. I thought you were a great one for night wanderings?'

'Glad to.'

'Goodbye, Vladimir Ivanovitch.' She kissed Moikov carefully on his stubbly cheek. 'Goodbye, Hotel Rausch.'

'I'm living on 57th Street now,' she said, once we were outside. 'Between First and Second Avenue. Borrowed, like everything always is with me. From friends who are out of town. Is that too far for you?'

'Not at all. As you say, I like to wander around at nights.'

She stopped in front of a shoe shop. There was no one inside. It was closed, but light poured over the leather and silk compositions. Maria studied them as seriously and intently as a huntsman, her head forward a little, her mouth half open, as though she were on the point of saying something. But she didn't speak. She just breathed more deeply, as though stifling a sigh, then turned away, half-smiled and walked on. I followed her in silence.

We passed a long line of aimlessly lit shop windows. Maria only stopped in front of the shoe shops; but then she stopped in front of each one and took it in, slow and alert. It was a strange, silent wandering from one side of the road to the other, taking in the sparkling cavernous shops with the young woman who seemed to have entirely forgotten I was there and was following a mysterious imperative of her own.

She finally stopped. 'You missed one out,' I said. 'Back on the left, on the other side of the road. It's not as brightly lit as the others.'

Maria Fiola laughed. 'It's a sort of compulsion of mine. Were you very bored?'

I shook my head. 'Not at all. It was lovely. And very romantic.'

'Really? What's so romantic about shoe shops?'

'The food shops in between. They always enthuse me. There are lots of them on this street. More numerous than shoe shops, even. Did you see something you liked?'

She laughed. 'It's not that simple. No, I don't think I did.'

'Shoes are something to run away in. Is that what you want – to run away somewhere?'

She looked at me in surprise. 'Yes – maybe. But what from?'

'A thousand possibilities. From yourself too.'

'No. It's not that simple. And who am I anyway? We'd just go round in circles.'

We got to 57th Street. On Second Avenue the homosexuals were walking their poodles. About half a dozen poodles were squatting over the gutter in a row, doing their business. They looked like a series of black sphinxes. Their owners stood by, proud and empathetic.

'Here's where I'm staying,' said Maria Fiola. She stood hesitantly in the doorway. 'How nice that you don't ask the questions that other people do. Aren't you curious?'

'No,' I replied, pulling her closer. 'I take what comes.'

She didn't resist. 'Shall we leave it like that?' she asked. 'Take what comes? Whatever chance allows? Not more?'

'Not more,' I said and kissed her. 'If there's more, you get lies and you get pain. Who wants that?'

Her eyes were open wide. The light of the street lamps reflected in them. 'Fine,' she replied. 'If we can do that. Fine,' she repeated. '*D'accordo!*'

10

I was sitting in the waiting room of the attorney Levin. It was early in the morning, but the room was almost full. In among cactuses and green, unflowering plants of the kind you might find doing duty in a butcher's shop to garnish a dead piglet, about fifteen people sat around on uncomfortable chairs. A small sofa was being hogged by a very fat woman in a tulle hat and a gold chain; she squatted there like a cockroach with a Maltese spitz beside her. No one dared to sit next to her. You could see right away that she was no emigrant. Almost all the others were; it showed in the way they tried to occupy as little space as possible.

I had decided to follow Robert Hirsch's advice, and give Levin a payment of a hundred dollars and see what he could do for me next.

I noticed Dr Brandt in a corner behind the door. He waved to me and I sat down beside him. He was sitting next to a little fish tank, in which little neon fish swam back and forth. 'What are you doing here?' I asked. 'Have you got a dodgy visa? I thought you were working in a hospital here.'

'Not as a gynaecologist,' he replied. 'As an assistant and locum, with exceptional leave. Of course I have to redo my exams.'

'So you're an illegal again,' I said. 'Just like in Paris, eh?'

'More or less. Not quite black; maybe grey, like Ravic.'

I knew that Brandt had been one of the best gynaecologists in Berlin. However, French law refused to recognise German medical qualifications and he hadn't been given a work permit. So he had worked for a French doctor friend of his, performing operations on his behalf. Just like Ravic, in fact. And in America, he too was required to start over.

Brandt looked tired. Probably he was doing unpaid work and was barely making enough to get by. He saw my look. 'They feed me in hospital,' he said with a smile. 'And I get some pocket money. Don't worry about me.'

A canary suddenly piped up. I looked around; I hadn't noticed it. 'Levin seems to be fond of animals,' I said. 'The fish must be part of the ambience of the waiting room as well.'

The yellow bird sang loudly in the dim room full of misery and worry. Its blitheness seemed almost offensive; it really had no place here. The Maltese spitz grew restless, then launched into a furious volley of barking.

A pretty, fragile secretary opened the door to Levin's consulting room. 'We don't allow barking dogs in here,' she said. 'Not even yours, Mrs Lormer.'

'What about the bloody bird?' retorted the woman on the sofa. 'My spitz was perfectly well behaved. The bird started it! Tell him to shut up!'

'I can't tell the bird that,' said the secretary calmly. 'He just sings. But I'm sure you can explain to your spitz that he shouldn't bark. He listens to you. Or haven't you trained him?'

'What's a canary doing in here anyway? Get him out,' retorted Mrs Lormer.

'And your dog?' said the petite assistant, now irritated. 'This isn't a vet's, you know.'

The atmosphere in the waiting room had shifted. There weren't submissive shadows perched in the chairs, but people who were alive and had eyes that were no longer quenched. They avoided taking sides, but their sympathies were engaged.

The spitz now barked at the secretary. She hissed back at him like a goose. Levin's head appeared in the doorway. 'What's all this commotion?'

His large, chalky teeth seemed to light up the dim room. He read the situation immediately and had a Solomonic solution. 'Come on in, Mrs Lormer,' he said, holding the door open for her. The fat woman in her lavender hat grabbed her dog and waddled through the ranks of waiting emigrants to the consulting room. The secretary followed her. A smell of lily of the valley spread through the room. It came from the empty sofa where Mrs Lormer had been sitting. The canary, alarmed, fell silent.

'Next time I think I'll bring a dog,' said Brandt. 'You get quicker service that way. There's a German shepherd at the hospital.'

I laughed. 'Then the bird won't sing. He'll be petrified.'

Brandt nodded. 'Or the dog will bite the secretary and Levin will throw us out. You're right: it's better for an emigrant to trust to chance. If he tries to improve his odds, it won't work.'

I put down a hundred dollars on the desk. Levin's large bony hand passed over it and it was gone. 'Are you working?' he asked.

I shook my head. 'You know I'm not allowed to,' I said cautiously.

'How are you managing to survive, then?'

'I find money on the pavement and I play the lottery, and I'm kept by rich old ladies,' I replied calmly, bemused by the stupid question. He must surely know that I couldn't tell him the truth.

He laughed his peculiar laugh and abruptly stopped. 'You're right. It's no concern of mine. Not officially. Privately and humanly it is, of course.'

'Private and human information has landed me in prison before now,' I said. 'I've been burned. I have yet to learn to be more trusting.'

'Quite. But we can proceed anyway. Dr Brandt was here before you. He vouched for you.'

I was surprised. 'Poor Brandt! But he's got no money.'

'He vouched for you in moral terms. He confirmed that you had suffered persecution and that he knew you.'

'Does that help?'

'Every little helps,' said Levin. 'It adds up. Your friend Jessie Stein organised it. You know, she sent Brandt here.'

'Was he just seeing you on my account?'

'Not exclusively. But he probably wouldn't dare see Jessie Stein again without having made a deposition concerning you.'

I laughed. 'That doesn't sound like Brandt at all.'

Levin whinnied. 'No, but it's Jessie Stein all over. That woman is a force of nature. We must have had a dozen cases here, all for her. Does she have no other worries? No ego?'

'Her ego is her concern for others. She was always that way. Gentle and implacable. Even in France.'

A cuckoo called loudly and melodiously behind me. I spun round in surprise. Another bird! From a wooden cuckoo clock a small, painted thing shot out of a hatch that opened and shut. 'Eleven o'clock already,' sighed Levin.

'You've got a real zoo in here,' I said after the bird had finished. 'Canaries, Pomeranians, tropical fish, and now this emblem of German cosiness.'

'Don't you like it?'

'I'm surprised to find it here,' I replied. 'I was once

interrogated to a cuckoo clock. Every time the bird called, I got hit in the face. Unhappily it was twelve o'clock.'

'Where was that?' asked Levin.

'In France. I was questioned in a German army post. By a uniformed schoolmaster with sergeant's stripes. Each time the cuckoo called, I had to go: "Cuckoo! Cuckoo!"'

Levin's face had changed. 'I didn't know that,' he muttered. And he got up to turn off the clock.

I stopped him. 'Don't bother,' I said. 'The one occasion has nothing to do with the other. Where would it get us if we were all so sensitive the whole time? It's among my more pleasant memories, in point of fact. They let me go soon after. The schoolmaster gave me an anthology of German poetry as a leaving present. I lugged it with me all the way to Ellis Island and lost it there.'

I didn't tell Levin that it was Hirsch who had sprung me from the place a day later, in his role as a Spanish consular official. He had given the sergeant a real carpeting for arresting one of Franco's protégés. It had all been a terrible mistake! The teacher thought it might cost him his stripes and gave me the book by way of apology. Hirsch had whisked me away in his car.

Levin stared at me. 'Did that happen because you were a Jew?'

I shook my head. 'No, it happened because I was helpless. There's nothing worse than being completely helpless and falling into the hands of civilised German barbarians. Cowardice, cruelty and absence of responsibility: those three things are mutually reinforcing. The teacher himself was pretty harmless. Not an SS man.'

★

181

I didn't mention that, following the cuckoo game the night before, the sergeant had become uncertain. He had wanted to edify his sentry by showing him what a circumcised Jew was. I was made to strip. To his consternation he had seen that I was uncircumcised. When Hirsch fetched up the following day, he was pretty happy to be rid of me.

Levin listened to his clock. It ticked audibly. 'An heirloom,' he murmured.

'It won't strike for another forty-five minutes,' I said.

He got up and came round the front of his desk to me. 'How do you feel here in America?' he asked.

I knew that every American always expected you to feel great. There was something so adorably naive about that. 'Great,' I said.

His face lit up. 'I'm so glad. Don't worry about your visa. Once you're in the country, you're unlikely to be deported. It must feel wonderful for you not to be persecuted any more. We have no Gestapo here and no militia.'

No, I thought. But dreams! Dreams and ghosts of the past that suddenly come to life.

I got back to the hotel at noon. 'Someone was looking for you,' said Moikov. 'Red cheeks and blue eyes. Female.'

'A woman or a lady?'

'A woman. She's still there. She's sitting in the palm court.'

I walked out into the lounge with the potted plants and the spindly palm tree. 'Rosa!' I said in surprise.

The Tannenbaums' cook got up behind the shrubbery. 'I wanted to bring you something,' she explained. 'The goulash. You forgot it yesterday.'

She opened a large, chequered bag, in which I could hear

it clinking. 'Goulash keeps,' she said. 'In fact, it's even better after a day or two.'

She lifted out a large lidded china tureen and placed it on the table. 'Is it the Szeged?' I asked.

'It's the other one, actually. It keeps better. And here are some gherkins, and silverware and a plate.' She unwrapped a napkin with a spoon and forks in it. 'This dish is fireproof. You can heat it up. I'll pick it up with the cutlery in a week.'

'But this is paradise!' I exclaimed. 'Thank you, Rosa, so much. And please thank Mr Tannenbaum for me too.'

'Smith,' replied Rosa. 'It's official from this morning. And here's a piece of the citizenship cake.'

'It's huge! Is it marzipan?'

Rosa nodded. 'Yesterday's was chocolate. Would you have preferred that? There's still a little left. Hidden.'

'No, no. Let's stick to the future. Marzipan is fine.'

'And here's a note as well. From Mr Smith. Now, bon appétit!'

I fished a dollar bill out of my pocket. Rosa refused point-blank. 'Absolutely not. I'm not allowed to take anything from an emigrant. Otherwise I'll lose my job. Strict orders from Mr Smith.'

'Only from emigrants?'

She nodded. 'I can accept tips from bankers, but they hardly ever offer.'

'And the emigrants?'

'They always want to give me their last cent. There's gratitude in poverty, Mr Sommer.'

I watched her go, astonished. Then I lugged the tureen past Moikov to carry it up to my room. 'Goulash!' I said. 'Made by a Hungarian cook! Have you had lunch already?'

'Unfortunately, yes. A hamburger at the corner pharmacy. With ketchup. And apple pie. Thoroughly American.'

'Me too,' I said. 'A portion of overcooked spaghetti. With ketchup. And apple pie to follow.'

Moikov lifted the lid of the tureen and sniffed. 'There's enough in there to feed a company. What a smell! What are roses by comparison? Onions, reduced!'

'You're invited, Vladimir.'

'Don't carry the dish up to your room. Leave it here in the fridge where I keep my vodka. Your room is too warm.'

'Sure.'

I kept the note and went upstairs. The windows in my room were open. I could hear the radio down in the courtyard, or from windows across the way. Raoul's curtains were drawn. A gramophone was playing the waltz from *Der Rosenkavalier*. I opened Tannenbaum-Smith's note. It wasn't long. I was to call the art dealer Reginald Black. Tannenbaum had spoken to him. He was expecting my call the day after tomorrow. Good luck!

Slowly I folded the note. It was as though the dirty hotel had fallen away and turned into a tree-lined avenue. I had a glimpse of something like a future. An open road – not a locked gate. Something ordinary and hence miraculous. I went downstairs and telephoned right away. I had to. Reginald Black answered the phone. He had a low, slightly hesitant voice. While I was speaking to him, I heard music on the line. I thought it was a hallucination – until I realised that Black was playing music as well. It was the same *Rosenkavalier* waltz that I had heard out of Raoul's room. I thought that had to be a good omen. Black asked me to come and see him in three days. At five o'clock. I hung up, but the music was still playing. I turned and looked outside. The windows of Raoul's apartment had been thrown open. His gramophone now outdid all the jazz trumpets in the yard and was therefore audible in the gloomy little cubbyhole next to reception where the telephone was. *Der Rosenkavalier* was everywhere.

'What is it?' asked Moikov. 'You look as though you'd seen a ghost.'

I nodded. 'I have. The ghost of the biggest adventure there is: the adventure of an orderly life and a settled future.'

'You watch your mouth! So you're getting a job, is that it?'

'Maybe,' I answered. 'Illicit, of course. But let's not talk about it. Otherwise the bluebird will fly away.'

'All right. But how about a discreet, hopeful glass of vodka?'

'Any time, Vladimir.'

He fetched the bottle. I looked down at myself. My suit was eight years old and very worn; I had inherited it from Sommer and Sommer had worn it a long time in his day. So far I hadn't given it any thought; I had had a spare suit, but that was stolen some time ago on the road.

Moikov noticed my critical self-appraisal. He laughed. 'You look like a worried mother-hen. The first sign of bourgeoisification. What have you got against your suit all of a sudden?'

'It's pretty ropy.'

Moikov gestured dismissively. 'Wait till the job's in the bag. Then you can see about a new one.'

'How much is a suit?'

'At Browning King, about seventy bucks. Give or take. Have you got that much?'

'As a member of the wage-earning proletariat, no; as a gambler – sure. It's what's left of the Chinese bronze.'

'Then blow it,' said Moikov. 'That'll take some of the sheepish flavour away from your new respectability.'

We drank. The vodka was very cold and flavoursome.

'Do you notice the difference?' asked Moikov. 'Of course you don't. It's zubrovka. Bison-grass vodka.'

'Where do you get bison-grass from? Russia?'

'That's a trade secret.' He recorked the bottle. 'And now off into the shining future as a petty accountant or shop-keeper. Like Hirsch.'

'Why like Hirsch?'

'Because he arrived as a Sir Galahad of the Maccabees – and now he's selling transistor radios to schoolkids. Some adventurers you are!'

Once I was out on the street, I forgot Moikov's words. I stopped in front of a little florist's shop on the corner. It belonged to an Italian, who also sold fruit. His flowers weren't always the freshest; but they were inexpensive.

The proprietor was standing in his doorway. Thirty years ago he had come from Cannobio; I had once been expatriated from Switzerland to that very same Cannobio. That united us. As a result, I got fifteen per cent off my fruit. 'How are you doing, Emilio?' I asked.

He shrugged. 'It must be lovely in Cannobio now; swimming in Lago Maggiore. If only the bloody Germans weren't there.'

'They won't be there much longer.'

Emilio looked worried and scratched his moustache. 'They will destroy everything when they leave. Rome and Firenze and beautiful Cannobio.'

I couldn't comfort him. It was what I was afraid of as well. So I said, 'Nice flowers.'

'Orchids,' he replied with animation. 'Very fresh. Or quite fresh. Cheap! But who around here buys flowers?'

'Me,' I said. 'If they're as cheap as you say they are.'

Emilio scratched at his moustache again. It was a little

toothbrush moustache, like Hitler's, and it made him look like a pimp. 'One dollar a stem. I've got two. That includes the reduction.'

I suspected Emilio of having a deal with a local funeral home and supplying himself from there. The bereaved left flowers on the coffins of their dear departed when they were taken to the crematorium; before they were incinerated, one of the employees would sort out the saleable ones and flog them. Wreaths were of course fed to the flames. Emilio often had lilies and white roses to sell. Too often, I thought. But I didn't want to think about that now.

'Do you do deliveries?'

'Where to?'

'57th Street?'

'Sure,' said Emilio. 'I'll even wrap them up nice.'

I wrote down Maria Fiola's address and gummed down the envelope. Emilio gave me a saucy wink. 'At last!' he said. 'It was about time.'

'It's not what you think,' I said. 'They're for my maiden aunt.'

I went to the gentlemen's outfitters. They were on Fifth Avenue, but Moikov had explained to me that their prices were lower than elsewhere. The reek of complacency met my nostrils as I walked down the aisle of men's suits. Moikov could inveigh all he liked; if you hadn't experienced it, it remained an extraordinary adventure. It was the opposite of life on the run, where you could only carry a light suitcase. It meant calm, relaxation, living, studying, books; a continuing, assured existence; culture, future, staying put.

'I'd suggest a lightweight tropical,' said the salesman. 'For the next two months New York is going to be very hot. And very humid.'

He showed me a light-grey two-piece. I felt the cloth. 'It won't crease,' said the man. 'It's easy to pack and won't take up much room in a suitcase.'

In spite of myself, I gave the suit another look; something like that was good for the run, I thought. Then I shook off the idea; I didn't want to go on thinking like a wandering emigrant. 'Not grey,' I said. 'Blue. Navy.'

'For summer?' asked the salesman doubtfully.

'Sure, for summer,' I said. 'Tropical weight. But dark blue.'

I would rather have taken the grey; but ancient memories of my upbringing surfaced in me. Blue was solid and serious. It was more versatile – it would do for Reginald Black and for Maria Fiola. It would do for morning, noon and night.

I was taken to a changing room with a long mirror to try on the suit. As I took off the old one, I looked at myself worriedly in the mirror for an instant. The last time I had owned a blue suit it was my father who had bought it for me. Three years later he was dead, murdered.

I stepped out of the changing room. The salesman put on his best enthusiastic expression and danced attendance on me. I saw he had an almost healed boil on his neck, with a plaster on it. 'It fits perfectly,' he said. 'Might have been tailor-made for you.'

I looked into the mirror again. A serious-looking man I didn't know looked back at me, uneasy and worried. 'Would you like me to wrap it for you?' asked the salesman.

I shook my head. 'I'll keep it on. But wrap my old one if you will. I'm not ready to throw it out yet.'

I was thinking of many things at once. There was something symbolic about the strange ritual of trying on and changing clothes. It was as though, in laying aside the dead Sommer's suit, I was dropping a little piece of my past. Not that I had forgotten it, or would forget it; but I was no longer present in it. Some sort of future was looming. My old suit had been heavy; the new one was so light I almost had the sensation of not wearing anything.

I made my way slowly down to the antique shop. Alexander Silver, eighteenth-century *putto* in hand, was doing some window-dressing. When he caught sight of me he dropped it. I jumped, but the frail wooden angel had the good fortune to land on a piece of velvet. Silver picked it up, kissed it and waved me in. 'So this is how you spend your days,' he said. 'I thought you were seeing a lawyer.'

'That too,' I replied. 'My lawyer and my tailor. It was high time.'

'You look like a con man. Or a pickpocket. Or a bigamist.'

'Got it. I'm launched on a career as all three. Sad to say.'

Silver laughed and clambered down. 'Notice anything?'

I looked around and shook my head. 'Nothing new here, Mr Silver.'

'That's right. But something's missing. Do you know what it is?'

He stepped up to me dramatically. I took another look around. The shop was so stuffed full, it was hard to say what might have been missing.

'A prayer rug,' announced Silver proudly. 'One of the pair you turned up. Ring a bell?'

I nodded. 'Which one? The one with the blue or the green prayer niche?'

'The green.'

'The more unusual one, then. But never mind. The blue is in better condition.'

Silver looked at me expectantly. 'How much?' I asked him.

'Four hundred and fifty dollars. Cash!'

'My respects. A good price.'

Silently, Silver pulled out his wallet. Like a miniature peacock he seemed to get bigger and put on girth. Slowly he peeled off five ten-dollar bills on to a silver-gilt prayer desk. 'Your commission,' he declared. 'Earned while you were at the tailor's. How much is your suit?'

'Sixty dollars.'

'With waistcoat?'

'With waistcoat and two pairs of trousers.'

'You see. So you've got it for nothing. Congratulations!'

I pocketed the money. 'Now what would you say to a Czech-Viennese double mocha with crumb cake?' I asked.

Silver nodded and opened the door. The evening din of the avenue poured in. Silver took a step back, as though he had seen an adder. 'Merciful Heavens! It's Arnold! And in a smoking jacket! All is lost.'

Arnold wasn't in a smoking jacket. He was in a little visiting outfit – a dark jacket, striped banker's trousers, stiff hat and light-grey, old-fashioned gaiters – traipsing through the dirty, fume-y, honey-coloured light of early evening.

'Arnold!' yelled the older Silver. 'Come here! Don't go! One last word! Come in here! Think of your mother! Your poor, devout mother!'

Arnold strode calmly across the avenue. 'I was thinking about Mother,' he said. 'And I'm not letting you make me crazy, you Jewish fascist.'

'Arnold! Don't talk like that. Didn't I always want the best for you? Look after you, as only an older brother can, tend you when you were sick, and how often you were sick—'

'We're twins,' said Arnold. 'My brother is older than me by all of three hours.'

'Three hours can be a lifetime. Those three hours made

190

me a Gemini and you a weak, dreamy Cancer, unworldly. I have to look after you. And you treat me like your arch-enemy.'

'Because I want to get married?'

'Because you want to marry a shiksa. A Christian! Look at him standing there, Mr Sommer, isn't he pitiful, like a goy going to the races. Arnold, Arnold, snap out of it. Be patient. He wants to present his suit, like an attorney. They've given you a magic potion. Think of Tristan and Isolde and all the misery that came of that. You're calling your own brother a fascist, just because he wants to save you from a disastrous marriage. Take a nice Jewish wife, Arnold.'

'I don't want any nice Jewish wife. I want to marry the woman I love.'

'Love. What's that!? Look at you, just look at you! He's going to offer his hand in marriage. Look at him, Mr Sommer, striped pants and a new smoking jacket. A banker.'

'I really can't comment,' I said. 'Seeing as I'm in a new suit myself. One for pickpockets and con men, if I remember?'

'That was just a joke.'

'It seems to be quite the day for suits,' I said. 'Where did you get the lovely gaiters, Arnold?'

'You like them? Picked them up on a visit to Vienna. Before the war, of course. Don't listen to my brother. I'm an American. Free from prejudice.'

'Prejudice!' Alexander Silver brushed a china shepherdess off a table, but reflexively managed to catch it before it shattered.

'Watch out!' yelled Arnold. 'Was that the old Meissen?'

'No, it was the new Rosenthal.' Silver senior held up the figurine. 'Nothing happened.'

After that near miss the conversation calmed down somewhat. Arnold took back the Jewish fascist. He swapped it for a Zionist, then for a mere zealot. Then Alexander made a tactical mistake. He turned to me and asked whether I would ever marry anyone but a Jewess. 'Maybe,' I replied. 'My father urged me to do that when I was sixteen, or else he said nothing good would come of me.'

'Nonsense,' declared Arnold.

'The voice of blood!' cried Alexander.

I laughed. The debate flared up again. By simple intensity Silver senior was gradually gaining ground against the dreamer and poet Arnold. It was exactly as I had expected. Arnold had not been very firmly resolved, otherwise he would never have turned up in the shop in his little visiting suit, but would have marched straight to the house of the inamorata with the blonde curls – dyed and bleached, according to Silver senior. He seemed not at all reluctant to be persuaded to wait. 'You won't lose anything,' Alexander Silver cajoled. 'You'll just think it over properly.'

'And what if someone else turns up?'

'Who?'

'She has lots of suitors.'

'No one else will come, Arnold. Haven't you learned anything in the course of thirty years as a lawyer and here in the shop? Haven't we claimed hundreds of times that there was another customer interested in this or that *objet* and on the point of buying it, and it was always a lie. Come on, Arnold!'

'We're getting on,' said Arnold, 'and we're not getting any prettier. Just sicker.'

'So's she. And at a much faster rate than you. Women age twice as fast as men. Now come in and take off that monkey jacket.'

'That I won't,' declared Arnold with unexpected rigour. 'I've got it on and I'm going out.'

Silver senior feared a new obstacle. 'All right, then, let's go out,' he said pleasantly. 'Where shall we go? The movies? There's a film with Paulette Goddard!'[3]

'The movies?' Insulted, Arnold looked down the length of his Marengo jacket. In the cinema that kind of thing didn't pull its weight; it was too dark for a start.

'All right, Arnold. Let's go eat. A good meal. A classy meal. With a starter! Chopped liver, and peach melba for dessert. Anywhere you like.'

'The Voisin,' said Arnold in a firm voice.

Alexander gulped. 'A luxury restaurant. Were you going to take her—?' He stopped.

'The Voisin!' repeated Arnold.

'Very well,' replied Alexander. He turned to me with a magnanimous gesture. 'Mr Sommer, will you join us? I note you're festively dressed already. What's in the package?'

'My old suit.'

'Leave it here. We can pick it up afterwards.'

I had the utmost admiration for Silver senior. The blow that Arnold had dealt him with the expensive choice of restaurant, where the livers wouldn't be chopped and chicken, but fine and goose, had been taken in exemplary fashion. Instead of flinching, he had responded with generosity. I decided, in spite of everything, to order goose liver myself. In a complicated way, I thought I owed it to Arnold and the twins' difficult racial problem.

I was back at the hotel at ten o'clock. 'Vladimir,' I said. 'The goulash will have to wait. I refereed a reverse racist battle. I dined at Voisin's!'

[3] A nod at the American actress (1910–90), star of *Modern Times* (and ex-wife of Charlie Chaplin), whom Remarque married in 1958.

'Good for you! All racist battles should be settled there. What did you have to drink?'

'A 1934 Bordeaux. A Cos d'Estournel.'

'Respect! I've only ever heard of it.'

'I came across it first in 1939. A French customs official gave me a half-bottle before he sent me packing across the border into Switzerland. He gave it to me because I was so depressed. It was the first evening of the Drôle de Guerre, in September.'

Moikov nodded abstractedly. 'It seems to be the day for presents. In the morning the goulash and this evening, at seven, another package came for you. The chauffeur of a Rolls-Royce dropped it off.'

'What?'

'A uniformed chauffeur in a Rolls-Royce. Discreet as the tomb. Have you and your blue suit become an arms dealer?'

'No idea! Is it addressed to me?'

Moikov got it out from under the front desk. It was a narrow, upright parcel. I opened it. 'A bottle,' I said.

I looked in the packaging for a note. There was nothing. 'My God!' I heard Moikov reverently utter over my shoulder. 'Do you know what this is? Real Russian vodka! Not the stuff we make here. How ever did that get here?'

'Aren't America and Russia on the same side?'

'Yes, gun-wise. But vodka? Are you a spy?'

'The bottle isn't quite full,' I noted. 'The cork has been opened.' I thought of Maria Fiola and Emilio's orchids. 'There's maybe two or three shots missing.'

'So it's personal, is it?' Moikov squinched up his parrots' eyes with their innumerable pleats. 'An act of some forbearance. Well, I propose we treat it with the respect it deserves.'

11

Reginald Black didn't have a gallery or shop. He dealt from home. I had expected a kind of shark on legs. Instead, I met a slight, rather quiet man with a bald patch and a neatly trimmed beard. He gave me a whiskey and soda, and asked me a couple of careful and restrained questions. Then from an adjacent room he got two pictures and put them up on an easel. They were a couple of Degas drawings. 'Which one do you like better?' he asked.

I pointed to the one on the right. 'Why?' asked Black.

I hesitated. 'Do I have to give a reason?' I asked him back.

'I'm interested. Do you know who they're by?'

'They are a couple of Degas drawings. Anyone can see that.'

'Not quite everyone,' said Black with a subtle smile that reminded me of Tannenbaum-Smith. 'Some of my clients can't.'

'Strange. So why do they buy?'

'To have a Degas on their walls,' replied Black mournfully. 'Pictures are emigrants, a bit like you. They often wind up in unlikely places. Whether they feel at home there is another matter.'

He took the two drawings down and came back with two watercolours from next door. 'Do you know what these are?'

'Yes, they are two Cézanne watercolours.'

Black nodded. 'Could you tell me which one you think is the better of the two?'

'Every Cézanne is good,' I replied. 'The more valuable one is probably the one on the left.'

'And why would that be? Because it's bigger?'

'No, not that. It's from his late period. It's almost Cubist. A pretty Provençal landscape, with the Mont St Victoire in the background. There was one a bit like it in the museum in Brussels.'

Black looked at me narrowly. 'How do you know all that?'

'I worked there for a few months.' I saw no reason to tell him the truth.

'As what? As a buyer?'

'No. As a student. But I had to give it up.'

Black seemed to be relieved. 'I really couldn't be doing with a buyer,' he said. 'I don't want to nourish a future rival.'

'I don't have the least aptitude as a dealer,' I hastened to assure him.

He offered me a cigarillo. That seemed to be a good omen; Silver had offered me one too when taking me on. That had been a Brazil; this one was a real Havana. I had never smoked one in my life, only heard of them.

'Paintings are like living beings,' said Black. 'Like women. You can't show them around everywhere if they are to keep their charm. And their value. Do you understand that?'

I nodded. I didn't understand it at all; it was an absurd form of words that made no sense.

'At least that's how it is for the dealer,' expanded Black. 'Pictures that are shown around too much are referred to as "burned" in the trade. The opposite are "virgins", which have always been in the same hands, privately owned and hardly ever seen. Connoisseurs rate them higher. Not because they're better pictures, but because the connoisseur's pleasure in making a discovery is factored in.'

'And so they command a higher price?'

Black nodded. 'That's their so-called snob appeal. Perfectly legitimate. There are other factors that are more abstruse. Especially today, in wartime. Fortunes change hands. Some are lost, others are rapidly made. Old collectors are forced to sell – new ones have plenty of money, but no judgement. It takes time, patience and love to make a connoisseur.'

I listened to him and wondered whether he would take me on or not. I wasn't sure; it felt a bit peculiar, him telling me all these things instead of testing me on my knowledge or suggesting a rate of pay. He put another picture on the easel. 'Does this one do anything for you?'

'A Monet.'

'Do you like it?'

'A fabulous painting,' I said.

Black gestured round the room, which was lined with grey velvet and, apart from the easel, contained a sofa, a low table and a couple of chairs. 'I often sit here in the mornings alone with a couple of pictures,' he said. 'Sometimes just with one picture. You're never alone with a picture. You can talk to it – or better, listen to it.'

I nodded. It seemed more and more doubtful to me that I would be offered the job. Black was talking to me as to a client, whom he was subtly trying to talk into making a purchase. But why was he doing it? He knew perfectly well that I wasn't a buyer. Perhaps he thought I might be touting for Tannenbaum-Smith – or again, he meant what he said, and he was a somewhat lost rich man who didn't feel altogether at ease in his profession. But he really didn't have anything to prove to me.

'A fabulous Monet,' I said. 'To think of all these things going on at one and the same time – that and war and concentration camps. It's hard to believe.'

'It's a French painting,' replied Black, 'not German. Perhaps that explains something.'

I shook my head. 'There are German paintings of that kind as well. A lot of them. Perhaps that's the unbelievable thing.'

Reginald Black took out an amber mouthpiece and inserted his cigar into it. 'Well, I'm happy to give it a go,' he said gently. 'I don't expect any great expertise. Discretion and reliability are more important. What would you say to eight dollars a day?'

He had almost hypnotised me with the unfamiliar cigar, the paintings and the quiet voice. Now I swiftly came to life. 'For what hours?' I asked. 'Mornings or afternoons?'

'From nine in the morning to five or six. With an hour off for lunch. It's not always easy to predict.'

'Mr Black,' I said, 'that's about what the better class of errand boy makes.'

I expected Black to reply that that was pretty much what the job was. But he was subtler than that. He worked out for me what the better class of errand boy got and it was less.

'I can't take less than twelve dollars,' I replied. 'I have debts I need to pay off.'

'Debts, already?'

'Yes, to the lawyer who's working on my residence qualification.'

Black shook his bald head disapprovingly and at the same time stroked his glistening black beard; a good exercise in coordination, two contrary motions at the same time. He did it. He gave me the impression of having to reconsider the whole matter of my hiring, gravely flawed as that made me. At last the tiger was showing his stripes.

But I hadn't studied with Ludwig Sommer for nothing. There was a man who could almost outdo Black in the area of careful expression. And I hadn't bought my new blue suit for nothing either. Black reminded me with a shy smile that I was working illegally and hence was paying no taxes. Also that my English wasn't exactly fluent. But then I had him. Perhaps not, I said, but I spoke French and that was an asset if his line of merchandise was French Impressionists. Black gestured dismissively; but he did agree to ten dollars and promised that if I got off to a good start, we could talk about remuneration again. 'You'll get a lot of time off as well,' he said. 'I often have to go away. Then there's nothing for you to do.'

We agreed that I would start in five days. 'Nine o'clock,' said Black. He sighed. 'The art business shouldn't be a business at all, if you ask me, just an occasional inspired agreement between connoisseurs to trade their treasures. Don't you think?'

I didn't think so at all; rather I thought it was an inspired agreement with each party trying to shaft the other for all he was worth. But I didn't say so. 'That sounds like the best case,' I merely said.

Black nodded and got up. 'By the way, why doesn't your friend Tannenbaum have any pictures?' he asked casually as he was seeing me out.

I shrugged. I could remember seeing some truly majestic still lifes at the Tannenbaum-Smiths'; but they had been flat on the table and were of the edible variety. 'Now that he's become an American, he should really think of buying pictures,' said Black. 'It does wonders for your social standing. And it's a superb investment, much better than the stock market. Well, you can't win them all, I suppose. Till next week, Mr Sommer.'

Alexander Silver was waiting for me excitedly. I had told him about my interview with Black. 'Well, how did things go with the old pirate?' he asked.

'He isn't exactly a pirate,' I replied. 'More a kind of conceited Assyrian.'

'What?'

'A bald, cultured, slightly opaque character, with an Assyrian's gleaming beard. Very polite and charming.'

'I know him,' said Silver. 'A cunning swindler with courtly manners. Apparently he's already managed to con you. Watch yourself!'

I had to laugh. 'Why? In case he doesn't pay me my wages?'

Silver was momentarily confused. 'No, of course not that. Just in other ways—'

I was charmed. He was jealous. It warmed my heart. 'He's a parasite,' Silver finally blurted out. He leaned against a Florentine Savonarola chair, the upper part of which was real. 'The art business is all about guilt,' he lectured. 'The dealer takes money that should have been the artist's. The artist starves – the dealer buys another chateau. Isn't that how it works?'

I didn't contradict him. Sommer hadn't owned any chateaux. 'It's less bad in the case of antiques and *objets*,' Silver went on. 'You make a little money. Sometimes you do well. But you risk being taken for a ride. It's high art that provides the worst cases. Think of Van Gogh. He never sold a picture in his life. All those millions that they fetch now, they all go to dealers. To parasites. Right?'

'In Van Gogh's case, yes. With others, I'm not so sure.'

Silver gestured impatiently. 'Well, I am. The dealers make contracts with the painters. Pay them a certain sum a month – a pittance. And in return, the painters hand over their works. Masterpieces for a hundred or a hundred and fifty francs. Right? I call that slave labour.'

'But Mr Silver! At the time the painter was working, no one wanted his paintings. He offered them everywhere. Almost nobody wanted them. In the end, only the art dealer bought them. And he wasn't sure he wouldn't be stuck with them.'

I wasn't speaking up for Reginald Black. I was speaking up for the late Ludwig Sommer who had lived and died in poverty. But Alexander Silver wasn't to know. 'There you go,' he said quietly. 'You too, Mr Sommer. Already on the side of the parasites. In a few more days you'll be running around in a top hat and gloves, and cheating poor widows of their nest egg on behalf of Mr Black. You've already got the blue suit. And to think that I trusted you. Duped! I've been duped again.'

I looked at him with interest. 'What do you mean, again? Who else has duped you?'

'Arnold,' whispered Alexander, suddenly wretched. 'The dinner at Voisin's, with pâté de foie gras and caviar and everything, it didn't do any good. I go out for a stroll at lunchtime and who do I run into? Arnold, arm in arm with his peroxided shiksa, Arnold in his top hat, looking like the president of a racetrack.'

'But Arnold never promised you that he would stop seeing the Christian woman. Over dessert, you remember those wonderful crêpes Suzette, he just said he would think about getting married. So he hasn't tricked you, Mr Silver. Or has he got married in the meantime?'

Silver went pale. 'Has he? How did you know that?'

'No, no. I'm just asking. So he hasn't duped you.'

'No?' Silver got a grip on himself. 'Then what do you call it if I see him coming out of Voisin's with the shiksa? That's where the ganef is taking her now. I introduced him to it and now he's taking the shiksa there! And that's no tricking? My twin brother?'

'It's terrible,' I replied. 'But that's love. It doesn't make people any better. It may exalt the emotions, but it destroys the character.'

The Florentine chair broke apart with a loud crack. In his excitement, Silver had been leaning against it too hard. We picked up the pieces. 'It can all be glued,' I said. 'Nothing's really broken.'

Silver was breathing hard. 'Think of your heart, Mr Silver,' I said. 'No one is out to cheat you. Not Arnold, not anyone. Everything is still in the balance. Arnold may still fall in love with a banker's daughter.'

'The shiksa won't let him out of her clutches,' muttered Alexander. 'Not if he's taking her to the Voisin every day.'

'I hardly think that's likely.'

'He'll bankrupt us if he carries on in that fashion,' declared Alexander Silver. Instantly his face brightened. 'Bankrupt! That's it! If we go broke, that super blonde will leap off him like a flea from a corpse.'

I could see the wheels turning. 'Isn't it time for coffee and poppy seed biscuits in the bakery across the way?' I asked cautiously. 'I hardly dare suggest it to you after the experience with Arnold at Voisin's. After all, you initiated me in the café as well. I think to be cheated twice on one day is more than any heart can stand. Still, I'd like to invite you. Or a piece of crumble with a cappuccino? Or a milky *café au lait*?'

Alexander Silver seemed to be coming out of a dream.

'That's it,' he murmured. 'Bankruptcy as a last resort.' Then he turned to me. 'That's different, Mr Sommer. After all, it was me who urged you to go and see Black. The fact that I happen to consider him a parasite is neither here nor there. Poppy seed biscuits, you say? Why not?'

We set off across the road. But Silver wasn't paying attention. He might still be wearing his pepper-and-salt trousers and his patent-leather slippers, but his thoughts were elsewhere. He made an ill-judged leap in front of a milk cart and was knocked over by a cyclist speeding along behind it. I was able to pick him up off the roadway and drag him across to the pavement, where he collapsed a second time at the feet of a woman with a laundry basket, who shrieked in alarm. 'Insect!' she screamed.

Silver staggered to his feet. I dusted him down. 'You had a near thing,' I said. 'Your reflexes are compromised today, Mr Silver. That slows you down. Revenge, outlook, ethics and declaring bankruptcy all are taking their toll on you as an athlete.'

Mizzi the waitress came running out of the café, clothes brush in hand. 'My goodness, Mr Silver! You were almost done for then.' She gave Alexander another dusting down, then she brushed the pepper-and-salt trousers. 'They really don't show the dirt,' she lamented. 'Now come into the café, Mr Alexander. My gentleman! Being knocked over by a nickel and dime bicyclist! If only it had been a Cadillac.'

'If it had been a Cadillac, Mr Alexander wouldn't be alive, Mizzi,' I said gravely.

Silver felt his anklebone. 'I wonder what that woman meant by "insect"?' he asked.

'That washerwoman? Presumably a superbly well-adapted form of life with highly evolved social structures,' I replied. 'Long before there were any human beings.'

Mizzi brought us our cappuccinos and a whole plate of fresh specialities. We chose the almond sponge with whipped cream. 'If you were dead now, Mr Alexander, the almond sponge wouldn't mean anything to you,' said Mizzi. 'That's how it goes. But now I want you to enjoy it twice as much.'

'Bravo, Mizzi, well said,' I declared and helped myself to another piece, this time *Sachertorte*. 'Unfortunately, these insights usually come too late. We live between longing for the past and dread of the future. But not enough in the present. Another cappuccino, please.'

Silver stared at me as though I were a fat bullfrog. 'Claptrap!' he muttered. 'Claptrap and shmonzes. But that's the annoying thing about banalities – in their fatuous way, they're truer than the most inspired paradoxes.'

'They are the paradoxes of yesterday. Tried and tested.'

Silver laughed. 'My word, how the *mots* are flying today! Is that always what happens after danger? You must know.'

'Only if it's surmounted. Generally, it's too high a price.'

'You know, I didn't really mean what I said about the parasite,' said Silver conciliatingly. 'It's just a tinge of contempt – but mostly it's consuming envy. We're shop owners and gypsies by contrast. Which is fine by us. If only Arnold—'

I interrupted him. 'Mr Silver, it's a practice among riders and bicyclists, if they've come to grief, to remount, and do the course again right away before they start to shake. That's the way to avoid a shock or trauma. Starters' orders? Or do you want to wait?'

Silver looked outside. He was hesitant. Then he looked again at his shop across the road. Someone was standing in front of the window, then pushed open the door. 'A customer,' whispered Alexander. 'Hurry, Mr Sommer!'

We crossed the bustling avenue. Silver was himself again.

Once safely back on the pavement, we slowed our pace. If there were customers, we never crossed directly in front of the window, but at a twenty-pace slant. That gave Silver time to stroll in calmly and authoritatively. Usually he would be on his own; I would come in after, as a chance authority on this or that, should I be required.

Everything this time went very quickly. The customer was a man of about fifty, in a pair of gold-rimmed spectacles. He was interested in the prayer rug with the blue edging.

'Four hundred and fifty dollars,' declared Silver, now winged by the danger he had been through.

The customer smiled. 'For a mediocre semi-antique Ghiordes? A hundred.'

Silver shook his head. 'I'd rather give it away for nothing.'

'All right,' said the man, 'I'll take it.'

'But not to you,' replied Silver.

'The prayer niche has been reattached,' said the man. 'The upper edge has been reinforced. Even the colour has been enhanced by indigo dye in several places. It's a wreck. A floor cloth!'

I could see through the window how Silver was getting angry. He motioned to me to come in and help. I walked in. The broad back of the customer looked familiar to me from somewhere.

'By chance, Mr Sommer from the Louvre happens to be in New York,' said Silver. 'He is just casting his expert eye over our stock. Let him give you an expert opinion.'

The customer turned round and took off his glasses. 'Siegfried!' I said in surprise. 'How did you get here?'

'And you for that matter, Ludwig!'

'The gentlemen are acquainted?' asked Silver curiously.

'And how! We both studied under the same master.'

Siegfried Rosenthal placed his fingers covertly across his lips. I understood and didn't give away his name. 'I work for the carpet dealer Vidal in Cincinnati,' he said. 'We're interested in buying old rugs.'

'Semi-antique, with newly reattached prayer niche, freshly enhanced colours, in a word: wrecks – that kind of thing?' I offered.

Rosenthal smiled. 'A man does what he can. What's the real price?'

'For you, three hundred and seventy-five, if Mr Silver's agreeable.'

Rosenthal flinched as though a wasp had crawled under his collar. 'Four hundred,' said Silver.

'Cash payment,' I put in.

Rosenthal was looking like a dying St Bernard. 'A fine friend you are!'

'I'm fighting to get by,' I replied. 'Unfortunately in the same branch as you.'

'As an expert from the Louvre in Paris?'

'As a freelance tout, same as you.'

Rosenthal got the Ghiordes for three hundred and seventy-five.

'Can we have a drink somewhere?' he asked me. 'Surely this meeting asks to be solemnised in some way.'

He winked at me. 'Go with God,' said Silver. 'Friendship is a sacred thing. Even friendship with rivals.'

We recrossed the avenue, Rosenthal with the Ghiordes rolled up under his arm. 'What are you calling yourself these days?' I asked.

'Same name. Only Siegfried had to go. You can't sell rugs nowadays with a name like Siegfried. Where are we going?'

'A Czech café. They have slivovitz. And coffee, of course.'

Mizzi wasn't surprised when we walked in. We were the only customers. Rosenthal spread the Ghiordes on the floor. 'That singing blue!' he said. 'I've been looking at it in the window for days. Ludwig Sommer would have loved it.'

Mizzi brought the slivovitz. It was Yugoslav, left over from before the war. We drank silently. Neither of us wanted to bring up the past. Finally Rosenthal said, 'Well, go on, ask away. You knew Lina too.'

I shook my head. 'No, I just knew she was interned.'

'So you didn't know her? I'm all confused. Well, I was able to get her out. She was sick and the doctor was a sensible fellow. He sent her to hospital. She had cancer. After six weeks, the hospital doctor sent her home; not back to the camp. We had a little room together, where we had left our belongings. The landlady was embarrassed when we called to pick them up. Lina had some jewellery sewn into a petticoat. The petticoat and her dresses were gone. The landlady claimed someone must have stolen them. There was nothing we could do; we were grateful really to be able to move back into the attic. "Your wife won't be needing any more dresses," the landlady said, to comfort me, I suppose. Lina was doing worse and worse. Two weeks later I came back from work and I just caught Lina being bundled out of the house by three Gestapo men. She could barely walk. Someone had denounced her. She saw me on the street. Her eyes suddenly grew big and round. I've never seen anything like it: her eyes were screaming: run! Her head hardly moved. She had no lips left. I stood there, frozen. I couldn't move. I couldn't do anything. Not a thing. I was only good for clubbing to the ground or hauling off to a concentration camp. I was totally indecisive. Everything came to a stop. There were only Lina's eyes. My head felt like a stone. Run! screamed her eyes. The Gestapo men were nervous. They dragged Lina into a car. She bent her head back as she was pushed in. She looked at me. Her mouth was moving. She smiled. She had no lips, but she smiled. That was the last I saw of her. Her smile. By the time I could move again, it was all over. I can't understand it. Not even now.'

He had spoken in a low monotone. All at once there were drops of sweat on his brow. He wiped them away. There were more. 'Then the papers came,' he went on. 'A week later. Too late. Her relatives in Cincinnati. The bureaucracy. Wheels turning. All too slow. Too late. Lying there in the consulate for days. Can you understand that? I can't. Not even today. Everything too late! And that was what we had saved our money for. The crossing. Always the crossing. Hope. The doctors in America. I can't remember much about those times. I wanted to stay. I wanted to find Lina. I wanted to hand myself in. Suggest an exchange. I was mad. The landlady threw me out. I was endangering her by staying. I can't remember much more than that. Someone helped me out. I didn't understand. Do you understand it, Ludwig?'

I shook my head.

'You go by Sommer now,' said Rosenthal. 'I take it he must have died?'

I nodded. 'The worst time was the first few weeks,' said Rosenthal. 'The fact that Lina was so sick when those monsters arrested her. It made no sense.' He started rolling up the carpet. 'It was like a wall. Then came the other thing I couldn't understand. I thought she might suffer less, because she was suffering so much already, from the cancer. The way you don't feel a wound, because you already have one that's hurting you a lot. They say it's like that if you're shot more than once. Mad, isn't it? And finally I thought she might not have survived the transport and there'd be no opportunity for them to torture her. For a few days that thought consoled me. Can you understand that?'

'Perhaps they put her in hospital when they saw what she had?' I suggested.

'Do you believe that?'

'It's possible. Everything is possible. What's your first name now? I can't call you Siegfried any more.'

Rosenthal smiled grimly. 'Our optimistic parents and their names for us, eh? I go by Irwin now.' He laid the carpet on the sofa next to him. 'Lina had some relatives in Cincinnati. I'm working for them now. Carpet salesman.' He looked at me for a long time. 'I couldn't stay on my own. Can you understand? I was going crazy. Six months ago I remarried. Someone who doesn't know anything about any of this. Can you imagine? I can't. Sometimes when I come back from a road trip I ask myself: who is this strange woman and what does she want? Just for a split second when I get in. And she's friendly and quiet. I can't live alone. The walls would crush me. You understand?'

I nodded. 'Don't you think your wife senses something?'

'I don't know. I feel she doesn't. I have terrible dreams all the time. I see Lina's eyes. Black, screaming holes. What are they screaming now? That I left her? She's long dead. I know it. Those dreams! What are they for? Do you dream?'

'All the time.'

'What do they mean? Are they calling us?'

'No. It's you calling.'

'Do you think? And what does that mean? That I should never have remarried? Is it that?'

'No. You would have had the dreams anyway. Maybe even worse.'

'I sometimes think I've betrayed Lina by marrying again.

But I was too done in. It's different anyway. Different from the way it was with Lina, do you understand?'

'Poor woman,' I said.

'Who? Lina?'

'No. Your present wife.'

'She never complains. She's quiet. Forty. She's happy not to be alone too, I think. I don't know.' Rosenthal looked at me. 'Do you think I betrayed her? You think so many things at night. Those eyes! That face. All white, except the eyes. Screaming. Questioning. Or maybe they're not questioning? What do you think? There's no one I can talk about it with. It's only because I ran into you that I can ask you. Don't mind me. Tell me what you think.'

'I don't know,' I replied. 'I'm sure the one thing has got nothing to do with the other. But it happens anyway. Things get mixed up.'

Rosenthal knocked over his glass. He picked it up. There was an oily mess of slivovitz on the table. I thought about many of the things in my life at once. 'What do you think?' Rosenthal pressed me.

'I don't know. Nothing seems to help. You've lost Lina. You need to be careful you don't lose the woman who's living with you now.'

'Why? What do you mean? Why should I lose her? We never quarrel. Ever.'

I felt myself writhing under his stare. I didn't know what to say. 'A human being's still a human being,' I muttered finally. 'Even if you don't love them.' I hated myself for saying that. 'And maybe a woman can only be happy if she feels her husband is, to some degree,' I said and I hated myself some more, because of the banality and the cliché.

'What do you mean, happy? Who said anything about happiness?' asked Rosenthal, vexed.

I gave up. 'I'm glad you've got somebody,' I said.

'You reckon?'

'Yes.'

'And it's not betraying Lina?'

'No.'

'OK.'

Rosenthal stood up. Mizzi appeared. 'Let me pay,' he said. 'Please.' He paid and picked up the carpet under his arm. 'Can you get a cab here?'

'On the corner.'

We stepped out on to the street. 'Goodbye, Ludwig,' said Rosenthal, putting on his gold-rimmed spectacles. 'I don't know if I'm glad to have run into you again. Maybe. Yes, maybe. But I don't know if I want to see you again. You understand?'

I nodded. 'I don't think I'll be coming to Cincinnati.'

'Moikov is out,' said Maria Fiola.

'Did he leave the fridge unlocked?' I asked.

She nodded. 'But I haven't stolen any vodka yet. Not today.'

'I need some,' I said. 'Some genuine Russian vodka. Donated by an unknown female spy. There's still some left. For you and me.'

I opened Moikov's fridge. 'It's not there,' said Maria. 'I've already been to check.'

'Here it is.' I took out a bottle with a big label gummed to it: Warning – Castor Oil. 'There! The label was to keep Felix O'Brien away.'

I took a couple of glasses out of the icebox. They misted over right away in the warmth of the kitchen. 'Ice cold,' I declared. 'The way it's meant to be.'

'Cheers!' said Maria Fiola. 'Cheers! Nothing like it, is there.'

'I'm not so sure. Doesn't it have a slightly oily taste? Like castor oil, say?'

I looked at her in astonishment. What a susceptibility, I thought. God have mercy on my life ahead. 'No, it doesn't taste in the slightest oily,' I said.

'All right, so long as one of us knows,' she replied. 'Then not much can happen. What's in the big dish at the bottom?'

'Goulash,' I said. 'The lid is stuck down with Sellotape. Again, on account of the greedy Felix. I couldn't think of a plausible label that would keep him out. He eats everything, even if you label it rat poison. Hence the Sellotape.' I ripped it off and lifted the lid. 'Made by a Hungarian cook. A present from a sympathetic patron.'

Maria Fiola laughed. 'It seems to me you get a lot of presents. Is the cook pretty?'

'She probably weighs two hundred pounds. She's pretty in the way a carthorse is pretty. Have you had something to eat yet, Maria?'

A gleam came over her eye. 'What do you want me to say, Ludwig? You know models live on grapefruit juice and coffee. And rusks.'

'Right,' I said. 'So they're always hungry.'

'They're always hungry and can never eat what they want. But they can make exceptions. Like today. Goulash.'

'Damn!' I said. 'I don't have a cooker to reheat it. And I'm not sure if Moikov does either.'

'Can't you eat it cold?'

'Heaven forfend! You'd get tuberculosis and brain disease. But I've got a friend who has a whole electric arsenal at his disposal. I'll call him. He'll help us out. Here are some gherkins for now. Very good with a second glass of vodka.'

I unwrapped the gherkins and called Hirsch. 'Can you

lend me a cooker for my goulash, Robert? I want to heat it up.'

'Sure. What colour would you like?'

'What does the colour have to do with it?'

'What colour hair does the lucky lady have? I want to lend you the appropriate model.'

'I'm sharing it with Moikov, the lucky so-and-so,' I replied. 'I'm looking for a bald cooker.'

'Moikov was here only two minutes ago, with vodka. He's on his way to Brooklyn. But come on over anyway, you useless liar.'

I put the receiver down. 'We can have the cooker,' I said. 'I'll just go and get it. Do you want to wait here?'

'With whom? With Felix?'

I laughed. 'All right. Let's go together. Or shall we take a taxi?'

'Not on a lovely evening like this. I'm not that hungry.'

It was a warm, somnolent evening. The children sat on the stoops, tired after their day. The garbage cans stank just enough to remind one of grapes fermenting in vats for mediocre wine. Emilio seemed to have profited from a mass cremation. Standing among banked lilies and bananas, he brandished a white orchid at me. No doubt a strategic new purchase. 'Look at the sun reflecting in the windows,' I said and pointed across the road. 'Like old gold.'

She nodded. She didn't pay any attention to Emilio. 'I feel I'm walking on air,' she said. 'As if I weighed nothing.'

We got to Robert Hirsch's shop. I went in. 'Where's the cooker?'

'Do you mean to leave the lady waiting outside?' he asked. 'Why don't you bring her in? She's very beautiful. Are you worried?'

I looked round. Maria was standing outside, among the passers-by. It was the hour of the young mothers returning from the bridge table and the neighbourly gossip session. Maria stood in their midst like a young Amazon fetched up among the humdrum rational. The shop window between us seemed to take her away from me. I barely recognised her. But Hirsch was right.

'Robert, I was just coming to pick up an electric hotplate.'

'It's not quite ready yet. I used it an hour ago to heat up my own Tannenbaum-Smith goulash. I was expecting Carmen for supper. The minx is forty-five minutes late. And tonight is the big fight. Why don't you stay? There's enough to eat. And Carmen will be coming. I hope.'

I hesitated for a moment. Then I thought of the hotel lounge and the room of the dead emigrant Sahl and of Felix O'Brien. 'Super!' I said.

I went out to my remote Amazon, shimmering miles away in the silver and grey light of the shop window. Once I was standing next to her, she seemed closer and more familiar to me than she had ever done. What a strange effect of light and reflection and shade, I thought.

'We've been invited to supper,' I said. 'And to watch the boxing.'

'What about my goulash?'

'It's all ready and on the table.'

The Amazon looked at me in surprise. 'Here? Have you distributed pots of goulash all over the city?'

'Only at certain strategic points.'

I saw Carmen arriving. She was wearing a light raincoat and no hat, and she looked so utterly relaxed, it was as though there were no one else on the street at all. I didn't understand what she was doing in a raincoat. It was warm and the evening was clear; probably she had just forgotten.

'I'm running a bit late,' she said. 'But that doesn't matter with goulash. It tastes better warmed up anyway. Did you get some cherry strudel as well, Robert?'

'We have cherry, cheese and apple strudels. All arrived this morning from the inexhaustible Smith kitchens.'

'And vodka and dill pickles,' said Maria Fiola in surprise. 'Vodka from Moikov's distillery. What a comprehensive surprise.'

The eyes of the TV sets grew bright and empty, and the advertisements began. The fight was over. Hirsch seemed a bit tired. Carmen was asleep, relaxed and at peace. The boxing had taken it out of her.

'What did I tell you,' said Hirsch to me, both ravished and annoyed.

'Leave her be,' whispered Maria Fiola. 'I have to go now. Thank you so much, for everything. It's the first time in my life I've had enough to eat. A wonderful feeling. Good night.'

We went out on to the street. 'I'm sure he wants to be alone with his girlfriend,' she said.

'I'm not so sure. It's not that easy with him.'

'She's very beautiful. I like beautiful people. Even if sometimes they make me sad.'

'Why so?'

'Because it doesn't keep. Nothing keeps.'

'Some things do,' I replied. 'The wickedness of people. But wouldn't it be awful if everything stayed the way it was? The monotony of it. We'd miss the possibility of change. And hope.'

'And death,' said Maria Fiola. 'The incomprehensible. Aren't you afraid of it?'

I looked at her. What a sweetly naive question. 'I don't

know,' I said. 'Maybe not of death itself. But of dying, yes. I'm not even certain what I feel is fear. But I know I would try to fight it as hard as I could.'

'That's what I thought,' she said. 'I am terribly afraid of it. Of death and being old and alone. Aren't you?'

I shook my head. What a conversation, I thought. No one talks about death. That was a conversation for the nineteenth century, when death was still natural − not brought about by bombs and artillery and a political morality of destruction. 'I love your dress,' I said.

'It's a *tailleur* for the summer. By Mainbocher. Borrowed for the evening, to try it out. I have to take it back tomorrow.' Maria laughed. 'Borrowed, like everything else of mine.'

'Which only makes it the more charming. Who wants to be themselves all the time anyway? The world is open to the one who borrows.'

She threw me a dart of a look. 'And the one who steals too?'

'Less so. Because he wants to own. That narrows things down.'

'And we don't want that, do we?'

'No,' I said. 'Neither of us does.'

We reached Second Avenue. The homosexuals' parade was going full tilt. Poodles of every colour were squatting in the gutter, or cocking a leg. Gold bangles glittered on the wrists of their owners. 'Do you think you're less frightened if you don't care about anything?' asked Maria, avoiding a couple of yapping things.

'More, if anything,' I replied. 'Then you won't have anything but fear.'

'No hope?'

'Yes. Hope as well. As long as you breathe. It tends to outlive its owner.'

We got to her building. She stood in the doorway, looking fragile, delicate and, I had the sense somehow, invulnerable. The headlights of the cars washed over her face. 'You're not afraid, are you?' she asked.

'Not just now,' I replied and drew her to me.

In the hotel, I caught Felix in front of the fridge. I had come in very quietly and he hadn't heard me. He had the goulash tureen in front of him and a big serving spoon in one hand, and he was guzzling away. His mouth was smeared with gravy and he had a bottle of Budweiser open next to him.

'Bon appétit, Felix,' I said.

The spoon fell out of his hand. 'Goddamnit!' he said. 'That's just my luck.'

He launched into a passionate self-justification. 'Mr Sommer, the flesh is weak, especially at night and alone—'

I saw he hadn't touched the Russian vodka. The warning label had done its job. 'Carry on, Felix,' I said. 'There's cake as well. Have you finished the dill cucumbers already?'

He nodded. 'Fine, then why don't you just finish off everything?' I said.

Felix's watery eyes slid over the open fridge. 'I can't do that. But with your permission, I could take the rest back to my family. There's a lot left.'

'Whatever you want. But be sure to bring the dish back. It's not mine. And in one piece, mind.'

'Of course it'll be in one piece. You're a Christian, Mr Sommer. Even if you are a Jew.'

I went up to my room. Fear, I thought. There are so many kinds of fear. I thought of Rosenthal and his displaced notions of loyalty. At night he knew what his place was.

And he wasn't so alien to me either. At night everything was different. Different rules applied than in daytime.

I hung up Sommer's old suit in the wardrobe and emptied out the pockets. There I found the letter from the emigrant Sahl, which I hadn't posted – 'how could I have known they would put women and children into their camps! I wish I had stayed with you. I deeply regret it. Dearest Ruth, I dream of you every night. You're always crying—'

I put the letter down carefully. Downstairs the Negro who emptied the trash started to sing.

12

Whereas I had worked for Silver in the catacombs of his basement, Reginald Black stuck me up under the roof. I sat in the attic and had to catalogue everything that Black had ever bought or sold in his life, to provide the photographs with labels giving information about the names of the paintings, the identity of the buyers and sellers, and research their provenance. It was easy work. I sat in a bright and spacious penthouse with a terrace that afforded a view over the city. With all the photographs around me, I sometimes had the feeling I was still self-absorbed in Paris, on the Quai des Grands Augustins overlooking the Seine.

Black came up to visit me from time to time, in a waft of Knize aftershave and Havana. 'Your work is condemned to incompletion,' he said, stroking his Assyrian beard. 'Of course we are missing many of the photos that the dealers in Paris took when they bought the paintings from the painters. But not much longer. Have you heard that the Allies have broken through in Normandy?'

'No. I didn't listen to the radio today.'

Black nodded. 'France is open. The next objective is Paris.' I was alarmed, without quite knowing why. Then it came to me: it was the centuries-old Teutonic cry from Blücher and Bismarck to Wilhelm II and Hitler. Only now the boot was on the other foot: the objective was a Paris under occupation by the Gestapo and the German General Staff.

'Merciful God!' I exclaimed. 'What will the Germans do to the city before they have to give it up?'

'The same thing they did in Rome,' said Black. 'Give it up.'

I shook my head. 'They gave up Rome without torching it because the Pope lives there, the Pope with whom they had their lousy concordat. He was indirectly an ally of theirs. To protect the Catholics in Germany he allowed the Nazis to catch Jews under the Vatican walls. He never raised his voice in protest even though he knew more than any other human being about the crimes of the Nazis; knew more than most Germans. The Germans abandoned Rome because they would have had the German Catholics against them if they had laid waste to it. None of that applies in the case of Paris. France is the ancestral enemy.'

Reginald Black looked at me in concern. 'You mean you think they'll bomb it?'

'I don't know. They may be short of air power; or perhaps they would get shot down by the Americans before they could do it.'

'You mean, they would actually go and bomb the Louvre?' asked Black, appalled.

'If they bombed Paris, they would hardly be able to miss out the Louvre.'

'The Louvre? With all its irreplaceable treasures? There would be a global outcry!'

'The world didn't cry out when London was bombed, Mr Black.'

'But the Louvre! The Jeu de Paume with all those Impressionist masterpieces! Impossible!' Black was at a loss for words. 'God can't permit it to happen,' he whispered finally.

I didn't say anything. God had permitted all kinds of worse things to happen. All Reginald Black knew about those was what he had read in the papers. It was different if you had seen them with your own eyes. It was easy to learn from the paper that twenty thousand people had been killed; it generally remained a mild shock on paper. It was something else to see someone slowly tortured to death in front of you, without being able to help. A single person you loved – not twenty thousand.

'Why are we living if such a thing is possible?' said Black.

'To prevent it from happening again, if that's possible. I don't believe it is.'

'No? But then what do you believe?'

'What's impossible, Mr Black,' I said, to calm him down. I didn't want him to take me for an anarchist.

He smiled suddenly. 'You're right there. And now leave your work for a moment. I came up because I have something I wanted to show you. Come down.'

We went down to the studio where Black showed his pictures. I was feeling rather stunned; the news that Paris might become part of the theatre had aroused me. I loved France and thought of it as a kind of second home, in spite of everything that had befallen me there. That is, I hadn't fared much worse in France than I had in Belgium, Switzerland, Italy and Spain; but I had been able to collect other, livelier impressions, which had quickly become clarified in the past. France was more colourful, sadder and more heartbreaking than other places, which had been dominated by the monotony of being abroad and on the run. Admittedly, that had changed with the coming of the war. But even danger hadn't completely displaced my affection for the place.

'There,' said Reginald Black and pointed to a picture that was up on the easel.

It was a Monet. A meadow with poppies, and in the background a woman in a white dress with a parasol, walking along a narrow footpath. Sun, green, sky, white clouds, summer, the flickering poppies, and a distant, indistinct woman.

'What a picture!' I said. 'And what peace!'

We gazed in silence at the painting for a long time. Black took out his cigar case, opened it, looked inside and put it away. Then he went over to a black lacquered cigar box, which was artificially cooled and kept fresh by a moist sponge. He took out two cigars. 'For a painting like that, only a Romeo and Juliet will do!' he said solemnly.

We lit our Havanas. I was starting to get used to cigars. Black poured a couple of glasses of cognac. 'Peace,' he said, 'and a little luxury. That's no blasphemy. Both are possible.'

I nodded. The cognac was fabulous. It wasn't the ordinary cognac for customers, it was Black's private supply. He was clearly feeling very emotional.

'And that's the kind of thing they'll be shooting at now,' I said, pointing at the picture.

'It's the world as God planned it,' said Black a little loftily. 'Do you believe in God?'

'I haven't got there yet,' I replied. 'I mean, not in life. In art I do. For instance, right now I'm praying, crying with dry eyes and enjoying the sun of France in the guise of this cognac. All at the same time. If you live as I do, you have to be able to do many things at once, without caring about the contradictions involved.'

Black listened to me with head inclined to the side. 'I understand you,' he said. 'As an art dealer you have to be able to do that too. To love art and be able to part with it at the same time. Every dealer is a Jekyll and Hyde.'

'You're not going to sell this painting, are you?' I said.

He sighed. 'It's already sold. Last night.'

'That's a shame. Couldn't you cancel the sale?' I asked impulsively.

Black looked at me with an ironic smile. 'How would you do that?'

'Yes. How? Of course not.'

'It's worse,' said Black. 'It's been sold to an arms manufacturer. To a man who makes weapons to overcome the Nazis. He thinks of himself as a benefactor of mankind. The fact that his weapons will also devastate France is something he regrets, but there's nothing to be done about it. A very moral man. A pillar of society and a support of the church. He loves peaceful-looking paintings.'

'Ghastly. Why doesn't he love warlike paintings and produce cosmetics instead? The picture will freeze and cry for help.'

Black shot me an amused glance and poured more cognac. 'There's been a lot of crying for help in the last few years. No one listens. But if I'd known that Paris was threatened, I wouldn't have sold the painting yesterday.'

I looked doubtfully at my Jekyll and Hyde. 'I would have hung on to it for another couple of weeks,' he said, confirming my feeling. 'At least until Paris was liberated.'

'Cheers!' I said. 'One shouldn't go too far in humanity either.'

Black laughed. 'Many things are replaceable,' he said pensively. 'Even in art. But if I'd known yesterday what I know today, I would have charged the cannon king another five thousand dollars. That would have been fair.'

I didn't immediately see what fairness had to do with it, I just had a sense of it as part of some devious cosmic balancing act between Black and the world. I had no objection.

'I mean there are replacements in galleries,' Black went on. 'The Met has a very good collection of Monet, Manet, Cézanne, Degas and Toulouse-Lautrec. But you knew that?'

'I've never been,' I replied.

'Why not?' asked Black in astonishment.

'Pure prejudice. I don't like museums. They make me feel claustrophobic.'

'How extraordinary! In all those spacious, empty corridors? It's got the only breathable air in New York; clean, fresh and cool, on account of the pictures.'

Black got up and fetched a little flower painting from next door. 'Let me show you something else to console you.'

It was a small Manet. 'Not yet sold,' said Black, and took the Monet down and turned it round. Only the flowers were left on the easel and they filled the grey room like something ten times their size. You thought you could smell them and smell the coolness of the water in which they were standing. They emanated a delicious quiet and a still energy that was wholly productive: as though the painter had created these flowers, as though nothing like them had existed before.

'A pure world, eh?' said Black meditatively, after a while. 'As long as you can flee to it, nothing is absolutely lost. A world without crises and disappointments. You believe in eternity so long as you're in that world.'

I nodded. The paintings were marvels. Everything Black said about them was true. 'Are you selling them anyway?' I asked.

He sighed again. 'What else can I do? I have to live.' He aimed a little spotlight at the pictures, which lit them up sharply. 'But not to a weapons manufacturer,' he said. 'They don't go for small paintings. To a woman, if possible.

One of the rich widows of America. New York is crawling with them. The men work themselves to death; their wives inherit their fortunes.' He turned to me and smiled conspiratorially. 'If Paris is liberated, there'll be access to its treasures again. There are private collections there that make ours look silly. The people will need money. So will the art dealers.' Black rubbed his strikingly white hands together. 'I know of two further Manets in Paris like these here. They are already teetering.'

'How do you mean, teetering?'

'Their owner needs money. When Paris is freed—' Black lost himself in dreams.

That's the difference, I thought. He sees the city as liberated; for me it's coming under siege. Black turned the lamp off. 'That's the beautiful thing about art,' he said. 'It's endless. You can always surprise a new enthusiasm in yourself.'

And sell it on, I thought crudely. I could understand him; he was sincere and straightforward. He had overcome the primitive possessiveness of the child and the barbarian. He belonged to the oldest profession in the world: the trader. He bought and sold, and each time indulged in the luxury of believing that this time would be different and he wouldn't do it. He was a happy man, I thought without envy.

'Go to the museum,' he said. 'They've got everything you could dream of and more. So long as you don't want to lug it home with you it's yours. That's democracy for you. It's free. The greatest beauties in the world: free for all to see.'

I laughed. 'If you love something, don't you want to own it?'

Black shook his head. 'Only when you don't want to own it can it be entirely yours. There's a line from your Rilke: "Because I never tried to hold you, I hold you fast."

Something like that. It could be a motto for any art dealer.'
He laughed too. 'Or an excuse for their Janus nature.'

I went to Jessie Stein that afternoon. The twins doled out
coffee and cake; the gramophone played Tauber songs. Jessie
was in grey. She was in mourning for the devastation of
Normandy and at the same time quietly gleeful because
the Nazis were being pushed back. 'A schism,' she said. 'My
heart is divided. I didn't know it was possible to be grief-
stricken and jubilant at the same time.'

Robert Hirsch took her in his arms. 'Yes, you did,' he
countered. 'You always knew that, Jessie. Your indestructible
heart kept forgetting it.'

She leaned against him. 'You don't think I'm being
frivolous?'

'Not in the least, Jessie. It's tragic. And we had better look
on the bright side – because otherwise our abused hearts
won't be able to stand it.'

Koller, the compiler of the bloodlist, was sitting in a
corner under the pictures with mourning frames with one
Schletz, an author of comedies, rapt in conversation. They
had added two generals to the list; traitors who would be
shot as soon as the war was over. And they had started work
on a second list, this time of the new German government
in exile. They were terribly busy; every other day they were
adding a new minister, or else deposing an existing one.
Right now, they were arguing; they couldn't agree whether
Rosenberg and Hess should be put to death or just given
life imprisonment. Koller was in favour of death.

'Who's going to execute them?' asked Hirsch, who had
walked up.

Koller looked up unhappily. 'Mr Hirsch, please leave us
alone with your defeatist remarks.'

'I'd like to put myself at your disposal,' replied Hirsch. 'I'll take them all on. So long as you shoot the first one.'

'Who said anything about shooting?' retorted Koller. 'A soldier's death? They should be so lucky! The guillotine's too good for them, I say. The Nazi Minister of the Interior, Frick, decreed that so-called traitors were to be killed with an axe. That's been the mode of death in the land of thinkers and poets for the last ten years. The same should apply to the Nazis. Or are you in favour of giving them a pardon?'

Jessie came fluttering up like a concerned mother hen. 'Don't get into an argument, Robert. Dr Bosse has just arrived. He wants to see you.'

Hirsch laughed and allowed himself to be pulled away. 'Too bad,' said Koller. 'I was just going to—'

I had stayed put. 'What were you just going to do?' I asked, taking a step closer. 'You may as well tell me as my friend Hirsch. Probably you're better off telling me, in fact.'

'What's it got to do with you? Don't meddle with things that aren't your concern.'

I took another step in his direction and gave Koller a mild shove in the chest. He was standing in front of a chair and tumbled backwards into it. It really was a very gentle push and Koller only fell because the chair was directly behind him. He didn't get up; he stayed sprawled in the chair, hissing at me, 'What's it got to do with you? You – storm goy! – you Aryan!' He hissed the words like a grave insult.

I looked at him in surprise, waiting for more. 'Anything else?' I asked. I was expecting the word Nazi. It wouldn't have been the first time.

But Koller stayed shtum. I looked down at him. 'Would you hit a man sitting down?'

I was suddenly aware of the comedy of the situation. 'No,' I replied. 'I would pick you up first.'

One of the twins was going round with sponge cake. Black's cognac had given me an appetite and I helped myself. The other twin brought me a cup of coffee. 'You see,' I explained to Koller, who seemed to take it as an insult, 'I don't even have a hand free. Anyway, I have a policy of not fighting actors; it would be like fighting a mirror.'

I turned round to find Leo Bach next to me. 'I've made a discovery,' he whispered. 'About the twins. Both are Puritans. Neither is a tart. It cost me a suit. I had to send it away to be cleaned. Those beasts are minxes with their coffee pots. They even throw cups of milk at you if you pinch them. They're sadists.'

'Is that your dry-cleaned suit?'

'No. This is my dark suit. The other is grey. Much more sensitive.'

'You should donate it to a museum for scientific research,' I said.

The new arrival, Dr Bosse, was a slight little man with a modest goatee. He was sitting between Schindler, the stocking seller who had once been a scientist, and Lotz the musician, who was now selling washing machines and was being plied by Jessie with coffee and cake as though he had been on a starvation diet. He had left Germany on the eve of the war; much later than most of the others.

'I should have learned modern languages,' he said. 'Not Latin and Greek. English. Then I'd be doing better.'

'Nonsense!' retorted Jessie vigorously. 'You'll pick up English soon enough. And the reason you're not doing well is because that rotter of an emigrant cheated you. Be truthful.'

'Well, Jessie, there are more important things than that.'

'Cheated and robbed you,' declared Jessie, so agitated that

her frills were shaking. 'Bosse owned a valuable stamp collection. He gave the best pieces from it to a friend in Berlin who was able to leave the country. He was supposed to keep them safe for him until Bosse got out. Now he's claiming never to have got them.'

'Did they take them off him at the border?' asked Hirsch. 'That's usually the line these people take.'

'This rascal was cleverer. That would have meant admitting he had once had them and giving Bosse a certain, albeit weak, claim on restitution.'

'No, Jessie,' said Hirsch. 'It wouldn't. You don't have a receipt for them, do you?' he asked Bosse.

'Of course not. Impossible. They might have found it on me.'

'And the stamps on your friend,' said Hirsch.

'Quite. And the stamps on my friend.'

'You would presumably both have been put to death, or . . .? You or him? That's why you didn't have a receipt.'

Bosse nodded awkwardly. 'That's why I haven't done anything about it.'

'There was nothing you could do.'

'Robert!' exclaimed Jessie angrily. 'You're not making excuses for the fellow as well, are you?'

'How much were the stamps worth?' asked Hirsch. 'Roughly?'

'They were my best pieces. A dealer would probably have paid four or five thousand dollars for them.'

'A fortune!' spluttered the indignant Jessie 'And Bosse unable to pay for college.'

'You're right,' said Bosse apologetically to Hirsch. 'Still, better than if the Nazis had got their hands on them.'

Jessie looked at him in exasperation. 'Always the same: better this, better that! Why don't you damn the fellow to hell?'

'It wouldn't do any good, Jessie. And after all, he did take a risk when he agreed to smuggle the stamps out of the country.'

'You drive me wild! Always that understanding. What do you think a Nazi would do in your place? He'd club the wretched man to death.'

'Well, that's where we differ. We're not Nazis.'

'And what are we, then? Eternal victims?'

In her silver-grey frills, Jessie resembled an angry, puffed-up parrot. Hirsch rubbed her back tenderly. 'You're the last of the Maccabees, Jessie.'

'Don't laugh! I could burst.'

She heaped more cake on to Bosse's plate. 'At least eat something, if you can't get your own back.' Then she got up and shook her clothes.

'Go to Koller,' said Hirsch. 'He intends to massacre everyone when he returns. He's your avenging angel, Jessie. He's written it all down. I'm afraid he's put me down for a few years in prison.'

'Ach, that idiot! All he'll do is run to the nearest theatre where they're giving out parts.'

Bosse shook his head. 'Let him play his little games. That's the last illusion to go: that they'll welcome us back with joy and contrition for all the things they did to us. They don't want us back.'

'Not now. But when the Nazis are defeated,' said the stocking seller Professor Schindler.

Bosse looked at him. 'I saw what happened,' he replied. 'I spent six years listening to the cries of Nazi supporters. I saw films with the gaping howling muzzles of tens of thousands of them at Party rallies; I heard the bloodthirsty joy of dozens who pressed their ears to their wireless sets; I read the newspapers.' He turned to Schindler. 'And I also followed the enthusiastic response from the German intelligentsia to the regime – the response of the law, and industry, and science, Professor – every day for six years.'

'What about the conspirators of the twentieth of July?' asked Schindler.

'They were a minority. A hopeless minority. They were betrayed to the gallows by their own caste. Yes, there were decent Germans; but only ever a minority. Of three thousand university professors in 1914, two thousand nine hundred were in favour of war; just sixty were opposed. It's always been that way. Tolerance was always in the minority; likewise humanity. So let the ageing actor keep his dreams. He will have a horrible awakening one day. No one will want him.' Bosse looked around sadly. 'No one wants us. We are an inconvenient reproach, best avoided.'

No one replied.

I went back to the hotel. The afternoon at Jessie's had made me melancholy. I thought of Bosse, trying to build a new life for himself. He had left his wife in Germany in 1938. She wasn't Jewish. In the space of those five years the woman had become a nervous wreck. Every other week Bosse was hauled off to be interrogated. He and his wife had trembled every morning between the hours of four and seven; that was the time they usually came for him. The interrogations generally happened a day or several days after. In the intervening time Bosse was locked up in a cell with several other Jews. They sat together stewing in the cold sweat of fear. In the course of those hours they bonded into a strange fraternity. They whispered together, without listening to each other. They only listened to the outside – the outside was the sound of boots. They were a fraternity whose members tried to help each other with the little advice they could offer, and who in their hideous affection and revulsion almost hated each other, as though there were only a certain limited amount of hope for all of them and each one took from the chances of the others. Sometimes the elite of the German nation would drag one of them out with kicks and blows and abuse that fearless twenty-year-old warriors deemed necessary to drive on a helpless human being. Then no one in the cell would speak. They all waited. They stopped breathing, and avoided looking at one another. When, often hours later, a quivering bloodied bundle of flesh was deposited back on the floor of the cell, they straight away silently got to work. Bosse had been through it so many times that he instructed his wife to leave a couple of spare handkerchiefs in his suit pockets for the next time he was picked up; he would need them for bandaging. He didn't dare to pack actual bandages. They would have accused him of believing negative publicity and would have kept him in detention. Even bandaging people up in the cells was an action that demanded courage. People were sometimes battered to death for 'obstructing justice'. Bosse remembered the victims when they were lugged back. Often they could hardly move, but some whispered, with voices hoarse from screaming and wild eyes from where the last possibilities of communication had fled, so that they stared out of the hacked faces hot and shining, 'I was lucky – they didn't detain me!' 'Detain' meant being slowly kicked to death in the basement, or tortured in the concentration camp before being chased into the electric wires.

Bosse had always come back. He had had to hand over his practice to another doctor long before. His successor had offered him thirty thousand marks for it and paid just one thousand – it was valued at perhaps three hundred thousand. A Nazi officer, a Sturmführer, related to his successor had turned up one day and given Bosse the choice between concentration camp for continuing to practise medicine illegally, or take the thousand marks and write out a receipt for thirty thousand. Bosse knew what he had to do. He wrote out the receipt. Over those years his wife had gradually been driven mad. But she still refused to agree to a divorce. She thought she was the only thing that stood between Bosse and the concentration camp, because she was a non-Jew. She would only divorce him if he was allowed to leave the country. She wanted to know he was safe somewhere.

Then Bosse had a stroke of luck. The Sturmführer, who had by now become an Obersturmführer, came to see him one night. He was in civvies and after some initial hesitation came out with his request: he wanted Bosse to perform an abortion on his girlfriend, who was pregnant. He was married and his wife was no great admirer of the Nazi idea that it was necessary to bring as many children as possible into the world – even if they came from two or three reputable bloodlines. To her, her own bloodline was sufficient. Bosse refused. He sensed a trap. Cautiously, he suggested that his successor was a doctor as well and why did the Obersturmführer not turn to him; he was even a relation who – Bosse expressed this delicately – was under a certain obligation to him. The Obersturmführer was having none of it. 'The bastard won't do it,' he said. 'I put it to him discreetly. He gave me the whole Nazi spiel about genetic purity and all that crap. So much for gratitude! When it was me that got him his prac-tice.' Bosse found not a trace of irony in the eyes of the well-fed Obersturmführer. 'It's different with you,' said the man. 'With you, everything stays between ourselves. My brother-in-law, the fink, might leak under certain circum-stances. Or even blackmail me for the rest of his life.'

'You could blackmail him back for performing forbidden operations,' Bosse dared reply.

'I'm a soldier,' replied the Obersturmführer. 'I don't know about those things. With you, it's simple. We understand each other. You're not allowed to work and I'm not allowed to solicit an abortion, so where's the risk for either of us? The girl comes round here at night and in the morning she goes home. All right?'

'No!' said Mrs Bosse from the doorway. She had been eavesdropping out of apprehension – and overheard everything. She stood by the door like a disturbed spirit, holding on. Bosse jumped up. 'Let me speak,' said his wife. 'I heard everything. You're not doing anything. Not until you've got an exit permit. That's the price. Get him one,' she said, turning to the Obersturmführer. He attempted to tell her that he had no way of getting such a thing. She was implacable. She threatened to blackmail him herself; she would denounce him to his superiors. He laughed in her face. Who would believe her? It was his word against hers, the wife of a Jew. An Aryan like himself, she countered, and it was the first time in Bosse's hearing that she had used the ridiculous word. Anyway, it wasn't one person's word against another's – they were two against one. The girl was pregnant, that was a perfectly unambiguous state of affairs. Bosse stared at his wife; he had never seen her like this. She was shaking, but she held on. She even managed to convince the Obersturmführer. He offered her assurances; she wasn't having any. First the permission – then the abortion. The near-impossible happened. The Obersturmführer pulled some strings; then the woman agreed the divorce. Both things helped. In the chaotic bureaucracy of terror, there were unexpected, hidden oases. The girl came a fortnight later, one night. When it was all over the Obersturmführer told Bosse he had had another reason for choosing him; he had more confidence in a Jewish doctor than in his duffer of a brother-in-law. Right up until the end, Bosse was expecting a trap. The Obersturmführer gave him a fee of two hundred marks. Bosse gave it back. The Obersturmführer stuffed it in his pocket. 'Doctor, I know this will come in handy.' He loved the girl.

Bosse was so suspicious and eccentric that he didn't say goodbye to his wife. He hoped to bribe destiny like that. If he had said goodbye to her, he believed they would have gone after him. He made it. First France. Then Lisbon. Now he was sitting in a hospital in Philadelphia, regretting that he hadn't kissed his wife goodbye. He was a sensitive man and he couldn't get over it. He loved his wife dearly. He hadn't heard from her since. It was hardly possible for him to have done so; soon after he had left the war had begun.

There was a chauffeur-driven Rolls-Royce parked in front of the Hotel Rausch. It looked like a gold bar in a pile of ashes. 'Here comes the escort you want,' I heard Moikov say to someone in the lounge. 'I'm afraid I can't make it.'

Maria Fiola came out of the palm corner. She was wearing a riding costume and she looked very young. 'Is that your Roller outside?' I asked.

She laughed. 'Borrowed! We needed it for some sporting shots. Borrowed, like everything else of mine – the clothes I am photographed in and the jewellery I wear with them. Even this riding costume. You know I can't ride to save my life. Nothing about me is genuine.'

'Marie Antoinette's tiara is genuine enough. And so is the Rolls-Royce, it seems to me.'

'Fine. But they're none of them mine. I am an illusionist who works with real props. Is that better?'

'That's more dangerous,' I said, looking at her.

'She's looking for an escort,' said Moikov. 'She's only got the Rolls-Royce for this one evening. It has to be returned tomorrow. Wouldn't you like to glide through the world like a criminal for one evening?'

'I've been doing it for many years. But never in such style. That would indeed be new.'

'All right, then.'

In my mind, I checked over my funds. I had enough; even for the Rolls-Royce. I still had Silver's commission for the blue rug to come. 'Where shall we go?' I asked. 'What would you say to the Voisin?'

The Voisin was the only good restaurant I knew. The foie gras with Alexander Silver and his brother Arnold had been unforgettable.

'They wouldn't let me in to the Voisin at night in this monkey suit,' said Maria Fiola. 'Anyway, I've eaten already. The chauffeur too. The sports company laid on a buffet. What about you? Do you have any more deposits of the infinite goulash waiting for you anywhere in town?'

'No, just the remains of a chocolate cake. And a few gherkins and a piece of rye bread. Pathetic, really.'

'We could take the gherkins. And the bread too. There's a bottle of vodka on board.'

Moikov pricked up his ears. 'Russian?'

'I think so,' said Maria Fiola. 'Walk us over to the car, Vladimir Ivanovitch, and see for yourself. Take a big glass with you.'

We followed her. It was Russian vodka. Maria Fiola filled Moikov's glass. It was ice cold. The Rolls-Royce had a small fridge on board. Moikov took a reverent sip and rolled his eyes heavenward like a pigeon. 'I'm a humble moonshiner, compared to this.'

'The despair of the true artist, faced with the original,' I said. 'Learn from it, Vladimir. Don't give up. Your zubrovka is at least as good.'

'It's better,' declared Maria fondly. 'It has a secret too: it chases away the blues. Cheers, Vladimir Ivanovitch!'

We drove up Fifth Avenue to Central Park. It was very hot. From the zoo, we heard the evening roars of the lions. The ponds lay there as sheer as glass or lead. 'This suit is killing me,' said Maria Fiola. She lowered a blind in front of the window that separated us from the driver. The windows all had blinds as well and we quickly turned the car into a private room. Maria opened a bag. 'I need to get changed into something lighter. Just as well I brought my old dress along.'

She took off her jacket and the low brown riding shoes of soft leather. Then she started tugging at her jodhpurs. She didn't have much room, even though the car had very wide, comfortable seats. I couldn't do much to help her. I sat there quietly in the humming dusk with the green shadows of the park slowly going by and scented the perfume that spread as she undressed. She was completely unselfconscious; probably she was thinking I had already seen her almost naked while changing for the photographer. This was true, but there had been a lot of people and lights around then. Now we were pressed close together, it was warm and half-dark, and we were all alone.

'How brown you are,' I said.

She nodded. 'I never go completely white. I always find some sun to lie in somewhere. Either in California or Mexico or Florida. Somewhere is always warm enough to run away to. And we're always being sent off to those places for fashion shoots or shows.'

Her voice sounded lower than usual. I thought about women speaking differently when they were naked from when they were dressed. Maria Fiola stretched out her long legs and folded up her jodhpurs. She packed them into her bag and pulled out a white dress. She was very beautiful, slim, but not a bag of bones; what the French call '*fausse maigre*'. I desired her very much, but I didn't move. Consummations in cars weren't my thing. Anyway, the driver was still there as well.

Maria opened the window next to her without pulling up the blind. A breeze came up from one of the ponds and mingled with the perfume in the car. She took a deep breath. 'A moment more,' she said, 'and I'll get into my dress. The vodka's in the little fridge. And glasses too.'

'I think it's too hot for vodka,' I said. 'Even Russian vodka.'

She opened her eyes. 'I think there are little miniatures of champagne as well. The car is fully equipped. The man it belongs to is something to do with foreign affairs. Hence the vodka. There's a Russian embassy in Washington. And the Russians are our allies, of course. Can I have a gherkin?'

I peeled back the greaseproof paper and held out the parcel to her. She wasn't wearing a brassiere and I could see she didn't need one either. All she had on was a pair of silk panties. She seemed cool and very self-assured. 'Ah, lovely,' she said and took a bite out of a gherkin. 'And now just a little sip of vodka. Maybe a finger, not more.'

I found the glasses. They were of very delicate crystal. The man who owned the car had excellent taste. 'Won't you have one yourself?' asked Maria.

It didn't seem to me that the owner of the Rolls-Royce wanted me to help myself from his cellar on wheels. 'I'm becoming a parasite,' I said. 'Against my will, of course.'

She laughed. Her laughter too sounded darker than when

she laughed by day, clothed. 'Why not be it willingly, then? It's much nicer.'

'True.' I poured myself a glass. 'To you.'

'To you, Ludwig.'

Maria Fiola pulled her dress on and slipped into a pair of white sandals. Then she pulled up the blinds in the car. The late evening light flooded in. The sun was just going down. We were in the neighbourhood of the Metropolitan Museum. The red glow filled the car so dramatically that I felt alarmed. The museum, the heroic sunset – where had I seen such a thing before? I didn't want to admit to it, but I knew right away. The dark bulk outside the window, the overwhelming light, the unconscious men on the ground and the apathetic voice with the Bavarian accent: 'Carry on – next.'

I heard Maria Fiola say something, but I didn't take it in. A wave of memories pulsed through my brain like an electric saw. With a sudden jerk I was back there again. Mechanically I reached for my glass and drank. Maria Fiola again spoke. I nodded and looked at her. I still wasn't taking anything in. I looked straight ahead, disturbed. She seemed very remote from me. She made a move with her glass. I raised the bottle. She shook her head and laughed. Then all at once I could understand her again. 'Shall we get out here?' she was saying. 'This is Yorkville. Your people's part of town.'

'All right,' I said.

I was pleased to get out. Maria exchanged a few words with the driver. I took a look around and drew a few deep breaths. A wide avenue, buildings, sky and air. 'Where are we?' I asked.

'86th Street. In Germany.'

'In Germany?'

'In Yorkville. The German neighbourhood. Have you never been up here?'

'No.'

'Shall we go on?'

I shook my head. She was watching me from the side. I didn't know exactly why she had brought me here, but I was damned if I was going to ask. Not magnanimity for sure.

In spite of its breadth, the avenue reminded me straight away of a hateful German town centre. Cafés, beer joints and sausage shops lined the street. 'There's the Café Geiger,' said Maria. 'With its famous cakes. The Germans are great ones for cake, aren't they?'

'Sure,' I said. 'Cake and sausage. Just like the Italians are great macaroni eaters. You can't beat a nifty generalisation,' I added amiably. I didn't want to get tied up in one of our silly arguments. Not now.

We walked silently through the neighbourhood. It felt oppressive. It was as though I were seeing everything double in a weird way. I heard German spoken all around me and almost jumped out of my skin; I half expected to see the Gestapo lurking behind the shop doors, so strong was my double sense that sent me ricocheting between safety, hatred and fear, as if I were an unpractised tightrope walker without a net, walking between these businesses with their German names. The names hit me like blows. They were harmless, though not to me. For me they had a kind of double, sinister meaning, just like the people who walked around and looked so ordinary. I knew them in a different context.

'The Café Hindenburg,' announced Maria Fiola.

She walked at my side with her supple, rhythmic model's steps, desirable and shockingly unattainable. She seemed not to get the small-town atmosphere that almost choked me – the mixture of priggishness and airless *Gemütlichkeit* and unconditional, reflexive obedience that at any moment could turn to violence.

'It's so peaceful here,' said Maria.

I knew the peacefulness. In the concentration camps, geraniums were planted outside the death barracks and on Sundays the laager band struck up; while the convicts were whipped or slowly hanged. Not for nothing was it known about Himmler that he doted on the angora rabbits he bred. He never let one of them be slaughtered. Jewish children, though – another matter. By the thousand.

I felt a little quivering in my veins. In that moment I could no longer imagine ever returning to Germany. I knew that that was my plan; but that was as far as it went. It wasn't the whole story either. I wanted to go back to look for the murderers of my father; not to go back there to live. At that moment I felt I no longer could. There would always be that double vision – the harmless small-town citizen and the obedient killer. I would never be able to prise them apart. I didn't want to. The doubleness had appeared too often. There was a sheer black wall I couldn't scale. There were the murders that had broken my life apart. I couldn't even think of them without feeling wound-up for days. Nothing could happen before they were repaid. Repaid, mind, not avenged. Expunged by the life of the murderer.

I had almost forgotten Maria Fiola. Now I saw her again. She was standing outside a shoe shop, studying the display, leaning forward like a huntsman over his rifle and so engrossed that it seemed she had forgotten me as well. A wave of warmth rose in me – just because we were so different and knew nothing of the other. It made her invulnerable and precious, and gave her an intimate joyfulness that would never be coarsened into stodgy familiarity. It made her secure and me secure as well, because our lives could proceed side by side without being tied together. There might even be room for a little crystalline joy – without becoming betrayal or interfering with the past.

'Did you see anything?' I asked.

She looked up. 'All too heavy,' she replied. 'Too solid for me. What about you?'

'Nothing,' I said. 'Nothing at all!'

She looked at me carefully. 'We shouldn't try and go back, then, should we?'

'You can't go back,' I said.

She laughed. 'That gives you a certain freedom, don't you think? Just like the birds in the fairy story that had only wings and no feet.'

I nodded. 'Why did you bring me here?'

'Just chance,' she said lightly. 'You wanted to get out too, don't forget.'

Perhaps it was chance, I thought; but I didn't believe in those chances. It was too obvious to compare the peace of this Nazi citadel with the devastation wrought in Maria's Florence. Each of us had hidden resentments only waiting to emerge. But I didn't say anything; as long as she didn't speak, an answer was just an unnecessary provocation and a waste of breath.

We came to a café that was jammed full. Oom-pah-pah music boomed out. German folk songs. I stared inside. I thought, any one of those individuals, stuffing themselves on whipped cream and Frankfurter ring cake with shining eyes, could be transformed into a werewolf in a death squad obeying orders. The fact that they were living in America hardly toned that down. If anything, it intensified their patriotism.

'The Americans are very generous,' I said. 'They're not locking anyone up.'

'Not quite,' replied Maria. 'They're locking up Japanese in California. And German emigrants have to be at home by eight at night, and they're not allowed to travel more than eight miles. I've been there.' She laughed. 'It always gets the wrong ones.'

'That's right.'

Brass band music was coming from a big bar. German marching tunes. Blood sausages hung in the windows. I expected to hear the Horst Wessel Song any moment.

'I've had enough,' I said.

'Me too,' replied Maria. 'The shoes all seem to be made for marching, not dancing.'

'Shall we go back?'

'Let's go back to America,' said Maria.

We were sitting in a restaurant in Central Park. There was parkland spread out ahead of us, a cool breeze blew over the water and we could hear the sound of oars splashing in the distance. Evening came on and the blue shadows of night were already hanging between the trees. It was quiet.

'You're so brown,' I said to Maria.

'You said that before, in the car.'

'That was a hundred years ago. I've been to Germany and back in the meantime. You're so brown. And the sheen of your hair in this light! It's an Italian light. The evening light of Fiesole.'

'Have you been there?'

'I've been close. In prison in Florence. But the light was the same.'

'What were you in prison for?'

'I didn't have papers. But I was thrown out and had to

leave the country. And I know the light from Italian paint-ings. It's mysterious; a light assembled from luminous, colourful shadows. Like your hair now, and your face.'

'My hair is dull and frowzy when I'm unhappy,' said Maria. 'And my skin suffers too, when I'm alone. I don't like to be alone for long. I'm nothing when I'm alone. Just a collection of poor qualities.'

The waiter brought us a bottle of Chilean white. I felt as though I'd escaped from a great danger. Disturbed fear, disturbed hate and disturbed despair were once more settling inside me, where I had tried to banish them at a time when they could have destroyed me. They had brushed me in Yorkville with the red mouths of memory, but I felt as though I had just got away. Now I felt a deep peace, of a kind I hadn't felt for a long time, and I felt there was nothing more important than the birds hopping about on our table, pecking for crumbs, the pale wine and the face in front of me looming out of the shade. I took a deep breath. 'I got away,' I said.

'Cheers!' said Maria Fiola. 'So did I.'

I didn't ask what she had got away from. It was bound to be something different from what I had in mind. 'I once saw a one-act play in the Grand Guignol in Paris,' I said. 'Two people in the basket of a balloon. A man staring down with a telescope. Suddenly there's a deafening pop. The man puts down his telescope and turns to his companion: "It's just blown up," he said, "the earth. What do we do now?"'

'That's a good beginning,' said Maria. 'How did it end?'

'As ever in Grand Guignol, with a catastrophe. But it doesn't have to be that way.'

Maria laughed. 'Two people in a balloon. Without a planet to call home. What can happen if you hate loneliness and think happiness is a mirror? An endless mirror reflecting itself. Cheers, Ludwig! It's nice to be free, so long as you're not alone. Is that a contradiction?'

'No. That's a cautious happiness.'

'That doesn't sound good, does it?'

'No,' I said. 'But you're safe enough.'

She looked at me. 'Where do you want to live when everything's over and you can go anywhere?'

I thought about it for a long time. 'I don't know,' I said at last. 'I really don't know.'

13

'What kept you?' asked Reginald Black.

I pointed to the clock. It was ten past nine. 'Lawyers don't open before nine,' I said. 'I had a bill to pay.'

'The convenient way to pay a bill is with a cheque.'

'I don't have a bank account yet,' I replied. 'Only bills.'

Black surprised me. This wasn't the man of the world with the casual manners. He was tense today, nervous, and reluctant to show it; even his face looked different. His slightly puffy softness was gone; even his beard had changed – not Assyrian, more Levantine. A tiger going after prey.

'We don't have much time,' he said. 'We need to rehang some pictures. Come on!'

We went to the room with the two easels. From the adjacent room, behind a steel door, he brought out two paintings and set them up. 'Tell me without thinking which of them you would buy. Now!'

They were a couple of Degas; both dancers. Both unframed. 'Which one?' asked Black. 'You've got to take one. Which?'

I pointed to the one on the left. 'I like this one better.'

'That's not what I wanted to know. Which one would you buy if you were a millionaire?'

'Same. The one on the left.'

'Which one do you think is more valuable?'

'Probably the other one. It's more developed, less sketchy. But you don't need me to tell you that, Mr Black.'

'Not in this case. I am interested in the naive, spontaneous judgement of a man who doesn't know an awful lot. A client, I mean,' he added, seeing my look. 'Don't be offended. I know the value of the paintings; the unknown quality is always the customer. Do you understand?'

'Is that part of my job now?' I asked.

Black laughed and in that moment he was the dangerous, not quite trustworthy charmer he had been previously. 'Why don't you show the client both pictures?' I suggested.

Black gave me an amused look. 'That would be a disaster,' he said. 'He would never be able to decide and would end up not buying anything. You show the client at most three or four pictures and never more than one by the same master. Different artists. If he can't decide, you let him go, and you certainly don't panic and show him everything you have. You wait for him to come back to you. That's a hallmark of the genuine art dealer; the ability to wait. Then, when the client comes again, you tell him that two of the pictures he looked at last time have been sold; even if they are still there. Or that they have been lent to an important exhibition. After that you show him two or three of the original pictures again – plus two or three or at the most four others. You claim that a picture has been sent out on approval. That stirs up interest as well. Nothing is a stronger inducement than the thought of buying something from under someone else's nose. The whole thing is to get the client's juices going.' Reginald Black blew out a cloud of smoke. 'As you see, I hadn't the least intention of causing you any offence; I just want to train you to be a good art dealer. Now, let's frame the pictures. Law number two: never show a client an unframed picture.'

We went to another room, where frames of all sizes were hanging. 'Not even a museum director,' added Black. 'Maybe – maybe – another dealer. Pictures need frames, just like women need dresses. Even Van Gogh dreamed of expensive frames. He could never afford any, of course. He never sold a picture. Which frame would you choose for the Degas?'

'Maybe this one?'

Black looked at me approvingly. 'Not bad. But we won't take that one.' He pushed the dancer into a heavy, ornate Baroque frame. 'Well?' he asked.

'A bit pompous for a picture that's not even finished.' Both pictures carried the red stamp of the Atelier Degas. They weren't signed; they came from the estate.

'Precisely,' replied Black. 'The frame can't be too ornate, precisely because the picture is a bit sketchy.'

'I understand. The frame covers.'

'I'd say it lifts. It's so utterly finished that the picture seems more finished.'

Black was right. The precious frame changed the picture. Suddenly, it shone. It was a little glitzy, but that was the point. It shone. Its perspectives didn't recede into infinity – they were held in the frame's rectangle and so acquired purpose. What had appeared to go off into space was instantly collected. Chance detail became essential; even the bare places that hadn't been touched seemed to belong.

'There are dealers who economise on frames. They're little better than dime stores, if you ask me. They think the client won't notice if they get out a pressed plaster gilt monstrosity. Well, he may not right away, or not directly – but the picture will look all the worse for it. Pictures are aristocrats,' said Black.

He looked for a frame for the second Degas. 'You're not

going to break your rule and show two pictures by the same artist after all, are you?' I asked.

Black smiled. 'No, but I want to have the second picture in reserve. You never know what will happen. You shouldn't be too rigid with your principles, anyway. What do you think of this frame? It fits. Louis XV. A beauty, isn't it? It puts five thousand dollars on the price right away.'

'How much is a Louis XV frame?'

'Nowadays? Between five and seven hundred dollars. It's all the fault of the bloody war. It's impossible to get anything.' I looked at Black.

The pictures were framed. 'Put the first one in the side cabinet,' said Black. 'And I want the other one in my wife's bedroom.'

I looked up in surprise. 'That's right,' he repeated. 'My wife's bedroom. Come along, I'll go with you.'

Mrs Black had a pretty and very feminine bedroom. A few drawings and pastels were hanging among the furnishings. Black surveyed them with his field marshal's eye. 'Take down the Renoir drawing over there and put up the Degas. Then move the Renoir over there above the dressing table, and take down the Berthe Morisot drawing altogether. Close the right-hand curtain a little. A bit more – there, that's a good light.'

He was right. The gold of the half-drawn curtain gave the picture sweetness and warmth. 'A battle plan is half the sale,' said Black. 'The client doesn't really want to catch us out in sober morning light, when pictures just look cheap. We're ready for him.'

He gave me further tips on dealer strategy. I was to bring out the pictures he wanted to show into the easel room one at a time. After the fourth or fifth picture, he would tell me to get the second Degas out of the cabinet. Then I was to remind him that the picture was up in Mrs Black's bedroom. 'You can use all the French you like,' he said. 'But when I ask you for that picture, I want you to reply in English, so that the client understands.'

I heard the doorbell. 'That's him,' said Black cheerfully. 'Wait here till I ring for you.'

I went into the cabinet, where the pictures were perched on their wooden stands, and sat down on a chair. Black hurried light-footedly downstairs to let his guest in. The cabinet had one little window with glass bricks and stout bars. It gave me the feeling of sitting in a prison cell, where for a change a few hundred thousand dollars' worth of pictures were housed. The milky light reminded me of the cell I had occupied for two weeks in Switzerland for being in the country without documents – the standard emigrant crime. The cell was just as clean and tidy, and I wouldn't have minded staying there longer – the food was good and the cell was heated – but after two weeks I was taken out to Annemasse on the French frontier, given a cigarette and a friendly clout on the shoulders: 'There's France, off you go! And don't show your face here again.'

I must have dropped off. All of a sudden I heard the bell. I went in to Mr Black. A heavyset man with big red ears and little eyes was with him. 'Ah, Monsieur Sommer,' warbled Black. 'Would you kindly bring us the bright Sisley landscape.'

I brought in the landscape and set it down. For a long time Black didn't say anything, just watched the clouds beyond the window. 'What d'you think?' he drawled. 'A Sisley from his best period. A flood scene – just what everyone wants.'

'Bullshit,' said the client, sounding even more bored than Black.

Black smiled. 'Well, it's a point of view,' he observed sarcastically. 'Monsieur Sommer' – he turned to me again. 'Perhaps you'd take this magnificent Sisley out.'

I waited for a moment for Black to tell me what he wanted brought in next, but seeing as no instruction followed, I took the Sisley out and just caught Black saying: 'You're not in the mood, Mr Cooper. We can do it some other time.'

Pretty canny, I thought, in my milky closet, he's putting the onus on Cooper. When I was called in again some time later, they were smoking a pair of Black's customer cigars, Partagas, I established, as I brought in the other pictures one by one. Then I heard my cue being given, and said, 'The Degas isn't here, Mr Black.'

'But of course it's here, no one's stolen it.'

I approached him, half leaned down to him and stage-whispered in his ear, 'The picture's upstairs – in Mrs Black's room—'

'Where?'

I repeated in English that the picture was in Mrs Black's bedroom.

Black smote his temple. 'Of course it is. I forgot. Our wedding anniversary – well, that takes care of that, I suppose—'

I admired him extremely. Once again he was putting the ball in Cooper's court. He didn't tell me to go and get the picture anyway; nor did he claim the picture was his wife's. He just broached the subject and waited.

I wandered back to my cubbyhole and waited likewise. It seemed to me that Black had hooked a shark and was playing him. It was possible the shark would eat Black, but it seemed to me that Black's position was stronger. Really, all the shark could do was bite through the line and swim off; it was impossible that Black would sell for too low a price. The shark made some interesting moves, though. As my door was open a crack, I heard the conversation turn to economic questions and the war. The shark was a gloom merchant: another Wall Street crash, debts, new state expenses, new battles, crises, even the looming prospect of Communism. Everything was going to tank. Cash was the only thing that would keep its value. He recalled the grave crisis after 1929. Whoever had cash then could buy anything he wanted for half-price – what was he saying, a third, a quarter, a tenth. Pictures too. Pictures most of all. Pensively the shark added, 'Luxury goods like furniture, carpets and pictures for as little as a fiftieth of what they had once commanded.'

Unmoved, Black offered him some first-rate cognac. 'After that, everything started to climb back up,' he said. 'And money went down. You know yourself the dollar is worth half what it was then. It hasn't risen since – and pictures have gone up many times over.' He laughed a quiet, artificial laugh. 'Inflation, eh! It began two thousand years ago and it's just kept on going. Goods get more expensive and money loses – that's the way it is.'

'That's why you should never sell anything,' retorted the shark with a merry shout of laughter.

'If that were possible,' said Black calmly. 'I sell as little as I can anyway. But there are taxes. And you need capital to keep the business turning over. Ask my clients. They think of me as their personal Santa Claus. I lately bought back a Degas dancer I sold five years ago – for twice the price.'

'Who from?' asked the shark.

'I couldn't possibly tell you that. Do you really think I broadcast the prices you pay? Or get back from me?'

'Why not?' The shark wasn't falling for the bluff.

'Well, some people don't like it. I have to respect their

feelings.' Black made a move to get up. 'I'm sorry you haven't found anything to suit you, Mr Cooper. Maybe another time. Though my prices may have changed by then, you know how it is.'

The shark got up as well. 'Didn't you have a Degas you wanted to show me?' he asked casually.

'Oh, you mean the one in my wife's bedroom?' Black hesitated. Then I heard the bell. 'Is my wife in her room?'

'She went out half an hour ago.'

'Then why don't you bring down the Degas that's hanging beside the mirror.'

'It will take a minute, Mr Black,' I explained. 'I had to insert a dowel peg because the plaster's a little loose. The picture is screwed to the wall. I'll only be a couple of minutes.'

'Oh, never mind,' replied Black. 'We'll just go up and take a look. What do you say, Mr Cooper?'

'Sure.'

I squatted back down like Fafner among the treasures of the Rheingold. After some time the two of them came back, and I was sent upstairs to unscrew the picture and bring it down. Since there was nothing to unscrew, I just stood there for a minute or two. Through the window on to the yard I saw Mrs Black at the kitchen window opposite. She made a questioning gesture. I shook my head vehemently; no, the coast was not yet clear; Mrs Black should remain in the kitchen.

I carried the picture down to the grey velvet viewing room and left. I could hear nothing now of what was said; Black had closed the communicating door. I would have liked to hear the subtlety with which he gave it to be understood that the picture was a present for his wife on their tenth wedding anniversary and that she was very attached to it; but I was sure he would do it in such a way that the shark wouldn't smell a rat.

It took about another half-hour; then Black himself came in and relieved me from my luxury prison. 'There's no need to rehang the Degas,' he said. 'Just take it round to Mr Cooper tomorrow.'

'Congratulations.'

He made a face. 'Absurd trouble. When I know perfectly well that in two years' time the fellow will be gloating because prices will have gone up so much.'

I repeated Cooper's question: 'Why do you sell, really?'

'Because I am addicted. The trade fascinates me. I'm a gambler. Even though there's no one around these days to take on. Basically I'm playing against myself. By the way, your little idea with the dowel – not bad. You're coming along.'

In the evening I went to Jessie Stein's. I found her with tear-stained eyes and very upset. Some of her friends were there, comforting her. 'I can come back tomorrow if today's difficult,' I said. 'I really just wanted to thank you.'

'What for?'

Jessie looked at me with sad eyes. 'For talking to my lawyer,' I said. 'And for sending Brandt along too. My permission to stay has been extended by two months.'

She burst out crying. 'What's happened?' I asked the actor Rabinovitz, who had his arm round Jessie and was comforting her quietly.

'Don't you know?' whispered Lipschitz. 'Teller is dead. It happened the day before yesterday.'

Rabinovitz motioned to me not to ask any more questions. He sat Jessie down on a sofa and came back. He played vicious Nazis in little 'B' films; in fact, he was a very gentle man. 'Teller hanged himself,' he said. 'Lipschitz found him. He must have been dead for two or three days already. It was in his room. He was hanging from the chandelier. All the lights were on, the chandelier as well. Perhaps he didn't want to die all alone, in the dark. He must have hanged himself at night.'

I made to go. 'Stay,' said Rabinovitz. 'The more people are around, the better for Jessie. She mustn't be left alone.'

The air in the room was humid and stale. Jessie didn't want to open a window; from some enigmatic, archaic belief she thought the dead would suffer if the survivors' grief were allowed to be dispelled in the fresh air. Once, many years ago, I had heard about people opening the windows when there was a dead body in the house, to free the soul wandering about the rooms; but never about them being shut to shelter grief, while the dead man was already with the undertakers.

'I'm a silly old cow,' said Jessie and she vigorously blew her nose. 'I should pull myself together.' She got up. 'I'm going to make coffee for everyone. Or do you want something else?'

'Nothing, Jessie, really. Nothing.'

'Yes, I'm going to make coffee.'

She bustled off into the kitchen in her rumpled dress. 'Does anyone know of a motive?' I asked Rabinovitz.

'Does there have to be a motive?'

I remembered Hirsch's theory about life being layered like slate and how the rootless individual was particularly vulnerable to several layers being ruptured at once. 'No,' I said.

'He wasn't completely impoverished; it won't have been that. He wasn't sick either; Lipschitz saw him maybe two weeks ago.'

'Could he do his work?'

'He was writing all the time. But of course he couldn't publish anything. He hasn't published anything for ten years,' said Lipschitz. 'But there are a lot like that. It can't have been just that.'

'Did he leave something? A note?'

'Nothing. He was hanging there from the chandelier with the blue face and the swollen tongue, and flies were crawling over his open eyes. He looked ghastly. It happens so quickly in the warm weather. The eyes—' Lipschitz shuddered. 'The worst thing of all is that Jessie wants to see him to say goodbye.'

'Where is he now?'

'With the undertakers – they call them morticians here. My God! Morticians! That's where they spruce up the dead. Have you ever been to one of those places? Don't go. The Americans are a young people; they can't cope with death. The deceased are made up to look as if they were just sleeping. Many are embalmed.'

'If they make him up, Jessie will be able to—' I said.

'That's what we thought too; but there's nothing left to cover with Teller. There can't be that much slap in the world. And it's expensive too. Dying in America is very expensive.'

'Not just in America,' threw in Lipschitz.

'And not at all in Germany,' I added.

'It's very expensive in America. We went to a very modest firm of undertakers. Even so, the cost will run to several hundred dollars at a minimum.'

'If Teller had had that much, he might still be with us,' suggested Lipschitz.

'Maybe.'

I saw that the arrangement of photographs in Jessie's

room had already been changed. Teller's picture was no longer among the living. It didn't have a black frame like the other dead on the opposite side, it was still in its old gold, but Jessie had looped a piece of black tulle over it. There was Teller, smiling and fifteen years younger. It was a youthful portrait, bland in its black tulle surrounds. But there was real pain and loss.

Jessie came in with cups on a tray and poured from a flowered coffee pot. 'There's sugar and cream too,' she said.

Everyone drank. I as well. 'The service is tomorrow,' she said to me. 'Will you come?'

'If I can.'

'All his friends must come,' Jessie replied, shrill and excited. 'Tomorrow at half-past twelve. We've timed it specially so that everyone can make it.'

'I'll come, Jessie. Of course I will. Where is it?' Lipschitz told me the place. 'Asher's Funeral Home on Fourteenth Street.'

'Where is he being buried?' asked Rabinovitz.

'He's not being buried. He's being incinerated. The crematorium is cheaper.'

'What?' I asked.

'He's being burned.'

'Burned?' I repeated and several things went through my mind at once.

'The Funeral Home is organising it.'

Jessie stepped up. 'There he lies now alone, among complete strangers,' she lamented. 'If only he could have been laid out among friends till it was time for the funeral.' She turned to me. 'What else did you want to know? Who put up the money for you? Tannenbaum.'

'Tannenbaum-Smith?'

257

'Yes of course. He's our capitalist. He's paying for Teller's funeral as well. So will you be sure to come tomorrow?'

'Of course,' I said. There was nothing else to say.

Rabinovitz walked me to the door. 'We're having to trick Jessie,' he whispered. 'She can't possibly see Teller. Not in the shape he's in. Because it was suicide, there was an autopsy. Jessie doesn't know any of that. And you know how she expects always to have her way. It was lucky she made coffee. Lipschitz put a sleeping pill in her cup. She didn't notice anything, that's why we all drank her coffee and praised it. Jessie can't resist praise; left to herself she wouldn't have drunk it. We offered her a sedative. She won't take anything like that; she thinks it would be betraying Teller. Just like opening the windows would have been. Perhaps we'll manage to smuggle another tablet into her food tonight. The crisis will be tomorrow morning. Will you come?'

'Yes. The funeral home. How will Teller get to the crematorium? Is it at the funeral home?'

'I don't believe so. But the funeral home will make the arrangements. Why?'

'What are you saying there for such a long time?' called Jessie from the room.

'She's getting suspicious,' whispered Rabinovitz. 'Good night.'

'Good night.'

He went back along the half-dark corridor, lined with photos from the Romanisches Café in Berlin, into the stifling drawing room. I went out on to the street, whose usual chaotic noise felt vaguely soothing. Crematoria, I thought. There's no getting away from them.

I sat up in bed with a jolt. I wasn't immediately sure I had been dreaming, but I switched the light on to dispel the

dream. It wasn't one of the usual emigrant dreams that I
had so many of – being chased by the SS because you had
foolishly crossed the border and now the murderers were
on your trail. You often awoke screaming out of those dreams;
but they were normal. It was your own stupid fault for
winding up in their toils again. Then you had to stretch,
look out of the window into the reddish city night and
you knew everything was more or less OK.

This dream was different, put together from incoherent,
unspecifiable pieces, tough, glutinous, dark like pitch, without
beginning or end. Sibylle was in it, silently crying for help.
I was trying to get to her, but my knees repeatedly gave
way in the thick morass of tar, swamp and old blood. I
could see her eyeing me in terror, silently screaming: Run!
Run! and then: Help! I stared into the black hollow of the
screaming mouth, with the sticky mass rising towards it, and
then it wasn't Sibylle any more, it was the wife of Siegfried
Rosenthal, a sharp voice with an unendurable Bavarian
accent was issuing commands, there was a form silhouetted
against a mighty red sunset, pale smell of blood, flames from
a chimney and the sweetish reek of burnt flesh, a hand on
the ground moving very slowly, someone stamping on it,
then a scream that seemed to come from every direction
and that was still resounding.

I hadn't had many dreams in Europe. I had been far too
concerned with survival. If you're in danger you don't have
the leisure to reflect on it. Dreams are sapping; so the primitive survival instinct suppresses them. Then the sea had
interposed itself between me and my memories, and I
thought its constant murmur would keep me hidden from
them, like the dark ship that slipped past the lurking U-boats.
I had the usual refugee dreams that everyone had – but
now I knew that I hadn't escaped from anything, however

hard I tried, so as not to fall to pieces before I could avenge myself. I couldn't control my dreams, my memories had leached into the spectral world of sleep that unfurled new laws and conditions every night, and broke apart before the day. These dreams, though, refused to break apart.

I stared out of the window. The moon had climbed up above the roofs. Somewhere a cat yowled. There was a rustling among the garbage cans in the yard. A window opposite flared and straight away went out. I was afraid to go back to sleep. I didn't want to call Robert; it was too late for that and he couldn't help me either. I had to deal with it myself.

I got up and dressed. I thought I might wander around the city until I was exhausted. But even that would have been just an escape. I had done it often before, and in the unconscious effort to try and find support, something to lean on and forget with, thoroughly over-romanticised it. As though shining skyscrapers were not built on a dark ground of greed, crime, exploitation and egoism, and as though miserable slums formed no part of it. I had built up my cult of the city by night as a counterweight to the bloody years of the European past that I wanted to disperse. It wasn't true, I knew that – crime was at home in these Parsifal castles as much as it was at home anywhere else.

I went downstairs. Moikov had to be around. I wanted to cadge a couple of sleeping pills off him. However much I wanted to cope with my problems by myself – in this acute case it would have been absurd to scorn the chemical recipes of the time.

The plush lounge was still dimly lit. 'Vodka or seconal?' asked Moikov, who was closeted with the Contessa behind the palms. 'Or company? To shake at the pillar of existence? At our ur-fears.'

The Contessa had come down in her scarves. 'If only one knew,' she said. 'I think it's company first, then vodka, then seconal, then all of them – and finally I run around like a headless chicken and don't know any more.'

Moikov opened his parroty eyes. 'And then we begin again,' he replied. 'Everything goes around in circles, Contessa.'

'Do you believe that? And is it the same with money as well?'

There was a bell in reception. 'That'll be Raoul,' sighed Moikov. 'It's a restless night.'

He got up to answer it. The Contessa looked at me with her bird face, where the eyes flashed like sapphires on crumpled silk. 'Money doesn't come round again,' she whispered. 'It runs and runs away. I hope I die before it's completely gone. I don't want to die in a home for paupers.' She smiled bitterly. 'I'm doing my best to accelerate things.' From one of the scarves a bottle of vodka peeped out and disappeared without my seeing the hands that were holding it. 'What about a good cry?' she suggested to me. 'Crying is soothing, if you can do it. It tires you out. Then you arrive at a dull peace. But it's not always possible. The time for tears quickly goes by. Only later do you see how much good it did you. Then along come fear, rigidity and despair. The only thing that keeps me alive is my memories.'

I looked at the pallid face of frail silk. What was she talking about? The opposite was true, at least for me, I thought. 'How do you mean?' I asked her.

The Contessa's face became a little animated. 'Memories,' she repeated. 'They're alive. They're warm and shining, and full of youth and love.'

'Even if they're memories of the dead?'

'Yes, of course,' said the delicate lady after a pause. 'If the

261

people were still alive, there'd be no cause to remember them.'

I stopped asking her questions. 'Memories keep you alive,' she said quietly. 'They live for as long as you do. What else? But they stand in the shadows in the evening and they beg you: Stay! Don't kill us please! All we have is you! And you feel desperate and tired, and you want to stop, but they're even more tired and desperate, and they beg and beg: Don't kill us! Summon us again and we'll be there, to the tinkling of the clock mechanism; and there they are again, the glass faces, there are their bows and there is the dance, there are the dear faces again, come back to life, a little paler, and they're begging you: Don't kill us, please, we need you. Who can say no to them? But can you endure it? Ah,' lamented the Contessa abruptly. 'But I don't want to go to the poorhouse with so many others, trash that still breathes—'

Moikov reappeared. 'All the heroes,' he said. 'Where are they now? The wind does not know them and the grass grows.' He raised his vodka glass. 'None for you?' he asked me.

'No.'

'Grief is still like a lump in his throat,' Moikov said to the Contessa. 'In us, it's already turned to earth, collecting in our feet, and climbing up to our hearts and burying them. But we can live without a heart. Isn't that right, Contessa?'

'Those are words, Vladimir Ivanovitch. You love words. You're a poet. Perhaps you can. But what for?' The Contessa got up. 'What about two for tonight, Vladimir? Good night, Monsieur Sommer. What a nice name. We learned a little German when we were children. And sweet dreams.'

Moikov walked the frail lady to the stairs. I looked at the bottle from which he had shaken two pills for the Contessa. They were sleeping tablets. 'Will you give me a couple as well,' I said when he came back. 'Why does she always get them from you two at a time?' I asked. 'Can't she have a bottle of them on her bedside table?'

'She doesn't trust herself. She's afraid she might swallow them all one night.'

'In spite of her memories?'

'Well, not because of them anyway. She's afraid of poverty. She wants to stay alive as long as she can. But she's afraid of sudden fits of despair. Hence her caution. But I've had to promise her to let her have a whole big bottle full if she asks. But there's time till then.'

'Will you do it?'

He looked at me with his lidless eyes. 'Wouldn't you?' Then he slowly opened his mighty hand. In it lay a small old-fashioned ring with a ruby. 'She has to sell it. It's not a big stone, but just take a look at it.'

'I don't know anything about them.'

'It's a star ruby. Very rare.'

I looked at the ring again. It was a very clear red, in which, if you turned it against the light, a star with six little rays appeared. 'I wish I could buy it,' I said unexpectedly.

Moikov laughed. 'Why?'

'Just because,' I said. 'Because it's not something that men have made. It's pure and incorruptible. Not for Maria Fiola, as you suppose. Anyway, she wears emeralds the size of your fingernails in diadems worn by empresses. Where are all the duchesses now?' I quoted. 'Did you write that? The Contessa called you a poet. Were you, once upon a time?'

Moikov shook his head. 'The professions all – where are they now? In their first twenty years the Russians talked all the time about what they were and they lied about it horribly. More every year. Then less. In the end they forgot everything. You are still a very young emigrant with all the sores of your profession. You still cry for vengeance, and take it for justice and not egoism and megalomania. Our cries for vengeance! I remember them. Where are they now? The wind blows and doesn't know them. And the grass grows and grows.'

'Your generation wasn't given an opportunity,' I said.

'There were some, you trembling scholar on the first step to becoming a cosmopolitan. What did you want? You didn't come down for nothing, did you?'

'The same as the Contessa. Two sleeping pills.'

'Not the whole bottle?'

'No,' I said. 'Not now. Not in America.'

14

Reginald Black sent me to Cooper, the arms dealer who had bought the Degas, to hang up the picture in his place. 'It'll be interesting for you to see the house,' said Black. 'It'll be instructive in all sorts of ways. Take a taxi; the dancer's frame is genuine and it's genuinely frail.'

Cooper lived on the ninth floor of a building on Park Avenue. It was a duplex apartment with a roof garden. I was expecting a maid, but Cooper received me in person, shirtsleeved, at the door. 'Come on in,' he said jovially. 'We'll take a little time finding a place for the green–blue lady to go. Do you want coffee? Or would you prefer whiskey?'

'Thank you. I'll stick to coffee.'

'I'll have whiskey. It's the only thing that makes sense in this heat.'

I didn't contradict him. The apartment was very cool; it had the graveyard air of artificially cooled and ventilated rooms. All the windows were closed.

Cooper carefully unwrapped the Degas. I took a look around. The furnishings of the room were French, Louis XV, almost of all them small, good pieces, delicate, lots of gold, with the addition of two Italian armchairs and a gorgeous little Venetian bureau in yellow. There were Impressionists on the walls. I will confess I was surprised. I hadn't expected Cooper to have so much taste.

He set the Degas down on a chair. I was expecting an attack; the coffee wouldn't have been provided for nothing, I knew that. 'Were you really an assistant at the Louvre?' he asked me.

I nodded. I didn't want to leave Black in the lurch. 'And before that?' he asked.

'Before that I worked in the museum in Brussels. Why?'

Cooper laughed. 'You can't trust these art dealers. That notion that the Degas belonged to Mrs Black, that was just so much hooey.'

'Why? It doesn't make it a better or worse picture.'

Cooper glanced at me. 'Of course not. That's why I bought it anyway. You know how much Black wanted for it, don't you?'

'No idea,' I said.

'How much do you think?'

'I really have no idea.'

'Thirty thousand dollars!'

Cooper eyed me. I knew right away that he was lying and was testing me. 'A lot of money, eh?' he said.

'That depends. For me, it would be an awful lot of money.'

'What would you have paid for it?' he asked quickly.

'I don't have that sort of money.'

'And if you did?'

I had the feeling I had earned my cup of coffee already. 'Everything I had,' I replied. 'A love of art is great business these days; the prices seem to go up from week to week.'

Cooper whinnied with laughter. 'You're not trying to tell me what Black said was true? That he bought a picture back for fifty per cent more than what he'd sold it for?'

'No.'

'Well, then.' Cooper was grinning.

'I'm not trying to tell you so, because it is true,' I said.

'What?'

'It's true. I've seen it in the books. You can easily have it checked. Offer him the picture back in a year or two.'

'That old canard,' said Cooper dismissively, but he seemed to be relieved. Just then he was called away to the telephone. 'Take a look around,' he called out to me. 'Maybe you'll find a good place for the Degas.'

The girl who had called him showed me around. Cooper must have some excellent advisers. The apartment didn't feel like a museum, but every object in it would have found a place in one. I didn't understand it; Cooper didn't come across like a connoisseur. But there were such people, I knew that from Paris.

'Here is Mr Cooper's bedroom,' said the maid. 'Perhaps it can go in there.'

I stopped in the doorway. Over a wide bed in worst Jugendstil, in a massy gold frame hung a forest scene with a bellowing stag and a couple of hinds and a stream in the foreground. Speechless, I stared at the picture. 'Does Mr Cooper hunt?' I finally asked the maid.

She shook her head. 'Did he paint it himself?'

'As if! Though I'm sure he'd like to have done! It's his favourite picture. Isn't it lovely? So true to nature. You can see the pink steam rising from the muzzle of the stag.'

'You're absolutely right,' I said and went on looking.

On the opposite wall I found a Venetian scene by Felix Ziem. My eyes almost misted over with emotion, because I had found Cooper's secret, not least once I saw a few tankards set out on a sideboard. Here, in his bedroom, Cooper had licence to be human and himself. The rest of the apartment was stage set, investment and vanity, at most a kind of tepid admiration. But this yelling stag was passion and that mawkish Venetian scene was romance.

'Lovely, isn't it?' said the pretty maid.

'Wonderful. But it's too perfect the way it is. This picture wouldn't fit.'

The maid led me up a little flight of stairs. From the study I heard Cooper's rough voice barking orders into the telephone. I stopped at the door to the terrace. Below me lay New York, looking like a white African city with skyscrapers, no trees, only concrete and steel, not an organically grown city over centuries, but determined and rapid, and impatiently built by people who weren't impeded by tradition and whose watchword wasn't security but function. But just because of that the city acquired a new, bold, anti-Romantic, anti-Classical, modern beauty. I looked down in ravishment. So you didn't have to see New York stiff-necked, from below, I thought. The skyscrapers looked different too, from alongside, as though they belonged there, a stone herd of zebras, gazelles, rhinos and giant tortoises.

I heard Cooper puffing up the stairs. His face was, inasmuch as it could, beaming. He must have sold several thousand bombs on the phone just now. He was glowing like a tomato. Death made him happy; he even had morality on his side. 'Did you manage to find a place for it?' he asked.

'Here,' I said. 'On the terrace. A dancer over New York. But the sun would soon destroy the pastel colours.'

'That would be crazy,' said Cooper. 'Thirty thousand dollars.'

'Worse still,' I said. 'A work of art. But we could hang it next door in the living room; on the side that doesn't catch the sun. Over the two blue Han bronzes.'

'Do you know something about that Chinese junk?' asked Cooper. 'What are they worth?'

'Do you want to sell them?'

'Of course not. I only bought them two years ago. For five hundred dollars the pair. Did I pay too much?'

'That was a snip,' I said bitterly.

Cooper laughed. 'What about those terracotta thingies there? What are they worth?'

'The Tang dancers? Maybe three hundred dollars each,' I said in spite of myself.

'I paid a hundred.' Cooper's face beamed. He was one of those types that got turned on by good deals.

'Where shall we hang the Degas?' I asked. I wasn't in the mood to go on feeding the weapons dealer's ego. But Cooper was insatiable. 'What's this rug worth?' he asked greedily.

It was an Armenian dragon carpet from the seventeenth century. My namesake Sommer would have been in raptures over it. 'The bottom's gone out of the rug market,' I said. 'Ever since apartments have come with fitted carpets, no one's interested any more.'

'What? But I paid twelve thousand dollars for it! Isn't it worth that any more?'

'I'm afraid not,' I replied spitefully.

'How much do you think? Everything else has gone up, for heaven's sake!'

'Pictures have gone up, not carpets. That's because of the war. A new type of buyer has appeared on the market. A lot of old collectors were driven to sell; the new ones want to show off their culture. They can do that better with a Renoir on the wall than with an ancient worn carpet on the floor, that visitors track with their muddy boots. There are only a few, fine old-school collectors like you, Mr Cooper' – I looked him full in the face – 'that appreciate such good carpets.'

'So what's it worth?'

'Maybe half what you paid? People just don't buy these

great masterworks any more; at most they buy little prayer rugs.'

'God damn it!' Cooper stood up angrily. 'All right, hang the Degas where you said. But don't make a mess of the wall.'

'It's just the barest little hole. We use special hooks.'

Cooper went out to bewail his loss. I hung the Degas quickly. The blue-green dancer was now floating over the two almost blue Han bronzes, and all three threw the light of their velvet patina back and forth to each other.

I ran my hand carefully over the two Chinese bronzes, and felt the gentle cool warmth of their patina. 'You poor little aliens,' I said, 'ending up in the magnificent nest of an arms seller and barbarian, hail to you! You give me a strange feeling of being at home, a sort of home where geography is replaced by perfection, patriotism by artistry and war by the blissful moment when you see that this horde of restless, short-lived murderous nomads has nevertheless from time to time succeeded in making something that feels eternal, and that is set in pure beauty, whether it be in bronze, marble, pastel or words, even if you happen to run into it in an arms dealer's apartment. And you too, frail dancer, should not protest about your emigration. It could have been worse. Your present owner could have chosen to garland you with hand grenades, or show you flanked by machine guns and flame-throwers. As an expression of him and his life, that would have had more validity. But his greed for possessions saved you from such a fate. As it is, you will dream away your exile here, just like two terracotta dancers of the Tang period, excavated by grave robbers a century ago in Peking from a mandarin tomb and deflected, like so many of us, into this strange existence.'

'What's that you're muttering to yourself?'

The maid stood behind me. I had forgotten she was there. Cooper had sent her back to keep an eye on me, to make sure I didn't break or steal anything. 'Magic charms,' I said. 'Just some magic charms.'

'Are you not feeling well?'

'No,' I said. 'I'm fine. I'm even feeling particularly well. You know, there's a certain resemblance between you and that charming dancer here.' I pointed to the Degas.

'With that gross bitch?' she replied in disgust. 'She needs to go on a crash diet! Cottage cheese and lettuce!'

Outside Asher's Funeral Home stood two bay trees whose crowns had been shaped to balls. I had got the time wrong and was almost an hour early. A record was playing organ music, and the air smelled of candle wax and disinfectant. The room was half-dark; two stained-glass windows afforded a dim light and, coming out of the sun as I was, I saw almost nothing to begin with. I only heard a voice I didn't know and was surprised it wasn't Lipschitz. Lipschitz normally spoke at the emigrants' funerals. He had done that in France already, generally hastily and with difficulty, so as not to attract the attention of the police. Here in America he could finally draw himself out to his full length; no one was waiting for him at the cemetery exit or the undertakers' door, to ask him for his passport. Hirsch told me later that he saw it as his sacred duty to speak over the bodies of emigrants. He had been a lawyer in another life and missed not being able to address the court; and so he had discovered eulogies.

By and by it dawned on me that I was at the wrong funeral. The coffin was far too precious for one thing, and I could make out the mourners and saw there was no one I recognised. I quietly slipped out. Outside I ran into

Tannenbaum–Smith. Jessie in her excitement had told him the wrong time as well. 'Did Teller have any relatives?' he asked.

'I don't believe so. Didn't you know him?'

Tannenbaum shook his head. We stood in the blazing sun. The mourners at the other funeral came out, blinking, into the light and quickly dispersed. 'Where is the coffin?' I asked.

'It will be put in a back room and collected later. The storeroom is temperature controlled.'

Last to come out was a young woman. An older gentleman was with her. He stopped and lit a cigarette. The woman looked around. She seemed lost in the trembling heat. The man threw away his match and quickly followed her.

Lipschitz arrived. He was wearing a light tropical suit with a black tie. 'I made a mistake with the time,' he said. 'We weren't able to notify everyone. It was all on account of Jessie. She was adamant that she wanted to see Teller; so we gave her the wrong time. By the time she comes, the coffin will already be closed.'

'So when is the funeral?'

Lipschitz looked at his watch. 'In half an hour.'

Tannenbaum–Smith looked at me. 'Shall we have a drink? There's a drugstore on the corner.'

'I won't,' said Lipschitz. 'I'd better stay here. The others will be along soon.'

He already felt like a master of ceremonies. 'I also have to see to the music,' he explained. 'So that there's no confusion. Teller was a baptised Jew. A Catholic. But since Hitler's accession he felt more Jewish. I fixed it so that the Catholic priest blessed him yesterday. It wasn't easy, because Teller killed himself. He shouldn't have been able to get a consecrated site in the cemetery either. But luckily that's sorted, because Teller is being incinerated. But that priest! The amount of persuasion it took to get him to make the sign of the cross over the body! Finally he understood that it was tragic and complicated, and after that he became a little bit human. You can understand his point of view – after all, the Pope made a concordat with the Nazis, to protect the Catholics. Then a Catholic Jew is sort of a borderline case, especially when it's a suicide.'

Lipschitz was sweating. 'What about the music?' I asked. 'What have you arranged?'

'First off, a Catholic hymn: "*Jesus meine Zuversicht*". Then Bruch's "Kol Nidri". The funeral home has two gramophones; so there won't be a delay for the change of records. The one will follow directly after the other. Not that the rabbi minds; he's very easy-going.'

'Shall we go?' suggested Smith. 'It's terribly humid.'

'Yes.'

Lipschitz remained at his post, dignified in his half-mourning. He got his speech out of his pocket to memorise it, while Smith and I walked to the drugstore, to be greeted by a relieving blast of chill air. 'A lemon ice,' said Smith. 'A large one. What will you have? These affairs always make me terribly thirsty, I can't help it.'

I ordered the same. I hadn't thanked Smith yet for the job at Black's and wanted to demonstrate that we were of the same mind. I didn't know whether this was the right moment to discuss my future. But Smith broached the subject himself. 'How are things with Black?'

'Fine. Thank you. It's going very well.'

Smith smiled. 'A man with lots of strings to his bow, wouldn't you say?'

I nodded. 'An art dealer. It comes with the territory. He sells the things he loves.'

'That's not the worst. Some just lose them. At least he takes in some money for them.'

About twenty or thirty people turned out. Lipschitz spoke. I was stunned by the strong, dampish smell of the flowers on the coffin. They were tuberoses. The coffin was plain, it didn't have the chrome of the one from the earlier funeral, which had sparkled like an automobile. It was pine and it was there to be burned. Lipschitz had explained to me that funeral homes didn't have their own crematoria; in that way they weren't as luxuriously equipped as German concentration camps. The coffins were sent to a centralised crematorium. That relieved me; I wouldn't have liked to attend an incineration. I had been through too many and repressed the memory as well as I could. Even so, the thought buzzed like an angry wasp in my head.

Robert Hirsch had brought Jessie. She hung on his arm and sobbed jerkily. Carmen sat behind her, apparently asleep. There were various other writers there. Teller had been fairly well known in Germany before Hitler. Everything had the typical inconsequence of a funeral; something unimaginable had happened, and people tried to change it by means of prayer, organ and words into something imaginable, and to cut it down to size, so as to be able to withstand it.

Suddenly two men in black suits and black gloves were standing on the stage next to the coffin, they lifted it quickly and easily into the air with a practised manner that suggested executioners' assistants, and carried it swiftly and silently out on rubber soles. It happened so quickly that it was over before anyone was ready. They passed close by me. I thought I could smell the corpse in the draught and then to my surprise I noticed that my eyes were wet.

We went outside. It was a strange thing – in the

274

emigration we kept losing one another from view. That was how it had been with Teller as well, otherwise he wouldn't have died so abjectly. But then, when he was dead, it seemed like a lot of people had died, and we didn't understand it and felt guilty, and felt the strangeness of the lost little diaspora we belonged to, thrown together without any will of our own.

Jessie was taken by the Dahl twins to Tannenbaum-Smith's car. She didn't put up any fight; her red, puffy face looked odd against the blue sky and the trembling noonday heat; then she clambered into the Chrysler, whose black lacquer briefly reminded me of the earlier coffin and was now about to carry Jessie away.

'She's got a grip on herself,' said Hirsch. 'She has to attend to a few last details of the funeral buffet. She and the twins have been working on it from early morning. That helped her over the worst. Now she's desperate to have everything perfect. She feels she owes it to Teller. The logic may be flawed, but it's sincere.'

'Was she close to Teller?' asked Tannenbaum-Smith.

'No more than any of the others; maybe even a little less. That's partly why she feels such a deep sense of obligation to do all she can for him now. She feels responsible, as she does for all of us. The Jewish mama. We have to go to her. It will help her. We can depend on her. If no one else cries at our funerals, once it comes to be our turn — then we'll be able to rely on Jessie — as long as she's there.'

Lipschitz was the last one to emerge from the funeral home. 'Here is the receipt, Mr Smith,' he said. 'The crooks put another fifteen dollars on the bill. There was nothing I could do about it. Teller's coffin was standing out in the sun. They had me over a barrel.'

'You did the right thing,' said Smith, folding the receipt. 'Will you make my excuses to Jessie,' he then said to Hirsch. 'I don't like the custom of taking leave of the deceased with alcohol. And I didn't know Teller personally.'

'Jessie made herring salad especially for you,' said Hirsch. Smith shrugged. 'I leave it in your hands, Mr Hirsch. You'll find the right form of words.'

He tipped his hand to the brim of his panama hat and walked slowly down the dusty avenue. 'Where would we be without him,' said Lipschitz. 'We couldn't even get ourselves buried. He paid for everything. But what made Teller do it? Now of all times? With the Russians and Americans going from victory to victory—

'Yes,' said Hirsch bitterly. 'And the Germans fighting and fighting, as though they were defending the Holy Grail. Don't you see how it could make someone despair?'

'Have you been to the Metropolitan Museum yet?' asked Reginald Black.

I shook my head.

He looked at me in astonishment. 'Still not? You surprise me! I'd have thought you would know it like the back of your hand. That's a grave defect in your education as an art dealer. Go there straight away. It's still open. You don't need to come back today. I'm shutting up shop. Take your time.'

I didn't go to the Met. I didn't yet trust myself. I had the feeling I was on thin ice and had only just avoided crashing through. My last dream had upset me for longer than I had expected and had given me the feeling of uncertainty I had fought so long. Nothing was over, I knew that now; also Teller's death had affected me more than I would have thought possible. We were saved; but not from ourselves.

I found myself standing in front of Silver's antique shop again. Between two white armchairs with gold braid, in the pose of Rodin's *Thinker*, sat Arnold Silver, staring dreamily out into the street. He gave a jump when I rapped on the window and came trotting out to greet me.

'A rare pleasure to find you here, Mr Arnold,' I said.

Arnold glinted mildly. 'Alexander isn't in. He's eating a kosher lunch in Berg's restaurant. I'm not. I eat the American way.'

'In the Voisin, I hope,' I replied. 'The foie gras there was remarkable.'

The Silver twins were a study in contrast, even though born three hours apart and monozygotic. They reminded me of Siamese twins I had heard about, one of whom was an alcoholic and the other teetotal, who unhappily had to endure all the drunkenness and hangovers of his brother without any of the benefits except nausea and headaches. He was the only sober drunk I'd ever heard of. It was like that with Arnold and Alexander; they were contrasts, but at least they weren't attached.

'I found a bronze,' I said. 'At Spanierman's auction house on 59th Street. In an auction of carpets, the day after tomorrow.'

Silver Junior gestured wearily. 'I'm not in the mood for business now. Talk to my fascist brother. I'm thinking about my life. Can you understand that?'

'Of course. What's your star sign again? When were you born?'

'What? Oh, the morning of 22 June. Why?'

'So you're a Cancer,' I said. 'And Alexander?'

'Late at night on 21 June. Why?'

'So he's a twin.'

'A twin? Of course he's a twin. Bloody stupid!'

'I mean, astrologically a twin, born under Gemini, on the last day of the sign. That explains a lot.'

'Like what?'

'Character. You're opposites.'

Arnold stared at me. 'And you believe stuff like that? That star sign nonsense?'

'I believe in much more nonsensical things than that, Mr Arnold.'

'And what character does a Cancer have? Horrible word, anyway.'

'It's nothing to do with the illness. Just the animal, which is among the great delicacies of the old world; finer than lobster.'

'And the character?' asked Arnold the bridegroom.

'Deep. Profoundly emotional. Sensitive, artistic, devoted to family.'

Arnold perked up. 'And in the area of love?'

'Romantic. Idealistic. Fiercely attached; you would rather lose a claw than let go.'

'Another horrible image!'

'It's meant symbolically. In a psychoanalytical reading it means something like: one would have to remove your sexual organs before you let go.'

Arnold went slightly green. 'And my brother? What's his story?'

'As a twin, he has a far easier time of it. Janus-faced, a double. A double man. Slips easily from one mask into the other. Quick, glib, smart and dazzling.'

Arnold nodded.

Just at that moment the double twin walked into the store, gleaming from his heavy kosher lunch, puffing away at an unkosher cigar.

Arnold gave me a look that said: None of this gets out.

Alexander greeted me benevolently and pulled out his wallet. 'We owe you the commission on the latest prayer rug,' he said. 'A hundred and fifty.'

'Shouldn't that be a hundred? Or even eighty?' Arnold, the deeply emotional crab, interrupted him.

I looked at him speechlessly. The traitor! And for the difference he would probably take his bride out to the Voisin, or even to the Pavillon.

'A hundred and fifty dollars,' said Alexander firmly. 'Honestly come by in the struggle against his friend Rosenthal.' He handed me two notes. 'What will you do with it? Buy yourself another suit?'

'Let's see,' I said and shot a look at Arnold the astrological tightwad. 'I think I'll escort a very stylish lady to the Voisin and make another payment to my lawyer.'

'Also at the Voisin?' asked Alexander.

'In his office. And then I'll bid on a little bronze at the Plaza Auction that Mr Arnold refused to interest himself in,' I added in another poke at the crab.

'Arnold isn't quite himself at the moment,' said Alexander. 'Will you give us an option if you buy it?'

'Of course! You're my principal dealers.'

'And how are things going with the arch-parasite Black?'

'Beautifully, thanks. He's trying very hard to imbue me with the philosophy of an art dealer in the Buddhist sense: someone who loves art, but in such a way that he also loves selling it. Don't own for the love of ownership.'

'Shmonzes,' replied Alexander.

'Museums have everything you need to worship art, Black likes to tell me. You can enjoy the pieces without worrying about a fire or break-in in your house. Also, museums have the best pieces; no private citizen could ever hope to find the like.'

'Double-shmonzes! And what does Black live off, if that were the case?'

'Off his even deeper trust in human avarice.'

Silver laughed in disgust.

'God has no pity, Mr Alexander,' I said. 'As long as you remember that, your sense of the world won't go too badly awry. And justice isn't a basic part of mankind, but an invention of the Decadent period. Possibly their best. So long as you know that, you won't expect too much and you won't die from the bitterness of existence. Not to say life.'

'You're forgetting about love,' the traitorous Arnold spoke up.

'I'm not forgetting it,' I replied. 'But it should be an ornament, not the essence of existence. Otherwise it makes a man a gigolo.'

I had got my own back on him for trying to rob me of fifty dollars' commission; but I didn't entirely like myself in that role. 'Except for natural Romeo types,' I added a little lamely. 'And of course artists.'

In the forecourt of the Plaza Hotel I spotted Maria Fiola, heading for Central Park. I was surprised to see her and realised that I'd never seen her in the daytime; only ever in the evening or at night. I set off after her, to give her a surprise. I felt the money from the Silvers in my pocket. I hadn't seen her for several days and in the honeyed light of late afternoon she looked like a vision. She was wearing a white linen dress and it suddenly hit me just how beautiful she was. Previously I'd only seen it piecemeal, a face, a pair of shoulders, her hair in the gloaming in the lounge, a movement, a few steps in the garish artificial light of the photographic studio or the nightclub, and the pieces had never really come together. Preoccupied with myself as I generally was, I hadn't really been aware of it. To think what I'd missed or only half perceived, as though it were so self-evident, scattered and half absent! Maria Fiola crossed the street to the Sherry Netherland with her long, supple strides, a little leaning forward, circumspect, briefly hesitating, between the steel colossuses, and then swiftly, almost dancing, reached the other side.

I had to wait a moment before I could follow her; but I stayed where I was anyway. Through a gap in the traffic I saw a man step out of the hotel lobby in her direction and kiss her on the cheek. He was tall and slim, and he didn't look like someone with two suits to his name; he looked more like someone who might be staying at that expensive address.

I followed the pair of them along the opposite side of the street, as far as the next set of lights. There I saw the Rolls-Royce parked in the cross street. I saw Maria Fiola climb into it. The unknown gentleman helped her in. All at once she seemed appallingly strange to me. What did I know of her? Nothing that the wind mightn't have blown away. What did I know about her life? And for that matter, what did she know about mine? It's over! I thought and at the same moment felt utterly ridiculous. What was over? Nothing. I felt a loss that wasn't real; but I felt it all the more strongly for that. Nothing had happened. I had seen someone I knew fleetingly in a situation that didn't concern me; that was all. Nothing was broken, because there hadn't been anything in the first place.

I walked back to the Plaza. The fountain in the middle of the court was dry. My spectral sense of loss persisted. I walked past the windows of Van Cleef & Arpels. The two diadems of the dead queen sparkled on black velvet, regardless of whether the guillotine had cut off her foolish head or not. The stones survived because they were not alive. Or were they after all? In a stiff, mute ecstasy? I stared at the glittering jewels and immediately I had to think of Teller. It came over me like a black wind. Lipschitz had told me how he was dangling from the chandelier in the hot night, in his best suit, a clean shirt and no tie. He had left off the tie, thus Lipschitz, because he thought it might impede his death or make it more protracted. Apparently in his death throes he had kicked about him, as though to reach a table near him. A plaster cast of the head of Amenophis IV was in pieces on the floor. Then Lipschitz had gone on to speculate whether Teller would be burned today or later; he hoped as soon as possible, because bodies deteriorate rapidly in the hot weather. I looked at my watch. It was past five o'clock. I didn't know whether American crematoria closed or not. The German ones I knew didn't. They went on firing through the night, to deal with all the gassed Jews.

I turned round. Everything around me seemed to totter for a moment and then be completely incomprehensible. I looked at the passers-by. I had the feeling I was cut off from them and their existence by a thick pane of glass, as though they lived by different rules from me, and were appallingly remote from me with their simple emotions, their rational unhappiness and their harmless indignation that happiness was no lasting state, but something like a wave in water. How happy and how enviable they were, with their successes, their jokes, their flip cynicism, their harmless mishaps, in which financial loss or love or a natural death was already as far as it got. What did they know about living in the shadow of an Orestean commitment to revenge, of sinister innocence and the compulsory involvement in the guilt of a murderer and the bloody laws of a primitive justice, what of the mob of Erinyes who kept watch over memory, waiting always to be sprung? With dazzled eyes I saw them, unattainable, sitting there like the ornamental birds of another century, and I felt the sharp bite of envy and despair that I could never be as they were, but in spite of all, remained subject to the laws of the land of the barbarians and murderers which held me, because I couldn't escape without either submitting to them or killing myself.

15

'Will you accompany me on a mission?' asked Robert Hirsch.

'When?'

Hirsch laughed. 'You haven't changed yet, have you?' he said. 'When, you ask, and not why. So the rules of Rouen, Laon, Marseilles and Paris still obtain. Thank God!'

'I can guess what it is,' I replied. 'A crusade. On behalf of the cheated Bosse.'

Hirsch nodded. 'Bosse's given up. He went to see the cheat twice. The second time the fellow lost his patience and threw him out, and threatened to charge him with blackmail if he ever came back. Thereupon Bosse lapsed into his old emigrant fear of being expatriated and gave up. I know all this from Jessie. And from her I have the name and address of the crook. Can you do two o'clock?'

'Yes,' I said. 'For something like that always. Anyway, Reginald Black has left town for a couple of days. When he's not there the business is closed down. I can't sell anything myself. It's very convenient. I'm still paid.'

'OK. Let's have lunch beforehand. In the King of the Sea.'

'Let me treat you, Robert.' I earned some extra money yesterday and spent less than I had it in mind to spend. I know another fish restaurant; let's blow my savings there.'

Hirsch darted a look at me. 'Have you fallen out with Maria Fiola?'

'Not in the least. We're miles away from anything like that.'

'Really?'

'Yes, Robert.'

He shook his head. 'Don't wait too long. Something like that doesn't run around for ever – not with legs and a face like that. Where are we going?'

'To Seafare. Cheap and very good. The prawns are cheaper than hamburgers are elsewhere. What's the name of the vulture we're going to pay a call on later?'

'Blumenthal. Adolf Blumenthal. Strange how many Jews are called Adolf. In this case the name fits.'

'Does he know you're coming?'

Hirsch nodded. 'I called him.'

'Does Bosse know you're going?'

Hirsch laughed. 'Of course not. He would be so worried he'd denounce us.'

'Have you got anything you can use on Blumenthal at all?'

'Nothing, Ludwig. He was very canny.'

'So nothing but item one of the Laon Breviary.'

'Exactly. Bluff, Ludwig.'

We walked down First Avenue. In the window of a pet shop we saw two Siamese fighting fish, sparkling and rainbow-coloured, butting heads against the glass wall that kept them apart, waiting to have a go at each other. In a bakery we saw Viennese cakes on display – Gugelhupf and Linzer and Sacher cakes. A bespectacled salesgirl waved to Hirsch. I watched him from the side as he strode along. His walk was quite different; his face too looked tauter. He reminded me of how he had looked in France, when he was Consul Raul Tegner – no longer a dealer in wireless sets and electric irons.

'All the Jews were victims,' he said. 'But that doesn't mean to say they were all angels.'

It was a building on 54th Street. Red stair carpets, engravings on the walls, a man in charge of the elevator, all mirrors and wood panelling, the man in a fantasy uniform. Modest affluence. 'Fifteenth floor,' said Hirsch. 'Director Blumenthal.'

We sped upwards. 'I don't think he'll have a lawyer there with him,' said Hirsch. 'I threatened him with evidence. Seeing as he's a crook, he'll want to see it first; because he doesn't have American nationality yet, there will still be a bit of that good old fear in him, and he'll want to know what it's about before taking his lawyer into his confidence.'

He rang. A girl opened. She led us into a room where copies of Louis XVI furniture stood around, some of it gilded. 'Mr Blumenthal is just coming.'

Blumenthal was a plump fifty-year-old man of average height. A German shepherd accompanied him into the golden salon. Hirsch smiled when he saw the animal. 'The last time I saw a dog like that it was working for the Gestapo, Mr Blumenthal,' he said. 'They used them to hunt Jews.'

'Quiet, Harro!' Blumenthal patted the dog. 'You wanted to talk to me. You didn't tell me you weren't coming alone. I don't have much time.'

'This is Mr Sommer. He has heard a lot about you. I won't keep you long, Mr Blumenthal. We're here on behalf of Dr Bosse. He is sick, doesn't have any money and is having to give up his studies. You know him, isn't that right?'

Blumenthal didn't say anything. He carried on patting his dog, which growled quietly.

'So you know him,' continued Hirsch. 'You even know him fairly well. But I don't know if you know me or not. There are a lot of Hirschs, just as there are a lot of Blumenthals. You can call me Gestapo Hirsch if you like. Perhaps you've heard of me. I spent quite a bit of time in France, waging war on the Gestapo. It wasn't always very pleasant; not from either side, Mr Blumenthal. Certainly not from my side. This is just by way of saying that having a German shepherd for an escort would have made me laugh in your face in those days. Just like today, really. Your pet would be dead before it got anywhere near me, Mr Blumenthal. And presumably you with it. But I don't care about either of you. We're here because we're collecting money for Dr Bosse. I assume you'd like to help him. How much can we put you down for?'

Blumenthal stared at Hirsch. 'Why should I do any such thing?'

'There are a number of reasons. One might be called compassion.'

Blumenthal seemed to be chewing on something. He didn't take his eyes off Hirsch. Then out of his jacket pocket he pulled a brown crocodile wallet, opened it and pulled out two notes from a side compartment, first licking his fingers. 'Here are forty dollars. I can't give you any more than that. Too many people come to me in similar predicaments. If every emigrant were as generous as I am you would soon have got enough to cover Dr Bosse's studies.'

I thought Hirsch would throw the bills down on the table, but he took them and pocketed them. 'Thank you, Mr Blumenthal,' he said calmly. 'We still need another 1,160 dollars from you. That's how much Dr Bosse will need, if he lives very modestly, doesn't smoke and doesn't drink, till he can take his exams.'

'You're joking, aren't you. I'm afraid I don't have any more time . . .'

'Oh, you have time all right, Mr Blumenthal. And please don't tell me your lawyer is sitting next door. He is not sitting next door. But I want to tell you something now, something that will interest you. You don't have American citizenship yet and are hoping to acquire it next year. One thing you don't need is any injurious gossip at this stage; the United States can be quite fussy about that. My friend Sommer the journalist and I would like to save you from such a thing.'

Blumenthal appeared to have come to a decision. 'Too kind,' he said. 'Now would you have anything against it if I informed the police?'

'Not in the least. They will be interested to see our evidence.'

'Evidence!' Blumenthal pulled a face. 'Blackmail carries quite a high tariff in America, I hope you know that. If I were you I would clear off while I still can.'

Hirsch sat down on one of the golden chairs. 'You think you've been clever, Blumenthal,' he said in a different tone of voice. 'You weren't clever. You should have given Bosse the money you owed him. In my pocket I have a petition signed by a hundred emigrants addressed to the immigration authorities, asking them not to give you American citizenship. Here is a further petition not to give it to you because of your dealings with the Gestapo in Germany, signed by six people, and with a detailed account of how it was that you left Germany with more money than anyone else – including the name of the Nazi who brought it to you in Switzerland. I also have a newspaper clipping from Lyons about the Jew Blumenthal who, under questioning from the Gestapo, betrayed the whereabouts of two refugees, who were both shot as a result. It's no good protesting, Blumenthal. Perhaps it wasn't you, you know, but I will insist that it was.'

'What?!'

'I will testify that it was you. People here know what I did in France. They will believe me more readily than you.'

Blumenthal stared at Hirsch. 'You mean to give false witness?'

'False only in the sense of a crude understanding of the law; not the sense of an eye for an eye and a tooth for a tooth. You've practically destroyed Bosse; therefore we're destroying you. We don't really care what's true and what isn't. I already told you I learned from my time with the Nazis.'

'And you a Jew?' whispered Blumenthal.

'Just like you, worse luck.'

'And you would persecute a fellow Jew?'

For a moment Hirsch was dumbfounded. 'Yes,' he then said. 'I've already told you I've picked up a trick or two from the Gestapo. I've also learned something from the ways of American gangsters. Plus, Blumenthal, if you like, some native Jewish intelligence.'

'The American police—'

'And I've learned from the American police as well,' Hirsch interrupted him. 'Quite a bit, in fact. But I don't even need them. To finish you off, all I need is the papers in my pocket. I don't even care whether you go to prison or not. All I want is to have you interned in a camp for suspected Nazis.'

Blumenthal raised his hand. 'That needs someone other than you, Mr Hirsch. And that needs evidence of a different order than your false accusations.'

'Do you think?' Hirsch laughed. 'Now – in wartime? For an ostensible emigrant, born in Germany? What would happen to you in an internment camp? You'll be held in humane conditions. They don't need too much in the way of evidence before doing that. And even if you avoided internment, think what it would do to your case for citizenship. Things like doubt and gossip can make quite a difference.'

Blumenthal's hand clasped at the collar of the dog. 'And what about you?' he replied softly. 'Think what would happen to you if this got out. Blackmail, false witness—'

'I know exactly what would happen to me,' replied Hirsch. 'Well, do you know something, Blumenthal, I don't care. I just don't care. I don't give a shit! All right? All those things that matter to you, you stamp robber with your dreams of a big future I don't give a shit about! I don't care and that's something you need to get your head around, you bourgeois earwig. Even in France I didn't care. Do you think I would have been able to do what I did otherwise? I'm not a megalomaniac with a bleeding heart. I don't care what happens. If you try to pull something against me, I'm not going to run wailing to the judge, Blumenthal. I'll take care of you myself. It wouldn't be the first time. Haven't you understood how little it takes to get a man killed these days?' Hirsch gestured dismissively. 'What do we need all this for? It's not about your life. It's just about paying back a portion of what you stole from Bosse, nothing more than that.'

Once again, Blumenthal seemed to be silently chewing something. 'I don't keep money in the house,' he finally said.

'I can take a cheque.'

Blumenthal let go of the dog. 'Basket, Harro!' He opened

a door and the dog slipped through it. Blumenthal locked the door behind him.

'At last,' said Hirsch.

'I'm not giving you a cheque,' said Blumenthal. He suddenly looked tired. 'You understand, don't you?'

I looked at him in surprise. I hadn't expected him to fold so quickly. Maybe Hirsch was right; the anonymous fear of the emigrant mingled with his actual guilt had undermined Blumenthal. He seemed to be thinking and acting quickly now – perhaps he was even now finding a way of giving us the slip.

'I'll come back tomorrow,' said Hirsch.

'And the papers?'

'I'll destroy them tomorrow, before your eyes.'

'I'll only give you the money in exchange for them.'

Hirsch shook his head. 'So that you find out who's prepared to give evidence against you? Out of the question.'

'What guarantee do I have that you'll destroy the actual papers?'

'My word,' said Hirsch calmly. 'That'll have to do for you. We're not blackmailers. We're just giving justice a little push. As you very well know.'

Blumenthal chewed some more. 'All right,' he said at last, very quietly.

Hirsch stood up from his golden chair. 'Same time tomorrow.'

Blumenthal nodded. He was running with sweat. 'My son is sick,' he whispered. 'My only son! And you – you come here – you should be ashamed of yourselves,' he said aloud. 'I'm in despair – and you—'

'Bosse's in despair too,' replied Hirsch quietly. 'And he'll certainly be able to recommend a doctor for your son. Just ask him.'

Blumenthal didn't say anything. He went on chewing and chewing. His face was a strange mixture of fear and hatred. I knew that financial loss could show itself in exactly the same way as personal loss; but this seemed to be something else. It was as though Blumenthal suddenly understood the secret connection between the suffering of his son and his cheating Dr Bosse. That was what caused him to yield so quickly and his helplessness only added to his detestation.

'Do you think his son is really ill?' I asked Hirsch, once we were back in the luxurious elevator, heading down.

'Why not? He didn't use it as a way of paying less.'

'Has he even got a son?'

'I think so. A Jew doesn't go making macabre jokes about his family.'

We dropped down to the street, surrounded by dazzling mirrors. 'What did you bring me with you for?' I asked. 'I didn't even open my mouth.'

Hirsch laughed. 'From old friendship. Because of the Laon rules. To complete your education.'

'I've got enough people working on my education,' I replied. 'Everyone from Moikov to Silver to Reginald Black. Anyway, I knew that all Jews aren't angels.'

Hirsch laughed. 'But you didn't know that people don't really change. You still believe misfortune can change them to the good or to the bad. A serious error. I took you along because you look like a Nazi — to intimidate Blumenthal.'

We stepped out into the steamy laundry air of the hot street. 'How can you intimidate anyone in America anyway?' I asked.

Hirsch stopped. 'My dear Ludwig,' he said. 'Haven't you

understood yet that we are living in the age of anxiety? The age of real and imaginary fear? Fear of life, fear of the future, fear of fear? And that as emigrants we're never going to be able to shake this fear, whatever happens? Don't you ever dream?'

'Yes, I do. Sometimes. Who doesn't? Americans dream too.'

'Yes, but not like us, they don't. We've had fear branded into our bones. By day you can do something against it, but what about at night? What happens to willpower then? And self-control?' Hirsch laughed. 'Blumenthal knows all about that. That's why he was in such a hurry to give up. That, and the fact that he's still got away with murder. The stamps he stole were worth twice that. If I had asked him for the full amount he would have fought to the limit, sick son and all. Even crime has its rules.'

Hirsch strode through the soupy early afternoon. It was as though we were back in France, his face looked so animated; for the first time in America I thought he was in his element.

'Do you think Blumenthal will pay up tomorrow?' I asked.

He nodded. 'I'm certain. He can't take the risk of being denounced.'

'Have you got anything to denounce him with?'

'Nothing whatever. Just his fear. And that's enough. Why would he risk his citizenship over a paltry thousand dollars here or there? It's the old Laon bluff, Ludwig – in a new variation. Not very stylish, a bit crude in fact, but you need something to help justice along.'

We stopped in front of the electrical goods shop where Hirsch worked. 'What's the beautiful Maria up to?'

'Do you think she's so beautiful?'

'Carmen is beautiful. But your friend is trembling with life.'

'What?'

Hirsch laughed. 'Not the shouty life of surfaces. But the intense life of pure despair. Haven't you noticed?'

'No,' I said. I felt a sharp pain go through me. Lost, I thought.

'The absolute diamond of despair,' said Hirsch. 'No bitterness.'

I looked at him attentively. 'And no remorse,' he went on. 'The other side; the side beyond the future. The side of pure present. Not even sullied with hope. The serene calm of sheer despair. The happiness of not-wanting-any-more. How else could you stand all this?' He rapped against his window, where the wireless sets and electric vacuum cleaners sparkled. Then he laughed. 'Back to business! But don't forget: the earth is still quaking underneath our feet. Only if we quake along can we be saved. And the danger is greatest when we think we are already saved. Into battle!'

He barged open the door. Cold air-conditioned air surged out; it was like walking into a tomb.

'Cafard?' asked Moikov.

'Average,' I replied. 'Not vodka-sized. Simple cafard of existence.'

'Not of life?'

'Of life too, Vladimir. But a little more optimistic than that. One should make more of it and live more consciously. More intensely. Quake a little. Advice from Robert Hirsch.'

Moikov laughed. He wasn't in uniform; he was wearing a very loose suit that seemed to billow all round him and a big slouch hat. 'Life is always an interesting subject,' he said. 'Only you forget to live it. A comfortable substitute.

Unfortunately I can't stay and chat now. I must defend the hotel. Raoul, the cornerstone of my earnings, wants to move out. He wants to rent an apartment. That would be the ruin of the hotel. Pray to God he stays – otherwise I'll have to put up everyone's rent.'

I heard a voice on the steps. 'There he is already,' said Moikov. 'I'll leave you a bottle of vodka for every eventuality. Dusk deepens the melancholy of life. Or of existence.'

'Where are you going?'

'Toots Shor.[4] Tender steaks. Air conditioning. Good place to talk someone round.'

Moikov walked off with Raoul, who was in a white suit and red shoes. I sat down under the bedraggled palm and tried to learn some English. Quake, Hirsch said, the subterranean movement of the earth, of life and of the heart, which one shouldn't ignore because one was safe and sink down into the comfortable morass of bourgeoisie. The trembling of being saved, the dancing that saw all things anew with wet eyes, the spoon in the hand, the breath, the light, the next step, the continually new flare of consciousness, of not being dead, of having got away, of not having perished in the concentration camp or in leaden despair in a basement somewhere.

The Contessa came floating down the stairs like a ghost in her dark lace. I thought she was looking for Moikov and brandished the bottle. 'Vladimir Ivanovitch has gone out,' I said. 'But he has left some of the elixir of consolation.'

The delicate person shook her head. 'Not today. I'm going out. A memorial dinner for Archduke Alexander. A magnificent man. We were practically engaged once. Murdered by the Bolsheviks. Why?'

---

[4] At 51 West 51st Street.

I didn't know what to say. 'Where is the dinner?' I asked instead.

'In the Russian Tearoom. With friends. Russians. All of them poor. And all of them generous. They make a celebration and then eat nothing but bread for days afterwards. But they have their celebration.'

A car hooted outside. 'That'll be Prince Volkovski,' said the Contessa. 'He has a taxi business and he's picking me up.'

She sashayed out in her dress that was made from pieces of old lace, a delicate scarecrow. Even she had somewhere to go tonight, I thought, and tried to learn some more vocabulary.

All at once Maria Fiola was standing in front of me. She had slipped in silently and was looking at me. She was wearing a yellow dress and, from the look of it, nothing underneath. She had no stockings and was carrying her yellow sandals in her hand.

Her apparition was such a surprise that I could only sit there and stare. She pointed at the bottle of vodka. 'Much too hot!'

I nodded and got up. 'Moikov left it here, but the Countess declined it. I did too.'

'Where is Vladimir?'

'Taking Raoul to dinner at Toots Shor. Steaks. The Countess is at the Russian Tearoom. Pirogi and stroganoff, at a guess. What about us?'

I held my breath. 'Lemon ices in the drugstore,' said Maria.

'And then?' I asked. 'Are you free afterwards? Is the Rolls parked round the corner?'

She laughed. 'No – not tonight.'

The sentence gave me a little pang. 'All right,' I said.

'Then why don't we have dinner? But not at the drugstore. I have learned too many lessons about life today. What about a little French restaurant with air conditioning and a good wine list?'

Maria Fiola looked at me doubtfully. 'Have we got enough money for that?'

'More than enough. I've pulled off some extraordinary deals since we last went out.'

At that moment everything felt very easy. The other side of life, I thought. The side that knows nothing of the grim circles of revenge and murder. There she was in front of me, glowing, mysterious, unattainable, provocative. 'I was waiting for you,' I said.

Maria Fiola's eyes seemed to burn. 'Why didn't you say so?'

'Yes, why indeed?'

I brushed against her as we walked out. She really was wearing next to nothing. I hadn't been with a woman in a long time. Outside, Felix was leaning against the wall, evidently harbouring a powerful thirst. I went back in and locked the vodka in Moikov's fridge. Then I saw Maria's face in the street outside the hotel. She was framed in the doorway like a painting. I felt almost happy. 'There's a storm on the way,' said Felix.

'And why not, Felix,' I replied. 'Why not.'

There were vivid flashes of lightning as we came out of the restaurant. Puffs of wind threw up dust and scraps of paper. 'Felix was right,' I said. 'We'd better try and find a cab.'

'Oh, let's walk,' said Maria. 'Taxis all smell of sweat and old shoes.'

'It will rain. You don't have a raincoat or an umbrella. It's going to chuck it down.'

'So much the better. It'll save me washing my hair.'

'You're going to get soaked, Maria.'

She laughed. 'This dress is nylon. You don't even need to iron it. Let's just go. If it gets worse, we can take refuge in a doorway. There are no taxis anyway. The wind! Do you feel it? Isn't it exciting!' She sniffed the air like a foal and leaned into the gale.

We stayed close to the house fronts. The lightning flashed, bathing the dim antique shops in momentary candescence, from which the furniture and the Chinese temple guards loomed almost drunkenly, as though they had been lashed by brightness and needed to find their old places again. It flashed on all sides of us, even up and down the skyscrapers, as though coming out of the tangle of pipes and wires under the asphalt, and split, white sheets of it, over the roofs and streets, followed by solemn booms of thunder that drowned out the traffic. Then it started to rain, big dark splotches that we saw scattered over the asphalt, before we felt them on our skin.

Maria Fiola held her face up into the rain. Her mouth was half open and her eyes squeezed shut. 'Hold me tight,' she said.

The storm increased. All at once the pavements were swept clean. People huddled in doorways, here and there a stooped form ran along the frontages, which were glistening now under the silver light of the smashing downpour that transformed the asphalt into a frothing dark lake pocked by lucent arrows and spears.

'My God!' Maria exclaimed. 'I forgot you're wearing your new suit!'

'Too late,' I replied. 'It won't come to any harm. It's not paper or woven nettle extract.'

'I was just thinking about me. I'm not wearing anything.'

She pulled her dress up to her hips. She was half-naked and the rain spattered round her sandals like lots of tiny explosions from the heavenly machine guns. 'But you,' she said. 'Your new blue suit you haven't even paid for yet!'

'Too late,' I repeated. 'Anyway, I can dry it and iron it. And it is paid for. So we can go on serenading the elements. The hell with my blue suit! Let's splash around in the fountain in front of the Plaza.'

She laughed and pulled me into a doorway. 'At least we can protect our linings and horsehair. They're not so easy to iron. There are more storms than suits.'

I kissed her wet face. We were standing between two shop entrances. On the one side there were corsets for elderly, heavyset ladies, lit in flashes by lightning; on the other was a pet shop with fish tanks. An entire wall was full of shelves of fish tanks with their silken green light and coloured fish. I had kept fish when I was a boy and I recognised some of the species again – the little poecilia who had live births, the guppies shining like precious stones and the kings of the cichlids, the half-moon-shaped silver-and-black-striped Scalaria, that swam like exotic sails through the jungles of vallisneria. It was a weird feeling to see a piece of my childhood so abruptly, silently looming up, a world beyond any of the horizons I was now familiar with, crepitating with lightning and untouched by the present, left by some soft magic intact, not aged, not streaked with blood. I held Maria in my arms and felt her warmth, all the while part of myself was far away, leaning down over a forgotten fountain that had long since ceased to bubble, listening to a past that was strange to me and all the more compelling for it. Days spent among forest streams; a small pool where dragonflies trembled in mid-air; evenings in gardens where lilac tumbled over walls; all that blew past me like a hasty silent film, while I gazed at the translucent gold and green of the miniature watery worlds that for me spelled the ultimate of peace, though murder and mayhem obtained in them just as they did in the other world I was more familiar with.

'What would you say if I had a bottom like that?' asked Maria. I turned round. She was looking the other way, into the corset store. There was an off-pink armour for a Valkyrie, draped over a black model of the kind that tailors use.

'That would be ridiculous,' I replied. 'But you'll never need a corset, thank God. You're the most fascinating *fausse maigre* I know. Bless every ounce of you.'

'Then I don't need to go on a diet to please you?'

'Never.'

'I always wanted that. Down with lettuce and starving models!'

The rain had stopped, bar a few parting drops. I gave the fish tanks a last look. 'Look, monkeys!' said Maria, pointing to the back of the store. In a big cage with a tree trunk in it two agitated monkeys with long tails were doing excitable gymnastics.

'Those are real emigrants,' said Maria. 'In a cage! You'll never match that.'

'You think?' I asked.

She looked at me in surprise. 'I hardly know anything about you,' she said. 'I don't want to know either. And you don't know anything about me. That's the way I want it to stay. What do we care about the stories of our lives.'

'Nothing,' I replied. 'Nothing at all, Maria.'

She looked at the Brünnhilde corset again. 'How quickly life flows away! Do you think I'll ever fit into a suit like that, or belong to a woman's club?'

'No.'

'Then will we not have a settled future?'

'Absolutely not.'

'Have we got any sort of future?'

'I don't know.'

'Isn't that sad?'

'No. If you think about the future you're not there in the present.'

'Good.' She pressed herself against me from her legs up to her shoulders, it was like holding a naiad in my arms. Her wet dress felt like a bathing suit. Her hair hung down in hanks and her face looked very pale. But her eyes were gleaming, and she looked exhausted and smouldering and wild. She smelled of rain, wine and garlic.

We walked down Second Avenue. It had got cool and a few shocked stars were visible among the clouds. Car headlights reflected on the shiny asphalt as if they were driving over ice and the outlines of the skyscrapers stood against the torn sky, as though cut out of tin.

'Here's 57th Street. Home,' said Maria.

'Your own place?'

'No. I'm just sitting it. You remember, it belongs to friends who went to Canada for the summer.'

'Does it belong to the man with the Rolls?' I asked with a grim presentiment.

'No. He lives in Washington.' She laughed. 'I won't make you any more of a gigolo than I have to.'

I didn't say anything. I sensed that a mysterious frontier had been breached. Many things I had thought I could control were now in play. I didn't know what the outcome would be. It came out of the dark and flooded me, it was exciting and unreliable and deception was somehow involved, and yet it overwhelmed me and I didn't resist, it didn't extinguish everything but cast a quivering, flashing light over it, it made me breathless and simultaneously calmed me, it pushed me and burst over me like a wave that I couldn't feel, it melted away and made me so light that I could float away on it.

We stood in front of the building. 'Do you live here alone?' I asked.

'Why do you ask so many questions?' asked Maria Fiola.

16

I left the building very early the next morning. Maria Fiola was still sleeping. Only her head was visible, her body was draped in an apricot-coloured sheet. The bedroom was very cool. An air-conditioning unit was droning away quietly; the curtains were drawn. All over, there was the same mild golden light.

I went to the sitting room to pick up my clothes. They were dry and not too badly crumpled. I got dressed and looked out of the window. There was New York, the city without a past, the city that didn't grow but was built by people in a hurry, the city of stone, cement and asphalt. I could see as far down as Wall Street. There were no people; only alternating traffic lights and lines of cars. It was a futuristic city.

I shut the door quietly behind me and waited for the elevator. A sleepy dwarf pushed the buttons. Outside it was still cool. The storm had broken the pressure and brought in cool, fresh sea air. I bought a *Times* at a kiosk and took it into the drugstore across the street. I ordered coffee and fried eggs, and slowly started to eat. There was no one apart from me and the waitress. Everyone was still asleep, myself too, everything felt slow and silent, like in a slow-motion film. Every movement was calm and protracted, time crawled and didn't chase me, I was breathing more slowly than usual and the things around me breathed more slowly too, they became more significant than before; I felt a connection with them, they drifted by me in the same rhythm as my breathing; they were like friends I had long forgotten, I was one of them, they were no longer alien and hostile, but danced a curious solemn dance around me in which I participated, though without moving.

It was calm as I hadn't felt it for a long time. I could feel it in my veins and behind my brow; the leaden clump of fear that had to be shovelled aside every morning had dissolved without notice, and in its place there was something like a sunny forest scene with cuckoo calls and shining trees. I knew it wouldn't last, but I didn't want to disturb it, so I ate terribly slowly and attentively. Even eating felt like a ritual act that didn't disrupt the gentle rhythm. Everything felt so natural, I couldn't understand why it had ever been different. This was life before it fell into the restless hands of men. I thought and felt everything as though for the first time, like someone waking up out of a serious illness and feeling the world like a child, new and intense and unhurried, almost inexpressible and not yet subject to the eroding function of language, not sayable, still cosmic but already familiar, in a strange, wild and quiet way, a beam that pierced the heart and didn't hurt.

A couple of truck drivers wandered in and called loudly for coffee and doughnuts. I paid and left, and walked slowly over to Central Park. I thought briefly of going back to the hotel and changing my clothes, but I didn't want to lose my sense of effortlessness and drift, so I walked through the waking city to the park and looked for a bench. Ducks were swimming on the lake and bobbing for food. My eye only now happened to light on the newspaper I still carried and when I saw the headline I froze: Paris had capitulated. The Germans had lost it. It was free.

For a long time I sat there completely still. I hardly dared to breathe. I had the feeling the horizon was silently widening and brightening. I looked around; the world had indeed got brighter. Paris was no longer in the hands of the barbarians. And it wasn't in ruins either. Cautiously I picked up the newspaper and read the report, very slowly, then again. Hitler's orders to destroy Paris had not been followed. The general they had been given to had disobeyed. It wasn't clear why; perhaps it was already too late – perhaps he hadn't wanted to sacrifice a city and millions of civilians for nothing. At any rate it hadn't happened. For a moment, common sense had prevailed. Hundreds of other generals might have carried out the orders unblinkingly, not this one. An exception and a stroke of luck. Mass carnage and devastation had been avoided. Perhaps only because the German occupation army was already too weak and was forced to flee; but that didn't matter. Paris lived. It was free. It wasn't just one city that had been freed; it was more.

I thought about telephoning Hirsch, but I felt a strange reluctance to do so. Not yet, I thought. Not even Maria; and certainly not Reginald Black, or Jessie or Ravic or Bosse. Not even Vladimir Moikov. They could all wait, I thought. I wanted to hoard the news.

Slowly I wandered through the park, past the lakes and the pond where kids played with their sailing boats. I sat down on a bench and watched them. I thought of the pool in the Jardin de Luxembourg and instantly Paris no longer felt like an abstraction, but an almost painfully real assemblage of walls, streets, buildings, shops, parks, quais, rustling linden trees and chestnuts with their red and white candles, familiar squares, the Louvre, the Seine, backyards, police stations without torture, the workplace of my teacher Sommer and the cemetery where I had buried him. My past rose on the horizon, dreamily, without pain, my French past, full of melancholy and yet free, mercurial mornings, freed from the jackbooted barbarians and their inhuman laws of slaves, labourers and second-class people and others to be destroyed in crematoria and starvation camps.

I got up. I was near the Metropolitan Museum. It glowed yellow through the trees. I now knew where I wanted to go. Up until now I had been afraid of it; I hadn't wanted to rouse memories of Brussels without cause; it was bad enough to have them roiling my dreams. But now I didn't want to avoid them any more.

It was very early and there were very few visitors in the museum. I crept through the great entrance hall like a thief, quiet and on tiptoe, looking round from time to time, as though someone were following me. I knew that was ridiculous, but I couldn't help it; it was as though shadows were coming after me, vanishing when I turned to look. My heart was throbbing and I had to force myself to climb the broad staircase instead of slinking along the walls. I was surprised the impact was so great.

On the first floor I stopped. In two great halls hung old carpets. Some of them were familiar to me from books belonging to Ludwig Sommer. I walked slowly through the rooms and had the strange sensation of a double existence, as if I were Ludwig Sommer, returned to life for the space of an hour, and at the same time the missing student who had once gone by my former name. With Sommer's eyes I saw what Sommer had taught me to see and underneath felt the dead yearning of my youth, consumed in murder and fire. I listened to them both, just as you might listen to the wind bringing sounds of an unattainable distance, distorted and full of the charm of the past, only bearable in fragments, in discontinuous scraps, blown hither in this vacuum cathedral of art, briefly separated from the implacable stream of reality, painlessly, as though the air were full of opium, anaesthetising memories, so that you could even look at your wounds without feeling their pain.

How afraid I had been of it! And now it was no more than a picture book belonging to me, but strangely devoid of feeling. I looked at my fingers; they were mine and they were Ludwig Sommer's, and they were those of a third person as well, who seemed to have been extinguished by some mild form of magic. I walked slowly, as in a blissful dream, a dream of a kind I hadn't had for many years, without fear or loathing or the terrible sense of having missed something that could never be made good. I had been expecting the past to surge up at me, full of sin and remorse and incapacity, and the heavy grief that came from having failed − but now in this light temple to everything that men were still capable of, aside from murder, robbery and bloody egoism, the past didn't come and in its place the quiet torches of art were burning on the walls. They were silent witnesses whose mere existence was proof that some things survived.

I came to the room with Chinese bronze urns. There was a bronze altar on which they stood, green and sharp-edged, buried for a thousand years and now bathed in light like junks on a white sea, like green and blue primal rocks. There was no trace left of their original metallic colour; they were all patina and past, and had been resurrected to some new charmed mode of being. What I loved about them was what they had never been, I thought, and I passed quickly on, as though they had some hidden strength in them that might have shot out, ghosts I didn't want to rouse.

In the Impressionists I found Paris and the landscapes of France. It was odd; I had been a fugitive in France, pursued by the police and the bureaucracy; I had been put in an internment camp there, until I was freed by Robert Hirsch's trick. But in spite of that, it seemed to me more like sloppiness and negligence on the part of the government, not really evil, however many times the gendarmes took us in. Only when they joined forces with the bounty hunters of the German SS did they become truly dangerous. Not all of them; but enough to assist the German terror effectively. And for all that, I kept my affection for the country, stained with episodes of blood and ruthlessness like anywhere else where the police are involved, but also by almost idyllic intervals which slowly outgrew and overgrew the others.

In front of the paintings my objections and reservations about France disappeared. They were what the landscape was when the people were only accessories. They glowed and remained silent, they didn't shout and had no raucous nationality. They were summer and autumn and winter and timeless, the torment of their creation was dispelled like smoke, the loneliness of consumption was fixed in them to an earnest and happy today, they were a present that had overcome the past, just like the bronzes of China. I felt my heart thumping. The indescribable domain of art held life like a crystal ring, I felt; high over murdering, wriggling, lying and dying mankind, the work consumed its creator along with the murderer, and all that remained behind was what had been created. I suddenly remembered the moment in the museum in Brussels when I briefly forgot my fear for the first time while looking at a Chinese bronze – a moment of pure looking that had stayed with me, almost as intense as my earlier memories of dread and horror. Here it was again, stronger now than it had been at the time, and in that moment I understood that my time in America was a unique, baffling and brief present, an intermezzo between killing and killing, a lull between two storms, something I had yet to understand correctly and had only misused, an area of separation, a corner of silence, of kind silence that I had gone and filled with impatience, instead of taking it for what it was: a gift of time, a blue space between two clouds.

I left the museum. Outside, the traffic was now spinning its wheels, the sun had warmed up and a blast of heat pounded against the doors. But everything was different. It was as if a gate had been opened. The gate was the fall of Paris, it led outwards, my notional prison had given way to a pardon and the end, appalling, threatening and ineluctable, was all at once visible between the clouds, a double end, the end of the barbarians and of my country, inextricably tied together, a two-edged sword that struck them both, and with it my own destiny that loomed like a black wall in front of me full of revenge and self-destruction.

I walked down the steps. A warm wind tugged at my clothes. A gift of time, I thought. A brief, precious gift of time.

'It's as though a gate had burst open,' said Reginald Black, stroking his beard. 'An opening into the free world. And on such a day I have to go and sell that barbarian Cooper a picture. And another Degas at that. You know he's coming in an hour.'

'Call him and cancel.'

Black gave me his best beaming Assyrian smile. 'I can't do that,' he replied. 'It would be in violation of my unhappy dual nature. I have to grit my teeth and sell. My heart bleeds when I see the hands my pictures fall into; but I have to sell. And I know I'm a benefactor of mankind. Art keeps its value better than any shares. Pictures go up and up in price.'

'Why don't you keep them, then?'

'You asked me that once already. It's my nature. I need to keep reaffirming myself.'

I looked at him. I was still surprised, but I believed him. 'I'm a gambler,' he said. 'A gambler and a bohemian. It's not through any desire of my own that I've ended up as a benefactor of millionaires. I sell them pictures that will be worth twice as much in a year's time. And these people haggle with me over a couple of hundred dollars. It's an appalling destiny. They think of me as a cheat when all I'm doing is making them rich.'

I laughed. 'Well may you laugh,' said Black. 'It's the truth. Since last year, prices have risen by twenty to thirty per cent. Show me the company whose shares can keep pace with that. The depressing thing is that only the rich can profit from me. No one else can afford pictures. And what depresses me still more is that there are hardly any collectors left who understand them and love them. People today buy as an investment, or to be able to say they own a Renoir or a Van Gogh – as a status symbol. Poor pictures, I think.'

I was never quite sure how seriously to take him; what was incontestable was that he was right. 'What shall we do when Cooper comes?' I asked. 'Do we need to rehang a few of the pictures?'

'Not today. Not on such a day.' Black took a mouthful of cognac. 'I just do it for my own private satisfaction anyway. Earlier it used to be different, then it was part of it. But today? With those millionaires who buy pictures as though they were pork bellies? Don't you think?'

'It depends.'

Black shook his head. 'Not today. Cooper's probably done some roaring trade. Even so, he will probably be annoyed that Paris wasn't bombed – he would have earned even more. Every time there's a big battle, he treats himself to a little picture. Two hundred thousand casualties makes one middle-sized Degas, as a reward to himself for protecting democracy. Even the conscience of the world is on his side. Don't you agree?'

I nodded.

'You must be feeling strange,' Black went on. 'Happy and depressed at the same time. Happy because Paris is free again and depressed because your country has had to give it up.'

I shook my head. 'Actually, it's neither of those.'

Black looked at me piercingly. 'Well, let's leave it. Let's have a drink.'

From a shelf in a chest he produced a bottle. I looked at the label. 'Isn't that the cognac for important clients? For Cooper?'

'Not any more,' declared Black. 'Not since Paris has been liberated. We'll drink it ourselves now. Cooper can have the Rémy Martin. We're having the forty-year-old.'

He poured. 'Soon we'll get cognac from France again,' he said. 'Cognac that the Germans won't have intercepted at source. Do you think the French will have managed to keep some hidden?'

'Yes,' I said. 'The Germans don't know a lot about cognac.'

'What do they know a lot about?'

'Fighting. Work. And obedience.'

'Is that why they trumpet that stuff about their superiority and the master race?'

'Yes,' I replied. 'It's because they're not. A tyrannical bent doesn't make you a master race. Tyranny and authority aren't the same thing.'

The cognac went down like velvet. The whole room was full of the aroma right away. 'In celebration of the day, I think I'll ask Cooper for another five thousand dollars,' said

Black. 'The time of bended knee is over. Paris has been liberated. It won't be long till we can go shopping there again. I know of a couple of Monets – and Cézannes—'

His eyes shone. 'And you know what, they won't even be expensive,' he declared. 'The prices in Europe are much lower than they are here. You just need to be the first person to express an interest. The best thing is you take a little suitcase full of money with you. Cash is so much more sensual than any cheque; it makes them weak at the knee. Especially the French. What about another cognac?'

'Happily,' I said. 'But it'll take a while before it's all right to go touring around France.'

'I'm not so sure. The collapse could come very suddenly.'

[Cooper cancels his visit at short notice.]

'There is a God,' said Alexander Silver when I dropped in on his shop late in the afternoon. 'I can believe in Him again. Paris has been liberated. The barbarians will not take over the world. We're closing a couple of hours early, in celebration, and going to dinner at Voisin's. Will you come, Mr Sommer? How are you feeling? Wretched as a German, I suppose? But liberated as a Jew, no?'

'Still more liberated as a citizen of the world,' I replied. I had once again forgotten that I had a Jewish passport.

'Then please come with us. My brother will be there. He's bringing his shiksa.'

'What?'

'He made me a solemn promise that he wasn't going to marry her. Word of honour. Of course that changes things. It doesn't make them better, but maybe more agreeable.'

'Do you believe him?'

Alexander Silver gulped. 'You mean you can't trust where

feelings are involved? Maybe not. But it's better to know the risks. It's easier to control then. Not so?'

'So,' I replied.

'And you're coming? We mean to have pâté de foie gras as a starter again.'

'Don't make it too hard for me, please. I can't make it today.'

Silver looked at me in astonishment. 'Don't tell me you've been caught as well as Arnold?'

I shook my head. 'No, just another engagement.'

'Not with Mr Reginald Black?'

I laughed. 'No, Mr Alexander.'

'That's all right. Between those two poles you're safe. Business and love.'

Over the afternoon, I felt a gentle reluctance gradually getting stronger. I was thinking as little as I could about Maria Fiola and noticed that it was easy – as though I unconsciously wanted to displace her. On my way to the hotel the florist waved to me energetically. 'Mr Sommer! A wonderful opportunity!' He held up a fistful of lilies. 'White lilies. Practically for nothing. Look!'

I shook my head. 'Those are flowers for the dead, Emilio.'

'Not in summer. Only in November. For All Souls'. In spring they are Easter flowers. In summer they are flowers of purity. And very cheap.'

Emilio must have got a big batch from a funeral home. He had white chrysanthemums, too, and a few white orchids. He held out a stem, which looked lovely. 'You will make an unforgettable impression as a cavalier and Don Juan. Who else gives orchids nowadays? Look! Like a row of white butterflies dreaming.'

I looked up in surprise. 'A white that is only matched by gardenias at dusk,' Emilio continued.

'Enough,' I said. 'Or else I'll give in, Emilio.'

Emilio was on song. 'It's not possible to give in too much,' he said, laying a second stem next to the first. 'That makes you strong. Gorgeous for the lovely lady you step out with. Orchids are her flower.'

'She's not in New York.'

'Oh, too bad. But someone else? You must have a replacement!? You must celebrate. Paris has been liberated.'

Yes, with funeral flowers, I thought. Strange idea! 'Take one for yourself anyway,' Emilio pressed. 'Orchids last for three or four weeks. By that time the rest of France will have fallen.'

'Do you reckon?'

'Of course. Rome is free – and now Paris. Now things will move fast, very fast.'

Very fast, I thought, and to my surprise felt a sharp stab of pain that took my breath away. 'Yes, of course,' I muttered. 'Perhaps it will all go very fast now.'

I walked on with a strange feeling of something having been taken from me, something I hadn't even had – a flag, a sky of sun and clouds that sparkled and drifted on before I could reach up and grab it.

Felix O'Brien the stand-in porter was leaning casually in the doorway. 'You're expected,' he announced.

I felt my heart beat and I went quickly in. I hoped it would be Maria, but it was Lachmann, who greeted me with a wide smile. 'I've got free of the Puerto-Rican lady,' he reported without any preliminaries. 'I've found another woman. Reddish blonde, from Mississippi. Germanic, big, generous, a wonderful specimen.'

'A Germania?' I asked.

He laughed a little sheepishly. 'In love, the question of

nationalities is secondary, Ludwig. She is of course an American. What does that matter? Any port in a storm.'

'In Germany you'd be gassed for it.'

'But we're here in free America. She could be my salvation. I dry up without love. The Puerto-Rican was just stringing me along. Plus she – and her pimp – cost too much. A man can't sell as many rosaries and icons as you need to feed that Mexican who lives with her. Not even in New York. I was close to bankrupt.'

'Paris has fallen.'

'What's that?' he asked absently. 'Oh, Paris, yes. Of course! Well, it'll take another two years or so till the Germans are out of the rest of France. And then they'll go on fighting in Germany. It's the only thing they know how to do. As I know to my cost. It's not possible to wait for them, Ludwig. I'm getting on. The blonde Valkyrie is no pushover. But at least I have hope—'

'Kurt' I said. 'Wake up! Why should she go for you when she's so wonderful?'

'One shoulder is lower,' explained Lachmann. 'It's the suggestion of a very small hunchback. Barely noticeable, but she's well aware of it. It inhibits her. Even though her breasts are like marble and her bottom – sugar, I tell you. She works on the till of a cinema on 44th Street. If you want to see a film she can get you in for free.'

'Thanks a lot,' I said. 'I don't go to the cinema much. So you're happy?'

Lachmann's expression changed. His eyes gleamed. 'Happy?' he retorted. 'I don't know the word. An emigrant is never happy. We are condemned to uncertainty. We are aliens. We can never go back and we are here on sufferance. It's a terrible situation and worse if you are prey to your drives, as I am.'

'That depends. At least you've still got them. Other people have lost theirs.'

'Don't laugh,' sighed Lachmann. 'Even success in love is a drain; failure obviously too. But what does an emotional dunderhead understand about such things?'

'Enough to notice that happiness seems to make you more aggressive than failure, you fearless dealer in religious artefacts—'

I stopped. I remembered that I didn't know the address of Maria Fiola's new flat. Nor the telephone number either. 'Goddamnit!' I said.

'Typical goy,' declared Lachmann. 'When you don't know what to say, you swear. Or you shoot.'

Second Avenue at night was a homosexual *paseo*. They walked up and down, arm in arm; young singles waited to be approached and older men eyed them with careful, lustful regard. There was a carnivalesque atmosphere, a heated slow carousel turning, powered by an exotic engine that was forbidden but tolerated, hence risky and exciting as if the air trembled.

'Those pigs!' said the newspaper seller in his kiosk where I bought the evening paper.

'How can you say that? Aren't they your customers?' I asked.

'I'm not talking about the homos,' he replied. 'I mean their fucking dogs. By law they should be on a lead, but the queens let them go. They are besotted with their animals. Once it used to be dachshunds, then terriers were all the rage and now it's poodles. Look at them! Droves of them.'

I looked around. He was right. The street was dense with men taking their poodles on walkies.

'There's that wretch again,' shouted the newspaper seller and tried to get out of his round kiosk. He was slow in getting out. A bale of magazines got in his way. 'Give that animal a kick up the backside,' he yelled.

A little champagne-coloured poodle had sauntered up and cocked a leg against the newspapers that were hanging underneath the counter outside. I shooed him away. He yapped at me and disappeared in the parade that was sashaying back and forth. 'That was Fifi,' said the newspaper seller, furiously and dismally examining a well-drenched copy of *Confidential*. 'He's managed to do it again! That little rat always picks my kiosk to pee on. And I tell you, he must have a bladder like an elephant's. The worst of it is I can never get out in time to nab him.'

'He seems to have some taste,' I said. 'Only peeing on things that are worth peeing on.'

The newspaper seller clambered back into his kiosk. 'I can't see him from here,' he said. 'Fifi knows that, the smart bitch. He creeps up from behind and cocks his leg. I don't see him till he's trotting away – and sometimes I don't see him at all, if he leaves the same way he came. Why can't he be like a normal dog and piss on a tree? Every day he costs me a couple of issues.'

'That's galling for you,' I said. 'Couldn't you do something like sprinkle pepper over the bottom row of your publications?'

The newspaper seller looked at me. 'Would you read an erotic magazine if it made you sneeze? If your eyes were weeping? I'd like to poison all those poodles. I have dogs myself – but not like these.'

I took my newspaper and looked in. What's keeping me back? I thought. What gives me this unreasonable reluctance? I had no idea. It was a mixture of all sorts of feelings, oddly spun together out of lightness, excitement, impatience, a small, flickering happiness and a remote feeling of guilt. I folded up the paper and walked into the building, which I recognised.

In the elevator I ran into Fifi, the champagne-coloured poodle, and his owner, who immediately addressed me. 'I think we're going to the same floor,' he said. 'Didn't you come in last night with Miss Fiola?'

I nodded, surprised. 'I saw her come in,' he explained. 'I'm José Kruse.'

'I already know Fifi. He's the darling of the newspaper kiosk.'

Kruse laughed. He wore a heavy gold bracelet and had too many teeth. 'Our floor is supposed to have been a high-class brothel once upon a time,' he said. 'Not unfitting, is it?'

I wouldn't have known what floor Maria's apartment was on. Kruse stopped the elevator and let me out first. He followed directly on my heels. 'Here we are,' he said and looked at me. 'You're over there and I'm here. Perhaps we can have a cocktail together some time. I have a superb view.'

'Yes, perhaps.' I was relieved to have located Maria Fiola's apartment with so little trouble. José Kruse watched me and waved.

Maria Fiola opened the door a crack and looked out. I could see an eye and a lock of hair. 'Hello, fugitive,' she said, laughing. 'You really are a refugee, aren't you. Leaving me there on our first day without saying goodbye.'

I took a deep breath. 'Hello, fragment of an eye and a shoulder and a lock of hair,' I said. 'Can I come in? I bear greetings from Fifi the poodle and your neighbour José Kruse. But for them, I don't think I'd have found you.'

She opened the door some more. She was wearing shoes, but was otherwise naked. A knotted towel sat atop her head like a turban. She was very beautiful. At her back, New York's skyscrapers gleamed in the honey light of evening. The windows flashed like sculptures made from mirrors.

'I'm just getting dressed,' she said. 'I have to go and get my picture taken. Why didn't you call?'

'I didn't have your number.'

'And why did you take off so early this morning?'

'Out of regard. I didn't want to wake you and I didn't want to expose you, later on, when all the poodles get their walkies. This seems to be a particularly animal-friendly building.'

She looked at me critically for a moment. 'I wouldn't think quite so much if I were you,' she said. 'Apparently, this used to be—'

'A brothel. But a high-class one, hundred dollars a pop or more. José told me all about it.'

'Did he invite you to cocktails?'

'Yes, as a matter of fact he did,' I said, surprised. 'How did you know?'

'He always does that. Don't go. He's charming and vicious. The upper reaches of this building is all fairies. We have to be careful.'

'You too?'

'Me too. There's no shortage of female fairies here.'

I went up to the window. Below me lay New York, white and stone like a city in Algeria.

'The homosexuals always look out the best parts of a city to live in,' said Maria. 'They're very clever like that.'

'Does this apartment belong to a homo as well, then?'

Maria laughed. Then she nodded. 'Does that calm you or offend you?'

'Neither one,' I answered. 'I just thought this is the first time we've been together in an apartment, instead of in bars or hotels or studios.' I pulled her to me. 'You're so brown.'

'I tan easily.' She freed herself. 'I must go. Only for an hour. To try on some hats. For the spring. I'll be finished soon. Stay here. Don't go. The fridge is full, if you want something. But don't go.'

She got dressed. I adored the complete unconcern with which she walked around naked or dressed.

'What if someone comes?' I asked.

'Don't let them in. Anyway, no one will come.'

'Are you sure?'

She laughed. 'The men I know tend to phone in advance.'

'That's good to know.' I kissed her. 'OK, I'll be here. Your prisoner.'

She looked at me. 'You're not a prisoner. You're an emigrant. An alien. A wanderer. And I'm not going to lock you in. I'll leave you a key.'

She waved. I walked her to the elevator, then watched the cage carry her down the yellow shaft and into the city. Then I heard some dogs barking below. I carefully shut the door and went back into the strange apartment.

She's made it easy for me, I thought. The tangle of contradictory feelings I'd run around with all day had simplified to a mix of naturalness and cheerfulness. I walked around the apartment. In the bedroom I saw her clothes scattered all over the bed. That moved me more than anything else did. A pair of high-heeled shoes stood in front of the mirror, one of them on its side. It was an image of delicious disorder. In a corner was a photograph in a green leather frame. It was the picture of an elderly man who looked as though he hadn't had much to worry about in the course of his life. I thought I recognised the man I'd seen Maria with a couple of days ago. I went into the kitchen and put the bottle of Moikov I'd brought with me in the fridge. Maria was right; the fridge was full. I discovered a bottle of real, Russian vodka, the same make that Maria had sent round for me in the hotel and that had been in the Rolls-Royce as well. I hesitated momentarily, then I put mine in there too, separated by a bottle of green chartreuse.

I sat down by the window and looked out. Outside, the great evening show was in progress. The evening sky went pink, then blue, and the skyscrapers changed from being functional things to modern cathedrals. The windows came on, rows of them at a time, and I knew the cleaning women were getting going in the empty offices. After a little while the towers stood there like great hives of light. It reminded me of my time on Ellis Island, when I'd stared from the dormitory out at the unreachable city, after I'd woken up out of one of my nightmares.

A piano began playing next door. I could hear it slightly muffled by the walls. Maybe it was José Kruse, but the music didn't seem to me to go with José Kruse and Fifi. It was someone practising a few of the easier pieces in *The Well-Tempered Clavier*. I remembered practising them myself once upon a time, before the barbarians overran Germany a hundred years ago. My father was still alive and at liberty, and my mother was lying in hospital with typhoid and worrying whether I would pass my exams. All at once I felt a slicing pain; it was as if a piece of the film of my life were being pulled through at breakneck speed – far too quick to follow, but still painful anyway. Faces and scenes appeared and disappeared, people crying, Sibylle's shocked and brave face, the corridors of the museum in Brussels, Ruth dead in Paris, with her eyes coated with flies; dead. Too many dead for one lifetime and the black reflexive salvation of a desire for revenge.

I got up. The air conditioning was buzzing and the room felt almost cold; even so, I felt as though I was dripping with sweat. I opened the window and looked out. Then I picked up the newspaper and read the war reports. The Allies were already beyond Paris; they were advancing along a broad front, and it seemed as though the Germans were on the run and not offering much resistance. I studied the little sketched maps avidly; I knew that part of France very well, its bars and roads and hamlets – it was the Via Dolorosa, along which the emigrants had fled. Now it was the victors who were fleeing along it, the soldiers, the SS, the torturers, the drag hunters and killers. They were fleeing back to Germany – the victors, of whom I was one, though they had hunted me too. I dropped the newspaper and stared into space.

I heard the door and then Maria's voice. 'Is no one home?'

It had got dark in the room. 'In here,' I answered and stood up. 'I didn't switch the light on.'

She came in. 'I was thinking you might have run away again.'

'I don't run away,' I said, and drew her to me. In that moment she felt like all the life in the world.

'No,' she murmured. 'You mustn't run away. I can't be alone. I'm nothing when I'm alone.'

'You are the life of the world,' I said. 'You are all the warmth it has: Maria, I adore you. You are all light and all colours.'

'Why were you sitting in the darkened room?'

I pointed to the shining skyscrapers. 'Outside the world is alight. I forgot to turn a light on inside. Now you're here, I don't need light.'

'But I do.' She laughed. 'I get depressed in dark rooms. And I need light to unpack. I've brought some supper for us. Tins and jars full. In America you can buy everything ready made.'

'I brought some vodka,' I said.

'I had a whole other bottle left.'

'I saw it. Genuine Russian.'

She leaned against me. 'I know. I prefer yours from Moikov.'

'I don't. I'm not prejudiced.'

'But I am. Take the Russian vodka with you,' she said. 'I don't want it here any more. Give it to Moikov, it'll make him happy.'

'All right,' I replied. She kissed me. I felt her perfume and her young, fresh skin.

'You have to treat me carefully,' she murmured. 'I can't stand to suffer any more. I'm vulnerable. I don't know what will happen otherwise.'

'I won't hurt you,' I said. 'Not on purpose anyway, Maria. Accidentally, you never know.'

'Hold me tight. I want you to hold me tight.'

'I will. I will hold you tight.'

She sighed happily, like a little girl. She stood very slim and frail before the shining wall of light of the skyscrapers in which a thousand cleaning ladies were mopping up the dirt of an office day, and at the same time filling the sky with magic. She said something in Italian. I didn't catch it and replied in German. 'My sweet life,' I said. 'Lost and resurrected and indestructible—'

She shook her head. 'I can't understand you. And when we really try to talk to each other you can't understand me either. An odd sort of love. Love in translation.'

I kissed her. 'I don't think there are translations in love, Maria. And if there are, then I'm not afraid of them.'

We lay on the bed. 'Do you have to go out again tonight?' I asked.

Maria shook her head. 'Not till tomorrow night.'

'Good. Then we can stay in. We can have something more to eat, pastrami and cheese with rye bread. And beer – and then the rest of the Sara Lee cake with coffee. Such an adventure!'

She laughed. 'A very simple adventure.'

'The biggest adventure I know! I can't say how long it is since I've last experienced such a thing. When I was a refugee, I always stayed in cheap rooms and I felt happy enough if I found one of those. Then I would sit on a dirty window seat and scarf something down out of waxed paper, and I was happy to have that. And today—'

'Today you've eaten out of waxed paper again,' Maria put in.

'Today I've eaten with you. In your apartment.'

'It isn't my—' she replied sleepily. 'It's borrowed like everything else of mine – my clothes, my jewels, my crowns, even the seasons. Today we were busy doing next spring at the photographer's.'

I looked at her. She lay on the bed all naked and brown and she was very beautiful. Next spring, I thought. I wonder where I'll be? Still in America? Or would the war be over by then, and I trying to make my way back to Europe? I didn't know, but something in me flinched. 'What were you modelling?' I asked.

'Jewellery,' she said. 'Big, bright, fake, cheap jewellery. Fake like me.'

'Why do you say that?'

'Because I feel it. I don't think I have a real self. Not one that doesn't change and is always clear. I'm like a figure dancing between two mirrors; it's there, but when you reach out your hand to touch it, it isn't. A bit grim, don't you think?'

'No,' I replied. 'Dangerous. Not for you. For others.' She laughed and got up. 'I want to show you something else we modelled. Very small hats – velvet and brocade caps and berets. I took a couple of them home with me. Until tomorrow.'

She walked out of the room into the corridor. The air-conditioning unit hummed softly in the window. The little flat was so high up that the noise of the street was almost inaudible. Suddenly everything felt a little unreal – the deep, tinted twilight in the room, without artificial light, only lit by the glittering glass walls of the skyscrapers. It was as though we were flying in a silent balloon, briefly lifted out of time, war, uncertainty and smouldering fear into a zone of peace that was so unfamiliar to me that its silence gave me palpitations.

Maria returned. She was wearing a soft beret, some barbarous-looking gold collar round her neck, a pair of high-heeled slippers on her feet and nothing else. 'May I present: Spring 1945,' she said. 'Negro ornaments of brass to look like gold. And coloured glass stones.'

Spring 1945! It was as though she had said: never and tomorrow. It almost felt as though it was tomorrow. The artificial chill of the room tightened. I stood up and embraced Maria. 'Do you want to go?' she asked.

I shook my head. 'I'm just going to the kiosk to fetch the evening paper. I'll be back right away.'

'You're bringing the war into our room,' she said. 'Can't you wait till tomorrow?'

I looked at her in surprise. 'I'm not bringing the war into our room,' I said. 'I'm going downstairs to look at the headlines; then I'll hurry back to this room, where I know you're waiting for me, and I'll feel a kind of happiness that I no longer knew: to have someone waiting for me, and a night and a room with you. It's the biggest adventure I can imagine: conventional life without fear – even though it sounds so philistine, but not for us the modern children of Ahasuerus.'

She kissed me. 'Whoever makes such long speeches is only interested in concealing the truth. What will I do with a man who is prepared to forsake me for a newspaper?'

'You're a gypsy as well,' I said. 'More than I am. But I'll stay here. Let time stand still for the day.'

Maria laughed. I pulled her close. I didn't want to tell her why I wanted to see the newspaper. It wasn't because of the news. I wanted to see how much time I still had for this peace that had broken out over my existence. Beloved, alien life, I thought. Stay! Don't leave me before I have to go. And I knew how deceiving that was, with an undertone of betrayal and falsehood. But I couldn't go on thinking about it, Maria was too close to me and the other thing was still too far away. How much could happen in the meantime and who could say who would leave whom? I felt Maria's lips and her skin, and stopped thinking. Late at night I woke up and heard the piano next door again. Someone was hesitantly playing a Clementi sonata, which in another life I had once practised myself. Maria was asleep at my side, exhausted and taking deep breaths. I thought of my forgotten youth and stared out of the great window into the illuminated night. Then I listened to Maria's breathing again. And once again it seemed to me that we were both in a balloon hanging in the still point at the centre of a tornado. Thank you, I thought. You bit of wild peace in this night.

17

'Jessie Stein has to undergo an operation in the next few days,' said Robert Hirsch.

'Is it dangerous? What's the matter with her?'

'They don't know yet. It's a growth of some kind. Bosse and Ravic have examined her. They're not saying anything. Medical confidentiality. Probably the operation will tell them whether the tumour is benign or otherwise.'

'Cancer?' I asked.

'I hate that word,' said Hirsch. 'After Gestapo, it's the ugliest word I know.'

I nodded. 'Does Jessie have any sense of anything?'

'They told her it was a harmless little operation. But she's suspicious as a fox.'

'Who's doing the operation?'

'Bosse and Ravic, together with an American doctor.'

For a while neither of us spoke. 'Just like in Paris,' I said. 'When Ravic operated with a French doctor. Surgery as graft.'

'It's not quite like that, according to Ravic. Here it's more grey than black. He won't be facing prison if he's caught.'

'Did you get Bosse's money?' I asked. 'From our fishing expedition?'

Hirsch nodded. 'It was very straightforward. Of course Bosse didn't want to accept it. I practically had to beat him up to make him agree. He thought it was extortion. His own money! Some emigrants and their sense of honour. It makes you despair.' He laughed. 'Go and see Jessie, Ludwig. I've been once and I can't go again; it would make her suspicious. She's afraid. I'm not a good comforter. Other people's fears make me angry, sentimental and impatient. Go and see her. She's having a German day today. She says if you're ill, you don't have to stammer in broken English. She needs help. People.'

'I'll go along there tonight, when I've finished at Reginald Black's. What's happening with Carmen, Robert?'

'She's charming and unfathomable, as only the truly simple can be.'

'Is there such a thing as a truly simple woman? Stupid, yes, but simple?'

'Simple is just a word. Just like laziness or stupidity are words. For me it describes the wonderful area of baffling anti-logic − kitsch, if you like, beyond values and facts, pure fantasy, chance, feeling, without ambition, indolence without end; something that charms me because it's so completely alien to me.'

I looked at Hirsch doubtfully. 'Do you really believe all that, Robert?'

He laughed. 'Of course I don't − that's why it delights me so.'

'Have you told Carmen about it?'

'Of course not. She wouldn't understand.'

'You just used a lot of words,' I said. 'Do you really think she's so simple?'

Hirsch looked up. 'Are you suggesting I don't understand women?'

I shook my head. 'No, that's not what I mean at all − although that's part of being a hero. Conquerors don't usually understand women − that's why victims do.'

'Then why are the others still the victors?'

'Understanding doesn't make you a conqueror. Least of all understanding women. Life is unfair like that. But victors don't always remain victors, Robert. And if something's simple, it shouldn't be needlessly complicated; life is complicated enough.'

Robert waved to the white-clad man behind the bar of the drugstore, where we had just consumed two hamburgers. 'I can't help it,' he said. 'Those salesmen always look like doctors to me; and a drugstore is a chemist's shop. Even the hamburgers seem to have a taste of chloroform. Don't you think?'

'No,' I said.

He laughed. 'We've been bandying a lot of foolish words today. You too.' He looked at me. 'Are you happy?'

'What's happiness?' I said. 'A nineteenth-century term, I believe.'

'Yes,' he replied. 'What's happiness indeed. I don't know. I'm not on the lookout for it either. I don't think I would know what to do with it.'

We went out on to the street. I was suddenly worried for Hirsch. He didn't seem to me to fit in anywhere. Least of all in his electrical goods shop. He had been a type of conquistador; but what was a Jewish conquistador doing in New York, if the draft board had already rejected him?

Jessie was lying in bed in a salmon-coloured Chinese gown that in the imagination of its Brooklyn manufacturer was probably a mandarin robe.

'You're just in time, Ludwig,' she said. 'Tomorrow I'm off to the knacker's.'

She had a flushed face, fever-shining eyes and was full of fake cheerfulness. Her round face was rigid with the fear it tried to overcome. Even her hair had suffered; it stood on end like a fright wig.

'Oh, Jessie,' said Ravic, 'you're overdoing it again. It's just a routine examination. Just to be on the safe side.'

'In case of what?' asked Jessie quickly.

'Lots of things, big and small.'

'Tell me the big ones.'

'Jessie, I don't know. I don't have a crystal ball; that's why we're doing the operation. But I'll tell you the truth.'

'Promise?'

'Promise, Jessie.'

Her breathing was shallow. She didn't altogether trust him. Probably she had already asked him a dozen times. 'All right,' she finally said and turned to me. 'What do you say to Paris?'

'Paris is free, Jessie.' I didn't know what else I was supposed to say.

'To think that I lived to see it,' she murmured.

I nodded. 'You'll live to see the liberation of Berlin too, Jessie.'

She was silent for a while. 'Eat something, Ludwig. In Paris you were always hungry. Next door the twins have coffee and cake. Let's not be sad. Everything happens so quickly. Paris – and then this. And everything feels so close together. As if it were only yesterday. Don't think about it. You know, in spite of everything, they were good times – compared to this, now.' She pointed at her bed. 'Get yourself some coffee, Ludwig. It's freshly made. Ravic has gone to get some as well.' She leaned across to me conspiratorially. 'I don't believe him,' she whispered. 'Not one word!'

'Or me?'

'I don't believe you either, Ludwig. And now go and get something to eat.'

★

There were about a dozen people in there. Bosse too; he was sitting by the window, staring out. It was warm and overcast, as though there was rain on the way. The sky was the colour of white ash. The windows were shut and an air-conditioning unit was humming away on a walnut cabinet like a great tired fly. The Dahl twins came in with coffee and plum cake, tiptoeing like ponies; at first, I didn't even recognise them. They were wearing short, tight skirts and striped cotton sweaters with short sleeves.

'Luscious, no?' someone said behind me.

I turned round. It was Bach, the man who was unable to find out which of the twins, if either, liked her bottom pinched. 'Absolutely,' I said, pleased to be able to think of something else. 'It must be so confusing to have a relation-ship with one of the twins, if the other is so like her that you can't tell them apart.'

'You double up.' Bach nodded eagerly and speared a piece of strudel. 'If one of them dies, you marry the other. No bother! Where else in life do you get insurance like that?'

'That's a macabre thought. Last time you were just wondering how to get at their pretty bottoms without getting coffee thrown all over you. And now you're proposing marriage. You're a flexible sort of idealist.'

Bach tipped his bald head garlanded by black hair so that it looked like the back end of a baboon. He kept a suspi-cious silence. 'I wasn't thinking of marrying them succes-sively,' I said. 'And I wasn't thinking about dying either.'

'Of course not, you thoughtless goy. But what else do you think about when you're in love? That one party must die before the other and the other is alone. It's the oldest fear in the world, albeit possibly modified. Out of the archaic fear of dying, love makes fear for the other.' Bach licked the

sugar off his fingers. 'A torment. Twins are the rational solution. Especially these here.'

The Dahls were just tiptoeing past. Jessie had asked to
see her copper engravings of Berlin. 'Would you marry one
of them, just like that?' I asked. 'After all, you can't tell them
apart, probably not even their characters. There are such
cases. Or would you toss a coin?'

Bach eyed me mournfully over his pince-nez and under
his bushy eyebrows. 'Just you go on making your little jokes
about a man who's poor, bald, homeless and Jewish,' he said.
'Those aren't the girls for me, they're Hollywood fodder.'

'What about you? You're an actor too.'

'I play very small parts. Nazis, to my chagrin, nothing
but Nazis. Of course with dyed hair and wigs. It's curious,
though: in Hollywood almost all the Nazis are played by
Jews. Can you imagine what that feels like? Schizophrenic.
Luckily, some of the Nazis come to a sticky end – otherwise
it would be simply unbearable.'

'Wouldn't it be worse to be a Jew playing a Jew killed
by the Nazis?'

Bach looked at me in silence. 'I never thought of that,'
he finally said. 'The things you come up with! No, the Jews
are generally played by stars. By non-Jewish stars. What a
world.'

I looked around. Luckily, the keeper of the bloodlist was
not in attendance. Instead, I met the author Franke. He
had emigrated with his Jewish wife when the Nazis took
power. He himself was not a Jew. His wife had left him
after they reached America. He had lived in Hollywood
for six months. The studios had offered some prominent
authors work for a time so that they could familiarise
themselves with America; they had expected in return that
the authors would write something for them. Almost none

of them had been up to it. There was a big difference between books and film scripts, and the writers were too old to adapt. Their contracts were not renewed. They fell burden to charitable organisations and had to beg or else received private subventions.

'I can't learn the language,' said Franke despairingly. 'I just can't. And what good would it do anyway? There's a difference between writing and talking that's like day and night.'

'Aren't you writing in German?' I asked. 'For later?'

'What?' he asked. 'About my wretched life here? What for? I was sixty when I left Germany; now I'm past seventy. An old man. My books are burned over there and banned. Do you think anyone has heard of me?'

'Yes,' I said.

Franke shook his head. 'Ten years of poison in Germany can't be washed away overnight. Have you seen newsreel footage of the rallies over there? Those tens of thousands of jubilant, shouting faces? They weren't forced to do that. I'm tired,' he added. 'Do you know how I'm managing to live? I give German lessons to a couple of American officers to prepare them for occupying Germany. My wife put them on to me. My wife speaks fluent Russian, French and English. I don't speak any of them. But then my son, who is living with his mother, he doesn't speak German.' He laughed bitterly. 'Such cosmopolitans!'

I went in to say goodbye to Jessie. It was very difficult; she didn't trust the doctors or me or anyone else. She lay there under her sheets; only her eyes shone and darted this way and that. 'Don't say anything,' she whispered. 'It's good you've come. Now go home, Ludwig. And don't forget: nothing is truly bad as long as you have your health. That's something I've learned in the last few days.'

I passed Bosse. He was still sitting by the window, staring out. It had started raining. The pavements were glistening. There was no point in asking Bosse about Jessie. He wouldn't have given me any more of an answer than Ravic had. Instead I remarked, 'Paris has been liberated.'

He looked up. 'Yes,' he replied. 'And Berlin is being bombed. My wife is in Berlin.'

I set the bottle down on the table in front of Moikov. 'My God,' he said. 'The real nectar of the gods! Original Russian vodka! Another bottle. Where do you get it from? From the Russian embassy?'

'From Maria. It's her present to you for your eightieth birthday.'

'Is that today?' Moikov looked at the newspaper. 'Perhaps. I stopped thinking about it when I passed seventy. Anyway, the Russian and the Western calendars are different.'

'Maria knows them all,' I said. 'She knows the oddest things – and then there are other, perfectly ordinary everyday things she doesn't know.'

Moikov looked at me questioningly. Then his broad face broke into a smile. 'Like the Russian she isn't. God bless her.'

'She claims to have a Russian grandmother.'

'Women aren't obliged to be truthful, Ludwig. That would be boring. They don't lie either; but they are masters of embroidering. Just at the moment, a lot of women have Russian grandmothers. After the war that will change; then the Russians won't be our allies any more, they'll have gone back to being Commies.' Moikov examined the bottle. 'That's all I have by way of homesickness,' he said. 'No feeling for the land I was born in, just its drink. Why do your Jews make such a fuss about their longing for Germany? They

334

ought to be used to homelessness by now. They are the oldest emigrants in the world – ever since the Roman sack of Jerusalem two thousand years ago.'

'Longer than that, actually – since Babylon. But that's your reason. The Jews are incorrigible patriots wherever they fetch up. Because they don't have a home, they look for home tirelessly.'

'Won't they finally wise up?'

'Why? They need to live somehow and somewhere.'

Moikov cautiously opened the bottle. It had a very small, cheap cork. 'The Jews were the most patriotic Germans there were,' I said. 'Even the last Kaiser knew that.'

Moikov sniffed at the cork. 'Will they be that again?' he asked.

'There aren't many left alive,' I replied. 'Not in Germany. That takes care of the question for now.'

'Is it true they were murdered?'

I nodded. 'Let's talk about something else, Vladimir. What does it feel like to be eighty?'

'Do you really want to know?'

'No, I was just making conversation.'

'Thank goodness! I would have been very disappointed in you. You shouldn't compel people to give diplomatic answers. Let's try your vodka.'

Then from the entrance I heard Lachmann's unmistakable footfall. 'What's he still doing here?' I asked. 'He's found his cinema usherette, hasn't he?'

Moikov's broad, flat face slowly pulled into a smile. It was a many-layered smile, beginning with the eyes and ending with the eyes. 'Life isn't so simple. There is such a thing as inverse revenge. Jealousy isn't like a tap you can turn off when you've had enough.'

Lachmann came limping in. In his wake bobbed a blonde

335

who looked like a lion tamer in the circus; powerful, with granite chin and swarthy eyebrows. 'My sweetheart,' he introduced her. 'Miss McCraig.'

The lion tamer nodded. Lachmann took out a small parcel wrapped in red tissue paper. 'Your eightieth, Vladimir,' he announced. 'It wasn't easy to find something for your religion.'

It was a small Russian icon on gold ground. Moikov gazed at it in some astonishment. 'But Lachmann,' he finally said. 'I'm an atheist.'

'Poppycock!' replied Lachmann. 'Everyone believes in something. How would I make a living otherwise? Anyway, this figure here happens to be neither Jesus nor Mary. It's Saint Vladimir. Well, surely you believe in yourself, or don't you?'

'Myself least of all.'

'Poppycock!' repeated Lachmann with a look to me. 'I detect the paradoxical style of Ludwig Sommer. Give it up!'

In surprise I looked at Lachmann. I wasn't used to that brusque tone from tearful Kurt; love seemed to have done wonders for his character – it was as though he had been given an injection from a cement gun.

'What can I offer you two?' asked Moikov with a worried squint in the direction of his vodka.

'A Coke,' said Lachmann promptly, to our relief.

'And you, Madam?'

'Would you have some chartreuse?' chirped the nutcracker to our surprise in a high falsetto.

'Green or yellow?' asked the imperturbable Moikov.

'I didn't know there was yellow.'

'We have it here.' It was Raoul's favourite drink.

'Then I'll try yellow. Could you make it a double. The smoke in the cinema hurts my throat.'

'You can have a whole bottle if you like,' replied Moikov

gallantly and poured. Vodka for him and me. Lachmann and Miss McCraig sat hand in hand, smiling and staring at us in expectant silence. Is there anything more stupid than happiness, I thought. Especially when you're expected to ply it with bons mots. Luckily, Raoul and John happened to come down the stairs and the conversation perked up instantly. Both of them looked at Miss McCraig with such revulsion it was as though they saw a skinned seal, and since they were both aware of the fact, they compensated with courtliness. A minute later the Contessa tiptoed down the stairs. With her eagle eye she spotted the bottle of Russian vodka right away and burst into tears. 'Russia!' she whispered. 'Great, majestic empire! Home of the soul! Beloved mother.'

'There goes my birthday present,' whispered Moikov and poured.

'Swap the bottles. Yours is good too. She'll never know the difference.'

Moikov chuckled. 'The Contessa not know the difference? She remembers every banquet she had forty years ago. And the vodka that was served.'

'But she's happy enough to drink yours.'

'She'd drink eau de cologne if she had to. But she has never lost her good taste. Tonight we won't get the bottle out of her claws. Or else we'll have to drink it ourselves in a hurry. Are you up for that?'

'No,' I said.

'I thought not. Let's leave it to the Contessa.'

'I didn't want it anyway. Give me a shot of yours. I prefer it.'

Moikov glanced at me out of his lidless little parrot's eyes. I could see that he was thinking many things at once. 'OK,' he said. 'You're a gentleman in all kinds of ways, Ludwig. God bless you. And protect you,' he added.

'From what?'

He made his full glass disappear before the Contessa noticed it. He wiped his mouth with his giant fist and set it carefully down on the table. 'From yourself, of course,' he said. 'Who else?'

'Stay, Mr Sommer,' said Raoul. 'For an improvised party for Vladimir. It may be his last,' he whispered to me. 'Who lives past eighty?'

'Eighty-one-year-olds, for a start.'

'It's a biblical age. Would you like to get that old? Older than your desire, your appetite, your sex? What a grey world! Bring on suicide, I say.'

I had a different view from Raoul, but I declined to share it with him. I wanted to go. Maria Fiola was waiting in her borrowed apartment.

'Stay,' pressed Raoul. 'You're not a party pooper. And this is Vladimir's last birthday. You're his friend.'

'I need to go,' I said. 'But I'll be back later.'

'Promise?'

'Promise, Raoul.'

I suddenly felt pushed into something that felt like a little betrayal. For a moment I was disorientated; even though it was silly of me. I saw Moikov every day and I knew he didn't care about his birthday. Even so I said, 'I have to go, Vladimir. Perhaps I'll be back before all the fun's over here.'

'I hope not, Ludwig. Don't be a fool.' He gave me a pat on the back with his great paw and winked at me.

'There goes the last of your vodka,' I said. 'Down the tender throat of the Contessa. She's just divvying it up with Raoul's boyfriend. We haven't been paying attention.'

'That doesn't matter. I've got two more where they came from.'

'Real Russian?'

Moikov nodded. 'Maria Fiola brought them round this afternoon. I've hidden them away.'

He saw my rattled expression. 'Didn't you know?' he asked.

'Why would I know something like that, Vladimir?'

'Fair enough. God knows where she manages to find it. You can't buy it in the shops, that's all I know.'

'From a Russian would be the obvious answer. You keep forgetting that Russia and America are allies.'

'Or from an American diplomat who has a source in Russia; maybe even from the Russian embassy in DC.'

'Possibly,' I said. 'But the main thing is it's there. And you've got it securely hidden away. A man doesn't need to think about what he's got.'

Moikov laughed. 'A wise word. Too wise for one of your years.'

'Perhaps that's because of my rotten life. Too much too soon.'

I turned down 57th Street. The *paseo* of the homosexuals was in full swing down Second Avenue. Greetings flew here and there, extravagant waves and gestures, and everything bespoke a cheerful exhibitionism. Where on a conventional promenade with conventional couples there was secrecy and discretion, here it was the opposite, a flagrant demonstration of insouciance. José Kruse hailed me like an old friend and pushed his arm through mine. 'How about a cocktail with a few friends, mon cher?'

I carefully freed myself. I could see I was already being eyed up as a potential conquest. 'Another time,' I said. 'I have to go to church. My auntie is being consecrated.'

José stood there, shaking with laughter. 'Very good! Your auntie! You joker. Don't tell me you don't know what auntie means?'

'What do you mean? An aunt's an aunt. This one was old, quarrelsome and black.'

José laughed louder. 'An aunt is an old fairy, my dear. Enjoy the consecration.'

He patted me on the back. At the same instant I saw Fifi the champagne-coloured poodle cocking a leg against the display of the newspaper kiosk. The newspaper seller Kunovsky, who couldn't see Fifi from his place inside his kiosk, must have developed a sixth sense. He leapt up, shot out of the little door, upsetting a stack of *Life* magazines, and raced howling round his kiosk to catch Fifi with a kick. He was too late. Fifi was slinking along, all innocence, twenty feet away.

'That was your bloody dog!' Kunovsky yelled at José Kruse. 'This time he fouled a copy of *Esquire*. I want compensation!'

José Kruse raised his eyebrows. 'My poodle? I don't own one. Where is he?'

'Over there somewhere. The cunning beast has run off. Of course you've got a dog. I've seen you with him a hundred times.'

'A hundred times? But not today. My dog is back home, sick. Sick because you kicked him a couple of days ago. I should take you to court. He's worth hundreds of dollars.'

A group of co-religionists had gathered around us by now. 'We should inform animal welfare,' someone declared. 'What makes you think it was this man's dog anyway? Which one is he? If the dog was his it should be here, next to his master.'

Fifi was nowhere in sight. 'It was a sandy-coloured poodle,' said a slightly rattled Kunovsky. 'And this gentleman has a poodle that colour. All the others are black or white or brown.'

'What?' The man turned to look down 57th Street. 'Just take a look.'

Like an avenue of sphinxes, you saw a double row of squatting dogs at the pavement's edge – all in the melancholy-moronic attitude of moon worshippers defecating. 'There,' said the man. 'Second on the right, champagne-coloured, another one opposite him, then two in a row before the big white one. What do you say now? And here's two more just come out of the door of number 580!'

Kunovsky had already retreated in confusion. 'Those buggers stick together through thick and thin!' he gruffed and tried to recondition his *Esquire* with a wet rag, before offering it for sale as rain-damaged at a reduced price.

José Kruse followed me back to Maria's house, where Fifi was waiting for him in the doorway. 'That dog's a genius,' declared Kruse. 'When he does something like that, he knows he mustn't be seen together with me. Then he creeps home on his own. Kunovsky won't see him for a long time. And should he call a cop, Fifi will be up in the penthouse. The door's always open. We don't keep any secrets.'

He laughed again, setting everything shaking, gave me another pat on the back and let me go.

I took the lift up to Maria's flat. The encounter with Kruse had left me with a bad taste in my mouth. I didn't have anything against homosexuals, but I didn't have anything for them either. I knew that a lot of the great minds had been homosexual, but I doubted they had made as much of it as José Kruse did. For a moment my anticipation of Maria was spoiled by his slick, cheap superficiality. Nor did it help when I read the name of Maria Fiola's host on the door; I knew he too was of the fraternity. I knew that

341

models got on well with homosexuals, because they were safe from the usual crude advances.

Was that what it was? I thought as I rang the doorbell. I had heard something about people who swung both ways. I shook my head as I waited, as though to clear the cobwebs out of it. It wasn't just Kruse who was bothering me, I thought. There was something else too. Perhaps I was no longer used to knocking on doors behind which something like happiness awaited.

Maria Fiola cautiously opened the door a chink. 'Bathing again?' I asked.

'Yes. It's almost part of my job. I had a shoot in a factory this afternoon. The things those photographers come up with! With real dust! Come on in. I'm almost finished. There's vodka in the fridge.'

She went back into the bathroom and left the door open. 'Was there a little birthday party for Vladimir?'

'It's just getting going,' I said. 'The Contessa saw your vodka. It provoked her to a fit of homesickness. She was singing Russian songs in her quavery voice as I left.'

Maria let the water out. It gurgled and she laughed. 'Would you have wanted to stay?' she asked.

'No, Maria,' I replied and felt straight away that it wasn't true. At the same time, because I knew that was what had been bothering me, it instantly vanished from my head and that made it true again.

She walked into the living room, damp and naked. 'We can still go if you like,' she said, looking at me. 'I don't want you to miss out on anything you'd want to do on my account.'

I laughed. 'My God, what an awkward sentence, Maria. And what a lie, too, I hope.'

'Not quite,' she replied. 'But not in the way you think.'

342

'Moikov is happy with your vodka,' I said. 'The Contessa seems to have intercepted one bottle, but he was able to hide the others. Lachmann's new love is a chartreuse-swilling cinema cashier.'

Maria was still looking at me. 'I think you do want to be there.'

'To see Lachmann happily in love? In his Jewish lamentations he's at least original – when he's happy he's boring as hell.'

'Aren't we all?'

I didn't answer. 'Who cares?' I finally said. 'Other people, if that. Or someone who cares about his effect more than anything else.'

Maria laughed. 'A model, in other words.'

I looked up. 'You're not a model,' I said.

'No? What am I then?'

'What a silly question! If I knew—'

I stopped. She laughed again. 'Then that would be the end of love, eh?'

'I don't know. You mean, if the little bit of strangeness is accounted for, then our interest in the other person is over?'

'Not so clinical as that. But more or less.'

'Maybe not. Maybe that's when what people call happiness actually begins.'

Maria Fiola walked slowly through the room. 'Are we still capable of it?' she asked.

'Why wouldn't we be? Aren't you?'

'I don't know. I don't think so. There's something there that we no longer have. Our parents maybe still had it. Not mine. It's like something from another century, when people still believed in God.'

I got up and embraced her. For an instant I thought I could feel her trembling. Then I felt the warmth of her

343

skin. 'I think if we can say such silly things to each other, we must be very intimate,' I murmured into her hair.

'Do you really think that?'

'Yes, Maria. We were all launched into various types of loneliness too soon, so we know that nothing remains, only wretchedness, and we distrust all types of happiness. But there are thousands of other things we've learned instead to call happiness. Survival, for instance, or not being tortured or persecuted simply for being who we are. Don't you think that a fleeting happiness can be produced more easily than the ponderous conventional happiness of yore? Shouldn't we leave things as they are? And how the heck did we get started on this idiotic conversation anyway?'

Maria laughed and pushed me away. 'I don't know either. Do you want a drink?'

'Have you got any of Moikov's vodka left?'

She looked at me. 'Only his sort. The other sort I gave him for his birthday.'

'He and the Contessa were both very happy about that.'

'What about you?'

'I was happy too. Why wouldn't I be?'

'I didn't want to send it back,' she said. 'It would be too awkward. It's possible I'll be getting more of it. You don't want it, do you?'

I laughed. 'Strange to say, I don't. A couple of days ago I wouldn't have had any objection. Something's changed. Perhaps I've discovered jealousy?'

'I wouldn't mind if you had,' said Maria.

She stirred in her sleep. Outside, there was summer lightning among the skyscrapers. Silent flashes flickered through the room like ghosts. 'Poor Vladimir,' she murmured. 'To be so old and so close to death. Does he know it all the time, I wonder? How sad! How can you laugh and be happy if you know you'll soon be gone?'

'You know it and you don't know it,' I said. 'I've known people who knew they were going to die in three days and they were happy because their number wasn't up yet. They had two days to go. The will to live is harder to kill than life itself, I sometimes think. I knew someone who the day before he died beat an opponent at chess and he'd always lost to him before. That made him incredibly happy. And I've known people who were taken out to be shot and came back, because someone in the firing squad had a cold and couldn't be trusted to aim properly. Some cried, because they would have to die a second time; others were thankful because they got an extra day to live. Strange things, Maria, and no one knows what they will do until the moment comes.'

'Did something like that happen to Moikov?'

'I don't know. I think so. It's happened to a lot of people in our day.'

'To you?'

'No,' I said. 'Not to me. But I've seen it happen. It was far from being the worst. In some ways, it was almost the most civilised.'

Maria shuddered. A breeze seemed to blow over her skin as over a lake and curl the surface. 'My poor Ludwig,' she murmured, still half asleep. 'Will you ever be able to forget?'

'There are many kinds of forgetting,' I replied, while the silent lightning flew over Maria's young body like phantom scythes that touched her and left her untouched. 'Just as there are many kinds of happiness. You just have to be careful not to mix them up.'

She stretched out and fell deeper into the mysterious chambers of sleep, where she would soon forget me to be alone with the unknown images of her dreams.

'I'm glad you don't want to educate me,' she whispered with closed eyes. In the pale twitch of the lightning I saw that she had very long and delicate eyelashes, which trembled over her eyes like black butterflies. 'They always wanted to train me,' she said, very sleepily. 'But you don't—'

'No,' I said. 'I don't, Maria.'

She nodded and buried her head in the pillows. Her breathing changed, becoming slower and longer. She's slipping away from me, I thought. I'm nothing to her now, just a warm body and a familiar pressure, and that will be over in a few minutes. Then the part of her that is aware will drift along the channels of the subconscious; terrorised and fascinated by the flickering of dreams as of the pallid lightning outside the window; an altered person, foreign to everything that may have happened today; given over to the northern lights of different poles and the chance occurrences of subterranean forces; open to every influence, without the restraints of conventional morality and sense of self. How far away she was already from an hour ago, when we believed the lightning of our flesh and tried to become one in the blissful and sad deception of propinquity, under the great sky of childhood, when we still assumed happiness was a statue and not a cloud that was forever changing and sometimes melting away. The little breathless cries, the hands that clutched each other as if for ever, the desire that called itself love and behind which burned the remote and unconscious egoism of murder, the stare of the last moment in which all thought burst and one was just willing and receiving and barely recognised or knew the other, and so fell for the illusion of union and mutual self-abandonment, whereas in fact one was never more remote from the other and never more alien – and then the exhaustion, the blissful mildness of believing you found yourself in the other, the brief fascination of appearances, a sky full of stars that were already slowly bleaching and allowing the everyday or else the night of thought to lower itself.

Sleeping soul with no memory of me, I thought, beautiful scrap on which my name is fading into invisibility with every breath, how can you be afraid of being overly familiar to me, so that separation lurks behind each parting? Don't you slip away each night and I have no idea where you've been when you next open your eyes? You take me for a restless gypsy; but I'm only a misguided bourgeois with a set of terrible experiences, in the shadow of an Orestean vow to vengeance – you are the gypsy, searching for your shadow and a self. Beloved, homeless fragment, ashamed because you don't know how to cook. You should never learn. The world has enough cooks. More than murderers; even in Germany.

I heard a stifled hollow barking above me. It had to be Fifi, maybe José Kruse had found someone to help him through the night. I stretched out alongside Maria, without touching her. She felt me anyway. 'Oh, John,' she murmured, without awakening.

18

'We art dealers live from a simple and primitive human quality,' explained Reginald Black. 'From acquisitiveness. This is all the more surprising, as everyone knows he must die and can't take anything with him. And doubly surprising as everyone knows the museums are full of gorgeous pictures. Did you go to the Met?'

I nodded. 'I even went twice.'

'You should go every week, instead of playing chess in your dive with that Russian vodka distiller. Did you see *The Tower of Babel*? And El Greco's Toledan landscapes? They are just hanging there, it doesn't cost anything to look at them.' Reginald Black sipped his cognac – the one for clients who were buying for more than twenty thousand dollars – and dreamed: 'Priceless pieces. The sums they could fetch—'

'Is that human acquisitiveness you're expressing there?' I asked him.

'No, it's not,' he said crossly and having been going to refill my glass he took back his hand. 'That's the trader's instinct handed down to me by my forebears, which is forever in conflict with my love of art and unfortunately always prevails over it. But why do people not visit museums more often to look at the most wonderful paintings, instead of buying a couple of half-finished Degas to hang in their flats for a lot of money so that they can start being terrorised by fear of housebreakers and clumsy maids with broom handles, and guests mindlessly putting their cigarettes out on them? Museums have a much better class of picture than almost any so-called private collection.'

I laughed. 'It strikes me you're more of an anti art dealer really. If one took your advice, no one would ever buy a picture again. You're the Don Quixote of your guild.'

Black laughed, mollified, and reached for the cognac bottle. 'People talk about Socialism so much,' he said, 'when all the time the loveliest things in the world are free. The museums, the libraries and music – splendid concerts on the radio, Toscanini with all the Beethoven concertos and symphonies every week on the guest slot. If ever there was a time for a comfortable hermit's existence, then it is now. Look at my collection of art books! Sometimes I feel like chucking in my job and just living free as a bird.'

'Why don't you, then?' I asked, reaching for my glass, which he had refilled.

He sighed. 'It's that dual nature of mine.'

I looked at the unhappy benefactor of mankind (or the super-rich). He had the priceless quality of seeming to believe whatever he happened to be saying. The fact that at some level he also didn't believe it was what kept him from being an ear-bending idiot and allowed him to appear in a sort of scintillating halo. He was, without knowing or admitting it, the actor of his life.

'The day before yesterday I had a call from old Durant II,' he said. 'He's worth about twenty million dollars and he wanted to buy a little Renoir from me. He has final-stage cancer and knows it. The doctors are giving him days to live. I took the picture with me. The old geezer's room smelled of death, for all the antiseptics. Death has the strongest scent, you can't keep it out. The old man was a bag of bones with huge eyes and big brown stains on his parchment skin. He knows a thing or two about pictures, which is unusual. He knows even more about money, which isn't so unusual. I wanted twenty thousand dollars. He offered twelve. With a tremendous rattle in his chest he went up to fifteen. I saw that he wanted the picture, so I stayed firm. So did he. Imagine. A millionaire with days to live, haggling like a ragman for his last joy in life. You should know he also hates his heirs.'

'Millionaires have a way of pulling off miraculous recoveries,' I said. '"The experts are baffled" and so forth. You hear it all the time. What happened next?'

'I took the picture home with me. It's over there. Take a look at it.'

It was a beautiful little portrait of the young Madame Henriot. She was wearing a black velvet choker round her slender neck. The picture was painted in profile, and it showed her in all her youth and the expectation of the life ahead. No wonder the rotting old Durant II wanted it, the way King David once wanted his Bathsheba.

Reginald Black looked at his watch. 'Time to snap out of it. I'm expecting Cooper in a quarter of an hour. The American forces are on the march everywhere. The lists of casualties are growing. It's payback time for Cooper. He just keeps on supplying and supplying. His pictures should have black wreaths round them. And he should intersperse them with machine guns or flame-throwers.'

'You've told me that once before. When we were expecting Cooper that other time. Why do you want to sell him the other Degas?'

'I told you that before too,' said Reginald Black irritably. 'Because of my accursed Jekyll and Hyde dual nature. But Cooper's going to pay for his destructiveness. I'm going to take him for ten thousand dollars more than I would someone who sells fertiliser or thread.' Black listened out for the door. I heard the bell too. 'Ten minutes early,' gruffed Black. 'Another one of his tricks. He's either too early or too late. Too early, so that he can tell me he's just passing by and only has a couple of minutes, and needs to go to Washington, or Hawaii for all I care – or too late, so as to leave me on tenterhooks, like last time. I'm going to take him for an extra eleven thousand dollars and you can cut my arm off if I go down by as much as a cent. Now, hurry! Put away the private reserve and get out the cognac for average customers. That hyena of the battlefields is going to be treated to my blended cognac; unfortunately he knows no more about cognac than he does about pictures. And now, hurry off to your observation post; I'll ring for you when I need you.'

At my observation post I opened the newspaper. Black was right; the American forces were advancing along a broad front. Cooper's factories had to be working day and night to keep up – but wasn't the hyena in an odd way right when he claimed to be a benefactor of mankind, as right as the millionaires' friend Reginald Black? Wasn't Europe and the rest of the world delivered by killing from an even greater killer, who wanted to enslave Europe and eradicate whole nations? There was no answer to that, and if there was, it was just a mess of blood.

I lowered my newspaper and stared out of the window. How quickly killing could change names and roles. And how quickly the great concepts of honour, freedom and humanity could too. Every nation claimed them for itself, and the more savage a dictatorship, the more humane the qualities in defence of which it did its killing. And killing?

What was killing? Wasn't revenge killing too? Where did lawlessness begin and where the law? Hadn't the whole concept of law been murdered by those who would protect it? By the armchair theorists of Germany and their bent judges who willingly helped the criminal state? What was left of justice other than revenge?

All of a sudden the bell shrilled. I went downstairs, to be met by a cloud of Havana smoke. 'Mr Sommer,' said Reginald Black through the fragrant blue, 'did you tell Mr Cooper that this picture was inferior to the Degas he recently bought?'

I looked at Cooper in astonishment. The hyena was lying and he knew it; he knew, too, that I was caught in a jam, because I couldn't call him a liar without provoking a roar from him. 'In the case of a master like Degas, I would never claim that a given work was superior or inferior,' I said. 'That was the first principle of my education at the Louvre; at the most, a picture might be more fully realised than another; that's the difference between a sketch, a study and a signed painting. Neither of the Degas carries a signature. According to Professor Meier-Graefe that earns them both the exalted classification of incomplete, which leaves the most space for the imagination.'

Reginald Black looked at me, stunned by my expertise; I had picked up the reference five minutes before in my observation post, which included a small library. 'Well, then,' he said to Cooper.

'Poppycock!' protested the man with the beet-red face. 'Louvre, my eye! I don't believe it. He said the picture was inferior. I have good hearing.'

I knew it was talk, an effort to lower the price; but I didn't see why I should have to let myself be humiliated in the course of it. 'Mr Black,' I said, 'I think further discussion is unnecessary. Durant II has just called to say he wants the picture and would we bring it over.'

Cooper whinnied with laughter. 'Drop the pretence. I happen to know that Durant II is on his last legs. He doesn't need another picture, he needs a box.'

He looked triumphantly at Reginald Black, who stared coldly back. 'I know,' he said unpleasantly. 'I was with him yesterday.'

Cooper pooh-poohed. 'Does he want to line his coffin with Impressionists, then?' he mocked.

'Such a passionate and knowledgeable collector as Durant II would never do such a thing. But for whatever time remains to him, he wants to have all the pleasure he can. In such cases money is irrelevant, Mr Cooper. At death's door you stop bargaining. Durant II wants the Degas, as you have just heard.'

'Fine. Send it to him.'

Black didn't bat an eyelid. 'Pack the picture up, Mr Sommer, and take it to Mr Durant II.' He took the Degas off the easel and handed it to me. Then he stood up. 'I'm pleased this matter has been settled so amicably, Mr Cooper. It was very generous of you to pass up on the picture to please a dying man. There are several other Degas on the market. Perhaps in the next five or ten years we will find another picture of the same outstanding quality as this.' He got up. 'I'm afraid that's all I had to offer you; this was my best picture.'

I walked over to the door, not slowly as Cooper was probably expecting as part of a trick, but briskly, as though I couldn't wait to get to Durant II's sickbed. I was expecting Cooper's 'Stop!' at the door. It didn't come. Disappointed, I climbed up to my observation post; I had the feeling I had fouled up Black's deal.

But I didn't know Reginald Black. The call came fifteen minutes later. 'Is the picture gone yet?' asked Black's silky voice.

'Mr Sommer is just taking it downstairs,' I replied in falsetto.

'Run after him. I want him to bring the picture back.'

I hurriedly bundled up the picture and went back downstairs to unpack it. 'Just leave it packed,' said a glum-sounding Cooper. 'You can bring it round to my apartment in the afternoon. Then you can tell me you've got a third, even better Degas, you crook.'

'In fact, there is another Degas in the same category,' I replied coolly. 'You're right, Mr Cooper.'

Mr Cooper's head stuck up like an alarmed charger neighing. Reginald Black looked at me curiously. 'It's been in the Musée du Louvre in Paris for the last twenty years and it's not for sale.'

Cooper groaned. 'Spare me your little jokes,' he said and stomped off.

Reginald Black pushed the customers' cognac away and broke out the private supply. 'I'm proud of you,' he declared. 'Was there really a message from Durant II?'

I nodded. 'He wants to see the little Renoir again. Young Madame Henriot. It seemed to fit.' Black pulled a hundred-dollar bill out of his red morocco purse. 'A reward for bravery in the face of the enemy,' he said.

I pocketed it. 'Did you get the mark-up from Cooper?'

'Every last cent,' said Black. 'Nothing sounds as plausible as a half-truth. I had to swear to Cooper on the lives of my children that I visited Durant II last night.'

'What a ghastly oath.'

'I was there, of course. With the Renoir. But Cooper didn't specify Degas in his wording.'

'Even so,' I said. 'What a brute!'

Black smiled seraphically. 'And I don't have any children,' he said.

'Jessie,' I said in consternation. 'You're looking great!'

She was lying in a hospital bed, abruptly shrunken, grey, waxy, collapsed. Only the restless eyes seemed bigger than usual.

She forced a smile. 'Everyone says so. But I've got a mirror and that tells me the truth.'

The twins were bustling about. They had brought an apple cake and a thermos of coffee. 'The coffee here is gnats' piss,' said Jessie. 'I couldn't possibly offer it to visitors. The twins have brought some proper coffee.' She turned to Robert Hirsch. 'Have some, Robert. For my sake.'

Hirsch and I exchanged glances. 'Of course, Jessie,' he said. 'Your coffee was always the best – in Paris, in Marseilles and now in New York. It's pulled us out of more than one depression. Christmas 1941 in the catacombs in Paris; in the basement of the Hotel Lutetia. Upstairs the German jackboots were clumping around; downstairs the commercial councillor wanted to kill himself – as a Jew, he was sure he wouldn't survive the Christian feast of love. We had next to nothing to eat. Then you turned up like an angel bearing an enormous pot of coffee. And two apple cakes. You had given the hotel owner a ruby brooch in return and had promised him a ruby ring for not betraying us for a week. It was a time of panic and the first great fear. But you were laughing and you even got the old diabetic Busch to smile. You saved us all, Jessie, with your wonderful coffee.'

She listened to him greedily like one dying of thirst, and smiling. He sat in his chair like an Oriental teller of fairy tales. 'But then Busch died a year later,' she said.

'He wasn't murdered in a German concentration camp, but in a French internment camp, Jessie. And before that you smuggled him out of the Occupied Zone. In your second-best clothes, Jessie. With a wig and a smart Scottish wool suit, and a red ladies' coat. Just in case he was stopped and questioned, you had wrapped him in an enormous bandage, so that it looked as though he could only have croaked a reply. You were a genius, Jessie—'

She listened to him as though he were telling stories, when all the time it was the bleak and brutal truth, only here in the hospital amid the smells of dead blood, disinfectant, pus and the jasmine the twins had sprayed everywhere, it sounded unreal. To Jessie it was like a lullaby; she closed her eyes but for a small crack, and listened.

'But it was you that brought us over in your car, Robert,' she said. 'Your Spanish vice consul's car, with the dread CD plates.' Abruptly she laughed. 'All those things you went on to do afterwards! But by then I was in America.'

'Thank God you were,' said Hirsch in the same near-monotone as before. 'What would have become of us here without you? You walked your feet off for affidavits and collecting money to rescue us—'

'But not you, Robert,' said Jessie with an almost roguish smile. 'You could always look after yourself.'

It had got dark. The twins perched on their chairs like two delicate owls. Even the bird of the dead Lipschitz was quiet. The compiler of the bloodlist was counting to himself. He was the first to leave when the nurse came in to check the patient's bandages and take her temperature. He was a sensitive soul and couldn't endure the sight of blood, except in his imagination. Hirsch got up. 'I think they're throwing us out, Jessie. I'll be back soon. But perhaps you'll be back among us before that.'

'Oh, Robert! Who told you that?'

'Ravic and Bosse, your doctors.'

'And you're not lying to me, Robert?'

'No, Jessie. Didn't they tell you themselves?'

'All doctors lie, Robert. Out of compassion.'

Hirsch laughed. 'You don't need compassion, Jessie. You're Mother Courage.'

'Do you think I'll ever get out of here?' she asked him with a frightened look.

'Don't you, Jessie?'

'I try to believe it by day. But at night I can't manage.'

The nurse marked the temperature on her chart at the foot of the bed. 'How much is it, Ludwig?' asked Jessie. 'I don't understand their figures in Fahrenheit.'

'A shade over thirty-eight,' I said. 'That's normal following an operation.' I didn't know how to convert Réaumur to Fahrenheit, but I knew that a ready answer was best for patients.

'Have you heard that Berlin has been bombed?' whispered Jessie.

Hirsch nodded. 'Just like London, Jessie.'

'But Paris wasn't bombed,' she said.

'No, not by the Americans,' replied Hirsch patiently. 'The Germans didn't need to bomb it, it was theirs from the summer of 1940, Jessie.'

She nodded a little guiltily. She had heard the faint note of rebuke in Robert's answer. 'The British have hit the Bayrischer Platz in Berlin,' she said. 'We used to live there.'

'You're not to blame, Jessie,' said Hirsch very gently.

'I didn't mean it like that, Robert.'

'I know how you meant it, Jessie,' said Hirsch. 'But you should remember the second of the Laon Rules: One thing at a time – otherwise you'll be confused and the Gestapo

357

will catch you. And your thing right now is to get well. Quickly. We all need you, Jessie.'

'Oh, what do you really need me for? To make coffee. No one needs me any more.'

'People who think they're not needed are often precisely those who are needed the most. For example, I know I need you.'

'You, Robert,' replied Jessie, sounding flirtatious. 'But you don't need anyone.'

'More than anyone else, Jessie. Stay true to me.'

It was a peculiar exchange, almost like that between a hypnotist and his medium; but there was something in it also of a magician's tender, abstract declaration of love to an old woman who still followed him, a little weighed down by consolation and tiredness.

'You have to go now,' said the nurse.

The twins, who were still with us, straight away got up. In the cold overhead light they looked shadowy and pale. Both were wearing tight blue work trousers. They were still hoping to be discovered by the film industry. We walked down the bare corridor, the twins dancing ahead. What a sight for the bottom-fancier Bach. I said, 'I can't understand why some admirer hasn't snaffled them long ago.'

'They're not interested,' said Hirsch. 'They live with Jessie and they're waiting for their chance to play a pair of twins in something; that's what makes them stick together. You never see one without the other. On her own, each feels hopeless.'

We stepped out into the warm evening. The street was full of hurrying people who were unpreoccupied with death. 'How is Jessie, Robert?' I asked. 'Will she really be out of there soon?'

Hirsch nodded. 'They opened her up, Ludwig, and then

they closed her up again. There is nothing to be done. I asked Ravic. Metastases everywhere. In America they don't put people through pointless operations if it's too late. They let them die in peace, if peace is the word for someone screaming from pain all day when the opiates no longer help. Ravic hopes she might still have a couple of months of life ahead of her.' Hirsch stopped and looked at me in angry perplexity. 'A year ago they could have saved her. But she never complained; she thought they were just the normal aches and pains of old age. She had other priorities. There were always unhappy people around her for her to look after. That damned heroic self-sacrifice! Now she's lying there, past saving.'

'Does she sense something?'

'Of course she does. Like all emigrants, she's apprehensive. That's what my banter with her was all about. Ah, Ludwig. Come back with me and let's have a drink together. I'm taking it harder than I thought I would.'

We walked silently through the bright evening streets, where the light of September mingled with that of a thousand storefronts. I had watched Robert Hirsch while he talked to Jessie. Not only her expression, his too had changed in the course of it, and it seemed to me that on some level both of them took some consolation from their memories. A sudden fear befell me. I knew you had to keep memories locked away like poison as long as you wanted to use them, otherwise they could kill you. I sneaked a look at Hirsch. His face again had the tense, closed look of before.

'What happens when Jessie's had all she can stand?' I asked.

'Ravic won't let her suffer, as if she were in some concentration camp of God's, slowly being crucified,' Hirsch replied grimly. 'He will wait to hear from her, of course. She doesn't have to tell him in so many words. He will sense it. But I think Jessie won't give in easily. She's a fighter.'

Robert Hirsch unlocked the door of his shop. A chill blast of air conditioning blew in our faces. 'Greetings from the tomb of Lazarus,' he said and switched off the machine. 'I think we don't need this any more,' he added. 'That nasty, artificial air! In a hundred years we'll all be living in holes in the ground for fear of our fellow beings. This war won't be the last, you know.'

He produced a bottle of cognac. 'You're probably used to something a bit classier from Mr Black,' he said with a grin. 'Art dealers always keep a good cellar. For evident reasons.'

'My ex-namesake didn't,' I replied. 'And I'd rather have a glass of water with you any day of the week than a glass of Napoleon with Black. How's Carmen?'

'I think I'm boring her.'

'What nonsense! I'd find it easier to believe she's boring you.'

He shook his head. 'That's not possible. I already explained it to you. I can't fathom her, so she can't fathom me. She has the magical strangeness of utter naivety. Paired with her breathtaking beauty, it stops being stupidity and becomes an experience. And as far she's concerned, I'm just a slightly loopy seller of electrical goods and not even a good one. She's bored.'

I looked at him. He smiled glumly. 'The other stuff is over, behind us, it only exists to help a sick woman with memories at odd moments. We've been saved, Ludwig, but even our gratitude has washed off by now. It's not enough to fill my life. Look at the people we know. They escaped from a sinking ship on to a beach where they are gasping for breath, torn between being half alive and merely surviving. A few may actually adjust to their new circumstances. But I won't and I fancy you won't either. The great breathless experience of rescue is over. Day-to-day life has resumed – a life to no purpose.'

'Not for me, Robert. Not yet. And not for you either.'

He shook his head. 'More for me than for anyone else I can think of.' I knew what he meant. His time in France had been a hunt. He hadn't been a passive victim, he had become a hunter himself who pitted his own native wit and intelligence against the SS cannibals – and won. For him, almost uniquely, the occupation of France had been a private war and not the brutal rounding up of helpless victims. And then slowly the appalling thing started to happen: each danger overcome gradually took on in the memory the lustre of a bloodied romance, assuming that one has emerged unhurt. And Robert Hirsch was intact, at least from outer appearances.

I tried to distract him. 'Anyway, Bosse got his money,' I remarked.

He nodded and stood up. 'What are you doing tonight? Do you fancy the King of the Sea?'

I could see he needed me. I felt like a traitor when I answered, 'I've got a date with Maria. I'm picking her up from the photographer's. Come along.'

He shook his head. He needed to be alone with me and drink and talk. 'Go on!' I urged him.

'No, Ludwig, some other time. I'm not good company tonight. God knows why it is, but I haven't been able to stomach death since getting here. Especially when it comes sneaking up on someone, like with Jessie. I should have become a doctor like Ravic; then I could try and fight it. Perhaps we've all had too many dealings with death for our age.'

★

It was already late when I got to the photographer's place. Through the upstairs windows the beams cast their flat harsh light down on to the street. The white curtains of the atelier were drawn and I could make out shadows reflected against them. A yellow Rolls-Royce stood in a pool of light. It was the one in which Maria had taken me to 86th Street, to the Hindenburg Café.

I hesitated for a moment, wondering whether to go and be with Hirsch in his unlit shop instead. Then I thought I had made too many mistakes in my life through precipitate action and I set off up the stairs.

I saw Maria straight away. She was standing onstage, in front of an artificial white lilac bush, wearing a white dress with golden flowers. I sensed she had seen me, even though she couldn't move because she was just being photographed. She stood there very erect like a figurehead, reminding me somehow of the Nike of Samothrace at the Louvre. She was terribly beautiful and for a moment I could hardly believe she was mine, so wild and stormy and lonely did she look standing there. Then I felt a little tug at my sleeve.

It was the silk manufacturer from Lyons. His bald head was running with sweat, I noted to my surprise. I'd always thought bald heads were exempt from sweating. 'Gorgeous, isn't it?' he whispered. 'Most of the designs are from Lyons. Flown over by bomber. Since Paris has been liberated, silk is coming on stream again. By spring things will be almost back to normal. Thank God, eh?'

'Yes, thank God! You mean you think the war will be over then?'

'Sooner than that in the case of France. Just a matter of months, I think, and it'll be over.'

'Sure?'

362

'Very sure. I've just spoken to Martin from the State Department.'

A few months, I thought. A few months I still have for this bit of spotlighted youth standing up there on the stage, so infinitely strange and desirable and near. A moment later Maria broke her pose and hurried down the steps to me. 'Ludwig—'

'I know,' I said. 'The yellow Rolls.'

'I didn't know,' she whispered. 'He came as a surprise. I called you. You weren't in the hotel. I didn't want—'

'It's all right, Maria, I can go. I wanted to spend some time with Hirsch anyway.'

She stared at me. 'That's not what I wanted to say—'

I smelled her warm skin under the powder and the make-up. 'Maria! Maria!' called Nicky the photographer. 'Take! Take! Don't keep everybody waiting!'

'It's not that at all, Ludwig,' she whispered. 'Stay here! I want to—'

'Hello, Maria,' said someone behind me. 'What a wonderful shoot. Won't you introduce us?'

A tall man of about fifty pushed past me. 'Mr Ludwig Sommer, Mr Roy Martin,' said a suddenly calm-sounding Maria. 'Please excuse me, gentlemen. I've got to go back to the action. I'll be finished soon.'

Martin stayed by me. 'You're not an American, are you?' he asked.

'The accent gives me away,' I replied reluctantly.

'What are you? French?'

'Expatriate German, actually.'

Martin smiled. 'An enemy alien, then. Interesting.'

'Not for me,' I said quickly.

'I can well imagine. Are you an emigrant?'

'I'm a human being who's washed up in America,' I replied.

Martin laughed. 'So you're a refugee. What sort of passport are you travelling under?'

I watched Maria climb up to the stage. 'Is this an interrogation?' I asked calmly.

Martin laughed. 'Just curious. Why? Are you worried about an interrogation?'

'No. But I've been through enough of them to last me a while. As a refugee, as you say.'

Martin sighed. 'It's all because of the circumstances that Germany created.'

I sensed he was out to intimidate me. I understood his oblique warning not to disturb his circles as well. 'Are you a Jew?' he asked.

'Do you expect me to answer that?'

'Why not? I have a lot of sympathy for that unhappy, victimised people.'

'No one's ever asked me that in America before.'

'Really?' replied Martin. 'Not even at immigration?'

'Well, *they* did. They were officials doing their duty. But no one else.'

'Odd,' Martin said with a smile, 'how sensitive some Jews get when you ask them about it.'

'It's not so odd,' I replied, feeling all the while how Maria's eyes were levelled at me. 'They've been asked about it rather too often in the past ten years – and by all sorts of people: Gestapo murderers, torturers, policemen, to name a few.'

Martin's eyes narrowed for an instant. Then he was smiling again. 'Well, you don't look it, you see. You have nothing to fear in America as a Jew.'

'I know,' I said. 'Anti-Semitism here is confined to snobbish hotels and clubs that won't admit Jews.'

'You are well-informed,' replied Martin. Then he said

abruptly, 'I'm planning to take Miss Fiola out to dinner at El Morocco afterwards. Would you care to join us?'

I was briefly wrong-footed by the invitation, but I didn't have the least desire to be held up to ridicule in front of Maria by an official to whom I couldn't be truthful because of my uncertain situation. 'Too bad,' I replied. 'But I already have a date in Brooklyn with Chief Rabbi Nussbaum. He asked me to sabbath. Perhaps another time. Thank you very much.'

'Well, if you're devout—' Martin turned away with a barely concealed sense of triumph. I left when I saw that the stage was empty; the models were just getting changed behind a big umbrella. That was fine. I didn't need any further humiliation. I had a hundred dollars from Reginald Black in my pocket. I had been meaning to take Maria to the Voisin with that. I wasn't sure whether she actually had an assignation with Martin or not. But then why else would she have tried to call me from Nicky's? I didn't know. I'd had it anyway.

I walked fast, so as to catch Robert at home. On the way I was blaming myself for leaving him in the lurch. He would never have done such a thing, I knew. Well, I had my come-uppance. I felt ashamed, embittered and humiliated. Hirsch seemed to me to be in the right: we will only ever be here on sufferance, second-class humans, not belonging because of not having been born here, where we were permitted to stay as enemy aliens. Even if we could go back to Germany, we would remain aliens. No one would greet us with shouts of welcome. We would be treated as refugees and deserters because we had escaped from concentration camps and crematoria.

There was no light on in Hirsch's store, nor in his room.

I remembered he'd asked about eating at the King of the Sea, so I went there; I had a quick sense of impending doom and I ran almost all the way; I had been there often enough to know that a minute or two could make all the difference in these situations.

The broad windows of the restaurant glittered in the harsh light. I stood still a moment, so as not to walk in out of breath. The unhappy lobsters with their plugged claws moved slothfully on the unfamiliar ice – which must be torture to them, just as it was for the inmates of German concentration camps when oh-so-witty SS men poured ice water over them and let them freeze into pillars.

I saw Hirsch right away. He was sitting alone at a table, tucking in to a lobster. 'I'm back, Robert,' I said.

His face momentarily lit up, then just as quickly turned into a question mark. 'What happened?'

'Nothing, Robert. Strange that we still seem to think something terrible must have happened if we change our plans. That time is gone, Robert. We're in America; nothing much is going to happen to us any more.'

'No?'

'I don't think so.'

'You can still get in trouble with the police in America. Or the immigration people.'

I felt a quick shock, but those quick, hot shocks had happened to me for years. I probably wouldn't stop having them as long as I lived, I thought. It was a shock like the one I felt when Martin asked me about my passport.

'Sit down, Ludwig,' said Hirsch. 'Are you still opposed to lobster?'

'Yes,' I said. 'And I'm still in favour of life, whatever form it takes. Man has the great advantage of being able to end his whenever he likes, if it feels unendurable.'

'He can do that. But not always. Not in German concentration camps.'

'In them as well, Robert. I knew someone who was offered a rope every night to hang himself with. The third night he did it. He had to beg someone to help him. He had been beaten half to death and he didn't have any strength to tie the knot himself. He died half lying, on his knees.'

'This is some table talk we're having,' said Hirsch. 'And purely because I saved a wretched lobster in the window from further suffering. What would you like?'

'Snow crab. Even if they look like roast bones. They've at least been dead for a few days.'

'What a difference!' Hirsch looked at me searchingly. 'You're feeling macabre today. That usually means something has gone wrong in a person's love life.'

'Nothing went wrong. Just things can't always go the way you would wish them to. I'm glad I'm here, Robert. What does the Breviary say: Even running away at the right time is a fine art. Beats being slowly roasted.'

Hirsch laughed. 'Very good, Ludwig. There's a variation too: If you come back, don't hold any funeral orations. Forget what happened; or else don't bother. How much time have you got?'

'As long as I like.'

'Then let's go to the movies and lay into the cognac in my place afterwards. It seems to be an evening for getting drunk.'

I got back to the hotel late. Felix was waiting up for me. 'A lady called, twice. The same one. She wants you to call back.'

I looked at the clock. It was 2 a.m. and I didn't feel too steady on my pins or in my head. 'OK, Felix,' I said. 'If she calls again tell her I'm asleep. I'll call her in the morning.'

'It's all very well for you,' said Felix. 'The ladies are into you like maggots in a rancid bit of bacon. Whereas the likes of us—'

'That's a pretty metaphor, Felix,' I said. 'Your time will come as well. Then you'll remember how much you enjoyed freedom.'

'Freedom, my eye,' said Felix. 'I can smell cognac on your breath. Was it good?'

'To tell you the truth, Felix, I can't remember.'

I woke up because there was someone in the room. 'Who is it?' I asked.

'It's me,' said Maria.

'Where've you come from, Maria?'

She was an indistinct figure against the yellow light in the corridor, slender and dark. I couldn't recognise her. 'Who let you in?' I asked, still muzzy, and reached for my bedside light.

'Felix O'Brien, the only human soul with a grasp of unusual situations. Moikov is delivering vodka somewhere and you—' Maria replied with a strained smile. 'I wanted to see who you were deceiving me with.'

I stared at her. The cognac was dinning round in my head. 'That's—' I began, and in time remembered the Laon Breviary and Hirsch's variation: 'Stop!' I said. 'Where is Marie Antoinette's crown?'

'In the safe of Van Cleef & Arpels. I have to tell you—'

'What for, Maria. I have to tell you — let's just both of us forget it. Where did you eat?'

'In the fridge in 57th Street, steak tartare with vodka and beer. Very sad, like a pilgrim.'

'And I have a hundred-dollar bonus from Reginald Black in my pocket, to lavish on you. Serves us right. Why was I so childish?'

There was a knock. 'Damn!' I said. 'Is that the police already? They don't hang around.'

Maria opened the door. It was Felix O'Brien with a pot of coffee. 'Thought you might have some use for this,' he said.

'And how, you golden boy. Where did you magic that up from without Moikov?'

Felix O'Brien grinned adoringly at Maria. 'Every evening we keep a pot of coffee for Raoul when he goes out. He's not back yet. And some aspirin. He keeps a pack of a hundred there and I'm sure he won't mind if Mr Sommer takes the odd one. I think three will do you.' He turned to me. 'Or do you want more?'

'No thanks, Felix. The coffee is plenty. You've saved my life.'

'Keep the pot,' said Felix. 'I've got one in reserve for Raoul.'

'What a luxurious establishment,' said Maria.

Felix saluted. 'Now I'd better go back and put on the coffee for Mr Raoul. He could be in any time.'

He closed the door after him. I looked at Maria. I saw she wanted to say something, but then didn't. 'I'm not going anywhere,' she finally said.

'Good,' I said. 'That's better than all the explanations in the world. But I don't have a spare toothbrush and I'm pretty drunk.'

'I'm drunk too,' she said.

'It doesn't show.'

'I wouldn't be here otherwise,' she said, not leaving the door.

'What did you have to drink?' I was thinking of El Morocco and Martin.

'I told you. Vodka. Moikov's vodka.'

'I adore you,' I said.

She plunged towards me. 'Watch it!' I said. 'The coffee!'

It was too late. The pot was on its side on the floor. Maria jumped back. The coffee was all over her shoes. She laughed. 'Do we need it?'

I shook my head. She pulled her dress over her head. 'Can't you turn out the overhead light?' she asked from under its pleats.

'I'd have to be crazy to do that.'

She slept, exhausted, pressed against me. The nights weren't steamy any more the way they'd been in August. The air smelled of sea and the peace of the morning breaking ahead. The clock ticked by the bed. It was four o'clock. The coffee stain on the floor was the blackish colour of dried blood. I got up very quietly and spread a newspaper over it. Then I returned. Maria stirred. 'Where were you?' she murmured.

'With you,' I replied. I didn't know what she meant.

'What did Martin say to you?'

'Nothing special. What's his first name again?'

'Roy. Why?'

'I thought it was John.'

'No, it's Roy. John's dead. He died in the war, a year ago – why?'

'No reason, Maria. Go to sleep—'

'Stay with me?'

'Yes, Maria.'

She turned and went back to sleep.

19

'Today the Laskys are coming,' said Reginald Black. 'They're old customers for drawings and watercolours by great masters. They're not so bothered about the quality of the pictures, more the names of the artists. Typical status buyers. I don't know if they're currently in the market or not. We'll see soon enough. If Mrs Lasky is wearing her emeralds they're just here to look. If she comes without jewels, the chances of a sale are improved. Mrs Lasky thinks she's terribly subtle. Every dealer in New York knows about her and her games.'

'And Mr Lasky?'

'He worships his wife and allows her to terrorise him. And in return he terrorises his wholesale garment business on Second Avenue.'

'What are status buyers?' I asked.

'People who are socially ambitious, but not yet sure of themselves. New money. We function as facilitators. We tell the new millionaire that he is part of the elite if he becomes a collector. That his pictures will appear in the catalogues when there's a show and his name, too. It's crude, but it works. That way he's rubbing shoulders with the Mellons and Rockefellers and all the great collectors.' Reginald Black smirked. 'It's strange the way those big sharks fall for the little bait. Probably because there's truth in it. And more likely still, because their wives are the driving force.'

'What sort of cognac will you serve?'

'None. Lasky doesn't drink. At least not when he's in deal-making mode. His wife drinks before dinner. Martinis. But I don't serve cocktails. I'm not down to that level yet. Liqueur, yes. But not cocktails. After all, I'm not running a bar here, with a sideline in paintings. The whole business disgusts me anyway. Where are the great pre-war collectors now?' Reginald Black shrugged. 'Every war brings with it a rearrangement of personal fortunes. Old fortunes melt away, new fortunes are created. And the new-money types are keen to look like old-money types as quickly as possible.' Black stopped. 'Haven't I said this to you before?'

'Not so far today,' I replied to the benefactor of mankind (especially the millionaires).

'I'm going soft in the head,' said Reginald and stroked his brow.

'You've no reason to worry about that,' I said. 'At most you will be like our great statesmen. They repeat themselves until they end up believing what they're saying. They say of Churchill that he starts working on a speech in the bathroom in the morning. Then he tries it out on his wife, over breakfast. And so on, day after day, until everything's been tested. The listeners know everything he's going to say well in advance. It must be the most boring thing in the world to be married to a politician.'

'The most boring thing is to be boring,' said Reginald.

'Well, you're really not that, Mr Black. You have the great advantage of only believing in yourself at certain crucial moments, when it really matters.'

Black laughed. 'I'll show you something that will never be boring. Arrived here last night by plane from Liberated Paris. Noah's dove with the olive branch after the great flood.'

He fetched a very small picture out of his bedroom. It was a Manet. A peony in a glass of water, no more. He set it up on the easel. 'Well?' he asked.

'A marvel,' I said. 'The most beautiful peace dove I've ever seen. God lives! The collector Göring missed out on this little gem during the Occupation.'

'Maybe so. But Reginald Black hasn't. Take it up to your observation post and enjoy it. Pray to it. Change your life in front of it. Recover your faith in God.'

'Don't you want to show it to the Laskys, then?'

'Never!' exclaimed Reginald Black. 'I'm keeping that picture in my private collection. It will never be sold. Ever!'

I looked at him a little sceptically. I knew his private collection. It was by no means as integral as he claimed. The longer he kept pictures in his bedroom, the more sellable they came to be. Reginald in fact had the heart of an artist. He never believed in his success for very long, he had to keep proving it to himself anew. By new sales. There were actually three private collections – that of the house, Mrs Black's and finally Reginald's own. All three were subject to reappraisal, even Reginald's.

'Never!' repeated Reginald. 'I swear! By the life of –'

'Your unborn children,' I suggested.

Reginald stared at me. 'Have I said that before as well?'

I nodded. 'Yes, Mr Black, but at the right moment. There was a buyer present. It was a good idea.'

'I'm getting old,' he said. Then, with a grand gesture he turned towards me again. 'Why don't you buy it? I'd let you have it for the price I paid for it.'

'Mr Black,' I said. 'You're not getting old, otherwise you wouldn't be making those cruel jokes. I have no money. You know what I earn.'

'Would you buy it if you could?'

For a moment I couldn't speak. 'Like a shot,' I finally said.

'To keep?'

I shook my head. 'No, to sell.'

Black gave me a disappointed look. 'I wouldn't have thought that of you, Mr Sommer.'

'Nor would I,' I replied. 'But unfortunately I have much more important things to attend to in my life than collecting pictures.'

Black nodded. 'I don't really know why I asked,' he said after a while. 'I shouldn't ask questions like that. It's just unsettling and doesn't lead to anything. Right?'

'Yes,' I said. 'That's right.'

'Take the Manet upstairs with you anyway. There's more of Paris in it than there is in a dozen books of photographs.'

Yes, you do unsettle me, I thought, when I put the small oil painting on a chair in the room, beside the window with the view of the bridges of New York. You unsettle me by the mere thought of returning to France, which Black's thoughtless words unexpectedly caused to vibrate in me, like the blow of a hammer on an out-of-tune piano. Only a month ago, everything was still clear, my objective, my law, my revenge, the dark innocence, my Orestean entanglement and the pack of Erinyes watching over my memories. But almost unnoticed something else came along that didn't belong in that complex, something I couldn't shake, something to do with Paris, peace and hope – a different peace from the bloody peace that was all I had hitherto been able to imagine. We have to love something, Black had told me, otherwise we are lost. But are we still capable of loving? Loving not desperately or tenaciously, but simply and with devotion? Whoever loves is not entirely lost, even if he

374

should lose what he loves; an image, a reflection of the thing will remain in him, even if clouded by hate, a sort of negative of love. But – can we still love?

I looked at the small flower painting and thought about Reginald Black's advice. You have to love something, otherwise you might as well be dead. The safest thing to love is art. It doesn't change, doesn't disappoint, won't run off. Of course, you can also just love yourself, he added with a look aside, who doesn't do that? But it's a bit lonely and you're better off with art. Any form of art: painting, music, literature.

I stood up and looked out of the window into the warm September light. So much thought, just because a person made a chance remark. I felt the sun on my face like a caress. How did Paragraph 8 of the Laon Breviary go again? Think only of the present and its problems; the future will take care of itself.

I opened the Sisley catalogues. The picture that Reginald Black was going to offer the Laskys was of course in the main catalogue, but as I put together the pedigree I found it was also in an auction catalogue from Paris; it was even on the title page.

A quarter of an hour later I heard the bell. I didn't take the materials straight down with me, that would have looked overanxious and bad business style. I went downstairs, received Black's instructions, went back up, allowed five minutes to pass and came down again with the catalogues.

Mrs Lasky was an imposing-looking lady. She was wearing her emeralds. No prospect, then, of an imminent sale. I opened out the catalogues with the images, one after the other. Black's eyes lit up when he saw the title page. He showed it proudly to Mrs Lasky, who yawned. 'Mneh, it's an auction catalogue,' said Lasky dismissively.

That told me what we were up against. The Laskys were grumblers who liked to knock everything to get a better price. 'Take the catalogues back up,' said Reginald Black. 'And the Sisley too. And call Mr Durant II.'

Lasky grinned. 'To show him the Sisley? Those are old tricks, Mr Black.'

'Not to show him the Sisley, Mr Lasky,' replied Black coldly. 'We're not greengrocers here. Mr Durant wants to take receipt of his new Renoir.'

Mrs Lasky was fiddling with her emeralds. They were beautiful deep green stones. 'Have we seen the Renoir?' asked Lasky idly.

'No,' replied Black. 'It's on its way to Durant II. He has bought it and therefore owns it. On principle we don't show pictures that have already been bought or optioned by another party. Of course the Sisley doesn't come under that heading. Since you don't want it, I feel free to show it.'

I admired Reginald's cold-bloodedness. He wasn't doing anything to sell the Sisley. Nor did he introduce me as the expert from the Louvre who had known the picture in Paris. He started to talk about the war and French politics, and he let me go.

Ten minutes later he rang for me again. The Laskys were gone. 'Sold?' I asked as I came down. Reginald was capable of anything.

He shook his head. 'Those people are like sauerkraut,' he said. 'They need to be brought to the boil twice. And that Sisley picture is really good. You can take a horse to water, and you know the rest. Bloody people!'

I set the little Manet down on the easel. Black's eyes lit up. 'Did you pray in front of it?'

'I thought about everything that people are capable of, in a good way and a bad way.'

'They are. But the bad predominates, especially nowadays. But then again the good is longer-lasting. Men's evil dies with them – their good shines on in centuries to come.'

For a moment I was stunned. Evil didn't die with them, I thought. Rather, the bad man generally died without having been punished. Almost always, in fact. It wasn't for nothing that the primitive sense of justice had made blood revenge an imperative.

'Did you mean that about Durant II?' I asked with a little difficulty.

'I did. The old man is making a monkey of his doctors. Perhaps he'll even outlive them. He was always an underhand son of a bitch.'

'Don't you want to go in person?'

Black smiled. 'For me, the struggle is over. The old man would only start to haggle if I went. You go. Stick to the price I made. If he tries anything, ignore it. Tell him you're not authorised. Leave the picture there if he likes. Then I'll go along in a day or two and ask for it back. Pictures are the best agents. They have a way of creeping into the stone hearts of customers. They make a better case for themselves than the most eloquent dealer. The client gets used to having it there and doesn't want to hand it back. Then he'll even pay full price.'

I packed the picture and set off in a taxi to Durant II. He lived on the top two floors of a building on Park Avenue, on whose ground floor was a dealer in Chinese art. There were a couple of Tang figurines in the window, lovely, gracious clay forms that were given to the departed as funerary gifts. They struck me as oddly fitting to the drama that was in train on the upper floor. As though they were waiting. They and the charming picture of young Madame Henriot that I carried under my arm.

Durant II's apartment had an oddly abandoned feel to it. It wasn't so pompously set up as Cooper's place and felt all the more deserted for it. Museums always feel deserted, even when they're full of visitors. The word visitors is the key; no one lives there. Here I had the impression the owner had already died – he was still living in the two rooms he used, as far as the rest of the place was concerned he was already gone.

I was made to wait a while. In the hall there were a couple of Boudins and a Cézanne. The furniture was average Louis XV, the carpets were new and pretty nasty.

The housekeeper came along and wanted to take the Renoir away. 'I have to take it in in person,' I said. 'Those were Mr Black's instructions to me.'

'Then you'll have to wait a little longer. The doctor's just with Mr Durant.'

I nodded and unpacked Madame Henriot. Her smile filled the dead room. The housekeeper came back. 'That girl's cross-eyed,' she said with a look at the Renoir.

I looked at it in surprise. 'She has astigmatism,' I explained. 'In France that's taken for a sign of special beauty.'

'Really? And it's for that that Mr Durant threw out his doctor? To see that? Her right cheek is askew as well. And the silly choker isn't straight.'

'All these things don't happen with photographs,' I said mildly. I didn't feel like submitting to the critique of a cook.

'That's what I say. All that old junk! That's what Mr Durant's nephews say too.'

Aha, I thought. The heirs. I came to a very large room with an enormous window and stopped dead. There was a bed, with a skeleton half poking out of it. A powerful smell of disinfectant. But glowing in the warm September light were the pictures all over the walls, dancers by Degas and portraits by Renoir, pictures of life and its joys, far too many, even for the large room, and all hung in such a way that they could be viewed from the bed. It was as though the wizened ghoul in the bed had wanted to gather all of beauty and pleasure around him before finally slipping away.

A ruined, hoarse, but surprisingly steady voice croaked, 'Put the picture on the chair beside the bed.'

I set it down and waited. The skull gazed at the delicate Madame Henriot hungrily, almost obscenely. The far too large eyes seemed to suck on to it like leeches, eating the picture up. I looked around at the clutch of pictures there on the walls, like so many colourful butterflies, and I assumed that Durant II must have gradually brought them all in from the rest of the apartment as he slowly left it. Now the blithest and loveliest of them were gathered around him, his favourites in all probability, and he clung on to them as his actual life ebbed away.

'How much?' asked the living corpse after a while.

'Twenty thousand,' I replied.

He croaked, 'How much really?'

'Twenty thousand,' I said again.

I saw the big brown stains on the skull and the great teeth which were very white, chalky and a hundred per cent false. They reminded me of the lawyer's teeth on Ellis Island. 'That damned bastard,' croaked Durant II. 'Twelve.'

'I am not here to deal,' I said. 'Mr Black has given me no authority, Mr Durant.'

'Double-damned bastard.'

Durant stared at the picture again. 'I can't see it properly. It's too dark in here.'

The room was dazzlingly bright. The sun shone on the opposite wall, where three Degas pastels hung. I pushed the chair into the sun. 'Now it's too far away,' croaked Durant II. 'Use the beam.'

I found a searchlight by the window halfway up and switched it on. Its strong beam was full on the sweet face of the young woman. Durant stared at it avidly. 'Mr Durant,' I said, 'the three Degas pastels are in full sunlight. That's not good for them.'

Durant ignored me. After some time he turned in my direction and looked at me like an insect. 'Young man,' he said with a semblance of calm, 'I know. And I don't care. For the time I've got it's good. And I don't give a damn whether the pictures lose value for my fucking heirs. I can hear them slinking around downstairs, doing their sums. The bastards! Dying is difficult. Did you know that, young man?'

'Yes, sir,' I replied. 'I do.'

'Oh?'

He turned back to face Madame Henriot. 'Why don't you buy it,' I said finally.

'For twelve thousand I will,' replied Durant quickly. 'Not a penny more.'

He looked at me with his burning owl eyes. I shrugged. I couldn't say what I thought, even though I would have liked to go back to Reginald with everything settled. 'It would be against my honour,' Durant II added unexpectedly.

I made no reply. It wasn't my place. 'Leave me the picture,' croaked Durant II. 'I'll get in touch.'

'Very well, sir.'

For a moment it struck me as bizarre to show such respect

to someone who already stank of the rot in his body, in spite of all the disinfectants and air-fresheners; who was just a rearguard action, the last cells of a collapsing body and a slowly dimming brain.

I left the sickroom. The housekeeper stopped me. 'Mr Durant asked me to give you a glass of cognac. He doesn't do such a thing very often. He must have liked you. One moment, please.'

I didn't actually feel like staying, but I was interested to find out what sort of cognac Durant II drank. The house-keeper came back with a tray. 'Did Mr Durant buy it?' she asked.

I looked at her in surprise. What was it to her? 'No,' I ended up saying.

'Thank God! What does he need all that old junk for? That's what his niece, Miss Durant, keeps forever saying.'

I could easily imagine the niece; a bony, greedy piece of work who was waiting to inherit, just like in all probability the housekeeper, for whom each new purchase threatened to diminish her legacy. I reached for the cognac and put it down right away. It was quite the most unpleasant blend I had ever drunk. 'Is this the cognac Mr Durant himself drinks?' I asked.

'Mr Durant doesn't drink. Doctor's orders. Why?'

Poor Durant, I thought. Surrounded by furies who didn't scruple to adulterate his drinks. 'Strictly speaking, I'm not allowed to either.'

'Mr Durant ordered it personally only a year ago.'

It gets worse, I thought. 'Why isn't Mr Durant in hospital?' I asked.

The housekeeper sighed. 'He didn't want to. He doesn't want to say goodbye to his old junk. He has the doctor staying in the house, downstairs. Everything would have been so much easier in hospital.'

I got up to go. 'And does the doctor drink this splendid cognac?' I asked.

'No. He's a whiskey drinker. Scotch.'

'It's the language barrier,' said Georg Kamp. He was sitting in his stained white overalls in Hirsch's store. The working day was over. Kamp looked satisfied. 'It's over ten years ago that my books were burned in Germany,' he said. 'I can't write in English. A few have been able to. Arthur Koestler and Vicki Baum. Some others in the film industry, where style doesn't matter so much. It was always beyond me.'

Kamp had been a well-known author in Germany. He was now fifty-five. 'I became a painter and decorator; today I'm celebrating my promotion to gaffer; that's something like a bricklayer's foreman. I'll take you out for coffee and cake. Robert gave me permission to use his store. Everyone's coming in ten minutes. They've all been invited.'

Kamp looked around, proud and satisfied. 'Don't you write any more, then?' I asked. 'In the evenings, after work?'

'I tried for a while. I'm usually too tired in the evenings. I did for the first couple of years or so. I would have starved. I would have been crippled by complexes. As a painter I make ten times as much money.'

'I see a great career ahead of you,' said Hirsch. 'You know Hitler was a painter and decorator.'

Kamp waved his hand. 'He was an artist who didn't make it. I'm in the union. Fully paid-up member.'

'Do you want to remain a painter and decorator?' I asked.

'I'm not sure. I'll have to think about it, nearer the time. For now I'm just trying not to erode the bit of talent I have in reserve with too much introspection. Maybe one day I'll write the memoirs of a housepainter in New York, if I can't come up with anything else.'

Hirsch laughed. 'God is on your side,' he said. 'You're saved, Kamp.'

'Why not?' asked Kamp in surprise. 'Do you think I should have put on my brown suit?' He stared at the window display where Carmen had appeared. 'I could—' He stopped talking and just stared.

'Too late,' replied Hirsch. 'The coffee's already perking. I've sacrificed my best coffee-maker.'

Carmen walked in. On her heels came a little greenfinch of a woman, carrying a large cardboard box. This was Katharina Jellineck, the wife of a professor who had remained in Austria. Katharina was Jewish, the professor wasn't. They had come for her twice in Vienna; he had given her enough money for the crossing, sent her away and got a divorce. She had escaped through Switzerland and France, and reached New York just before the outbreak of war, small, tousled, almost penniless, but with an indomitable will. She had started off as a maid, then someone had made the discovery that she could bake and set her up in a tiny back apartment. She had to sleep with the man who did her the service; as she had also had to sleep with several others, for bits of help and advancement. She didn't complain. She knew life and she knew that nothing was for free.

She had also had to sleep with the SA man in Vienna who had given her a passport. She had done it and tried to think of her husband, assuming that would make it as if nothing had really happened. But in fact she had thought of nothing at all. In the instant the sweating SA man laid his mitts on her, she had become a machine. It hadn't been her at all. Something in her was iced over and didn't participate. Everything else was clear and cold and aimed at a single objective: her passport. She was no longer the wife of Professor Jellineck, twenty-eight, pretty and a touch sentimental – she was just a thing requiring a passport. There was neither sin nor disgust nor morals, all those were qualities of a bygone world. She passed through the squalor of existence like a moonbeam; it never touched her. Later on, when her little baking business was successful, someone wanted to marry her; she couldn't understand. She was walled in and inaccessible. And all the time she remained friendly, sweet and, in a birdlike way, homeless. She baked the best strudels in New York. Poppy seed biscuits, cheese and cherry and apple strudels, compared to which even Jessie's baking was amateurish.

'Katharina,' said Georg Kamp. 'Come in here and unpack your delectables.'

Hirsch lowered the shutters in the window. 'A precaution,' he explained. 'Otherwise we'll have the police here in no time.'

Silently and politely Mrs Jellineck unpacked her cakes. 'I love cake,' said Kamp to Carmen. 'Especially cheese strudel.'

Carmen awoke from her divine lethargy. 'So do I,' she declared. 'With lots of cream.'

'Just like me,' replied Kamp, beaming, without taking his eyes off her deceptive beauty. 'With coffee and even more cream.'

Carmen was thrilled. 'Carmen, this is the writer Georg Kamp,' I introduced them. 'The only jolly emigrant I know. Once, he was the author of deeply melancholy, heartbreaking books. Now he paints houses in cheerful colours.'

Carmen helped herself to a piece of cherry strudel. 'How wonderful,' she said. 'A jolly emigrant!' She gave Kamp an appraising look, then stretched out her lovely hand for a poppy seed biscuit.

Mrs Jellineck had also brought cups, plates and spoons. 'I'll come for all those tomorrow,' she said.

'But stay and celebrate our relief from the spirit of oppression,' cried Kamp.

'I can't. I have to go.'

'But Mrs Jellineck! What can you possibly have to go on to? The day's work is done. For you too.'

Kamp reached for her hand and pulled her nearer. She began to tremble. 'Please! Let me go! I must leave! Right away! Forgive me! I must—'

Kamp looked at her in astonishment. 'But what's the matter? We're not untouchables—'

'Let me go!' The woman was pale and trembling violently.

'Let her go, Mr Kamp!' said Carmen calmly in her deep voice.

He let her go right away. Mrs Jellineck bungled a curtsey and ran out. Kamp watched her go. 'An émigrée tizz,[5] I expect. We all go a little mad from time to time.'

Carmen shook her tragic head. 'She got a telegram today from Bern. Her husband has passed away. In Vienna.'

'Old Jellineck?' asked Kamp. 'The man who threw her out?' Carmen nodded. 'She wanted to return to him. That's why she was saving up her money.'

'She wanted to go back? After everything that happened here, and with him?'

'She wanted to go back. She thought that would undo everything that had happened and she could start over.'

'Stuff and nonsense!'

Hirsch looked at the painter. 'Don't say that, Georg. Don't you want to start over too?'

'Who can say? I live as I am.'

'That's the merciful illusion of emigrants. Forget and start over.'

[5] That phrase: *Emigranten Koller* again.

'The woman should be glad Jellineck's snuffed it. It's to her advantage. She doesn't need to hoick the man who put her out like a cat into her warm bakery and be his skivvy again.'

'People don't always grieve over the right things,' said Hirsch.

Kamp looked around a bit helplessly. 'Damn,' he said. 'We were going to be cheerful today.'

Ravic came in. 'How's Jessie doing?' I asked.

'She left hospital this morning and went home. More suspicious than ever. The better her wound healed, the more suspicious she became.'

'Better?' I asked. 'Really better?'

Ravic seemed very tired. 'What do you mean, better?' he said. 'Slowly dying, that's the most we can hope for. And it's bloody useless, if you read the papers. Hecatombs of healthy young fellows slaughtered over there and we bust a gut to try and keep a few sick old people alive a little longer. Have you got a cognac for me?'

'Rum,' I replied. 'Like in Paris.'

Ravic drank his rum. He looked outside. '*L'heure bleue,*' he said. '*Crépuscule.* The hour of shadows, where you're all alone with your wretched self and even less than that. The hour when the sick die.'

'You're in a bad way, Ravic. Something happen?'

'I'm not sad. I'm discouraged. I lost a patient. It shouldn't really depress me any more but it does. Go and see Jessie. She needs help. Laugh with her. What are you doing here among the cake eaters?'

'And you?'

'I'm picking up Robert Hirsch. We're going to eat in a bistro. Like in Paris. Is that Georg Kamp, the author?'

I nodded. 'The last optimist. A brave, naive fellow.'

'Bravery!' said Ravic. 'I wish I could go to sleep for years and not have to hear the word. It's the most misused word there is. Be brave and see Jessie. Lie to her. Cheer her up. That's bravery, if you ask me.'

'Does she need to be lied to?' I asked.

Ravic nodded.

'Let's go out somewhere,' I said to Maria. 'Somewhere superficial and jolly and casual. I feel as full of sadness and death as an old moss-grown tree. Here's my bonus from Reginald Black. Let's go and eat at Voisin's.'

She looked at me. 'I have to leave tonight,' she said. 'I'm going to Beverly Hills. To take pictures and model clothes for the Californians.'

'What time?'

'At midnight. For a few days. Have you got the blues?'

I shook my head. She pulled me inside. 'Come in,' she said. 'What are you doing standing in the doorway? Or are you planning to leave again right away? How little I know about you!'

I followed her into the dark room, which was lit up by the windows of the skyscrapers like a cubist painting. A very pale-looking half-moon stood in a space between them. 'Couldn't we go to Voisin's anyway?' I asked. '*Changer la crèmerie?*'

She looked at me alertly. 'Has something happened?' she asked.

'No. I just feel shockingly helpless all of a sudden. It happens from time to time. It's the colourless hour of shadows. It'll go away when the lights come on.'

Maria switched on the light. 'There we are,' she said in a voice that was halfway between challenge and apprehension. She was standing between two suitcases, with hats lying on top of them. One of the suitcases was open. Maria was naked, except for a pair of high-heeled shoes. 'I'll be done in a jiffy,' she said. 'Of course I'll need to get ready if we're going to the Voisin.'

'Why?'

'What a question! It's obvious you don't know the first thing about models.' She sat down in front of her mirror. 'There's vodka in the fridge. Moikov's.'

I didn't reply. I watched as in the space of a second or two she forgot all about me. The sharply lit face in the mirror grew strange to me like an animated mask, as the hands reached for the brushes as for the scalpels of a surgeon. With great concentration, as though it really were an operation, lines were drawn, powder tried out, and shadows and lights placed silently, like a huntress girding herself for the chase.

I had often watched women putting on make-up and they had never particularly liked being watched. Maria, though, was wholly uninhibited, just as she was when walking naked through the apartment. It wasn't just her job, I thought; it was much more the consciousness of her beauty that made her so casual. She was so used to changing clothes that nudity was something like her public mode.

I was captivated by the woman in the mirror. She was utterly engrossed in her narrow, brightly lit world, in her self, her face, which was no longer individual but generic, the face of the guardian of the species, that of the mysterious young woman in the depths of an archaic mirror. Her concentration was so absolute, it was almost hostile. She had gone back to something that would soon be set aside again – to remote beginnings before the dawn of consciousness.

She put down her brushes and powder puffs, and slowly turned round. It was as though she were returning from some distant place; she recognised me again. 'Ready,' she said. 'You too?'

I nodded. 'Me too, Maria.'

She laughed and came up to me. 'Are you still keen to waste your money?'

'More than ever. But for other reasons now.'

I could feel the warmth on her skin. She smelled of cedar, refuge and difference. 'How many useless things there are,' she said. 'And you're full of them. Why?'

'I really couldn't tell you.'

'Why don't you forget them? We could live so simply without the curse of memory.'

I laughed. 'People forget – but usually they forget the wrong things.'

'Me too?'

'No, not now, Maria.'

'Then let's just stay here. I've got the blues as well, but mine are at least sensible. I'm sad because I have to go away. Why go out to a restaurant if we're feeling like that?'

'You're right, Maria. It wasn't a good idea.'

'There's steak tartare in the fridge and turtle soup and salad and fruit. Also beer and vodka. Will that do?'

'That's plenty, Maria.'

'You don't need to take me to the airport. It would feel too much like goodbye. I'm just going to leave like someone who's coming back soon. You can stay here.'

'I won't stay here. I'll go back to the Rausch when you leave.'

She didn't say anything. 'Whatever,' she said. 'I'd have liked it if you'd stayed. When you go there, you always seem so far away.'

I held her in my arms. Everything seemed so simple. 'Turn the light out,' I said.

'Don't you want to eat?'

I turned out the light. 'No,' I said and carried her to the bed.

When time resumed we lay quietly together for a long while. Maria stirred in her half-sleep. 'You've never said you loved me,' she murmured, as though she were talking about someone else.

'I adore you,' I replied after a while, so as not to disturb her lovely deep breathing. 'I adore you, Maria.'

She laid her head against my shoulder. 'Never mind,' she whispered. 'Never mind, my darling.'

I didn't say anything. My eyes followed the hands round the clock on the night stand. I was thinking vaguely of lots of things at once. 'You'd better go, Maria, it's time.'

Then I saw that she was silently crying. 'I hate saying goodbye,' she said. 'I think we've had too many goodbyes between us. And too soon. Don't you?'

'It's what I've had to do for most of my life. But this isn't goodbye. You'll be back.'

'Everything is a goodbye,' she said.

I walked her to the corner of Second Avenue. The late evening *paseo* of the homosexuals and their poodles was on. José waved; Fifi barked. 'There's a cab,' said Maria.

I lifted her suitcases into the boot. She kissed me and climbed in. She looked very lost, all alone on the wide back seat. I watched until I could no longer see the taxi lights. Odd, I thought, after all it's only for a few days. But my European fear was with me – that it might be for good and that we might never see each other again.

20

Reginald Black held a newspaper aloft. 'He's dead,' he said. 'Gave us the slip.'

'Who?'

'Durant II. Who else?'

I sighed with relief. I hated news of deaths. I had had too many. 'Oh, him,' I said. 'Well, that was on the cards. An old man with cancer.'

'On the cards? What are you saying? An old man with cancer and an unpaid Renoir!'

'That's true,' I said, surprised.

'I phoned him the day before yesterday. He told me he would probably take the picture. And now this! He's duped us.'

'Duped us?'

'Of course! Twice over! He hasn't paid for the picture, and now it belongs to his estate and will be held in fief until the various claims on it are settled. It could take years. And in the meantime the portrait's lost to us.'

'But it's going up in value all the time,' I replied. It was the argument that Black the benefactor probably used for every single sale he made.

'This is no time for jokes, Mr Sommer. We have to act, and act fast. Come with me. You've no idea the kind of things that heirs are capable of. When someone dies, they turn into so many spotted hyenas. I need you as a witness. It's perfectly possible that the heirs will claim that the picture has already been paid for.'

'Has the funeral taken place yet?'

'I don't know, but I don't think so. The news broke this morning. But maybe he's been packed off to a funeral home already. That's the way they do things here, like sending a parcel by express delivery. Why do you ask?'

'If he's laid out, then for form's sake, we should maybe have a black tie apiece. Do you have one?'

'For an unpaid picture. Dear Mr—'

'A bit of piety and false sympathy will help things along,' I interrupted him. 'A tie doesn't cost anything, but it will improve the atmosphere.'

'If you say so,' growled Black and disappeared into his bedroom.

He came back with a black tie in patterned brocade for me. 'What a natty item,' I said.

'From Paris.' Black looked down himself. 'I feel like a chimpanzee with this black rag round my neck. It looks horrible with the suit.' He stared in aversion at the mirror. 'Ghastly!'

'If I might suggest: a dark suit.'

'Do you think? Maybe. All the lengths we go to to get our property out of the hands of a dead man and his heirs.'

Reginald Black disappeared and came back; this time in a quiet pinstripe. 'I couldn't go the whole hog and wear black,' he said. 'After all, a man has his honour. I'm not in mourning for Durant II. I just want to rescue my picture.'

Durant II was indeed laid out. He was no longer in his bedroom, but in one of the splendid public rooms downstairs. A servant intercepted us. 'Do you have an invitation?'

'I beg your pardon?' asked Reginald stiffly and disbelievingly.

'An invitation to the funeral.'

'When is it being held?' I asked.

'In two hours.'

'Fine. Is the housekeeper there?'

'She's upstairs.'

A man walked in who looked like a bull in subfusc. 'Do you want to see the deceased?' he asked.

Reginald Black made to decline. I nudged him and asked, 'Is there time to?'

'Sure. Plenty of time.'

The man smelled of good whiskey. 'Show them the way,' he said to the servant.

'Who was that?' Black asked the servant.

'Mr Rasmussen. A relative of Mr Durant II.'

'I thought as much.'

The servant left us outside a large, almost empty room, with two laurels flanking the entrance. Inside, dozens of wreaths had been piled up and vases stood around with roses of every colour, though principally white. I thought of Emilio, the florist; if he had an in with the mortician who had laid on this show, the roses would be cheap tonight.

'Why should I look at a stiff who only wanted to pull a fast one on me?' growled Reginald Black. 'I want my Renoir back and I don't want to have to pray for it.'

'You won't have to pray. You only need to lower your head diplomatically and think that we might not get Madame Henriot back; then you'll even shed a few tears.'

There were about twenty people present. Almost all of them were old; only a couple were children. One woman wore a black tulle hat with a black wig. She eyed us suspiciously. Death's receptionist, I thought, and remembered

Lachmann's new sweetheart, the chartreuse-drinking cinema cashier.

In among all these bored people Durant II lay there like a wax doll with closed eyes. He looked much smaller than I had remembered, almost like an old, tired child. In accordance with the peculiar rites of death, the ex-Wall Street shark had a cross stuck between his pudgy hands. The flowers smelled so strong, there might have been twice as many of them. Reginald Black eyed Durant II with close attention. The air conditioning was on; that gave the occasion something of the feeling of a morgue. None of the pictures in Durant II's collection was in the room with him; both Black and I would have registered it immediately.

'On to battle,' murmured Reginald. 'Rasmussen, here we come.'

'First the housekeeper.'

'Oh, all right.'

There was no stopping us now. From somewhere we heard a clinking of glasses. There had to be a bar somewhere around. We climbed a flight of stairs. 'There's an elevator,' said the servant, who knew us now.

We rode the elevator up to the floor I had visited before. The housekeeper, to my astonishment, received me like an old friend. 'He's gone,' she sobbed. 'You came too late. I expect you wanted to talk to him about the picture?'

'Yes, that's right. I had brought it on approval. It's the property of Mr Reginald Black. I thought we could just take it back. Where is it now?'

'Still in his bedroom. Nothing's been moved.'

I headed there with no further questions. The way was familiar. Black marched determinedly at my side. The house-keeper followed, sobbing.

'There's Madame Henriot,' I said at the doorway. 'Beside the bed.'

Black took a couple of large strides forward. Madame Henriot smiled sweetly at him. I looked into the deserted room where the pictures now enjoyed a curious, autonomous existence, full of sun and life, and remote from death.

The housekeeper followed Black. She stood in front of the Renoir. 'Stop!' she sobbed. 'We'll have to ask Mr Rasmussen's permission to take it away.'

'But it's my picture. You know that.'

'We still have to ask Mr Rasmussen.'

Reginald Black's beard trembled. For a moment he looked as though he wanted to barge the housekeeper out of the way. Then he stopped. 'Very well,' he said mildly. 'Would you get Mr Rasmussen?'

The duel began with a ritual exchange of pieties. Rasmussen, smelling more strongly of whiskey than before, played the grief-stricken survivor, who declined to talk about business while the departed was still waiting to depart. He was supported by a vixen with garish eyes, ill-fitting dentures and a veil flapping round her hair like a flag in a storm. Black stood his ground. He remained untouched by imputations of emotional coarseness and vulgar commercial thinking, and insisted on his property. He had seen at a glance that the housekeeper was not on the side of the phoney mourners. She was probably the only one with any affection for the dead man; and perhaps she knew too that her services would no longer be required. When Rasmussen therefore claimed that the picture was part of the estate and had probably long ago been bought and paid for, Black found he had an ally in the still sobbing woman. Rasmussen rejected her evidence; she was ignorant. That annoyed the housekeeper; she told him, when he said she should just shut up, that she wasn't taking orders from him, she had been engaged by Durant II. The grieving female heir joined in with a shrill voice, and a short, sharp fight developed between her and the housekeeper. Black pushed me into the fight as a further witness. The housekeeper gave me intrepid support. She insisted that the Renoir had been in the house for less than two weeks, and Durant II had told her that following his death it would have to be returned. Rasmussen was gobsmacked. He said everything would have to wait until the Will was opened. Black insisted on his point of view. Rasmussen took out his watch; he had to quit this undignified bickering and check that all the arrangements for the funeral were in hand.

'Very well,' said Black, 'then please be informed that I have an offer for this picture of 50,000 dollars and that I hold you personally responsible for such a sum.'

For a moment there was silence. Then the storm broke loose. 'What?' screeched the heiress. 'Who do you think you can fool! That daub isn't worth one thousand.'

Reginald Black ushered me forward. 'The Louvre's expert, Mr Ludwig Sommer, offered it to Mr Durant II at that price.'

I nodded.

'Outrageous!' stormed the heiress. 'Two hands' breadth of canvas! The corners haven't even got any paint on them.'

'It's a collector's piece,' I said. 'Not for day-to-day commerce. For a collector, it is beyond price.'

'Only if you're selling it.'

Reginald Black toyed with his Assyrian beard. 'There's no question of that,' he said with dignity. 'Anyway, you can't sell it. It's mine. I am only telling you what damages I want if you refuse to surrender the painting.'

Rasmussen suddenly folded. 'This is all nonsense. Come into my office. We need to indemnify ourselves if we hand over the picture.'

He led the way to a small study. I stayed behind with the housekeeper. 'The more money people have, the greedier they are,' she said bitterly. 'She wanted to put me out on the street on the first of the month, when Mr Durant stipulated that I was to be kept on till the end of the year. Well, they'll be in for a surprise when they see what he's gone and left me. I was the only one he trusted; he never cared for any of the others. They even bad-mouthed his cognac. Would you like some, by the way? You are the only one who liked it. I haven't forgotten that.'

'Happily,' I said. 'It was outstanding cognac.'

She poured me some of the devil's stuff. I knocked it back and beamed. 'Delicious!' I said.

'There you are! That's why I thought I'd help you out. All the others here, they just hate me. Well, see if I care.'

Reginald Black returned to the bedroom with a few papers. Rasmussen followed him silently. He handed him the sweet Madame Henriot as though it were a toad and locked the bedroom. 'Wrap it up,' he said curtly to the housekeeper and walked off without a goodbye.

The housekeeper went to find packing paper. 'Would you like some cognac too?' she asked. 'There's a lot left in the bottle. And no one will come here—'

I winked at Black. 'Very much,' he said.

'An outstanding make,' I said by way of cautioning him.

Black took a swallow, but he controlled himself impressively. 'Mr Sommer told me about it,' he managed to wheeze. 'I think he'd like another, if you have so much of it left. I'm restricted to a single glass a week. Doctor's orders. But Mr Sommer here—'

I ground my teeth as the housekeeper refilled my glass. 'I'm sure he'd appreciate a double,' volunteered Reginald.

A shy smile blossomed on the wrecked face of the old woman. 'Why not,' she said. 'I'm so glad you like it. Perhaps you'd like to take the bottle with you?'

I almost swallowed some the wrong way – with unimaginable consequences – and motioned no. 'I've learned in life that visitors come at the oddest times and it's best to be prepared.'

We left the grieving house with Madame Henriot under our arm, feeling we'd rescued a tender nymph from the hands of Arab slave traders. 'I need a drink,' Reginald panted into his beard. 'That was sulphuric acid. An abrasive, not a drink.' He craned around for a bar. Luckily a taxi came along at that moment. 'All right, let's just take it. It's best to flush out this nasty taste with some of my very best cognac. Those robbers! Death, greed and acquisitiveness.'

'Your idea with the 50,000 dollars was inspired,' I said.

'In our profession you have to be able to think on your feet and be fearless. Let's celebrate the safe return of Madame Henriot with candlelight and some of my private Napoleon.' Reginald Black laughed. 'Can you understand people?'

'You mean Rasmussen? And the grieving hyena?'

'Not them. Those are two open books. But Durant II. Why didn't he buy the Renoir when he knew what his heirs were like? He could have given it to his housekeeper. I'm sure he slept with her thirty years ago. Because it was cheaper than a wife or a mistress.'

In the window of the Silvers' antique store there was a poster: 'Sale! Everything must go! Big reductions!' I walked in. Alexander Silver received me in grey socks and chequered trousers, but paired with a black tie. 'Has something happened?' I asked.

'Everything,' replied Alexander bleakly. 'The worst!'

I looked at his black tie and remembered I was wearing one myself. I had forgotten to change out of it. 'Has someone died?' I asked.

Alexander shook his head. 'Not that – but hardly better, Mr Sommer. But what about you? You're wearing black too.'

'Grief as a business tactic. But you? Today seems to be a day for black ties.'

'My brother! The double-tongued Nazi! He got married. Secretly. A week ago.'

'Who to?'

'The shiksa, of course. The blonded, marcelled hyena.'

'It seems quite the day for hyenas. I ran into one this afternoon. Is that what prompted you to put the poster up? A closing sale?'

Alexander nodded. 'The poster's in the window. But not one customer. It's all in vain. Who wants antiques nowadays? Only my brother, the monster! And he's gone and married her.'

I leaned against a Dutch chair that was genuine except for the legs. 'Do you really want to close the business? That would be a pity.'

'Want to, want to! I tried to close it. No one wants it. I can't even get any customers to my closing sale.'

'What sort of business do you want to have?' I asked.

Silver looked at me narrowly. 'I don't know,' he answered cautiously. 'Do you want it?'

'Of course not. I couldn't even rent it. I don't have the money.'

'So why are you asking?'

'Plain sympathy. What about a cup of coffee over the road? May I treat you this time?'

Silver looked at me mournfully. 'I don't have the heart, my dear friend. Those were the good old days in the past. All finished! Do you know what my brother threatened to do? He threatened to go back into the law if I remained so stubborn. All I'm doing is standing up for the memory of our mother. If she knew about this! She would be spinning in her grave.'

'You never know. Perhaps she'd have taken a shine to her daughter-in-law.'

'What, my mother, a devout Jewess and that shiksa!'

I walked to the door. 'Come on, Alexander. A cup of coffee and a chat won't hurt. Do me a favour.'

All at once Silver looked a bit derelict. The wars of religion had taken it out of him; this wasn't the bohemian of yesteryear. His footwork had suffered too; he was almost run over by another cyclist as we crossed the road, a bit of a comedown for an old man who once had danced between sports cars and buses.

'The Gugelhupf is fresh,' said the waitress. 'I'd recommend it, Mr Silver.'

Alexander took in the samples without much interest. 'A Moor's head,' he finally said. The dark chocolate frosting seemed to go best with his black mood.

The waitress brought us our coffee. Alexander burned his mouth, it was so hot. 'It's really not my day,' he muttered wretchedly.

I embarked on a discussion on the transience of all earthly things, in the hope of making him pliant and melancholy. I took Durant II as my example. Alexander was barely listening. The next moment I saw him shoot up like a snake. He looked across the street at the shop. 'There they are!' he

400

whispered. 'Those two! Alexander and the shiksa! In the window! The impertinence! Do you see? The curled blonde beast with her wig and face full of teeth.'

I saw Arnold in his little visiting suit, Marengo jacket with striped trousers, and a rather scrawny, harmless-looking girl. 'She's casing the joint,' hissed Alexander. 'See those greedy eyes.'

'No, I don't,' I said. 'And nor do you for that matter, Mr Alexander. You have a vivid imagination. What are you going to do about it? Have another Moor's head, that's the most sensible solution.'

'Absolutely not! I have to go over there. Otherwise the shiksa will break in and empty the shop. Come. Help me.' Alexander Silver rampaged across the avenue, with almost the exuberance of the old days. Hate lent him wings. He performed an elegantly held half-salto avoiding a delivery van for diapers, then shot behind an omnibus.

I got up and paid. 'He's not himself,' said the waitress. 'It's eating him up, Mr Arnold getting married like that. As if it was the worst thing in the world. Forgetting it's wartime.' She shook her head sadly.

I approached the shop slowly. I wanted to give Alexander Silver time to recover his sangfroid in his own immediate family circle; after all, he did view himself as a gentleman, for whom even a shiksa was a woman and as such demanded respect.

Arnold introduced us; I offered modest congratulations, so as not to provoke Alexander needlessly. After that I listened. Arnold wanted to take down the Sale sign. There couldn't be a sale without his agreement, he explained mildly. 'Why do you want to sell, Alexander?'

'I want to resume my legal practice,' replied Alexander. 'As a divorce lawyer,' he added.

The shiksa, whose name was Caroline, laughed. 'How funny! But sad too.'

'We can talk about that later,' said Arnold, who seemed to have gained in stature. 'For now I'd like to show Caroline our business.'

Alexander shot me a look that spoke volumes. 'You don't object, do you, Alexander,' twittered Caroline. At the use of his first name the elder Silver flinched as though he had been stung by a wasp. 'Just as I thought,' she went on smilingly, 'a gentleman like you.'

She opened the door and went inside. Arnold followed with a grin. Alexander resembled the Prussian general from the time of Wilhelm who to his utter astonishment found his genitals being given a squeeze. 'Come along,' he murmured to me in stricken fashion. 'You come too.'

Caroline seemed oblivious to his icy demeanour. She twirled and twittered about, found everything delightful, continued to call him 'Alexander' and 'my dear brother-in-law', and even demanded to see the exciting catacombs. Arnold climbed down the steps in front of her with a broad smile on his face.

'Now what do you say?' groaned Alexander, after the newlyweds had gone on under the ground. 'She pretends everything's perfectly all right. What can I do about it?' He looked at me piteously.

'Nothing,' I said. 'It's done and I would take it graciously. Otherwise you'll end up with a heart attack.'

Alexander struggled for breath. 'That's your advice to me? I thought you were my friend.'

'I come from a country where Jews are murdered if they even touch a shiksa, Mr Alexander – never mind actually marrying one. It's not a thing I can be objective about.'

'That's precisely it,' said Silver. 'That's why we two have to stick together. My poor mother! She was devout and

402

believed, and raised us to be the same. Arnold the apostate would have been the death of her, if she hadn't happened to be dead already. Just as well. But how can you understand my suffering? You're an atheist.'

'Only in the daytime.'

'Ach, enough with the joking. What can I do? That woman with her grinning friendliness is impossible to attack.'

'Why not get married yourself?'

'What? Who?'

'A girl your mother would have liked.'

'Sell my freedom? Just because Arnold—'

'It would restore the balance of the family,' I said.

'Nothing is sacred to you,' said Silver. 'Worse luck.'

'Yes, it is,' I replied. 'Worse luck.'

'Here comes the legacy-huntress,' whispered Alexander. 'Careful! She has ears like a thief.'

The trapdoor opened. Arnold, already heavier from marriage and the cooking of his shiksa, clambered out. Caroline followed with happy laughter. 'Will you see what I found, Alexander,' she tooted. 'An ivory Christ! I can take that, can't I? You don't want it, do you? You people put him to death, after all. Funny that you want to deal in him all the same. Arnold doesn't mind if I take him with me; you won't either, will you?'

Alexander almost suffocated all over again. He mumbled something inaudible about art and freedom, and had to stand and be kissed by Caroline.

'Come and eat with us tonight,' she said. 'We're even having something – what do you call it – kosher. Chopped chicken livers with onions as an hors d'oeuvre.'

She beamed at him with all her teeth. Alexander seemed on the verge of an apoplexy. 'I have an engagement with Mr Sommer,' he finally managed to say.

'Couldn't you change that?' asked Caroline coquettishly and flashed me the smile.

'Not easily,' I replied, in answer to a beseeching look from Alexander. 'We have a date in Harlem. With a big collector.'

'In Harlem? In the Negro quarter? How interesting! In the Savoy Ballroom, by chance?'

'No, this is with a missionary with four children. Very boring, but rich. A councillor in South Harlem.'

'What does he collect?' asked the indefatigable Caroline. 'Negro plastics?'

'No, rather the opposite. Venetian mirrors.'

Caroline went into a peal of laughter. 'Isn't that funny! You never can tell. Come on, darling.' She linked arms with Arnold and blew Alexander a kiss. 'You are funny!' she twittered. 'So earnest! But so sweet and funny as well.'

I watched her leave. The word funny and all the laughter had rather caught me off-balance. It reminded me of a concentration camp doctor who was known as the Smiler. He found all the patients screamingly funny and cured them, amidst peals of laughter, by hitting them with a riding crop for so long until they declared themselves healed. That was how he examined patients.

'What's the matter?' asked Alexander Silver. 'You're all pale. Is it that you're so disgusted by that harpy? What can we do about her? She covers you in kisses and laughter and embraces no matter what. Arnold is lost, don't you see?'

'He looked rather contented to me.'

'People have been known to go to Hell laughing.'

'Just bide your time, Mr Silver. The divorce system in America is very simple and straightforward. The worst that can happen is that Arnold one day wakes up a wiser man.'

Silver looked at me. 'That doesn't show a lot of compassion.'

I didn't reply. It was too absurd. 'Are you really thinking of going back to the law?' I asked.

Alexander made an impatient gesture. 'Take down the Sale sign, won't you,' I said. 'It doesn't bring anyone in. And why should you sell for less than cost price?'

'Less than cost price? I wouldn't dream of it,' replied a suddenly animated Alexander. 'For Sale is not the same as less than cost price. Sale is just Sale. Of course we still want to make money.'

'Very well. Then leave it up. That's the spirit! And just wait calmly for Arnold to get a divorce. You are both lawyers after all.'

'A divorce costs money. Pointless money.'

'Experience always comes at a cost. As long as it's just money, it's not important.'

'And the soul!'

I looked in the worried and good-humoured face of the desperate Jewish pseudo-Nazi. He reminded me of an old Jew whom the Smiler had examined and whipped in the concentration camp. The victim had a bad heart and the Smiler had told him, amidst blows, that the concentration camp diet was just right for heart sufferers: no fat and no meat and plenty of exercise and fresh air. The old man had collapsed under an especially vicious blow and never got up. 'You won't believe me, Mr Silver,' I said. 'But you with all your worries are still a deuced happy man.'

I visited Robert Hirsch. He was just locking up. 'Let's go and eat together,' he said. 'There's nowhere you can sit outside in New York, but there's plenty of good fish restaurants.'

'We can sit outside,' I said. 'On the narrow terrace of the St Moritz Hotel.'

Hirsch made a dismissive gesture. 'Not to eat. They just have coffee and cake for homesick emigrants. And schnapps, to drown the hankering for the innumerable little pavement restaurants in Paris.'

'Yes, and the Gestapo and the police, who haul you off.'

'The Gestapo isn't there any more. The city's free of that plague. But the homesickness is still there. It's a funny thing: in Paris the emigrants felt homesick for Germany, in New York they feel homesick for Paris, each successive layer covers the one before. I wonder what will be the next one?'

'There are emigrants who didn't have either.'

'Yes, the super-Americans and those straining to be world citizens. They have homesickness too, but it's displaced, neurotic and anonymous.' Hirsch laughed. 'So the world is opening again. Paris is free; France is for the most part; Belgium too. The Via Dolorosa is open. Brussels is free. Holland can breathe again. It's all right to feel homesick for Europe again.'

'Brussels?' I said.

'I thought you knew,' replied Robert Hirsch in surprise. 'Yesterday in the paper I read an article about how it was freed. I kept it for you. I'll get it.'

He went back into the dark shop and gave me the newspaper. 'Read it later,' he said. 'We're going to have something to eat now. The King of the Seas.'

'The lobsters with their pinned claws?'

Robert nodded. 'To the hobbled lobsters on ice in the window waiting for their deaths in boiling water. Do you remember the first time we went there?'

'I'll never forget it. The streets seemed paved with gold and hope.'

'And now?'

'Different and the same. I haven't forgotten.'

Hirsch looked at me. 'That's a rare thing. Memory is the biggest traitor there is. You're a happy man, Ludwig.'

'That's what I said to someone else earlier. He almost punched me. Probably oneself is always the last to know.' We walked down Third Avenue. The newspaper with its piece on the liberation of Brussels was burning a hole in my jacket pocket. 'How's Carmen?' I asked.

Hirsch made no reply. The warm wind snuffled at the buildings like a dog. The damp laundromat heat of the New York summer was over. The wind carried a smell of salt and the sea. 'How's Carmen?' I repeated.

'Same as ever,' said Hirsch. 'She's a riddle without a mystery. Someone wanted to take her to Hollywood. I urged her to go.'

'You what?'

'It's the only way of hanging on to someone. Don't you know that? How's Maria?'

'She's also gone to Hollywood,' I said. 'As a model. But she'll be back. She's been there before.'

The windows of the King of the Sea lit up. The tied lobsters lay silently on the ice, waiting for their deaths in boiling water. 'Do they scream when they're thrown in?' I asked. 'I know that crabs can scream when they're put in hot water. They don't die right away. The armour that protects them when they're alive turns against them when they're dying. It makes their deaths slower and more agonising.'

'You really are the last person to take here,' said Hirsch. 'I'm going to order the snow crab legs tonight. You win.'

I stared at the black mob of crustaceans. 'That's the loudest cry of homesickness for the sea that I've ever heard,' I said.

'Stop it, Ludwig, or we'll have to go vegetarian. As for homesickness – that's nothing but sentimental feeling if you've left voluntarily. Safe, useless and unnecessary. But it's something else if you were forced to leave by the threat of death and torture and concentration camp; then your rescue can after a while turn into a creeping cancer gnawing at your vitals, unless you're very careful, very brave or very fortunate.'

'Who knows that about themselves,' I remarked and felt for the newspaper with the report from Brussels.

I was back at the hotel early. All at once there was time in abundance. It wasn't time to fill, this was time like a bottomless hole, an emptiness that only got emptier if I tried to fill it. I hadn't heard from Maria Fiola after she left. I hadn't expected to. A great part of my life had passed off without letters and phone calls, because I almost never had a fixed address. I had got used to it; I had also got used to expecting nothing but what there was. Even so, I felt the emptiness. It wasn't a panic because I thought Maria wouldn't come back, even though I knew that she had had to give up the apartment on 57th Street; it was just an emptiness as though there was something missing in me. I wasn't unhappy; that's what you were when someone died, not when they left you, be it for a long time or for ever. I had learned that.

It had turned into autumn almost without my realising it. The steam had gone from the air, and the nights were high and clear. The shadow existence went on, the war in the newspapers, the rumoured war on the other side of the world, in Europe, in the Pacific, in Egypt, the ghost war that was raging everywhere. Everywhere but here on the continent that was making it possible, the country where I was a restless shadow, tolerated and even gifted with a modest private happiness, unearned and almost unwanted. I thought of the black wall that was slowly parting in front of me, drawing me ever closer to the thing that had sustained me all these years and now held out its bloody peremptory demand to me.

I stopped under a street light and opened the newspaper with the report on Brussels. I had meant to wait until I was back in my room, but now I was almost afraid of being alone with it.

It took me a while to get back to myself. The article came with a photograph and many names of familiar streets and squares. I could hear a voice calling them out to me from another world, from a grey underground station abruptly lit up by a strong electric light like a hall at dusk, that then filled with a green and white cemetery light, silent voices and a feeling of almost unbearable sadness. To my astonishment I stopped in the middle of a street, amidst the noise of traffic and the light of a hundred shop windows, frozen, anaesthetised, and stood there whispering names to myself; disappeared, perhaps dead names, flat names garlanded with thorns and the pain of unallayable dismalness, behind which faces surfaced, pale, plaintive but not accusing, and eyes, turning to me for something, but what? For life? For help? What help? For memory? For what memory? For revenge? I didn't know.

I stood in front of a leather goods shop. Suitcases were piled up in the window, a teetering pyramid of them.

I looked around. Someone barged into me and muttered something. I missed it. I looked at the suitcases in front of me, symbols of insouciant voyaging of a kind I had never experienced. Travelling for me had always signified flight, I'd never had any use for leather suitcases and, as I understood on this autumn evening, I was still fleeing; I was fleeing from myself, from the thing inside me that was broken and confused and screaming, and was unable to heal itself without destroying what had destroyed me. I had avoided it, and would continue avoiding it, because I knew I could only make use of it when the time came, not before, otherwise it would only cut me to pieces. And the more the tangled and bleeding world revealed itself to me, the more my own contract would enclose me in a dark web of helplessness and the deed of which I knew only that it must happen, whether it spelled the end of me or not.

'There's someone waiting for you,' said Moikov. 'They've been here for an hour already.'

I looked inside the plush lounge without going in. 'Police?' I asked.

'I don't think so. He says he's known you for a long time.'

'Do you know him?'

Moikov shook his head. 'He's never been here before.'

I waited a moment longer. I hated myself because I felt afraid, but I knew I would never be able to shake that emigrant complex. It had eaten too deep into all of us. I walked into the lounge.

Someone got up under the palms. 'Ludwig?'

'My God, Siegfried, is it you? Are you still alive? What do you call yourself now?'

'The same as before. And you go by Sommer now, is that right?'

They were the usual questions when people saw each other at the cemetery and saw to their surprise that they each had survived. I had met Siegfried Lenz in a German concentration camp. He was a painter and could play the piano. His gifts saved him from a bullet in the neck. He gave the camp commandant's kids piano lessons. The commandant saved tuition and let Lenz live. Lenz taught in slow motion; just enough for the commandant not to wax impatient; but slowly enough to extend his life, as far as he could. He also played at SS and SA jollies. Not Party songs; that would have been racial transgression, because he was a Jew; but any amount of marches, dances and operettas, when the guards were issued with free schnapps for beating or torturing Jews and wanted music to get drunk to.

The commandant was replaced and his replacement was childless. Again, Lenz was in luck. The new commandant heard that not only did he play the piano, he also painted. He commissioned a portrait from Lenz. Again, Lenz worked in slow motion to extend his life. When he was finished, the commandant was promoted. He was given a new uniform and Lenz painted a new portrait. He painted one guard after the other, he painted the wife of the commandant and the wives of some of the senior officers, he painted for dear life, he painted the doctor who was waiting to give him a lethal injection, he painted until he was transferred to a different camp and I lost touch with him. I had supposed that in the race of paintbrush against death he had come second and had almost forgotten him. Now here he was in front of me, bearded, fat; barely recognisable.

'Why the beard?' I asked, for the sake of asking something.

'I can always take it off,' replied Lenz, puzzled by such a stupid question. 'That changes your appearance instantly. A great advantage, in case I have to flee. It's always better to be prepared, wouldn't you say?'

I nodded. 'How did you get out of the camp?'

'I was let go. A commandant managed to swing it. He wanted paintings of his entire family, grandparents, friends, the lot. I did it; before the last one was finished I ran away. Otherwise they would have locked me up again. I didn't stop running until I got to France.'

'And in France?'

'I painted,' said Lenz. 'In Germany I sketched people who put me up overnight, by way of thanks. It's not possible to do more in a single night; maybe a watercolour. On the border I drew the French guard; it's amazing where bad art gets you. I'm not a good painter; I'm a dauber who can get a good likeness. Van Gogh or Cézanne would never have made it; I was given a bottle of Beaujolais and a set of directions. I spent one Christmas among customs guards. They were so childishly grateful to have presents for their wives.'

Moikov came along, and silently set down a bottle of vodka and two glasses.

'If you happened to have Beaujolais, I'd rather drink that,' said Lenz. 'For old times' sake. Anyway I can't drink schnapps.'

'Do we have any wine?' I asked Vladimir.

'Raoul keeps some. I can call him and propose a swap? Shall I do that?'

'Yes, do that,' I said. 'Even champagne would be appropriate. This reunion that makes me believe in miracles. Not just in the Middle Ages. Were you caught in France during the war?'

Lenz nodded. 'I was just painting in Antibes, to get my Spanish and Portuguese transit visas. I got them and was promptly locked up. A couple of months later I was freed and drew the camp commandant in tempera. Getting out of the country was easy, seeing as I already had the visas.'

Moikov returned. 'Compliments of Monsieur Raoul. We all are pilgrims on this bloody planet, he asked me to say.' He uncorked a bottle of champagne.

'Is Monsieur Raoul an emigrant too?' asked Lenz.

'Of an exotic kind. How did you get across the Atlantic, Siegfried?'

'From Portugal on a freighter. I drew—'

I began to count on my fingers and thumbs. 'The captain, the first and second mate—'

'And the cook,' finished Lenz. 'I even drew him twice. He was a mulatto who made the most fabulous Irish stew.'

'And did you paint the American consul who gave you a visa for America?' asked Moikov.

'Not him,' said Lenz. 'He gave me a visa because I was able to show him my release papers from the concentration camp. I offered to sketch him, out of gratitude. He declined. He has a collection of Cubists.'

Moikov filled our glasses. 'Are you still doing portraits?'

'Now and again, to get by. It's really surprising how artistic people like officials, customs men, guards, tyrants and murderers are. Even in democracies.'

'Do you play the piano still?' I asked.

Lenz looked at me. 'Not often, Ludwig. That's why I don't paint much any more either. There was once a time when I hoped to make something of myself. I was ambitious. Concentration camp took care of that for me. I can't separate the experiences. My little bit of ambition is slathered with too many grim memories. Too much death. Not yours?'

I nodded. 'It's like that with all of us, Siegfried.'

'True. Well, for an emigrant music and art are preferable to writing poems and novels. What use would they be? Even if you happened to be a good journalist once? Even in Holland, Belgium, Italy, France, the language was always an obstacle. They muted you. And you too, I would guess?'

'Me too. How did you find me?'

Lenz smiled. 'The old Via Dolorosa still exists, even over here. The underground telegraph. A gorgeous woman gave me your address. I didn't know your new name. In a Russian nightclub.'

'What was her name?' For a moment I couldn't breathe.

'Maria Fiola,' said Lenz. 'I was talking about you. She said that sounded like someone she knew and she told me where you were staying. It so happened that I was going to New York anyway. So I came here.'

'How long are you here for?'

'Just a couple of days. I'm living in Westwood, California. About as far away from Europe as you can get. In an artificial town, an artificial society, surrounded by people who make films and think that's what life is. It's more remunerative, for sure. I've had enough of real life. Haven't you?'

'I don't know. I haven't really thought about it. If what we know of it is real life, then yes.'

'You don't know either?'

'Not today, Siegfried. Every new day is different.'

Moikov came back in. 'Full moon,' he said.

Lenz looked at him uncomprehendingly. 'Harvest moon,' explained Vladimir. 'It makes the emigrants unsettled. More skittish than usual.'

'Why?'

'I don't know why. Maybe like caged birds. They start to flutter too.'

Lenz looked around and yawned. The lounge looked a bit dispiriting. 'I'm tired,' he said. 'It's the difference in time zones. Can I stay here?'

Moikov nodded. 'On the second floor. Room 8 is free.'

'I'm going back tomorrow,' said Lenz. 'I just wanted to see you, Ludwig.' He smiled. 'Curious how little we have to say to each other when we see each other again after so long? Perhaps it's the monotony of misfortune.'

I walked him up to his room. 'Is it misfortune? Still?' I asked.

'No. But is it happiness? We're waiting. What for?'

'Do you want to go back?'

'No. I don't think so. I don't know. Do you remember how in camp we used to tell ourselves as long as we're alive nothing is lost? We were such idiots with our hopeless false heroism. As long as you're alive you can be tortured is more to the point. As long as you're alive you can suffer. Good night, Ludwig. Will I see you tomorrow morning?'

'Sure, Siegfried.'

Lenz smiled again. It was a resigned, cynical, sad smile. 'We used to ask each other that in camp as well. But we were never quite so sure. Do you know we two are probably the only ones in that camp still alive?'

'Probably.'

'That's something, isn't it?'

'It's everything,' I said.

I went back down to the lounge. The Contessa had just blown in. She sat like a tangle of grey lace and pale features in front of a brimming glass of vodka. 'I'm doing everything I can to die a decent death before I have to go to the poorhouse,' she whispered. 'I can't kill myself. My religion prohibits that. But why do I have such a strong heart? Vladimir Ivanovitch? Or is it that it's made of Indian rubber?'

'It's made of the most precious stuff there is,' replied Moikov carefully. 'Memories and tears.'

She nodded and took a large sip. 'But aren't they the same?' she asked hesitantly.

Moikov nodded. 'I believe so, Contessa. Even the happy ones. Maybe especially the happy ones.' He turned to me and opened his great hand. A few sleeping tablets were in it. 'How many?' he asked.

'Two,' I said. 'Or three. You're the clairvoyant.'

'Full moon. Take three, just in case. I need to keep a couple for the Contessa.'

I fell asleep, but awoke screaming a couple of hours later. It took me a while to reorientate myself. I had been dreaming of Sibylle's pale, silent face and of another face in Paris, rigid and flyblown, and in between of Maria Fiola as well, and I had felt like a cheat, a cheat of the living and the dead. I stared into space and got dressed to run around a bit in the night, and then I got undressed again and stared out into the courtyard and at work and life, and then I swallowed the rest of the tablets and thought of Siegfried Lenz and the Contessa who couldn't die, and of Jessie who didn't want to die, and of many others besides, and then I took the other sleeping tablets I still had, and slipped back down into that gurgling dark void whose shadow frightened me because I was helpless against it and had nothing but my contemptible and lacerated self.

21

I ran into Siegfried Lenz as I was leaving the hotel. 'I'm leaving in an hour,' he said. 'What about breakfast together?'

I nodded. 'There's a drugstore on the corner. How was your night?'

'Bloody awful, Ludwig, or whatever you go by these days. If only you could change your memories as easily as your name, that would be something, wouldn't it? You think you've got it all behind you, and you run into someone you used to know and the whole thing starts up again. In war, people forgot a lot over the years, or it became normal – but camp? It's different. War was stupidity, murder, almost aimless – it could happen to anyone. Camp was pure cruelty, pure evil, mass murder for the sake of it, for the pleasure of tormenting and killing. That never goes away – even if we live to be a hundred.' Lenz smiled feebly. 'There won't be any reunions of us with beer tables and sepia reminiscences? Or don't you think?'

'No, I don't agree,' I said. 'There will be that too, in Germany. But not the victims, the killers. You forget that our dearly loved fatherland is the home of the good conscience. German murderers and torturers were actuated by idealism and a first-class good conscience. That's what's so repulsive about them. They have reasons for everything. Don't you remember the humane speeches that were held under the gallows?'

'Do you think they'll protect each other once the war is over?'

'They don't even need to. Suddenly there won't be any Nazis any more. And they will all prove they only acted under orders if they happen to be caught. And they'll even believe it.'

'Ugh, what an idea,' said Lenz. 'All I can say is: I hope you're wrong.'

'I hope so too. But see the way they're continuing to fight. They'll defend every last dungheap as if it were the Holy Grail, and die on it. Are those going to be people who are appalled about what happened in their country over the past ten years? Genghis Khan was like a kindergarten teacher by contrast. My God, the Germans queued up to give their lives for the cause.'

Lenz pushed his plate away. 'Let's not talk about it any more,' he said. 'Why do we do it? We survived because we didn't talk about it and thought about it as little as we possibly could, isn't that right?'

'Maybe.'

'Not maybe. That's how it was. But here on this bloody East Coast in New York City, people talk about nothing else. Probably we're too close to it. Why don't you come out West? In Hollywood, on the Pacific, the nearest land is Japan.'

'The war in the Pacific is still going on.'

Lenz smiled. 'That one doesn't concern us so much.'

'Really? Is there such a thing?' I said. 'A war that concerns one less? Isn't that the terrible reason why we keep getting new wars?'

Lenz finished his coffee. 'Ludwig,' he replied. 'I'm leaving in fifteen minutes. I don't want to argue with you about ideology. Or egoism either, stupidity, cowardice and the killer instinct. I want to give you some advice. Staying here may well finish you off. Come out to Hollywood; it's an artificial, cheerful world. It's easier to wait things out there. We don't have a lot in reserve. We need to economise. And you're waiting, aren't you?'

I didn't say anything. I had nothing to say. There were too many different types of waiting. I didn't want to talk about mine. 'I'll think about it,' I said.

'Do.' Lenz scribbled his address on a napkin. 'Here, you can always find me at this number.' He picked up his suitcase. 'Do you think we can ever forget what happened to us?'

'Do you want to?'

'Sometimes, when I'm lying in the sun on the Pacific, then I do. Do you think it's possible?'

'Not for us,' I said.

'You don't exactly cheer a fellow up, Ludwig.'

'I didn't want to depress you. We're alive, Siegfried. That may be a great source of comfort; or maybe not. Still, we're alive; we could have rotted in a mass grave or gone up the chimney in smoke many times over.'

Lenz nodded. 'You know you can't stay here and rot away in your helplessness. You should think about Hollywood. We fit better in the crazy world of the dream factories over there, to get us through the winter.'

Translator's Afterword

Uncompleted novels: *Edwin Drood, Amerika, The Castle, The Man Without Qualities, The Promised Land* – can you really find it in you, dear reader, to think less of them than of their signed, sealed and delivered peers? All of them, certainly all of those named and of those certainly this one, are beautiful things to hold in the mind: the story of a season and a city, New York in the summer of 1944. A book that begins on Ellis Island, and that never strays more than a mile or two from the ponds and follies of Central Park. Turbulent but becalmed, pitched existentially between the bloody past and a sanguine future, the dissociated nerve-centre of a world at war.

The book it seems Remarque originally had it in mind to write was a story of return and revenge; the testing to its destruction of its author's 'militant pacifism.' There is a vague but extensive back story of camps and atrocities; references to the torturing and killing of Sommer's father; to the fallen comrades – Bär, Hasenclever, Ruth, Sibylle, and many more – who don't make it. In a disastrous earlier version of the novel called *Shadows in Paradise* (puzzlingly and rather destructively brought out by Paulette Goddard, Remarque's widow, in 1971, though Remarque had already rejected it), Ross (then) actually leaves New York and goes to Hollywood, and then to Europe. Plausibility and form and sympathy hiss out of the book like air from an inner tube. Remarque projected assassinations, court cases and suicides. There is no sign of any of this being about to come about any time soon, in *The Promised Land*. The book is all the better for it.

Sommer can't leave New York, here: his crucible, his laboratory, his unities. Love lies ahead, and murder behind, or is it the other way round? Or even both? The longer the book goes on, the more unthinkable that he leave. You can't go back: the more perceptive of the emigrants (Thomas Mann, Fritz Lang, Remarque himself) understood in their less deluded moments. America beckons with its lights and weathers. Meliorism tempts, self-improvement. A blue suit, a better job and a bigger room. A toehold and then a foot-hold. An ascent measured in cakes and drinks and dollar denominations. Why not Hirsch as the owner of a string of electrical shops, eventually?

This New York is a remarkable place peopled by human flotsam and jetsam, the lucky ones, the successful immigrants – oxymoron! – who crashed or burned their way through the walls of paper, and find themselves in a land of peace and plenty. Actual Americans in this book are occasional walk-ons: lawyers, policemen, businesspeople, tycoons. The main characters, the ones with inner lives, are the immigrants, who keep to themselves. The book is put together from their meetings and re-meetings, who wins and who loses, who is plunged deeper into traumatic memory, who is further along in the processes of normalization, who returns to the more pleasant and congenial circumstances. Because these people know all about survival, but very little about life. They are haunted but safe, or damaged but safe; they sleep with literal arsenic round their necks, or a metaphorical revolver under their pillows – except that they don't sleep.

They have vast moral projects, and endearingly trivial anxieties; for most of them it is a time of waiting or indecision: to stick or twist is a decision for later, when the war is over.

As the *donnée* for a book of existential reflection, it is probably not possible to improve on (and surely, the mesmeric 'New York, looking like a white African city with skyscrapers' (p. 268) is a nod at Camus and Oran). Punchy B-movie dialogue ('In the Ritz?' asked Silver. 'No, the Rausch. It doesn't have so many stars.'(p. 97)), punctuates spiralling bouts of strenuous introspection, with heady Beat notes of strange America, the food, the music, the machines and cars, the light, especially. Life comes down to moments, in a way that has rarely been better put over than here, in this book that Remarque, himself dying, was determined to write:

'Now I felt a deep peace, of a kind I hadn't felt for a long time, and I felt there was nothing more important than the birds hopping about on our table, pecking for crumbs, the pale wine and the face in front of me looming out of the shade.' (p. 244)

It seems to me there is actually very little for the reader to forgive here: occasional repetition (or, better, over-supply) of incident or detail. Barbara Hoffmeister took out the most egregious instances. But then, the reader should perhaps bear in mind that that's what life is: more of the same.

Michael Hofmann, 2014

www.vintage-classics.info